ONE
CARELESS
MOMENT

ONE

A PORTER CASSEL MYSTERY

CARELESS
MOMENT

DAVE HUGELSCHAFFER

Cormorant Books

FSC

Mixed Sources
Product group from well-managed
forests, controlled sources and
recycled wood or fibre

Cert no. SW-COC-003438
www.fsc.org
© 1996 Forest Stewardship Council

 Canada Council   Conseil des Arts
for the Arts   du Canada

ONTARIO ARTS COUNCIL
CONSEIL DES ARTS DE L'ONTARIO

The publisher gratefully acknowledges the support of the
Canada Council for the Arts and the Ontario Arts Council
for its publishing program. We acknowledge the financial support
of the Government of Canada through the Book Publishing
Industry Development Program (BPIDP) for our publishing activities.

Printed and bound in Canada

LIBRARY AND ARCHIVES CANADA CATALOGUING IN PUBLICATION

Hugelschaffer, Dave, 1967–
One careless moment / Dave Hugelschaffer.

ISBN 978-1-897151-08-2

I. Title.

PS8615.U315O54 2008   C813'.6   C2007-906475-2

Cover design: Angel Guerra/Archetype
Text design: Tannice Goddard/Soul Oasis Networking
Cover image: © Craig Aurness / CORBIS
Printer: Hignell Book Printing

CORMORANT BOOKS INC.
215 SPADINA AVENUE, STUDIO 230, TORONTO, ON CANADA M5T 2C7
www.cormorantbooks.com

I'M RIDING WITH BB the King — not the blues legend, but a guy of considerable talent. Last night at camp he took sixty dollars from me in a card game, saying it would ease his retirement. I can understand his concern — at well past fifty, Bert Brashaw is one of the oldest fire-fighters I've worked with. If I sit at the card table with him many more nights, I'll go home to Canada poorer than when I arrived.

"Take a right up ahead," he says, pointing. "But watch that curve."

Brashaw is local, the supervisor of a district hotshot crew, and knows the road. I take his advice, braking gently, and we hit the curve at a reasonable speed. Too late, I see washboard and the 4x4 dances sideways, clanging hand tools. I swear and brake harder. Brashaw has a hand on the dash to steady himself, the other on the brim of his hard hat. "Maybe I should drive," he says.

"Everyone's a critic."

"Do they have drivers' licences up north?"

"No," I tell him, jamming the shifter into a higher gear. "Buckle up sweetheart."

Brashaw looks for something else to hang onto. He's a big guy, fully occupying his half of the front seat. On this rough road, his folds and chins jiggle, but there's a lot of muscle underneath. At camp, he was loading cubies — five-gallon water jugs — like they were softballs. We pull out of the curve and I glance in the side-view mirror. Barely visible in a plume of dust behind us, the crew bus rounds the corner. Farther back is the rest of the convoy; two fire engines and a D7 dozer on a lowboy. We may move slow, but we're armed to the teeth.

"Cassel, this is Missoula Dispatch. What is your present location?"

I reach for the radio, give BB a questioning look. "Blood Creek Road," he says.

"Missoula Dispatch — we're approaching the Blood Creek Road."

There's a pause, then Dispatch gives us an update. "Revised location is nine miles northeast of a sharp bend in the Blood Creek Road — you should see the smoke pretty soon. Eight smokejumpers have been dispatched and are currently en route to the fire. This will be Incident 47. Upon arrival, you are to assume control as the incident commander."

"Copy that Dispatch. Any word on fire behaviour?"

Another pause. The dispatcher still has the radio keyed; other voices can be heard in the background, cutting in over each other. It sounds busy. The dispatcher says something clearly not intended for us, then we're told to stand by. Up ahead the road forks, and a small brown sign points the way to Blood Creek. We rattle over more washboard, then start uphill on a steep, winding grade. The trees — big ponderosa thick with fir understory — are so close to the edge of the road it seems the forest might slap together like a giant vise, trapping us.

I hope the fire isn't burning in the same type of fuel.

"Cassel, this is Missoula Dispatch. Jumpers are at location and report the fire is about thirty acres, burning in a canyon. Moderate rate of spread. Surface fire with some candling. Winds steady from the east at three miles per hour."

"What about access?"

"There's a narrow bush road. Sounds pretty steep, but you might make it."

"Copy that Dispatch." I hang the radio mike in its bracket below the dash, look over at Brashaw. He's got a map out and is frowning. "You know that area?"

"Yeah," he says, staring at the map.

"Rough country?"

He looks over at me, his normally jovial face pensive. "You could say that."

I glance at the map, looking for contour lines, roads — anything that might give me a clue as to where we're going and what we're going to be up against when we get there. But the map is a fuzzy photocopy and the road ahead is a bit distracting; I yank the truck off a collision course with a massive ponderosa.

"What kind of slopes are we talking about?" I ask Brashaw. "Can we use the dozer?"

Brashaw looks at me a moment longer, as if deciding whether to answer. He gazes ahead, and with a beefy hand wipes sweat from his brow. "From what they said, I think it's burning in Holder's Canyon."

I wait for more. Brashaw fidgets, building the suspense.

"Okay," I say finally. "What's so special about Holder's Canyon?"

"Well ... forget it." He folds the map, tucks it into the pocket of his yellow fire shirt.

"Forget what? You haven't told me anything. What kind of country is it?"

"It's rugged," he says. "Pretty inaccessible."

For a few minutes we drive without talking, listening to short bursts from the radio — smokejumpers talking to one another, checking in, regrouping after touching down. Mixed in are other conversations, from other fires. In this line of work, everyone gets a turn at burning up. This year it's the Pacific Northwest; Montana and Oregon are getting hit pretty hard. That's why I'm here, on loan from Alberta through the MARS — Mutual Aid Resource Sharing — agreement, a wonderful example of cross-border co-operation allowing firefighters to make a little overtime when it's raining back home. So far, I've done pretty well: nearly two weeks on a fire farther south; then, this afternoon, as I'm waiting for orders, this one pops up. And it's all mine.

"So tell me more about Holder's Canyon."

Brashaw lifts his hard hat and scratches his head, plops his lid back on and gazes out the side window. Green branches ripple past. "It's nothing you really need to know," he says.

He's playing me just right — now I have to know. "Tell me anyway."

"Okay," he murmurs. But he takes his time. He takes the map out of his shirt pocket, unfolds it and stares at it until I'm just about to say something, then folds it again and places it in the glove compartment. At this rate, the fire will be out by the time he tells me. "You gotta keep an open mind," he says.

"Open as a dumpster."

"Well ..." He shifts, looks uncomfortable. "That canyon has a reputation around here."

"Vampires?" I say, gearing down for a steep climb.

"People who go in never come out."

For a minute, neither of us say anything. The transfer case on the truck whines and I glance in the mirror to see if the fire engines are on the slope yet, but they're hidden by a curve in the road. They're going to have a bitch of a time getting up here. Brashaw isn't going to have it much easier getting me to believe the campfire tale he's spinning. At least, I'm pretty sure that's what it is — have a little fun, intimidate the new guy.

"So what happens to them?" I ask. I can play right along.

"They die," he says solemnly.

I wait, but he's not very forthcoming, which gives me an eerie chill. I've sat around a lot of campfires, heard a lot of tall tales, but most guys don't have Brashaw's sense of pacing. Between bends in the road, I glance over at him to see if he's smiling. We pull another steep grade, the steepest yet, then round a sharp corner. There's a trail forking to the left, just a set of brown dirt tracks with grass growing between them. Brashaw lifts a heavy arm. "Up there."

I slow to a crawl to make the turn, stopping just long enough to ensure the crew bus sees where we're going, then gear up. The trail is so narrow the side-view mirrors are knocked out of alignment. The forest closes in. Dense shadow. A scent of fir so strong it's nauseating. I'm about to prompt Brashaw again — we'll be at the fire soon and I want to hear the end of this little fable before we get there — but he starts on his own.

"There used to be a hunting camp a few miles south of the canyon, run by an outfitter from town. Most of his customers were out-of-state. Big shots who wanted a bear rug by the fire and a story they could use to impress their buddies back home. First thing the outfitter would tell them was they could hunt anywhere but the canyon, that it was cursed, and they generally stayed away — the canyon is so damn rugged no one wanted to bushwhack through there anyway. Until three hunters decide they have to check it out. The outfitter tried to talk them out of it." Brashaw pauses, gives me a wry smile. "But the customer is always right."

"Naturally."

"Well, they went in — by themselves. The outfitter didn't want anything to do with it. Two days later, he's getting worried. The hunters aren't back yet, and they haven't squared the bill with him. He waits another day, just to be sure they won't come back on their own, then jacks up his courage and goes after them. Wanna guess what he found?"

"Three zombies with their hearts ripped out?"

Brashaw is unflappable. "They were all dead," he says seriously. "Right next to the creek, shot through the heart. When the ballistics came back, they found three different slugs from three different rifles, all owned by the hunters. Seems they'd shot each other." He watches me, frowning in a challenging sort of way. "No one could figure out how they'd managed to do that."

I can think of a few scenarios, but maybe I'm just more creative.

The radio blares: Dispatch wanting an update. How close are we to the fire? Can we see it yet? I soothe her by saying we're five minutes back.

"So that's it?" I say to Brashaw. "A few hunters got shot?"

Brashaw looks mildly offended, scowling at the floorboards and shifting in his seat. But he rises to the occasion. "You think I'm making this up? Well, I'll tell you a little bit more about this canyon, although it might not help your peace of mind when you're in there. The canyon is named after Alister Holder. Holder was a miner back in the thirties who had a claim up there. One spring, he doesn't come to town like usual, for supplies, and the clerk at the store starts to get worried. After he's waited what he figures is a reasonable amount of time, he talks to the sheriff, and the sheriff saddles up and goes looking for Holder." Brashaw shakes his head, as though he might have known Holder personally. "They checked his shack and his workings along the creek, but he was nowhere to be found. Story is, the sheriff found him by accident on his trip out. There was blood on some of the branches along the trail, and when the sheriff looked up to see where the blood was coming from, he found Holder — up in a tree, like he was trying to get away from something. Dead as a post. When they got him down, they discovered that he'd cut his wrists."

I nod, impressed. A few holes, but not a bad story.

"Three weeks later, the sheriff had a heart attack."

"So the place is haunted?"

Brashaw nods. "I guess. They say it's the avenging spirit of the Indians."

There's a long uphill pull; the trail has turned to twin eroded gullies and I drift as far to one side as possible to avoid bottoming out. We're in another gully. Trees rise majestically on either side. At the top of the slope, the road levels and smoke hangs in gauzy suspension like early morning fog. Sunlight, sliced by the trees, projects ethereal beams through the haze. Ghosts don't seem entirely unrealistic. I stop the truck and get out, watch the progress of the convoy, worried they might not all make the hill. Below, the crew bus bounces over ruts. Behind them, fire engines labour forward in low gear. While I'm waiting I peer ahead, searching for the source of the smoke, but the forest is too dense and the fire remains hidden.

"Nothing like the smell of burning pine to get your blood roiling," says Brashaw. He's facing away from me, hunched, adding his contribution to the gully erosion.

"So why do they call you BB the King?" I ask.

He chuckles, zipping up. "State secret."

"I'll figure it out," I tell him as we climb into the truck again.

The road rises over the toe of a long ridge and suddenly we're at the fire. Dense white smoke rises in a slanting column from a steep valley. Judging from the width of the column at its base, I'd say the fire is pretty close in size to the jumpers' estimate. The whiteness of the smoke is a good sign — the fire is lying fairly low, not doing anything too crazy. But it's still early in the day and burning conditions are bound to worsen.

"This is going to be a bitch to get into," says Brashaw, leaning forward, a hand on the dash.

He isn't kidding. The canyon rises up the side of a rugged mountain, solidly carpeted with dense fir and brush — a smorgasbord of fuel for the fledgling fire. The north side of the canyon is a sharp, bony ridge, bisected by lesser gullies and ridges clogged with brush and deadfall. On the south flank, another ridge has been shorn away, leaving a high cliff. "We'll have to flank it," I say. "Create a safety zone at the tail and anchor from there."

Brashaw nods, chewing his lower lip.

I call Missoula Dispatch to let them know we've arrived, but get a broken response, the radio cutting in and out. Most of the message is garbled — too many ridges between us and them — and I relay through Kershaw Lookout, a local fire tower. After briefing Dispatch about what I see and how I plan to proceed, I request two more dozers for heavy line construction, another shot crew, and a helicopter. Dispatch confirms my order and tells me to stand by. While I'm waiting, I call the smokejumpers. The response I get is a little breathless.

"Cassel, this is Sue Galloway, smokejumper in charge. Welcome to Incident 47."

"Glad to be here. Where are you and what is the fire doing?"

"We're on the south flank, working our way toward the tail." Galloway's voice wavers, like she's walking on uneven ground. The pop and crackle of fire comes through like static. "We jumped into a bare area on the top of a ridge. It's pretty much a cliff from there on down, so it took us a while to get to the fire. It's candling quite a bit, but dropping down after a few trees go up. Lots of potential though, with this much understory. We get any more wind and it'll stay in the crowns."

There's a pause and I ask what action they've taken.

"Not much we can do with hand tools in this type of bush, so I started flagging a dozerline from the base of the cliff. I take it you're the new IC, so what do you want us to do?"

I watch the smoke pump up for a minute. The occasional dart of orange appears, then drops.

"Good thinking on the dozerline, Galloway. Keep going and we'll meet you at the trail."

Galloway copies, then Kershaw Lookout comes back on with a reply from Dispatch. The dozers and crew have been ordered, but probably won't arrive until sometime later. Resources are scarce. As for the helicopter, none are available — all machines are on higher priority fires, meaning fires where structures are threatened. I plead for a helicopter — I hate working a fire blind, without air support. The Lookout assures me my concern will be passed on to Command and signs off.

"Now what?" says Brashaw, staring at the canyon.

"Now we put your boys to work."

As we drop off the toe of the ridge, the trail curves and we lose sight of the fire. An indistinct mass of white smoke, like an approaching storm, is our only guide. The trail snakes around boulders and clumps of large trees at the mouth of the canyon, crosses a small creek, then makes a hard right and drops sharply to some hidden destination on the far side of the northern ridge. We stop just back from the bend.

"Where does this trail go?" I ask Brashaw.

He shrugs. "Nowhere. There are some squatters about ten miles farther up, but that's it."

"Squatters?" I can't imagine anyone making this drive frequently.

"Yeah. Old hippies and misfits. White trash."

"Would they be in the path of the fire?"

Brashaw shakes his head. "Not with this wind."

"Wind could change. We should think about evacuating them."

"You can try," he says, "but you might get shot. They're pretty anti-government."

I'm thinking that's not a very good reason to remain in the path of a fire, and make a mental note to call Dispatch about this later. For now, given the topography, they're relatively safe. We get out of the truck and watch the crew bus lumber to a stop behind us. It's a boxy, green vehicle, higher than a normal bus. The name of the crew — Carson Lake Hotshots — is printed in black on the side. The door squeaks open and young men in green pants and yellow shirts emerge. They cluster along the side of the bus, watch the bank of white smoke hanging above the canyon, and I hear one or two muted comments about a curse. Brashaw gets them moving, opening cargo doors, pulling out chainsaws and hand tools. Hard hats are donned, equipment belts strapped on, backpacks shouldered. Handheld radios are tested, squelches adjusted. Behind the bus, the first engine pulls up, squealing to a halt, its tank rocking. Engine is a bit of a glorification — it's just a big green water truck. A chubby, stubbled face peers out a side window.

"Jesus Christ," says the driver as I approach. "That was one mother of a hill."

Beside him, the engine module leader watches the smoke. He slips on a hard hat and climbs out of the truck, asks what the plan is. I tell him we're going to wait until the dozer is up, cut a line from the trail straight to the tail of the fire. Once that's done, he can pull in his engines and get to work.

"All right," he says, staring toward the canyon, looking concerned.

"Is there a problem?"

He hesitates. "No — no problem."

Brashaw saunters over. His men are ready, Pulaskis in hand, chainsaws resting on broad shoulders. I tell Brashaw that the brush is far too dense and I don't want anyone in there, even at the tail of the fire, until the dozer has pushed in an anchor line. He tells his men, but they don't budge, preferring to wait with packs and saws ready, despite the heat and weight of the equipment. It's all part of the image — hotshots are the elite ground-pounders of the firefighting world.

As we're waiting for the semi-trailer with the lowboy and dozer, the brush rustles and the other elite warriors of the firefighting world appear. Sweaty, curly hair plastered to her forehead under an oversized hard hat, Sue Galloway extends a fire-blackened glove, and we shake hands. Introductions ensue, during which several of the hotshots give Galloway disapproving glances. Firefighting is the ultimate macho career and not all of the participants are thrilled with the female presence. Personally, I like the variety.

"We've got a line flagged right to the cliff," says Galloway, brushing hair out of her eyes.

"Excellent. How far from the trail is the fire?"

Galloway pauses for a drink of water. "About a hundred yards."

"Any sign of the origin?"

"Not so far," she says. "But I haven't had time to look."

"Let's go for a walk."

I motion Brashaw over and the three of us head into the dense green. Shrub and understory fir crowd beneath older larch, three feet in diameter. Mossy black beards hang like rags. Galloway takes the lead, following her line of fluorescent orange flags hung on branches. It's cooler and dimmer in here, shade maintaining the humidity — a stroke in our favour. The advantage won't last much beyond noon, just giving us a lag period for line construction. We don't go far before we see the first flickers of orange, getting as close as we can until the heat from the flames becomes uncomfortable.

The perimeter of the fire is a sharp line on the ground, hissing and crackling, crawling relentlessly outward, sending up tendrils of fragrant smoke. Tongues of orange dance on twigs and dry moss, lick along dead-fall. In places, where the branches of understory fir touch the ground, fire races upward in a wild, ecstatic gush. We need to get that dozer rolling, cutting the monster from its fuel supply, and we need water.

I look at Brashaw. "We should check out that creek right away."

"I'll get someone on it," he says, reaching for his radio. As he makes the call, I gaze into the blackened, smoking heart of the beast, where a forest lies half-digested, trees stripped of their needles, trunks oozing smoke. I need a good look at this thing from above so I can judge its mood, see where it intends to go, and how we can stop it. I'm not sending men anywhere near the head until I've got a good understanding of the terrain, fuels, and fire behaviour. Doing that strictly from the ground is like a blind man trying to describe an elephant by touch.

"That ridge where you jumped in," I ask Galloway. "Is there a good view of the fire?"

She nods emphatically, her hard hat wobbling. "Oh yeah, you can see the whole thing."

"How difficult would it be to get up there?"

She frowns. "Tough. It was a bitch bushwhacking down to the shoulder of the cliff. Nasty understory. Gives me the creeps, jumping in above a fire like that, especially when it turns out there's ground access. I saw another trail farther back though, below the ridge when we were coming down. An old road or something. You might be able to 4x4 up there and walk in the rest of the way."

I nod, filing the information away for later, and we walk back to the trail. The smokejumpers are resting in the shade. The hotshots stand in the sun, still carrying their hand tools and chainsaws, trying to look tougher than the jumpers. They stiffen when we emerge from the foliage. The lowboy and dozer have finally arrived. The skinner is on the dozer, firing her up. He backs the dozer down onto the trail, treads clanking, pivots the big machine toward the bush, then shuts it down so I can climb up.

Standing on the tread, I tell the skinner — an old guy with dense, woolly grey hair and bright blue eyes — that I want him to start cutting along the flag line. I point out the start ribbon at the edge of the road, remind him to cut straight down to mineral soil, windrow everything on the side away from the fire. Don't get too close to the flames so nothing burning is pushed across. He assures me in a calm, gravelly voice that he's done this before.

The dozer roars and trees start to topple. Forest floor is peeled back like an old rug and everyone watches, in mutual appreciation, the massive amount of work being quickly completed. The smell of conifer sap and freshly torn earth mixes pleasantly with woodsmoke — the fragrance of the fireline. When the dozer is a tree length into the bush, the firefighters begin to follow. The drivers of the engines fire up their rigs, ready for action. I step onto a running board, have a few words with the module leader.

"You have foam with you?" I ask.

"Of course," he says.

Together, we track the progress of the dozer, listen to the progression of toppling trees. My gaze wanders toward the trail, to the crew bus and lowboy with its waiting driver. Boxes of hose and spare hand tools neatly stacked out of the way. Something along the edge of the trail catches my eye — red and barely discernable at this distance. It's probably nothing, but I go for a look. I recognize it before I get there.

It's a fusee cap, its pull-strip curled back.

A fusee is a red, cylindrical flare used by firefighters to burn out fuel between a fireline and the active edge of a fire, thus robbing the fire of potential intensity so it can't jump the fireline. It's also handy to burn a safe area in case of an emergency, as Wag Dodge did on the infamous Mann Gulch fire.

It's too early in this fire for anyone to have need of one, so I lift my radio and call around, just to make sure.

"Galloway, this is Cassel. Have any of your people used a fusee on the fire?"

There's a pause; the answer comes back negative. Same answer from Brashaw.

I stand on the trail a moment longer, pondering the little red cap. Most arsons are started right from the edge of a road or trail, with the arsonist nervous and wanting a quick getaway. But this fire was started deeper in the bush, which takes time, walking both ways. This probably means it wasn't a hot start but was rigged as some sort of time delay. The arsonist placed the device in the bush so no one would see it from the trail, then got careless with the cap — flung it aside or dropped it shoving it into his pocket. But why walk so far into the bush? Maybe he thought the distance from the trail would be less obvious and no one would look too hard for the cause.

He's wrong.

I call Brashaw and Galloway, tell them to be on the lookout. Then I head into the fire.

The engine crew is already at work, hoses run from where the engine sits on the dozerline, water soaking the perimeter. This is where I go in, stepping over slippery black logs, pushing aside the barbed, black swivel sticks of the burned understory fir. I go in about forty yards and look around, taking note of the charred tree trunks, the burn pattern on deadfall. A fire always points to where it's been and, if you can read the signs, you can usually get a pretty good idea of where it originated. You start with the knowledge that fire burns outward from its point of origin, its behaviour modified by fuel, weather, and topography. A fire in calm weather conditions, in continuous fuel, will burn a perfect circle. A wind-driven fire will form an ellipse, the width-to-length ratio a function of wind speed. But that's under ideal, predictable conditions. A fire in a canyon, with erratic winds, variable fuel, and unknown moisture conditions, can be a little more challenging.

I walk slowly, watching the ground, watching tree trunks, checking scorch patterns on rocks. The fire cleaned out the understory, reducing fir and brush to slender spikes. There's a certain voyeuristic aspect to walking in a freshly burned forest — a sudden, injured nakedness; trees stripped of their foliage. Solitary old growth larch, blackened but not entirely burned, stand like tall, determined, survivors. Deadfall, normally hidden and treacherous, forms a crisscross pattern like a relief map. My eyes track across smouldering devastation, thinking about the fusee. It would have been planted in duff or dry litter — fine enough fuels to easily ignite — and positioned securely so it wouldn't topple as it burned down. Either way, it wouldn't be set far from the road. A fusee burns for a maximum of thirty minutes, and the arsonist would want a quick, clear route back to his waiting vehicle. He must have made a dash for the trail then driven like mad, because we didn't meet any vehicles on our trip in.

Maybe the fire was started by one of the squatters, who then high-tailed it home. Or the arsonist is farther up the trail, waiting for night to sneak out. I make a mental note to post a guard on the trail and look for tire tracks.

There's a narrow creek in the burn, a dark meandering line bordered by dense black spears of incinerated spruce and fir. The creek is pretty shallow, but perhaps we could dam it and put a pump there. It's also an obvious route back to the trail, maybe a way to hide the scent of boots, so I go for a closer look. Branch stubs tug at my clothes as I struggle through the hedge, leaving long black marks. But the creek is clogged with deadfall and I revise my theory. Backing out, a branch stub tears a strip off the sleeve of my shirt, scraping my arm hard enough to draw blood. I stand for a minute, holding the abrasion, and look around. Char patterns on tree trunks point everywhere; the fire was pushed around by the wind playing across the canyon.

Other indicators may be equally unreliable. I'll have to approach this one differently.

The tail end of a fire grows slowly, backing into the wind. I notice the perimeter at the tail of this fire is different on both sides of the creek — the far side has burned closer to the road. This could mean a difference in fuel type, but I don't think so. The fire was started on the far side and took some time to build sufficient intensity to jump the creek.

On the other side of the creek, the view is much the same but, by using the difference in distance the fire backed into the wind on either side of the narrow drainage, I can estimate how much farther into the burn I should be looking. This, coupled with a quick calculation of the current spread rate, should put me in the right neighbourhood. I pace the distance and look around.

Then I see it: a game trail, beaten into the forest floor. It's faint but unmistakable, a thread of crushed moss not as completely burned. Only a short section of trail is visible, but it wanders toward the road and I get a shiver of anticipation. I don't follow it far before I find the origin.

Arsonists love fusees — they burn hot, they're easy to use, and they're common — but they leave plenty of evidence in the form of a white, ceramic residue. From the shape of the residue here, it's apparent this fusee was propped at a near-vertical angle. As it burned down into itself, the molten residue built a tube around the jet of flame, falling off at regular intervals. I pick up one of the pieces, white and hard like bone, and sniff it; the usual sulfur smell. Crystals tinted green and orange have formed inside the tube like miniature heads of cauliflower. I set the piece back where I found it and examine the blackened ground. Small splatters of white slag are scattered close by, castoffs from jetting through the casing of the fusee when the slag cap sealed off the top. These jets, which can eject hot slag several feet, are usually what starts the fire, which then burns both outward and back to the fusee. Even so, arsonists always pile fuel at the base, and this example is no different. There are delicate black threads of carbon: dried grass and moss. It's a simple setup, not very inspired, but dependable. I pull a roll of fluorescent pink ribbon from my pocket — a colour I use specifically for such occasions — and tie a generous portion to a nearby tree.

I unholster my radio. "Brashaw and Galloway, this is Cassel. I found something at the origin and marked it with pink ribbon. It's on the north side of the creek, maybe a hundred yards into the fire, but you should be able to see it from quite a distance. Make sure no one works the area or goes in for a look. Let's keep the scene clean."

"No problem," says Brashaw. Galloway gives me a double-click, the salutation of busy firefighters everywhere. While I've got the radio in hand, I call Kershaw Lookout, pass on that I have a confirmed arson and need a fire investigator. After a lengthy pause, the tower informs me that an investigator from the district will arrive in about two hours, and tells me to ensure I mark and protect the origin. And don't pass any sensitive information over the radio. The voice is filled with excitement, being part of the intrigue. Smiling, I assure her that I'll follow orders.

I'm part way down the trail, pausing for a look back to confirm the visibility of the pink ribbon, when the wind picks up suddenly, blowing ash. Flames along the perimeter quadruple in height. There's a merry campfire sound, but I'm not impressed — wind is what makes the difference between a small fire and a big one. Wind is what kills people. A cluster of trees go up together, flames licking wildly forty feet into the air. When their needles are gone, the trees flame out, trailing smoke like spent birthday candles. I call Brashaw on the radio.

"You catch that wind, BB?"

"Yeah." He sounds as concerned as me.

"All your men square if it starts to get squirrelly?"

"They're good. They'll stay at the tail, close to the road."

I check with Galloway. Her men are farther up, ahead of the dozer. They'll fall back.

For a few minutes, I stand and watch flames on the perimeter, gauging the wind, waiting to see what else it might do. The wind gusts a few more times, then settles down again, stronger than it was before. The tone of the fire has changed. Smoke, drifting like a fog bank above the canyon, has doubled in height. I need to see what the fire is doing.

"Brashaw, this is Cassel. Meet me at the road."

"Sure, what's up?"

"We're going up that ridge for a look."

Brashaw copies and I head out of the fire, following the narrow path of the game trail. Sometimes, as an arsonist exits the scene of a crime, they leave behind clues — called transfer evidence — such as footprints, scraps of clothing, or hair caught on branches. But there's nothing. Fire is a marvellous cleanser.

I arrive at the road to find two new water trucks with Carson Lake Fire Department printed on the side. Three firefighters stand behind one of the engines, talking and pointing toward the fire. They see me, and one ambles over.

"Looks like you got a bit of excitement here," he says.

I nod, offer a handshake, introduce myself as the incident commander.

"Name's Hutton," he says. "I didn't know you guys were already on this one." Hutton is tall and lanky, tanned, early forties. He's wearing black wraparound shades and no hard hat; his receding hair blows lightly in the breeze. "We could stick around for a while, if you'd like."

"Great." I'm not about to turn down help.

"At least until we dump these loads." He glances back at his engines. They're not big trucks, but every gallon counts. "If we get a call in town though, we'll have to leave."

"Understood."

"Where do you want us?"

I point toward the fresh scar of the dozerline. "We're cutting a line to the south. When the dozer has tied into that cliff on the south flank, he'll come back and start cutting on the north side. We've got two trucks on the south line already, so you may as well wait until the dozer gets back and starts going north."

Hutton nods, scuffing the hard surface of the rutted trail with the toe of his work boot. He's got a calm self-assurance about him. He doesn't have to be here — the local fire department is almost certainly volunteer — and although I don't doubt his dedication, there are certain aspects of a fire this big that his crew simply isn't trained to handle.

"I'll have you work with our smokejumpers."

Hutton nods again, but he's scowling a little. "Okay."

Brashaw trudges into sight along the dozerline, puffing, his folds jiggling. He looks over to where Hutton and his men are strapping on gear and they nod in mutual recognition. Brashaw mops his forehead with a kerchief that hangs around his neck bandito-style, watching the smoke rise into the sky. Big beads of sweat cling to his cheeks.

"Goddamn," he says. "That wind sure picked things up."

The trail to the ridge is overgrown. Trees lean threateningly and the trail winds like a goat path. Heavy green branches brush side windows, slapping the glass and thumping the roof. I've given up readjusting my side mirrors, and my radio antenna is in serious jeopardy. Brashaw stares gloomily at the wall of green around us.

"Piss fir," he mumbles. "Nothing but piss fir."

"What?"

"Alpine fir. Burns like piss."

We drive in silence for a few more minutes. The trail hugs the backside of the ridge, rising but still a good distance from the crest. It looks like we'll have a bit of a hike ahead of us, which makes me nervous. I don't like to be on foot anywhere near a fire in bush this dense. Wind direction is straight up the canyon too. We'll be fine, but I'm still nervous. Maybe it's Brashaw's spooky campfire story. He shifts his bulk and sits up, looking ahead intently. "I know this road," he says.

"How close does it come to the ridge top?"

"This is the road to that bear hunting camp."

"The one from your story?"

"Yeah." He has an almost comical look on his face. He's working on his story, building it up again. "We shouldn't be here," he says. "We should turn back."

"What?"

He looks at me. "This is a bad place."

I'm not sure if he's referring to the heavy timber or if he's just superstitious.

"We'll be fine. The wind is steady up the valley and there's a dozer-line to the cliff."

"Yeah, I know. But I got a bad feeling."

A bad feeling. He's played this about as far as I'm willing to take it. I'm about to tell him so when we come around a bend and find a small tree across the road. I brake and get out, expecting BB to follow and help move the tree, but he just sits in the truck. I give the tree a few tugs — it's just a big sapling from the understory — but it's too resilient to snap off. So I get an axe from the toolbox and whack it into a few chunks. By the time I've dragged them off the road, I'm sweating and in no mood for campfire stories. Brashaw must sense this, because he doesn't say anything. We gear up and lurch forward. The trail continues to rise, then levels for a short stretch, wider where someone cut out a few trees. Brashaw frowns and, looking ahead, points to the widened area.

"Pull over," he says. "We'll have to walk from here."

The fir on the slope is dense enough that I hang a few orange ribbons on the trek to the top of the ridge. The slope is steep and we grab onto slender tree trunks to heave ourselves up. When we break out of the trees near the crest of the ridge, we both lean forward, bracing arms against shaky legs until our breath returns.

"I'm too old and fat for this shit," Brashaw says between lungfuls.

The view from the ridge is worth the climb; it's like standing at the lip of a volcano. The fire has widened from its origin near the road and the head spans the width of the canyon. Smoke boils up in a dense grey column. Flames glow orange, like glimpses of flowing lava. The canyon is a perfect chimney up the side of the mountain. There's no way we're getting in front of that.

"Christ," says Brashaw. "That's a real burner."

We need aircraft. Heavy bombers. Helicopters with buckets.

I call Dispatch. Kershaw Lookout compliments me on my spectacular smoke, but relays the same response. Houses threatened on a

fire to the south. All available aerial resources committed. I grind my
teeth, wondering how they expect us to accomplish anything. I call
Kershaw Lookout again, get the winds and RH, request Dispatch do a
spot forecast. The wind feels stronger up here and the change of the
smoke from white to grey is not good.

Radio chatter from the crews on the fire indicates the show is heating
up on the ground. I call Galloway, confirm her men have fallen back.
They have. Brashaw calls his crew, tells them to make sure they're on
the dozerline, not in the dense fir and larch. They acknowledge and
pass on that the dozer is still a few hundred yards from the cliff. I pace
nervously, watching the fire. I'm not letting it out of my sight until we
get some aircraft. I call Kershaw Lookout and tell them that the fire
is now two hundred acres and growing rapidly, stressing the limited
window we have for air tanker drops.

Kershaw tells me to stand by.

I continue to pace, shale grinding under my boots. A strip of rock
just back from the drop off, about twenty yards wide, has been blasted
by wind and exposure. Nothing grows here except a few hardy junipers,
low to the ground. Perfect spot to jump into. There's a small pile of gear
from Galloway's crew: neatly-stowed parachutes and jump helmets. I
call Galloway on the radio, confirm Hutton and his men are working
with them. While I'm on the radio, Brashaw stands at the top of the
cliff, shaking his head and muttering. He squats and carefully takes a
seat on the edge of the cliff.

After a few more minutes of pacing, I join Brashaw at the lip of the
volcano, dangle my feet in the air. Rock drops a good hundred feet to
a jumbled talus slope, then to burnt trees farther down. The sound of
clanking treads and splintering wood drifts up like an overheard conversation. I look for the dozer but it's invisible from this angle.

"Nice view," says Brashaw, spitting, watching the foamy flecks
descend.

"Wonderful. So what happened to the Indians?"

"What?" He squints at me, his face glistening with soot and sweat.

"The Indians — the ones who cursed this valley?"

He shifts on the hard rock. "A long time ago, settlers and Indians were fighting over some valley land, farther down. Settlers wanted to put their stock there, but the Indians wouldn't let them. Kept killing the cows. One day, a girl goes missing — one of the settlers' daughters — and someone gets into their head that the Indians took her. They form a posse and raid the Indian camp, but the girl isn't there. So they figure the Indians killed her and there's a big fight. The Indians are outgunned and make a run for it, the posse in hot pursuit, and they chase the Indians into this canyon."

Brashaw pauses to dig a can of chewing tobacco from a pocket — the skilled storyteller.

"Well, they got the Indians trapped, but the bush is too thick to go in and find them. They know the Indians will hide in the canyon until they're gone. You want to guess what they did?"

Brashaw is watching me, his lower lip bulging with tobacco. I shrug.

"They started a fire at the mouth of the canyon. Burned them all up."

We both stare at the cauldron of fire and smoke in the canyon below. I'm getting an uncomfortable feeling that everything Brashaw has told me is true, and start to appreciate his reluctance. Firefighters can be a superstitious lot — comes from living so close to danger — and for a minute there's a hush. The dozer has paused in its operation and even the radio is silent. It's eerie. Then the radio barks, snapping us both out of our reverie. It's Kershaw Lookout.

"Cassel here."

"Dispatch says they'll free up a bomber group for one run, after they dump once more."

"Great. Any word on a helicopter?"

The voice on the radio is apologetic. "Not until tomorrow."

One tanker drop is better than nothing. If the drop is good, the wind dies down a bit, and we have a decent RH recovery tonight, we might be okay. I'm thanking the tower and getting an update on the winds when a worried voice cuts in.

"Break — break. This is Galloway. We've got fire over the line."

I turn to look toward the tail of the fire — the only place there is any line — and as I key the mike on the radio I see a sheet of grey smoke rising over the treetops of the ridge, feel an anxious clench in my gut. This is no little spot fire. This is in the crowns of the piss fir coming up the side of the ridge. Toward us. I should have seen it minutes ago but was looking the wrong way. I release the transmit button on my radio and Galloway's voice comes back on, controlled but wavering slightly.

"— didn't see it until just now. We thought it was in the canyon."

As Brashaw and I watch, radios in hand, the sheet of rising smoke quickly doubles in height. A fire on a slope preheats the fuel in front of it, the pitch of the slope acting like wind, accelerating the speed and intensity of the flame front. With the wind we already have, it's a dangerous combination. Curls of black smoke boil up — the fire burning so hot it's not getting enough air — and for a moment all I can do is stare at the wavering serpent rising above the treetops. Then Galloway's voice cuts through.

"It's really moving. You guys had better get the hell out of there!"

Together we bolt for the trees, knowing the only way out is on the trail, in our truck, but we can't find the ribbon line I'd flagged on the way up. Hearts thumping at the sudden precariousness of our situation, we run back and forth along a solid wall of green. Brashaw swears and crashes into the bush. I follow. Going downhill, we have to hit the trail. We're not far into the trees when Brashaw trips. I run side-slope, ducking branches, and help him to his feet.

He staggers when I let him go. "Twisted my damn ankle."

"You okay to keep going?"

He looks at me, knowing that he's far too heavy for me to carry. That I may have to leave him behind. It's not something I'm prepared to do. He takes a few steps to test the ankle. He can move on his own, but he's going to be slow and the fire is rapidly gaining on us. What was just a distant crackle is now a steady roar and when I glance toward the noise I see the space between the trees is filled with orange. A gust of hot air blasts across my face. We don't have much time to decide.

Keep going downhill and try for the truck? Return to the ridge and deploy our fire shelters in the open?

The truck is halfway down the slope. If it doesn't start, we're dead. If there's a tree farther up blocking the trail, we're dead. If the trail ends, we're dead. On the other hand, we're not far from the ridge, but it's uphill all the way.

"We're going back up," I yell at Brashaw. "Deploy in the open."

He nods, the look in his eye deeply concerned.

"Come on," I tell him. "I'll help you."

He drops his pack and together we start up the slope, using tree trunks and branches to heave ourselves forward. Barely audible against the roar of the fire, our radios blare a mix of urgent voices. Brashaw has an arm over my shoulder but he's doing most of the work. We divert around a massive old ponderosa — survivor of some earlier fire — and Brashaw pauses for a moment, wheezing. His cheek has a strange hue to it, a sort of glow, and I look past him. It's a mistake.

A hundred yards away, the forest is engulfed in pulsing orange. Tree trunks are slender stems amidst a mane of gushing flame. There's a pounding, thundering roar like standing under a waterfall. The skin on my cheek tightens against the uphill blast of heated air. We have a minute to make it to the top. I glance forward, pushing Brashaw ahead.

"Run, goddamn it!"

Brashaw surges forward, scrambling, lugging himself up. I no longer hear him wheezing; I hear only the growl of the beast at our heels, crunching up trees. Thirty more yards to go uphill, then another ten or so in the open until we can deploy. A rabbit blurs past me on the ground. Twenty yards. My shirt is hot against my skin. Ahead of me, Brashaw's damp shirt is steaming. I push him forward, trying to will him up the slope. His steps are awkward, stilting. Ten yards to the edge of the trees, the fire seems to pause, take a deep breath. I pass Brashaw and he looks at me, his brow deeply furrowed, a look of intense concentration on his face. We're almost clear of the trees when the fire exhales, knocking us both down, blowing my hard hat off my head. I scramble forward, grab my hard hat and cram it on, feel the hair at the back of my head curl and singe. We break from the timber and run in a crouch toward the cliff. I want to keep going, throw myself over into cooler air.

"Deploy! Deploy!"

I'm not sure if the voice is in my head or if I'm screaming it. We're in an oven. The rock around us glows orange. If we turn toward the fire we'll surely burst into flame. Brashaw is clawing at the yellow pouch on his belt. I pull my own fire shelter from its pouch, yank the pull cord down on the plastic package. The shelter comes out as a small, silver brick, unfolding in a zigzag pattern like some child's Christmas decoration. Hot wind tugs at the shelter as I open it, trying to tear it from my hands. A wave of pain flashes over my back and arms. It's too late.

Brashaw is down beside me, a small silver pup tent.

I pull the shelter over my head, step onto the other end, drop next to Brashaw and press my face against rock and dead moss. The temperature only inches above the ground may be dramatically higher. The flames are over us now, tugging at the shelter, trying to tear it off and flatten it out. The noise is terrible, like the meshing of immense gears in some horrible, angry machine. My radio squawks with distant, unrecognizable voices. Despite my hands and boots holding down the bottom edges of the shelter, my back feels as though it's on fire and I'm overcome by fear that the top of the shelter has been ripped open and I'm exposed to the full fury of the firestorm. A careful glance to the side confirms the shelter is still there. Bright orange spots show through pinholes in the foil.

My gloved fingers begin to burn where they touch the foil, and I want more than anything to let go. I try to focus elsewhere, remembering images from a training video where tests were conducted to determine the limits of a shelter. Silver pup tents, like the one I'm clinging to, are engulfed in whipping flames while the narrator calmly explains: "At five hundred degrees Fahrenheit, the glue holding the foil to the fibreglass breaks down, the layers separate and the foil can be blown out of place or torn by turbulent winds. At twelve hundred degrees Fahrenheit, the foil itself begins to melt —" The silver pup tents in the training video whip in the wind. Foil contracts and lifts. The shelters vaporize like houses during a nuclear bomb test. This isn't helping and my mind searches desperately for something reassuring. I close my eyes and think of my sister Cindy and her three kids. I think of Telson and our sometimes relationship, vow I'll spend the rest of my life with her if I survive this. I picture my parents at their coffee plantation in Jamaica, working on a lush green mountainside.

A splintering crash jolts my thoughts back to the present. I wince as something hits the top of my shelter, pulling it down and drawing a line of fire across my back. Instinctively I buck upward, knocking off the weight of the object and restoring a narrow air space. A line of pain remains on my skin like a brand. Flames gush louder and much closer than before. I feel a sudden rush of heat on my right side and close my eyes, grit my teeth, telling myself this can't go on much longer. Fire needs fuel to burn and fuel can't last indefinitely. But it doesn't stop. It gets worse.

A flash of light burns through my closed eyes and I push my face harder against the rock. The heat is unbearable and I realize with a sickening jolt that the side of the shelter must have lifted, exposing me to the fire. Carefully, I turn my head, see my gloved hand on the edge of the foil. Out of the corner of my eye, I see a bright light, turn my head a little further.

What I see confuses me.

A patch of orange behind a hazy film. Flashing ribbons of silver. Then I understand. A flap of foil on the right side of my shelter has separated and lifted, like opening a window. I'm looking through the white fibreglass mesh, the heat of the fire blasting through like a jet engine. The ribbons of silver dancing in the orange are from Brashaw's shelter, only feet away. Beyond that I see a heavy branch, like a fiery groping arm. Then the flap of foil settles back in place on my shelter, and the oven door closes.

"You okay BB?" I shout as loudly as I can.

There's no response.

2

●

THE FIRE BURNS interminably. I try to ignore the pain in my hands and feet and the searing welt on my back, my mind skipping between fragments of memory laid against a tapestry of heat and crushing noise. Time ceases to exist. I'm trapped in a single hellish instant.

It's the change in noise I notice first — still a steady roar, but not quite as overwhelming. I listen hard, my mind beginning to clear, afraid that I'm losing my hearing and the fire is still just as bad, but I'm convinced that the change in the pitch of the fire is real. The heat, too, seems to be diminishing and I lift my head. The light inside the shelter is different — whiter — than before.

"BB, you okay?"

Nothing. I call again but hear only the pop and sizzle of fire. Maybe if I call him on the radio. Cautiously, I slide my hand along the edge of the shelter until I feel the antenna, drag the radio up to my head and press it against my lips.

"Bert Brashaw, this is Porter Cassel. Do you read?"

No response, and I realize the radio has been silent for some time. I try once more.

"This is Cassel. Anybody out there?"

Silence. Not even static. I check to ensure the radio is on, find the plastic on one side is warped and rippled, and I suddenly feel very alone. I lay my head against the rock and let out a deep breath. The worst is over and I'm alive. The realization leaves me weak with relief and for several minutes that's enough. Then I start to worry about Brashaw. I want to check on him but I'm not sure how much longer I should remain in the shelter.

What if he needs me? What if there's something I should do?

Leaving my shelter too early would be disastrous. One breath of the hot gases released by a fire can sear the delicate membranes of the lungs shut, causing suffocation and death in minutes. But when I lift my head, the heat is no longer unbearable. We deployed in the open, which means there is nothing around us to burn. A little moss maybe, perhaps the odd juniper, but nothing with any real mass. The blast of heat preceding the flame front was the primary danger, and that has passed. Then I remember the brief glimpse through the hole in my shelter, the heavy blazing branch. The top of an old ponderosa, maybe the whole tree, must have come down. That would explain the weight across my back: a small branch had snapped off and landed on my shelter. That could also explain why Brashaw has not answered. Slowly, I lift the right side of my shelter, expecting flames and heat, until I can see the silvery bottom of Brashaw's shelter. All that comes in is a little smoke.

I pull back my own shelter and sit up.

There is a brief, agoraphobic moment of disorientation. On one side, mere yards away, the world drops off — I'm a lot closer to the edge of the cliff than I had thought. Beyond the rocky precipice is a great trough of black tree trunks. Brashaw's aluminum fire shelter is crumpled and misshapen, strips of blackened foil draped over the ridge like forgotten tinsel. I remember the heat when the small patch of foil lifted on my own shelter, and come to my feet slowly, filled with a heavy foreboding. When I step past the ruined shelter and see the far side I have to look away.

It takes a moment to build the courage to turn back.

The top of an old ponderosa, snapped off by a blast of superheated air, smoulders and crackles several yards from Brashaw's shelter. It was this mass of fuel that destroyed the side of his shelter, the wind-driven flames eating the thin foil. The underlying fibreglass mesh is blown in, leaving the side of the shelter fully open. As if that weren't bad enough, the intact interior wall of the shelter reflected heat back onto Brashaw's grotesquely burned body.

I didn't hear him screaming; I can only hope that means he went quickly.

I retch suddenly, the force of it bringing me to my knees. It leaves me weak and I kneel on the scorched rock, stare blankly at the scene before me. Where there was colour there is now only austere shades of grey and black, like stepping into an old photograph. The slope at the back of the ridge — where Brashaw and I struggled uphill — lies exposed, a precipitous wasteland of carbonized poles, talc-fine ash, and drifting smoke. Somewhere down there is what's left of the truck. As I search for it, I catch flashes of colour, tiny yellow forms working their way toward me.

When they're closer I stand; it seems disrespectful to be found just sitting here. Galloway comes first, puffing, her features anxious and strained. Others follow, moving a little slower. I walk around the fallen tree, meet her away from Brashaw's remains. From here, you can see very little.

"Cassel," she says, breathing hard. "Thank God you're okay."

I nod, frowning. She brushes sooty hair away from her eyes. "Where's the other guy?"

When I shake my head, Galloway winces. She takes a step toward the cliff and I grab her arm.

"You don't want to go up there."

She wrenches free her arm and stalks away, toward the cliff. I don't want to return to the ridge and face what remains of Brashaw. Galloway's entourage is almost past me when I turn and walk after her. I find her kneeling in front of the open side of Brashaw's shelter, her head hung.

"Jesus Christ," she says softly. "Jesus fucking Christ."

Other boots scuff up behind us. I hear heavy breathing but nobody says anything. Galloway lets out a low, half-stifled sob and I lay a hand on her sooty shoulder. She looks up at me, her eyes anguished. "I didn't see it in time," she says. "I didn't realize it was over the line."

"It's not your fault."

"It went so fast."

"I know." I look around, toward the tail of the fire where the trees are still green; into the canyon where the fire still crawls — anywhere but at what's in front of me. The way the two shelters are deployed, it's obvious Brashaw's shelter saved my life. "I'll need your radio."

Mechanically, Galloway unsnaps her belt radio and hands it to me.

"We should cover him," a voice says behind me.

"No," says another, hushed. "We have to leave him."

I turn, look at firefighters who stand like nervous pallbearers. "You guys don't need to be here. Maybe you could just back up, give us some room."

They back up, no doubt relieved. I key the mike.

"Kershaw Lookout, this is Cassel on Incident 47."

"Kershaw here. Go ahead Cassel."

I pause. There's no easy way to say this. "There's been a burnover. We have a fatality."

For a moment the radio is silent, then Kershaw comes on sounding strained.

"Cassel, this is Kershaw. Please confirm that you have a fatality."

I confirm.

"Are there any other injuries?"

"Negative."

"Stand by, Cassel."

"You hear stories," Galloway says quietly. "See things on the news. You never expect —"

Kershaw comes on abruptly, all business now. Help is on the way. So are investigators. Do not touch anything. No further radio communication regarding the whereabouts or identity of the *injured* firefighter. Is smokejumper Sue Galloway in the vicinity?

Galloway looks up sharply, lumbers to her feet. I pass on that she's in the vicinity.

I'm relieved of duty. Galloway will be the incident commander until help arrives.

I nod as though Dispatch were watching, hand the radio back to Galloway.

The helicopter, a silver A-Star, lands a hundred yards away on the ridge. It came in low and fast, banked once for a quick overview, then picked its spot, the skids sliding a little on the rock. There are two passengers, both wearing Forest Service brown. They duck as they exit the bird and run crouched, holding hard hats at their side. One of them carries a small duffle bag. We meet a dozen yards from Brashaw's shelter. The older of the two, a short rounded man with white hair and a bushy white moustache, is Herb Grey, chief ranger of the Carson Lake District. I met him two days ago at the station. He indicates the man with the duffle bag.

"Cassel, this is Wilfred Aslund. He's our district investigator."

Aslund and I nod to each other; no one is in a hand-shaking mood.

Galloway is introduced as the smokejumper-in-charge and by some general, unspoken consent we move slowly toward the crumpled fire shelters. Grey takes point and we give him plenty of room. He stands in front of Brashaw's shelter for a few long minutes, intent, his moustache twitching, then crosses himself and walks carefully around both shelters.

"You were in the other shelter?"

I nod, although Grey probably already knew this.

"You okay, Cassel? You burned anywhere?"

I shrug. My hands and feet hurt, and there's a line of fire across my back, but right now it seems insignificant. "I'm okay."

"You breathing all right?"

He's watching me carefully, like I might collapse. "I'm fine."

"No macho bullshit?"

"No sir."

He stares a moment longer, then nods, satisfied. "So what happened?"

Behind us, the helicopter winds down like a toy low on batteries. When the pilot kills the rotors it's suddenly very quiet and everyone is looking at me. I shift uncomfortably, remembering Brashaw's nervousness in the truck when he realized where we were. Now, the curse seems too real, but as I tell the story it's the one thing I leave out. I tell Grey about arriving at the fire, my concerns about assessing behaviour without an aerial perspective, finding the fusee cap and origin, the trip to the ridge. It's the condensed version, but it's fairly compelling. No doubt they'll want the full, unabridged version later.

"Arson," he says, scowling. "Goddamn it. Brashaw was a good guy."

"Yes sir."

"You didn't see anyone headed out when you drove up here?"

"No sir."

I'm talking like a Marine. Maybe there's some security in the formal approach. Maybe I just don't feel like talking. Grey must be able to see this. He claps a hand on my shoulder. "Try not to think about this for a while," he says, as if that were possible. "We'll fly you back to town. You can clean up, get some distance from what happened here. We've got a psychologist on contract you can talk to, off the record of course. We'll get your statement tomorrow."

Aslund looks disappointed. He's tall and wiry, full of energy. By the way he's been glancing around and shifting on his feet, he obviously has questions he wants to ask. Galloway keeps peeking at him out of the corner of her eye. I think she's worried he might try to pin this on her.

"I'd like to stay for a while," I tell Grey.

He gives me a hard look. "You sure?"

I nod.

"Okay," he says quietly. "For a little while, anyway."

The radio barks. A sheriff's deputy and an emergency medical technician are at the tail of the fire and need transport to the fatality scene. Grey calls the pilot and tells him to get down there, pick those

boys up. After the helicopter augers away, Grey turns to Aslund, tells
him to do his thing, then stands away from the ruined shelters and
looks downwind, toward the head of the fire. On the south flank the
fire has burned to the top of a parallel, lower ridge, throwing up a veil
of smoke. The horizon, once occupied by mountain peaks, has been
blotted out. While we wait for the helicopter to return, Grey makes use
of his radio, leaving no doubt about who is in command.

"Where are those goddamn bombers?" he barks at Kershaw Lookout.

"Stand by Mr. Grey."

"Don't tell me to stand by, goddamn it. Tell them we've got a fire
rolling up the mountain here and we need resources. I need a full Type
II Incident Management Team with air support. Order three more
crews, two more dozer units, and two more engine modules. Tell them
to start working on a base location and get someone in line to handle
the media right away. And have them call the Missoula Technology
Development Center, get some of their boys out here to check over the
shelters and personal protective equipment. You got all that?"

"Uh, yes sir." I can almost hear her scribbling. "Just one thing
Mr. Grey —"

"Go ahead."

"They want to know when you'll have a Wildfire Situation Analysis
ready."

"Tell them they'll get their damn analysis when I get my bombers."

Kershaw copies. Grey glares at us, his moustache twitching. No one
meets his eye.

"Where are the rest of your men, Galloway?"

Galloway briefs him on the status and location of resources presently
on the fire. Dozerline cut nearly to the cliff, but overrun. Three of
the four engines gone to refill. I wander away, no longer part of the
command structure. I'm a witness now. A survivor. The helicopter
returns, coming straight in this time. But it doesn't land, hovers
alarmingly close, rotorwash rippling Brashaw's shelter, threatening to
blow it away. It's a different helicopter.

Grey snatches up his radio. "Get the hell out of here," he hollers, pointing at them.

The helicopter swings up and around, over the ridge. I can see the cameraman hunched in the front seat, pivoting to follow the action. In the back seat, a woman in a blue business suit cranes her neck. We're probably live, beaming into every living room in Montana, maybe the entire country.

"Listen up," Grey hollers into the radio. "We've got a TFR on this fire."

The pilot acts dumb, buying video bytes. "Come again?"

Grey's face is red. "A temporary flight restriction. Five thousand feet and five miles."

There's a brief pause, then the pilot acknowledges and the machine begins to rise.

"Assholes," Grey grumbles, watching them go. High above us, the helicopter begins to circle. Grey checks Brashaw's shelter, shaking his head. The whap of our own helicopter grows louder. The deputy sheriff and EMT join the growing crowd on the ridge. The deputy's name is Wayne Compton. The EMT is referred to simply as Hal. Everyone seems to know everyone else. Except Galloway and me — we hang back a bit, beyond the inner circle. Our importance in the grand scheme of things continues to diminish.

"Let's clear the site," says Compton, waving a hand. "No non-essential personnel."

A few firefighters, the ones who came up with Galloway, are shooed farther back. The deputy and EMT approach Brashaw's shelter, the EMT crouching beside the body, checking vitals. Given the state of the corpse, it's a formality. "Gone," he says, glancing over his shoulder. Compton flips open a small notebook, checks his watch. His uniform is dark green with a crest on the sleeve, his rank in yellow bars. SHERIFF is printed in bright yellow letters across his back. He's very crisp, very clean. Not for long out here, though.

"Can you confirm the deceased's identity?" he asks Grey.

"Bert Brashaw," Grey says curtly. "Crew boss. One of my men."

Compton nods, looking around at each of us. I've seen the look before; he's taking a photocopy, a reasonable facsimile, storing us away for later reference. That done, he crouches next to the body, pulls on white surgical latex gloves. When they're snapped in place, he begins to examine Brashaw, peering, gently moving aside scraps of clothing. Aslund crouches over him, breathing in his ear. Compton stops, looks back at him.

"Need a hand?" Aslund asks.

Compton pulls a roll of yellow crime scene ribbon from a pack. "Here, flag off the scene."

Aslund hesitates, obviously wanting to get in on the real action. Personally, I'd prefer a little distance. Aslund frowns and starts stringing the ribbon. Since there are no trees here he lays it on the ground, anchoring it with slabs of shale. The deputy reaches across and under the corpse, turning him onto his side. Brashaw rolls over like a burned log.

"You looking for anything in particular?" Grey asks.

Compton doesn't look up from his work. "It's just procedure."

"You don't seriously think there's foul play here do you?"

"You never know."

Grey draws himself to his full stubby height but the effect is lost on Compton, who continues his work, looking for knife wounds or whatever. Grey coughs, grumbles under his breath.

"Perhaps there's something you can do," says Compton.

Grey scratches under the brim of his hard hat, smoothes his moustache. Clearly, he thinks this is a Forest Service affair. He stares at the back of the deputy a minute longer, then turns toward me. "Come on Cassel, let's go for a look at this fire."

Fires appear different when seen from the air. They're silent and look smaller against the surrounding forest. They can appear deceptively benign, almost beautiful in their own way. But there's nothing beautiful about this one. It's a killer, belching flames and poisonous fumes.

A real dragon. The helicopter banks and we circle to the beast's spiny tail.

Two engines have returned and sit on the narrow bush road like bright red and green toy trucks. Men in yellow stand next to the tankers. Others walk along the dozerline — now surrounded by black on both sides — as if trying to figure out what happened. The dozer toils up the south flank, cutting line along the new fire perimeter. It looks disorganized down there. In my headset I hear Grey giving directions, getting things rolling. He pauses and I see his head shake.

"Damn," he mutters through the intercom. "What a cluster."

He's in the front seat and I can't read his expression, but he must not think much of my leadership abilities, letting something like this happen. That makes two of us. I wait until Grey is done giving orders from his lofty perch before asking to set down at the tail. I want to look at where the fire jumped the line, but Grey shakes his head.

"Negative, Cassel. As soon as they're done with you, you're headed out of here."

We fly in silence for a few minutes. The bombers arrive, a group of old Navy P2Vs. We rise to five thousand feet and the fire looks smaller, more abstract. Grey talks with the lead plane, a small Cessna which flies ahead of the three bombers, guiding them in for their drops. I stare down at the canyon — from here it looks much steeper as it rises up the side of the mountain — and think of other fires I've heard of where more than trees were burned. Mann Gulch. Storm King. Winthrop. Over the years, hundreds of firefighters have been killed on the line, in dozens of notorious fires.

Now there's another name to add to the list — the Holder's Canyon Fire.

Brashaw mentioned squatters at the end of the road and I strain to make out buildings beyond the north ridge. I catch a glimpse of something shiny, like a signal mirror from the trees. Then it's gone. So are the bombers, headed back for a refill. A long red streak across the canyon ahead of the fire attests to their work; a line of hope, drawn on the forest canopy. They'll be back in about forty-five minutes. Our fire is now priority number one.

"Have you had other arsons like this?" I ask over the headset.

"No," says Grey. "Nothing like this."

The radio squawks. My presence is requested on the ridge and the machine swings wide, giving us another view of the crushed little shelters. When we're down, I get out. Grey doesn't. The machine augers away and I'm left at the edge of the cliff with no radio, my ears still buzzing from the turbo whine of the engine. I trudge along the ridge toward the shelters. A half-dozen firefighters huddle a good distance back. I recognize Galloway, shorter and slimmer. I want to talk to her again, find out more about the excursion that burned us over, but as I pass Compton and Aslund, standing by the border of yellow crime scene tape, Compton waves me over.

"I've got a few questions for you, Cassel, if you don't mind."

I nod, mentally brace myself for the start of a painful inquisition, but Compton is in no hurry. He checks the recording on a small video camera, kneels to stow it in his pack. I get a good view of the holstered pistol on his hip, then he stands, takes out a little flip notebook. "You're from Canada, right?"

"Yeah. Alberta."

"And you're here as part of the US Forest Service command structure?"

"Yes. Upon arrival at the fire, I was assigned command."

Compton frowns. "So, you're responsible for what happens here?"

Normally, this is a simple yes or no question, but today it seems a little leading.

"Yes, I'm responsible for the safety of the men under my command."

"I see." Compton scribbles something in his notebook. "What are your qualifications?"

Qualifications are a matter of record; he could get the information from the Forest Service, either here or back in Alberta, but I remind myself that Compton is not part of the Forest Service. He deals with criminals, which takes a different style. "I'm a certified Type II Incident Management Commander."

"And how did you end up on the ridge?"

A simple question, loaded with significance; I'm sure I'll hear it more than once. They'll want to know if my actions followed procedure, or if they were careless. They'll question my judgment — I don't blame them, I'm starting to do the same. If I'd listened to Brashaw and his superstitions, this might never have happened. But you can't fight a fire that way.

"I needed an aerial view of the fire. Given the fire behaviour, this location appeared acceptable."

Both Compton and Aslund make notes in their flip pads. They don't press further on my use of the ridge. That'll come later, in a task force investigation. Compton asks the next question without looking up.

"When did you discover the fire was an arson?"

I tell them about finding the fusee cap on the side of the road, searching for and finding the origin. They're both watching me but I talk to Aslund. If conditions were different, it would be me in his boots, investigating the arson. I conclude with a brief description of the way the fusee appeared to have been set, based on the residue; how I marked the spot with ribbon.

"You didn't post a guard?" says Compton.

"No, but I communicated a warning to all staff on the fire to stay well back."

Compton frowns, writes something in his flip pad.

"I'll need you to show me the origin," says Aslund.

"No problem."

"You saved the fusee cap?"

"Yes, I bagged it. Unfortunately, it was in the truck."

"The one that burned up?"

I nod and they both take notes. I can't help wondering, in a situation like this involving both a fatality and arson, what the protocol is between the Sheriff's Office and the Forest Service. So I ask. Aslund and Compton exchange glances and it occurs to me that they're not sure. In fact, I doubt they'll be the ones conducting the investigation. They're front-line people, beat cops — senior staff will undoubtedly take over an incident of this magnitude. Compton glances toward Brashaw's fire shelter.

"Due to the arson, Mr. Brashaw's death will be considered a homicide."

Aslund and I hike down the backside of the ridge, through a stand of blackened, branchless tree trunks. He doesn't like helicopters, he tells me. Damn things tend to crash. A plane is one thing, but that main rotor goes and you fall like a stone. So we walk.

Ash, whipped by wind, envelops us in a choking grey cloud. With the understory stripped away, the slope is visibly steeper than I remember and I marvel that Brashaw and I managed to scramble back up to the ridge so quickly.

"So you found the fusee cap by the road," he says, reviewing.

"Yes. It was a few yards into the trees."

"Like someone threw it?"

"Maybe. Or they were walking off the road, to avoid footprints, and dropped it."

Aslund nods, thinking about this. He's in his early forties, lean to the point of emaciation. Hair, shaved to stubble, blends with stubble on his neck and chin. Adam's apple like the wedge of an axe. Eyes like a falcon, alert and inquisitive. "What about tire tracks?" he says.

"Not that I noticed. But we moved a lot of vehicles and the ground is as dry as concrete."

The slope begins to level as we near the trail to the old bear hunting camp. Visible through a picket of black trunks, twin ruts snake their way along the side of the slope. The truck can be seen from a distance, blackened and sitting strangely low. I notice as we approach that it is resting on its rims, tires vaporized. Everything not metal is gone, even the paint, giving the vehicle a skeletal look, like the husk of a dead beetle. The windows have melted out, blobs of glass on the ground like dropped marbles. Coil springs from the seat lie in perfect formation on the metal floor, looking strangely out of place. I reach through the vacant window, pull open the glove compartment. It yields with a painful scrape.

"Anything left?" says Aslund, coming up behind me.

"Nothing but ash."

"Why did you put the cap in the glove compartment?"

"For security. In case there were fingerprints."

Fusee caps are waxy and would hold a good print, in case the arsonist was careless enough not to wear gloves. Aslund nods but doesn't say anything and we continue down the trail.

"You're a fire investigator?" Aslund says, walking beside me.

"Yes. I have a contract with the Alberta Forest Service."

"You get many arsons up north?"

"Too many," I say, thinking about the previous summer. "What about you guys?"

"Nothing like this," he says, echoing Grey's comment.

"No fusee fires?"

He shakes his head. "This is the first wildfire arson around here in years."

"You have any idea why someone might want to start a fire here?"

"Not yet," Aslund says with a half grin. "But I'm working on it."

At the road, we're mobbed by firefighters from Brashaw's crew. They've been monitoring the radio and know the fatality must be their leader. They want details. More information doesn't always make it easier but I tell them most of what happened. They're suddenly silent, listening to me, the horror of it clear on their faces. This is every firefighter's worst nightmare and they stare at their boots, scuffing dirt listlessly.

"I'm sure it happened quickly," I tell them. It's not much, but it's something.

"Don't tell anyone," Aslund cautions. "We've got to notify the family first."

"This is going to kill Del," says a young firefighter with long hair.

"Does this mean we're going home?" asks another.

We push through the crowd, leave them to discuss the day's events. It doesn't take long to find where the game trail leaves the road and we follow it into the burn. I stop once or twice and look around to be sure we're on the right trail. We seem to be, but I can't see any ribbon.

I pass the spot I'm sure was the origin and stop.

"Where is it?" asks Aslund.

"I don't know," I tell him, looking around. "It was right here."

3

●

THE FIREFIGHTERS, WITH nothing to do but work the tail of the fire, have progressed farther into the black than usual, mopping up the area to keep busy. Commendable behaviour, except they have obliterated the origin — sprayed it down and trampled the area with bootprints and hose drags — which is odd; in the openness of the burn, the pink fluorescent ribbon should have shone like a beacon. Wind might have blown down the ribbon, but this seems unlikely as I tied it tightly to the hardened branch of a burned tree. Even if the ribbon was lost for some reason, there should still be the hard, white slag tubes from the fusee; they're not water soluble. But there's absolutely nothing here.

"Maybe we're at the wrong spot," says Aslund.

I don't think so. There are enough burned trees that look the same to create some doubt as to exactly where the ribbon was tied, but I've got a good memory and this is definitely the right area. I look around, trying to remember where I found the fusee slag. There has to be something left.

Aslund shifts beside me, getting impatient. "Let's look around some more."

"No, it was here."

The firefighters chewed up the ground pretty good with the high-pressure hoses. I landmark at a bend in the trail, walk a dozen paces, squat on my haunches and inspect the ground, looking for flecks of white. "I'm positive it was right here."

Aslund stoops over me. "What exactly did you see when you found it?"

"Three or four slag tubes," I say, pointing, as if that might help. "Some fine fuel residue."

He waits a moment longer. "I'm going to look around a bit more."

While Aslund prospects in the burn, I examine the immediate area more carefully, working in a grid pattern. I start well back from where I think the origin was, walking slowly and studying the ground. The ribbon and fusee residue had to go somewhere. A gust of wind could have carried the ribbon some distance beyond the origin. A firefighter could have mistaken the ribbon as marking a hotspot and pulled it down once he was sure the spot was out. Maybe the high-pressure jets of water chewed up the ground enough to obscure the slag, or blew it beyond the area we've searched. But after a half-hour of searching, I find nothing, even though I've covered and re-covered a large area around the origin.

Aslund returns, asks if I've found anything.

Nothing, I tell him. He frowns, shaking his head. "I don't know, Cassel —"

"Well, it was here. I saw it."

"If you say so."

"You don't believe me?"

"Sure," he says. "I believe you."

"But?"

Aslund shifts on his feet. He seems distracted, uncomfortable. "Nothing."

"Look," I say. "Something is clearly bothering you. What is it?"

"You mean other than the absence of any physical evidence?"

"If everything is gone, then it's not by accident."

"You think someone purposefully tore down the ribbon? Pocketed the residue?"

"Maybe. It had to go somewhere."

He thinks for a minute. "What did you make of the burn patterns?"

"Inconclusive. The wind in the canyon whipped the fire around quite a bit."

Aslund nods. I can see where he's going with this. No physical evidence of arson and no conclusive pattern of fire travel to support that this is where the fire started. Good thing I called it in before the burnover, or they might have suggested my origin identification was a trauma-induced hallucination. Thankfully, Aslund is too professional to push this further. "Given the origin may have been sabotaged," he says, "what do you suggest we do?"

"Ask the firefighters. They may have seen something."

Aslund gives me a look mirroring my own thoughts: Or they may be responsible.

After the burnover, Brashaw's crew was pulled from the fireline and told to muster at the main staging area along the road. There's nothing more dangerous than a distracted firefighter. Most of the mobile equipment has been moved to this new clearing and the firefighters sit in the shade of their crew bus. When they arrived, they were broad-shouldered warriors, ready for battle. Now their shoulders are slumped; they're listless and tense. Beaten. The squad bosses are the only ones who bother to stand when Aslund and I approach. We pull the three of them aside, away from the rest of the men.

"I need to ask you guys a few questions," Aslund tells them.

They nod, solemn and weary. All three are young, in their mid-twenties, stubbled and stocky. They could be brothers. Aslund gets right to the point.

"Did you fellows see any pink ribbon out there?"

They shake their heads. One of the men introduces himself as Brad Cooper, senior squad boss, meaning he's second in command. "I heard you call BB," he says, his voice filled with a southern twang. "After you told him about that origin, we kept our eyes out for it, but we didn't see any pink ribbon. Just orange."

"Were you aware of the location of the origin?" says Aslund.

"Yeah." Cooper has a crooked nose; an old barroom wound by the look of it. "I copied your call when you hung the ribbon," he says, looking at me, his expression indignant. "None of our guys would have disturbed it."

"Which squad did you have in the area?"

Cooper frowns, turns to his co-worker. "You were workin' that spot, weren't you Phil?"

Phil nods. He's wearing a bear-claw necklace. "Didn't see no pink ribbon."

"When did you get in there, Phil?" I ask. "How long after I called BB?"

Phil gives this some thought. "Half-hour maybe."

"Did you see anyone else in the area?"

"I didn't," Phil says, squinting. "But I could ask the boys."

Phil is about to head back to the bus to question his men when Aslund stops him, tells him not to worry about it. They'll do that later, at the debriefing. I'd prefer an answer now, but it's not my investigation, so I bite my tongue.

"You worked that area with the hose?" says Aslund.

"Yeah," says Phil. "Wasn't much else we could do."

"And you're sure there was no ribbon?"

Phil's expression tells us he's pretty sure.

"What about stuff on the ground?" I ask. "You see any white residue?"

"Why?" he says, looking concerned. "Should I have?"

"There may have been some fusee slag," says Aslund, his glance flickering in my direction. "You see any little white tubes or splotches or anything like that?"

Phil shakes his head, frowning. Once again, he could ask the boys.

"You sayin' we screwed up the origin?" asks Cooper.

"Someone worked it over," I say. Aslund looks annoyed.

"Damn," says Cooper. "You sure?"

I nod.

"We're not sure of anything right now," says Aslund.

Cooper's brow furrows. "Well, if I fucked up, I'd sure like to know."

"Believe me," I tell him, "when you fuck up, you'll know."

Aslund gives me a strange look. I'm not sure if it's because of what I said or how I said it. Cooper, fortunately, hasn't seemed to notice. "Anyway," I tell him, "if you didn't see any ribbon, you have nothing to worry about."

"No ribbon," he says, shaking his head.

"What about your guys? Could they have taken down the ribbon?"

Cooper stares at us. "You mean, like, accidentally?"

Both Aslund and I don't say anything and Cooper's eyes narrow.

"Maybe they thought it marked a hotspot or something like that," I offer.

Cooper crosses his arms. "No way. We briefed them. They knew it marked the origin."

"So you wouldn't mind if we had them check their pockets, would you?"

Cooper's eyes narrow even further and Aslund gives me a startled look. "One minute," he says, raising his index finger like a referee. He tows me away, behind a dozer on a lowboy, his face pinched and frowning. "Listen Cassel, I know you're an investigator, but at this moment your continued participation in this event is strictly as a witness. If you have something of value to contribute, then I'm all ears. But when it comes to conducting an interview, you're just an observer. I'm allowing you to observe as a professional courtesy. Perhaps you could extend the same courtesy to me, and allow me to do my job."

"Fair enough," I say. "My apologies."

Aslund takes a deep breath, seems to relax.

"So, are you going to check their pockets?"

"No, I'm not going to check their pockets."

"Why not?"

Aslund scowls, looks away for a minute. More vehicles arrive, churning up dust. Fresh firefighters troop out of buses. Another green Forest Service engine lumbers to a stop along the road. A uniformed

Deputy stands next to his angled vehicle, controlling access. Aslund looks at me again, trying hard to be patient.

"Where are you going with this Cassel?"

"Nowhere yet. But we need to find that ribbon."

Behind us the dozer fires up, belching and roaring, puffing diesel fumes. A skinner looks down at us, waiting, and we move away. Cooper, Phil, and the other brother stand together, watching us. "Those firefighters have just lost their crew boss," says Aslund, shouting to be heard over the rumble of heavy equipment. "They're pissed off and confused. Thinking we don't trust them won't help matters."

"But what if they have the ribbon?"

"What would it prove? They couldn't have started the fire."

"What if they found the ribbon somewhere else?"

"So what?" says Aslund, raising his hands, clearly exasperated. I'm trying to get through to him, without telling him how to do his job, that you don't overlook anything at a crime scene. Trivial details can become key later. Once the participants have dispersed and the scene is released, you've lost your chance.

"It could have fingerprints on it," I say. "And this is now a homicide."

Aslund considers, glancing toward the Deputy along the road.

"Okay," he says quietly. "But I'll handle this."

Cooper is not impressed and does little to hide the fact. Never, in all his years of firefighting, has he been humiliated like this. Aslund is a little tense as well. The three squads form a loose line by the crew bus. Cooper, being senior, breaks the news to them.

"The pink ribbon at the origin is missing," he says, standing with his arms crossed. He sticks out his chin, straightens a crick in his neck. "Since we were working in the area, there's a possibility someone pulled down the pink ribbon, accidentally, maybe stuffed it into their pocket."

"Doubt it," says Phil. "They'd have to be colour-blind."

"Anyone colour-blind?" Cooper bellows.

Amused looks. No one is colour-blind.

"Good," says Cooper. "Cause no one here would pull down that ribbon on purpose, right?"

Vigorous nods of assent.

"I know that," says Cooper. "But not everyone knows you guys like I do. So, these two gentlemen here would like y'all to empty your pockets."

There's a stunned silence. For a moment, none of the firefighters move, waiting perhaps to see if we're serious. Finally, one of them pulls out a rumpled handful of orange ribbon.

"This is bullshit, man," he mumbles.

Amid furtive glances in our direction, the rest of the firefighters commence rummaging in their packs and the pockets of their green fire pants. Granola bars, sticks of gum, and tins of chewing tobacco are produced. And lots of orange ribbon, but no pink. It's a little hard to tell with everyone doing this at once, and I suggest, in a tone only Aslund can hear, that maybe they should do this one at a time. Aslund grinds his teeth and ignores me.

I see a flash of pink. "Over there," I say, pointing. "What was that?"

Heads turn and everyone stops what they're doing, hands half-full. One of the firefighters is staring at me, looking stricken. "What have you got there?" I ask, trying to sound calm and unaccusing.

"Nothing," he says. He's young, maybe nineteen, and looks terribly guilty.

"I saw something," I say. "Come on, empty your pockets."

He looks at Cooper. "I'd rather not, sir."

There's a tense moment, then Cooper waves him off. "Do it."

Slowly, with great trepidation, the eyes of his co-workers on him, the young firefighter reaches into his pocket and, blushing deeply, pulls out a wad of pink. He holds it up reluctantly. It's a rumpled pair of lacy pink panties. There's a ripple of laughter and he crams them quickly back into his pocket.

"What the hell you got them for?" asks one of his buddies.

"I hope those aren't yours, Bickenham," says another.

Blushing even harder, Bickenham says, "They're for luck."

"What kind of luck might that be?" someone hollers over the chuckling.

Bickenham's lip quivers and he stares furiously at the ground. Aslund finally reins them in.

"Okay guys, sorry for the inconvenience. Put everything back in your pockets."

Teary-eyed and still chuckling, the firefighters pocket their goods, punching each other on the shoulder, slapping Bickenham on the back. If nothing else, they're in a better mood.

"Hey," says one firefighter. "What about those guys?"

The three members of the local volunteer fire department stand by one of their red pumpers, looking at the crowd of rowdy, jostling firefighters. Aslund shakes his head.

"Oh, come on," says Cooper. "You made us do it."

"Yeah," says Phil. "Who knows what they might have in their pockets."

More laughter. Aslund hesitates and, grimacing, waves them over.

Hutton and his two workers smile cautiously, like men who aren't sure if they're going to be let in on a joke, or if they are the joke. "What can I do for you?" asks Hutton.

"Well, umm ..." Aslund stammers.

"Empty your pockets," hollers one of the firefighters.

Hutton frowns. "What?"

It's Aslund's turn to blush. "We're conducting a check. To see what's in your pockets."

Hutton squints at him. "This is a joke, right?"

Something in Hutton's voice makes it not so funny anymore. The laughter dies down.

"You know you need a search warrant to do that," says Hutton.

There's a silence — as quiet as it gets at an active staging area anyway. Hutton stares at Aslund and me, looks over at the firefighters.

He looks disgusted, disdainful. "You let them do this?"

"What's the matter?" says Cooper. "You got something to hide?"

Hutton reaches into his pockets, pulls out the lining. They're empty. His two men do the same.

"Have a nice day," he says, and stalks away.

"You happy?" says Aslund, under his breath.

"There you are, Cassel."

Herb Grey strides along the road, his belt radio slapping against his stubby legs. Aslund and I have parted ways and I'm sitting in the shade of a service truck, watching the staging area. The new crews are out on the line, working with the dozers and engines. The air is filled with the whine of pumps, the crash of trees, the buzz of chainsaws. Everyone is busy except me — I have nothing to do but wait and think, neither of which I'm keen on at the moment. Hard physical work is what I need right now to blot out the memories.

"Aslund all done with you?" says Grey, puffing as he nears the service truck.

"For the time being."

"Good. We're headed out of here."

I'm suddenly aware that I'll never be back. I've squandered valuable time.

"Do you mind waiting a few minutes? There's something I want to check."

"Negative." Grey shakes his head, still catching his breath. "We've got to get rolling."

I look into the burn, where I think the fire crossed the line. "I'll be quick."

Grey gives me an intent look. "What's so goddamn important all of a sudden?"

"I just want to look at where the fire jumped the line."

"What the hell for?"

"I'm not sure. I just need to see it."

Grey's stern, commanding expression softens just a bit. "Don't blame yourself."

"It was my fire," I say quietly. "I was responsible for Brashaw and his men."

"Shit happens, Cassel. Fires are not entirely predictable."

Despite Grey's reassurance, we both know there'll be plenty of scrutiny later and we share a moment of silence. I'd like to have a look at where the runaway fire started. Maybe I just need to know it was inevitable. Maybe I'm just a sucker for punishment. Grey frowns, his patience at an end.

"Come on," he says. "You're out of here and I'm your ride."

Still, I hesitate. Grey sighs heavily, uses a sooty hand to massage his forehead.

"We've got to get going, Cassel. I have to break the news to Brashaw's family."

Brashaw's family — I have a sudden anxious clench in my gut, thinking about BB's children. They'd be grown by now, with children of their own. I'd never thought of BB as a grandfather, and somehow this makes it worse. I take a deep, unsteady breath. Let it out slowly.

"You all right, Cassel?"

"Fine," I say numbly. "I was the lucky one."

Grey shakes his head. "No one was lucky today."

4

WE DRIVE BACK in a green minivan, Grey at the wheel. Considering how rutted and steep the trail is, I'm not sure how they got the damn thing up here. Grey hugs the side of the trail, riding the ridges. He hits a cross-rut and the minivan thumps down hard, its suspension scraping. At the bottom of the hill, Grey unsnaps his belt radio, calls the new incident commander who flew in. "It's Grey again," he barks into the radio. "You might want to send one of those dozers down the road, smooth things out before someone breaks an axle and cuts off your ground access."

We ride in silence the rest of the way down the narrow trail to the Blood Creek Road, Grey no doubt wondering how he'll break the news to Brashaw's family.

"Were there any other injuries?" I ask Grey.

He shakes his head. "What about you? Any burns?"

"Nothing serious."

"You did get burned?"

He looks concerned but my burns are minor. "I'm fine."

"You sure? I could drop you at the hospital."

"No, thanks."

There's an awkward silence. Any injuries, even minor ones, are to be reported and given appropriate first aid, but the last thing I need is a nurse fussing over me while Brashaw lies dead on the ridge. I ignore Grey's searching look, stare out a side window, watch trees and ranchland slide past. We're on the highway now and the minivan is quiet, like riding in a vacuum tube. My thoughts seem loud, self-evident. The first commandment of firefighting is to fight fire aggressively but provide for safety first. I could have waited until the next day for an aerial view of the fire, but by then it would have been lost. The ridge appeared safe, so I took what I thought was a minor risk for a strategic advantage. Somewhere though, I missed a clue, and now Brashaw is dead. Grey's belt radio crackles to life, catching a clear line of transmission from the fire, and we both flinch. He reaches down and shuts it off. Carson Lake comes into view, long and narrow below the highway. Grey shifts in his seat, clears his throat.

"Cassel, I want you to know how sorry I am you had to go through this. God knows this is a hard enough business as it is. No one should have to lose their life fighting a fire. No one should have to go through what you went through."

He's looking at me with the sad, tired eyes of a disappointed father and I suddenly feel weak.

"What happens next?"

"Well, there's going to be an entrapment investigation. The investigators will look at every aspect of the fire, try to learn exactly what happened. They'll look at weather records, dispatch logs, talk to those who were on the fire when it blew up. They'll examine personal protective equipment — which reminds me, I'll need yours. Then, after a lot of meetings and discussion, they'll make some recommendations so this won't happen again."

He's tactfully avoided any reference to my role, my possible mistakes.

"What about the arson?"

Grey smoothes his moustache, frowning thoughtfully. "That's a bit more complicated. Arson in a national forest is usually a Forest Service matter, but this fire had a fatality, which makes the arson a crime against a person. You see, when someone lights a fire intentionally, they can be held accountable for anything that occurs as a result of the fire. So, at a minimum, it'll be involuntary manslaughter. Most of the investigation will be handled by the Sheriff's Department."

"Will the Forest Service still have a role?"

"I'm sure we'll have some of our people on it."

"Aslund?"

Grey gives me a wry smile. "No, he's just local. Something this big, they'll bring in the boys from Washington." He shifts in his seat again, frowns slightly. "Used to be, we did our own investigating, but that's handled by a separate branch within the Forest Service now. Strictly law enforcement people. Supposed to get around local politics."

We pull into the Carson Lake Ranger Station, a sprawling shake-roofed wooden building overlooking the lake, and Grey tells me to grab my overnight bag. While he vanishes inside, I walk around back to where several wall tents have been erected on a grassy slope. I grab my pack and bedroll from one of the tents, spend a few minutes watching boats roar back and forth on the lake, pulling kids on tire tubes. Grey sticks his head out the back door, hollers at me. He's changed into his dress uniform. You know something serious has happened when a forest ranger wears a suit.

We continue into town. In his crisp dress uniform, Grey looks very official. He's going to visit Brashaw's family. I'd like to be there with him, to answer any of the questions I know they'll have. To apologize. But I can't go there looking like this, covered with soot and grime, so I ask Grey if we could stop somewhere so I can clean up.

"Sure," he says, distracted. "I'm bringing you to a motel."

I hesitate. "I'd like to come with you, to see Brashaw's family."

"Not a chance," he says, flashing me a startled look.

"I feel a certain obligation —"

"That's a definite negative, Cassel. This is a district responsibility."

It's clear from his tone there's no room for negotiation and I let it go. Before I head back to Canada, I'll visit Brashaw's family on my own, pass on my condolences. In their shoes, I would expect the same courtesy. Grey pulls the minivan into the Paradise Gateway Motel at the edge of town; it doesn't get more generic than that. At the front desk, it's clear that everything has been arranged.

"How long will Mr. Johnson be staying?" the clerk asks Grey.

Grey gives me a sideways glance. "Put him down for two nights."

I have a room at the end of the second floor with a splendid view of the parking lot. Grey stands in the doorway, his moustache twitching.

"Okay Cassel. Get yourself cleaned up. Have a rest. There'll be a debriefing here in the conference room at twenty-hundred hours. The whole crew will be there. Until then, if you need anything, call the ranger station, ask for Mark in Fire Ops. He knows the situation."

I thank Grey and he vanishes. From the window, I watch the green minivan turn onto the highway. My fingers and toes ache from being scorched and there's a line of pain diagonally across my back. I sit on the edge of the bed and stare at the phone. I want to call my sister Cindy in Edmonton, and Telson. But Cindy is at work and Telson could be anywhere. I stand, look around, feeling a bit lost. There's a black horse-shoe on the bed sheets where I was sitting. Grey forgot to pick up my fire clothes for analysis.

In the bathroom, I get a shock when I look in the mirror.

My face is dark grey, streaked with black. Even my teeth are stained with soot, my eyes bloodshot orbs, my hair black and coarse, sticking out like wire. I look like the face of Death, as though I'd clawed my way up through the earth on a moonlit night.

It takes a long time in the shower to wash off the ash. When I shut off the water, I hear someone knocking at the door, and I lean my head against the wet tiles, hoping they'll go away. My fingers and back blaze with pain and I'm in no mood to socialize. The knock comes five or six times, hesitates, then comes again, as persistent as a woodpecker. I take my time toweling off, pull fresh clothes out of my pack, thinking the woodpecker will give up, but the knocking continues. Finally, I throw the bolt and fling open the door.

"Mr. Cassel?"

It's a man in his mid-forties, a full head shorter than me. He's wearing a white shirt and narrow tie. A blue blazer is hung over his arm. He's nearly bald, the top of his head shining like his polished black shoes.

"I'm Cassel."

"I'm Irving Groves. Sorry to disturb you. I was concerned when you didn't answer."

"I was in the shower."

"Yes, of course." Groves looks a little embarrassed. "I should have given you time to clean up."

"What can I do for you, Mr. Groves?"

Groves extends a pale hand and my first thought is he's a reporter, which would explain his tenacity. "I'm a psychologist," he says. He's got a firm handshake for a head doctor; probably part of the prescription when dealing with a firefighter. Handshakes aside, we're a world apart and I'm in no mood to bare my soul to this stranger.

"Sorry, but I'm not interested."

I start to close the door but he reaches forward, holds it open. "I understand your reluctance Mr. Cassel, but it always helps to talk about these things after the event to prevent repression. This would be completely confidential and at no cost to yourself."

"I'm fine with repression."

"If you could just give me ten minutes of your time —"

"No thanks."

Groves yields the door. "I'll be available later, at the session in the conference room."

The door closes. I throw the bolt, collapse on the bed, and stare at the ceiling.

Eight o'clock comes way too fast.

My legs are a little shaky when I arrive at the conference room. A page ripped from a notebook is taped to the door, the message written in black felt pen: Incident Debriefing. I hear voices and the shuffling of chairs, and hesitate — behind these doors are all the firefighters I let down.

There were maybe forty firefighters on the Holder fire, but the room is packed with close to a hundred people. Chrome and plastic stacking chairs form ragged rows, rearranged by groups wanting to talk together. In one huddle are a dozen members of the Carson Lake Hotshots, their bright red T-shirts emblazoned with a cartoon logo of a superhero brandishing a Pulaski and shovel. Others stand in groups of three and four, talking quietly. I barely recognize Galloway without her hard hat and gear, long hair spilling over her shoulders. She sees me looking and glances away.

"How you holding up, Cassel?"

It's Aslund, wearing a ball cap and canvas shirt with too many pockets. I tell him I'm doing okay, all things considered. Grey is on a dais at the front of the room, talking to Groves. Grey has reverted to field gear, wearing jeans, a fire shirt, and fire boots. Groves is wearing a navy blazer and tie. They're at opposite ends of the fashion spectrum. This may not be the only divergence here; I think about Groves's pitch to me earlier, hoping he has something a little more practical for the masses. Grey hollers for order and the chatter dies off. He waits, stern and commanding, while the crowd takes their seats.

"For anyone doesn't know me, I'm Herb Grey, chief ranger of the Carson Lake District. Thanks for coming. I know you're all a bit stressed out, so we thought it would be a good idea to have a little session and get things into the open. Mr. Groves here is a clinical psychologist and he'll guide us through the process." Grey looks over at Groves. "They're all yours."

Groves surveys the room, nervously smoothes his tie. He's got a flip chart next to him. A hundred firefighters and support workers watch as Groves turns to his flip chart, and carefully flips up the blank first page. The next page is a flow chart, vivid orange letters against an azure background.

"There are five discernable stages to the grief cycle," says Groves, pointing to the chart. "We'll look at all five stages in more detail but, as an overview, this is how they flow. The traumatic event initially sparks denial, a natural defensive mechanism allowing one to immediately cope with the situation. This is followed by rage, bargaining, depression, and, finally, by acceptance, or resolution."

A professional pause as Groves flips the chart. There's a single word: DENIAL.

Groves drones on as though giving a lecture — Psychology 101 — oblivious to the impatient shiftings of his audience. We learn about the value of denial, the difference between short- and long-term repression. When he's done with denial, he flips over another glossy page. The single word — RAGE — is accompanied by a line drawing of a man with spiked hair and little puffs of steam coming from his ears. Rage, we're told, follows the collapse of denial.

"This is horseshit," someone mutters, loud enough to be heard across the room.

Another loud whisper: "Where'd they get this guy?"

"Isn't this supposed to be a debriefing?" says a smokejumper.

Groves smoothes down imaginary hair, takes a moment to assess the changing mood of his audience. Chairs scrape the floor as firefighters turn to talk to one another. Grey sits with his arms crossed, waiting. Groves glares at the crowd, but no one pays him any attention. He clears his throat conspicuously. "If we could just continue —"

"Just a minute, Sigmund," says Cooper, standing and looking around.

"If you'll just be so kind as to take a seat —"

"What I want to know," says Cooper, "is why someone had to get killed before our fire became a priority. If we'd had a helicopter, we could have plucked those guys off the ridge."

"And what about the bombers?" says a firefighter in front of me.

"They were on another fire," someone shouts. "Protecting buildings."

"Buildings!" Cooper roars. "We're more important than some damn structures."

There's a murmur of angry support; they've skipped denial and moved right along to rage. Groves tries once more to bring his lecture back on course, but it's clear the crowd was expecting something different. They want to talk about the fire. They want answers.

"Look," Groves says loudly, "I wasn't brought here to discuss that. If we could just —"

But he's drowned out by more shouting.

"They never should have been up there —"

"What about the arson? Are there any leads?"

"This is fucking pointless —"

Groves's attempt at bargaining has failed and he's slipping into depression. Grey walks onto the dais and stands silently, arms crossed, staring at the crowd. Despite his stubby stature, he has a foreboding presence. The arguing and cross-talk dies down.

"Sit down, Cooper."

Cooper sits. "Sir," he says. "With all due respect, what is this horseshit?"

There's a murmur of support. Grey holds up a hand, turns to Groves.

"Is the rest of your presentation like this?"

Groves looks offended. "It's on the grief cycle. It seemed appropriate."

"I'm sure it is," says Grey, looking at the crowd of restless firefighters. "In university."

There's a ripple of relieved laughter. Groves scowls; he's having trouble with acceptance.

Grey addresses the crowd. "As ineffective as it may seem, this stress debriefing was intended for your benefit. But it is completely optional and I won't hold it against any of you if you choose to diffuse your stress by other, more conventional means."

"Thank God," says Cooper, standing. The rest of Brashaw's crew stands with him and they troop out, quickly followed by the smoke-jumpers and most of the support staff. Groves watches them go, clearly distressed at his inability to soothe their anguish.

"If anyone has need of further counselling," he shouts. "I'm in Room 223."

The counselling session continues in the Pine Room — a bar in the motel with knotty pine wainscotting and a wall covered with video gambling machines. Chairs are pulled around small circular tables, quickly covered with glasses of draft, rum, and whisky. Cooper, the centre of gravity for Brashaw's crew, sits at one end of the room. He sees me looking, motions me over.

"Have a drink, Cassel," he says aggressively. "Have a fucking drink."

The bar reeks with the scent of smoke and sweat; these boys have come straight from the fire. Cooper's tanned face is streaked with black like a weary commando. I motion that I'm going to the bar for a drink but a waitress swings past, her tray loaded, delivering another bomber drop of alcohol. Cooper grabs a glass and thrusts a rye and Coke at me. "Pull up a stump," he says.

I look around, drink in hand, searching for a chair.

"Get the fuck up," Cooper hollers at one of his men. "Make a hole for this survivor."

Three firefighters stand and offer their chairs. I hesitate, then take one. I was expecting recriminations and accusations from the men on Brashaw's crew. But they're friendly in a belligerent sort of way, and crowd around, jostling and talking. Cooper holds up a hand for attention, leans forward and looks at me. "So tell us, what happened up there?"

Talk around me dies down but it's still deafening in here; the room vibrates with country music, shouting, and the chime of gambling. Young, stubbled faces watch me expectantly, as if I might have some answer that will make everything clear. I don't want to disappoint them but all I have to offer are details I'd rather forget: the fire roaring through the trees, the mad scramble up the hill. I drain my glass of whisky — it burns inside, like the scorch across my back. Another whisky is slid in my direction. I pick up the cool glass, hold it without drinking, wonder where to start.

"We needed to get to the ridge," I say slowly. "To look over the fire."

I pause, expecting someone to challenge me, to say this was my fault, that I never should have dragged Brashaw up there with me. But if they have doubts, they don't show it. I was the incident commander and my decision is not questioned. I relax a little, begin to relate the sequence of events starting from the drive up the old trail behind the ridge. Once again, I avoid mention of Brashaw's preoccupation with the canyon's curse, reluctant to shift blame to an old superstition. When I pause to sip my drink, I notice the crowd around me has deepened; the entire bar has come to hear my story. Even the waitress stands listening, her tray held at her side.

"After the call, we both stood there, hypnotized by the flames. They were something to see, like a snake rising over the hill, and for a few seconds, we couldn't move. Then we made a run for the truck, down through the trees, until BB twisted his ankle."

Around me, the faces of his men cringe, no doubt imagining themselves in our position. Someone takes the empty glass from my hand, gives me another.

"What'd you do?" asks Bickenham.

"The fire was coming up the hill pretty fast and I wasn't sure how far away the truck was. So we went back upslope, to deploy in the open, away from the fuel. It was a bitch of a climb though, with his bad ankle. He's not someone you can just pick up and carry."

"That takes guts," says a firefighter, slapping me on the back. "Not abandoning him."

Someone punches my shoulder. "You're a fuckin' hero."

There's a roar of approval and I wince. "I'm no hero."

"Sure you are," says Phil, the squad boss. "Anyone who has the balls to —"

"No — goddamn it! It was my fault we were up there to start with."

There's an uncomfortable silence. Men stare into their drinks.

"Fuck that," says Cooper. "You did what you had to."

"No —"

I feel like an idiot, don't want to explain what seems so obvious to me, set aside my drink and stand. Reeling. Hands support me on all sides but I shake them off. Everyone watches but no more questions are asked. They clap me on the shoulder, tell me to hang in there. I'm overcome by a deep, embarrassing gratitude for their support. The waitress, slim and dark-haired, offers me a drink on the house. I thank her, switch to beer, which has a higher LD50. There's a pay phone near the washroom and I take my beer with me. I know it's not a real good time, but I gotta make a call.

I dial Cindy's number. Breathlessly, she accepts the charges.

"Porter, God almighty. Are you okay?"

"I'm okay, Cin. The guy I was with didn't do so good though."

"I know. It's all over the news. It must've been terrible."

I tell her some of what happened, leave out the gruesome details. I'm starting to slur. Cindy listens and offers friendly support. Her voice makes me intensely homesick. I want to be playing cards with her, watching a movie with the kids.

"You really okay, Porter? You sound a little depressed."

I assure her I'm hanging in there, tell her I'll be home soon. The bar seems a little louder, a little more alien, when I hang up. I finish my beer, start another. I'm past the point of caring how much this will hurt tomorrow. Past the point of caring that I vowed never to do this again. Someone buys me a blue shooter. It looks like Windex but goes down easy enough. So does the next drink.

Someone slaps me on the back. It's Grey. "You okay, Cassel?"

I nod, my head bobbing to the music. I know I'm drunk when I enjoy Willie Nelson.

"That's good," he says. "Get this out of your system."

I nod and he moves on, consoling the troops. There's a bit of a ruckus and I turn to see Cooper standing unsteadily on his chair. He steps onto a small round table, knocking over glasses of beer and whisky. Bleary-eyed, he gazes across the room and raises his drink.

"Draw nigh, ye drunkards!" he hollers over the music. "Ye cowards, ye dissolute men."

Cooper sways, his face glistening with sweat. Glass crunches under the thick soles of his boots.

"— ye are sots. Ye bear the mark of the beast on your foreheads —"

It takes me a minute to place what he's saying. Dostoevsky, from *Crime and Punishment*. At the moment, it seems oddly appropriate. He staggers again, nearly falling; hands reach up to steady him. He grins down at them, anointing his faithful with spilled beer. Looking solemn, he tries to continue, but he's lost his train of thought. He raises his empty glass once again.

"Here's to Bert Brashaw — the King!"

There's a thunder of approval. Boots stomp. Tables are thumped. Cooper, smiling in a bemused fashion, is about to say something more when the table begins to wobble. For a few seconds he keeps his balance, but is defeated by gravity and alcohol, and returns to earth with an undignified crash, landing partway on his companions, partway on the table. Cooper, with minor wounds, is laid on the floor, where he commences snoring.

The waitress comes around and I fumble in my pockets for money.

"Don't worry," she says, smiling. "They're charging it all to Room 223."

"Yeah," shouts a smokejumper. "Further counselling."

I don't quite make it to Cooper's level of therapy. One by one, Grey leads us out of the bar and to our rooms. I'm dimly aware that I'm leaning on him as I stagger up the stairs. At my door, I feel I have to say something, although I don't know what, and make frustrated mumblings.

"I know, Cassel," he says. "I know."

5

●

LATE THE NEXT morning, I wake up on the floor, my pants around my ankles, an arm pinned under my thigh. Apparently, I didn't make it far from the door after Grey escorted me to my room. I was probably trying to undress and lost my balance. Motel rooms should come with emergency pull-cords, like hospital bathrooms. It takes me a while to roll over and sit up, longer to come to an upright position. Then I stumble again and crash onto my elbows.

"Sorry Lord, I'll be good now."

The higher powers are not impressed and when I stand again, I'm in purgatory. There's a funeral in my head for the dead brain cells, complete with drums and chanting. I limp into the bathroom, rinse my mouth with water. The chlorine taste isn't much of an improvement. In the mirror I can see the weave of the motel carpet on my cheek. Nice to know I can still make a good impression. I want a long shower, but the water burns the scab on my back.

In the motel restaurant, I order apple juice. The waitress, a weary-looking woman in her fifties, tells me the special is bacon and eggs, but the mere suggestion of grease causes an unpleasant turbulence from below and I order waffles — food I can empathize with.

It's a lovely morning. I wander down main street, not really sure where I'm going. I just want to get away from the motel, want to be on the move. What I really need is a long drive and plenty of loud music, but since I have neither, I content myself with a roaring headache and a long meandering walk in the heat.

The town of Carson Lake is strung along the highway, conveniently forcing through traffic to slow down and stop at a half-dozen lights. While stopped, the discerning commuter can peruse a selection of grocery stores with casinos, gas stations with casinos, and restaurants with casinos. In fact, every building seems to advertise gambling and cold beer. There's even a laundromat and casino; if you're short on change, you'll have to decide if you want to play the slots or wash your underwear. I stop in the shade of a tiny ice cream parlour, buy an extra-large vanilla. The girl behind the counter offers me a selection of scratch-and-win tickets. I buy one, just to fit in.

I push on, taking advantage of patches of shade thrown by buildings and dim verandas. I'm downtown now, where buildings are closer together and there are fewer trees. A guy standing in the parking lot of the Chicken Coop Casino and Lounge is using the side mirror of his truck to shave. Kids on skateboards practise their moves in front of a grocery store. Pop's Family Restaurant sits across the highway from Mom's Grill and Souvenir Shop — they must have had a falling out. The door of a service station is plastered with purple ribbons and I begin to notice them everywhere. Passersby wear them like Memorial Day flowers and I realize with a jolt that is exactly what they are. A big rental sign along the highway proclaims, "We Miss You BB" and the flag at the post office is at half-mast. I pull my cap a little lower. Standing in the shade of a service station, a scruffy-looking kid sidles up to me.

"Hey man," he says quietly. "You looking for something?"

He's maybe seventeen, with ripped jeans and a baggy jacket.

"My sanity," I tell him. "Have you seen it?"

He ignores the remark. "I can hook you up with some good weed."

"No thanks."

"Homegrown." He grins, showing me his two teeth. "No additives or preservatives."

"I'm trying to cut down on mind-altering substances."

But this is good shit, he persists — practically health food. I'm starting to lose my temper when he suddenly turns away, vanishes into the service station. A black-and-white sheriff's suv pulls to the pump. Deputy Compton scowls from behind reflective sunglasses.

I'm not in a socializing mood and swing away from Main Street, past the back of the service station. Beyond this the streets are narrower. Large ponderosa cast shadows. Despite marginally cooler temperatures, the backside of town is somewhat less attractive. Trailers and old stucco houses sit amicably next to metal-clad shops and industrial storage yards. Swing sets and sandboxes share space with dead cars. What the area lacks in presence, it makes up for in churches — an interesting contrast with the casinos along the highway.

The streets wind and I find myself at the edge of town, among the trees.

I rest in the shade of a massive sign announcing the new Lazy Pine subdivision. A cheery, rotund face beams at me from the sign, espousing the virtues of Lazy Pine, a quiet neighbourhood of architecturally controlled single-family homes. It's quiet all right — there's nothing here but a maze of dead-end gravel roads with electrical service wires sticking out of the ground. I'm suddenly very thirsty and start back for the motel.

These streets were probably wagon trails at one time, the way they meander. Does Juniper Drive continue all the way to the highway? No, it ends at Birch Street. Naughty Pine Lane sounds interesting but dead-ends at a machine shop. I spend a bit of time going in circles around Larch Crescent until finding a secondary road leading straight to the highway. A service station lures me in and I buy a bottle of deliciously cold grapefruit juice, which I drink at the checkout. A woman standing by the window watches me.

"Are you Porter Cassel?"

I don't like being identified by strangers and pretend not to hear her, quickly stepping outside. I don't make it far before I hear the door open. There's a van with a familiar logo at the gas pumps. I've got to stop hanging around service stations.

"I'm a friend of Christina Telson," she says, trotting up beside me. Reluctantly, I stop and turn to face her.

"You are Porter Cassel, aren't you?" she says, her eyebrows arched. She's quite attractive even without the blue business suit and cameraman.

"If you're a friend of Christina's," I tell her evenly, "you know that I don't give interviews."

"Yes, well, we're colleagues," she says, giving me a six o'clock smile.

I turn away, keep walking. She calls after me, asking for a few minutes of my time — that's all. Just a few questions. This is an opportunity to tell my side of the story, to set the record straight. I didn't know the record wasn't straight but pass on the opportunity. I think she's given up until the van rolls quietly beside me, the window down. She's got her microphone ready.

"Mr. Cassel, I understand it was your decision to go up on the ridge."

I keep walking but she continues her rolling interview, so I switch directions. The van lurches, then backs up. Just as they catch me, I go forward again and the van rocks. So does the reporter, trying to steady herself with one hand on the dash. She sticks her head out the window.

"You were the incident commander —"

I switch directions again, but the novelty has worn thin and I make an undignified retreat across the service station lot, into a narrow walkway between two buildings. The van circles around, trying to corner me, but I double back and run across the highway, dodging logging trucks. A horn blares but I make it to the other side, dash into a pocket of trees. When I glance back, the van is still circling the service station.

I chuckle, head for the motel, keeping to back alleys. But the last laugh is on me. The parking lot of the motel is full of media vans. Cameramen are setting up, reporters doing sound checks.

I fade back, start looking for a phone booth.

A green minivan pulls to the curb, and for a second I think it's the reporters again, but it's Grey and a few unfamiliar faces. The door slides open and I'm practically yanked inside. Three serious-looking individuals in suits frown at me. Grey wasn't drinking last night, but he looks hungover.

"You should have stayed at the motel," he says.

The minivan pulls away from the curb, turns down a back street.

"Good morning, Mr. Cassel," says one of the suits, sitting beside me. He introduces himself as Mark Castellino, principal death investigator for the Missoula County Sheriff's Department. Behind me is Robert Haines, a sheriff's department arson specialist and, in the front passenger seat, Kirk Noble, a Forest Service special agent from Washington.

"Quite a zoo you got going here," says Noble, looking back.

"Yeah. I had to run from one of them earlier."

Noble looks concerned. He's chunky, balding, and sunburned. "You tell them anything?"

I shake my head.

"Good," he says. "This is a sensitive situation. We don't have many arson-related fireline fatalities, and even fewer investigations involving out-of-country service people. In fact, I'd have to say this is a rather unique situation." He loosens his tie as he talks. He's got a big neck and a few more chins pop out. "The plan for the next few days is to set you up out of town, where you'll be away from prying eyes. We'll be set up close by as well. We may need to speak with you on a fairly regular basis, until the circumstances are clear in everyone's mind."

I thought they were already clear — I screwed up and someone got killed.

"How does this all fit together?" I ask. "The different jurisdictions?"

"I operate out of Washington," Noble says, in case I didn't catch this the first time. "Our organization is a little different from the Canadian model. The US Forest Service has an autonomous law enforcement branch. We handle most criminal violations occurring in national forests, and arson is certainly one of them. But we don't handle crimes against people — that's the jurisdiction of the local sheriff's department. In this case, the fatality does complicate things. We're looking at a potential homicide now, and this is where Mr. Castellino and Mr. Haines become involved. They'll be the leads from the sheriff's department."

"Is the Forest Service conducting their own arson investigation?"

Noble frowns. "That hasn't been entirely worked out yet. Because the arson is essentially the homicide, the Forest Service likely won't conduct a separate investigation into the cause of the fire. We'll function as an attachment to the sheriff's team, provide some expert advice."

I glance over at Haines. "Have you investigated wildfire arson before?"

Haines shakes his head. He's pale, with a long face and thin sandy-blond hair. "Just structure arsons, but the concepts are the same."

I nod, thinking this could be an awkward arrangement.

Noble gives me an appraising look. "I understand you're a wildfire investigator as well."

"I do a little work with the Forest Service in Alberta."

"Yes, I've heard about you," he says ambiguously, which makes me a little nervous. "I'll be interested in your observations regarding the origin, since there doesn't seem to be any physical evidence remaining."

It sounds vaguely like an accusation but I let it slide.

"What about the burnover itself?" I ask. "How is that investigated?"

"There'll be an entrapment investigation team," Noble says, craning his neck — he's getting a kink from looking over his shoulder. "They'll try to determine exactly what happened; identify the contributing factors. I'll serve as liaison, but Mr. Grey here will be the lead."

Grey doesn't say anything and we ride in silence for a few minutes.

"Have you had any contact with the Forest Service in Alberta?" I ask Noble.

He nods. "Our director called your director."

I think about Gil Patton, Provincial Director of Forest Protection. With his blood pressure, this might kill him — I'd have two bodies on my hands. Maybe by the time I return, he'll have calmed down. Maybe I'll just move to the Caribbean and sell T-shirts on the beach.

We turn off the highway onto a secondary road, pass a log-building company with several partially constructed houses in their yard, and a small sawmill. We turn down another narrower road where a sign announces Lakeside Estates. Carson Lake flashes through the trees as we pull into a meandering driveway. Log cabins are set amid towering ponderosa. Lawns are manicured and there's a private beach. This is definitely a step up from the Paradise Gateway Motel. We park in front of a cabin, beside another unmarked minivan and a sheriff's black-and-white.

Inside, it's obvious the cabin is being used as an operations centre. Maps are tacked to the walls, the fire boundary, origin, and fatality site marked. Photographs are pinned to a portable corkboard, images I'd just as soon forget — a bit of a contrast to the homey, fishing-lodge atmosphere of the room. We pull out chairs around a wide dining-room table. The chandelier is made of artfully interlaced elk horns. Paintings of serene mountains hang on the walls. The domestic splendour does little to quell my nervousness as we sit down.

"We've got a few things to discuss," says Castellino. "We'll try to keep this informal."

He pulls a mini-cassette recorder from an inside suit pocket, sets it on the table, the microphone pointing at me. Noble, Haines, and Grey all have pads of paper in front of them, pens poised to take notes. It looks like Castellino will be the ringleader.

"Let's start with the origin," he says. "What was your first indication this was an arson?"

"I found a fusee cap," I say, staring at the tiny recorder. "It was along the road, a short distance into the trees, as though someone tossed it as they ran to their vehicle."

"Did you encounter any vehicles on your way in?"

"Nothing after we left the highway."

"What about vehicle tracks?"

I shake my head. "The road surface was very hard. And our own vehicles didn't help."

Castellino frowns. He's short and swarthy, with black hair going grey, receding at the temples, and a thin, fifties-style moustache.

"Did you search further up the trail?"

"No. I was a little busy."

Noble looks at Grey. "Where does that road lead?"

"Goes another ten or fifteen miles, then dead-ends."

"Someone said there were people living up there."

Grey doesn't look terribly impressed. "Bunch of old hippies."

"Do they have a lease or something?"

"Yeah, right," Grey snorts.

"You're just letting them squat up there, on government land?"

"They dragged a couple of beat-up trailers onto an old wellsite," says Grey. "Land belongs to the Bureau of Land Management, and the wellsite is still under some company's name. I think there's even a wellhead there. Either way, it's not really our concern. They'll stay until winter, grow their organic vegetables, or whatever the hell it is they grow, then give up when it gets cold and move on."

"You ever have a problem with them?"

Grey looks thoughtful, shakes his head. Castellino and Haines exchange glances. "Nothing substantial from our end," says Castellino. "You see them in town once in a while, buying groceries, but they pretty much keep to themselves."

"What do you know about them?" says Noble.

"Nothing really," admits Castellino. "They've only been there since spring."

"Could they have started the fire?"

"I doubt it. They're not crazy about drawing attention to themselves."

"Could someone be trying to get rid of them?" I ask.

"Not that we know of," says Castellino. "But anything is possible."

"Seems unlikely," says Grey. "They're quite a bit north of the canyon, on the far side of a ridge."

"Doesn't take a fire long to cross a ridge," says Noble, giving me a critical look. There's a brief, uncomfortable silence during which everyone does a remarkable job of not looking at me.

"Have there been other fires like this?"

More silence. No one seems eager to answer my question. Castellino thoughtfully rubs his chin. Haines is redesigning a paperclip. Grey is twisting the end of his moustache. He glances around when my eyes reach him, seems to accept that he'll have to answer. "It's been a few years since we had anything we could say for certain was arson. Last time, it was some guy using homemade napalm. Glue and gasoline. He'd slosh the stuff around on the trees, then stand in one spot, throwing matches until one caught. We nabbed him at the hospital after his leg caught fire. Burned himself pretty good."

"Could that be related?"

"I doubt it," says Grey. "He's in the loony bin now."

"What about motive? What's the employment situation like?"

Grey shakes his head. "Our crews are on all summer, and they've been busy."

"Any contentious timber sales or land developments?"

"Not in that area," says Grey. "Too rugged."

Haines scribbles in his notepad. Castellino realizes I've been asking more questions than him and frowns. "Let's get back to this fusee cap you found near the road. What did you do with it?"

"I bagged it, to preserve any prints, and locked it in the truck."

Castellino glances at Grey. "We'll have to get that cap to the lab right away."

Grey nods, makes a note of this. "I don't think so," I say.

"What?" Castellino gives me a dark look. "Why not?"

"It was in the Forest Service truck behind the ridge."

"The vehicle that was incinerated?"

"That's the one. I told this to Aslund. It's probably in his report."

"Did you mark the spot where you found this cap?"

I hesitate. "No."

"Can you identify the location?"

"Sure. Unfortunately, the location has been disturbed."

Noble looks irritated. "Like everything else."

"What sort of disturbance?" asks Haines, his knobby fingers laced together.

"The D8 type of disturbance," I tell them. "The area is now a parking lot."

Noble stands, goes to a wall map printed on orthophotography — aerial photos corrected for scale so measurements can be taken from the image. The photo is a few years old but, other than the fire, little has changed. He taps a pen at a spot where the perimeter of the fire, marked with a heavy black line, approaches the main trail.

"Can you mark where you found the fusee cap?"

I oblige, put a red dot about where I think I found the cap.

"About a hundred and twenty yards from the origin," says Noble. He tugs at his tie, still too tight for his thick neck. He mops his forehead with a kerchief pulled from a pants pocket and looks at me.

"Could you show me how you traced the fire back to the origin?"

Using the red marker as a pointer, I relate where I entered the fire, what signs I noted. Haines and Castellino join us at the map. Castellino has the recorder in hand, pointing it at me like a reporter. Noble frowns when I tell them about the mixed char patterns, how I used the fire spread rate and game trail to locate the origin.

"So, I wouldn't necessarily find the same origin," he says.

It's my turn to frown. "What do you mean?"

He points to the origin marked on the map. "If I relied on char patterns, and other traditional indications of fire spread, I could easily draw a different conclusion."

"Maybe," I say slowly, wondering where he's going with this. "But I doubt it."

"Why might that be?"

"Have you been out there?"

"This morning," he says. "First light. But indulge me."

"Okay. Like I said, the char patterns are multidirectional, indicating variable winds and correspondingly variable directions of fire spread; no doubt a result of complex terrain patterns. Unless you know something I don't, you'd have to rely on the same indicators — the rate of fire spread and the likely route of access into the origin area. What was your conclusion?"

"Based on what I found, I couldn't draw a conclusion."

"You couldn't draw a conclusion?"

He shakes his head and I get an uncomfortable feeling he doesn't believe me.

"Are you questioning my origin?"

"Not at all," Noble says hastily, raising his hands. "I didn't have the benefit of the physical evidence you found, or your early arrival at the fire. I was merely curious how you determined the origin. Given the char patterns, you did a hell of a job."

There's a silence. Haines and Castellino study the map. Grey leans back in his chair, looking critical. Despite Noble's assurances, I can't help wondering if he doubts I found the origin at all, and it's making me a little defensive.

"I did find the origin," I say. "And there was fusee slag there."

"No one is questioning whether you found the origin," says Noble. "You were there; we weren't. As for the contamination, it's not that uncommon. First priority is knocking down the flames. People tend to forget about the subsequent investigation, and its requirements."

Haines is nodding. "I can't tell you how many times that's happened."

There's an awkward pause, filled with the sound of a dripping coffee machine.

"You mentioned fusee slag," Castellino says quietly. "Was there anything else?"

"I didn't dig around looking for a nail or the end of the fusee. I didn't have the time to do a thorough crime scene investigation, so

I didn't want to disturb the site any more than necessary."

"Understandable," says Haines. "You were there as the incident commander, not a forensic specialist."

"But you are a wildfire investigator," says Noble.

"We've established that," I say flatly. "Did you find anything further this morning?"

"Nothing," says Noble.

"No droplets or small blobs of slag?"

"Not yet, but they're still looking."

"What about soil and ash samples? There should be traces."

"I don't think we'll be taking soil samples," says Noble. "Too expensive. Even if we knew exactly where to look, which we don't, we'd have a lot of material to analyze. We'd have to move truckloads of dirt just to look for a few microscopic castoffs."

"But it would give you some physical evidence."

"We had physical evidence," Grey mumbles under his breath. I give him a look he pretends not to notice. Castellino catches this little exchange, fixes me with a stern look. He has the expression of a man used to asking uncomfortable questions.

"Tell me about the ribbon," he says.

"I marked the site with pink ribbon and notified the crew leaders."

"Did you consider posting a guard?"

Here it comes. "We were pretty short-handed."

Given what happened, it's a lame excuse. A moment of carelessness. Nobody says anything, which makes it worse. I try to look as though it doesn't bother me, my statement hanging in the air like an accusation. "Anyway," Castellino says charitably, "at least you marked it. I understand you did a search of the firefighters before releasing them from the site."

I nod, thinking about Bickenham and his panties.

"How did that go?"

"No one had any pink ribbon."

"Did you search all the firefighters?"

"No. We missed the smokejumpers."

"You gotta be careful about that," says Noble. "Searches are tricky legal ground."

There's a pause as the investigators refer to their notes. I think about Noble's earlier comments regarding my identification of the origin, Castellino's question about guarding the site, the complete lack of physical evidence to support my claims. Searches may not be the only tricky ground.

Castellino gives me a dismissive nod. "Thanks for your time, Cassel."

I settle into my cozy little log cabin; this takes about two minutes after Deputy Compton drops off my bedroll. Then I'm left wondering what to do. I'm supposed to stay out of sight; avoid the road and don't leave the grounds. I wander through the ponderosa, inspecting my cage. There's a razor-topped wire fence hidden in the greenery. Minimum security — all that's missing are a few guard towers. I check out the beach, wade up to my ankles, kick pebbles into the water, but I'm not really in the mood. So I sit in the shade, whittle a round stick into a smaller round stick. I call Telson's cellphone but there's no answer, so I leave a message. I call my sister, talk for an hour, run up the Forest Service phone bill.

I'm sure I won't be able to sleep, but suddenly it's morning.

Breakfast. Then I'm wandering the compound again, standing on the dock overlooking the calm waters of the lake. Despite the tranquil setting, there's a storm raging in my head. I need another look at the fire. There must be something left at the origin; some clue in the vicinity. But they've left me without transportation and it's a long walk back to town — longer to the fire. I stand at the gate, contemplate the road. I'm about to hitchhike when a Forest Service truck rattles around a bend. The driver sees me and brake lights flash. It's Grey. He looks strained, the lines in his face a little deeper. The truck stops in a cloud of dust and he rolls down the window.

"Going somewhere?" he says.

"Just looking over the fence, Warden."

Grey looks worried. "You just take it easy for a day or two — you've been through quite an ordeal. I'll get someone to bring you back to town. Hell, I'll do it myself. Where do you want to go?"

"I don't need a babysitter," I tell him. "I just need a truck."

6
●

THE ROAD TO the fire has improved considerably. A grader has been hard at work, smoothing over ruts and filling potholes. A steady stream of water trucks and service vehicles rumble in both directions. A few minutes later, I arrive at the toe of the south ridge and stop for a moment — the same location where I stopped with Brashaw.

Smoke hangs in the air, thick and pungent, obscuring the northern ridge. The canyon is a dark trough filled with branchless trees. The southern ridge where BB died rises beside me like a great, ashy monument. Helicopters circle through the haze, audible over the thrum of the truck's engine. No problem getting aerial resources now. In a fresh clearing at the tail of the fire, a city of tents has sprung up. Base camp. The radio blares, announcing a wide load coming up behind me, and I ease down the toe of the ridge, create a parking space next to a grumbling generator. A sign announces all visitors must check in at the Service Tent.

I skip the check-in protocol, walk north along the road. I pass the area where I think I found the fusee cap, spend a few minutes looking around. Everything looks different. Trees have been pushed back to make room for parked equipment. A few minutes of searching between the black knuckles of burned tree roots yields nothing. If there was anything here, it's gone, turned to ash. I leave the burn, stand on the narrow road, picture an approaching vehicle. The road dead-ends, so somewhere up ahead the vehicle would have to turn around. The arsonist would likely do this before starting the fire, so he would be positioned for a quick getaway. There may be tracks up ahead, where the vehicle backed off the hardened trail. Looking ahead, I cross the creek — the washout repaired with a new culvert — pick up the start of the game trail, and enter the burn.

Ahead, the origin beckons, marked with yellow crime scene tape.

I duck under the tape, look around. Despite the attention this area has received, there isn't much here. Ash has been trampled into the ground in a brownish patchwork of trails. A red pin flag is planted where I located the origin for Aslund. More pin flags are scattered throughout the area — other possible origins identified by Noble? Or evidence markers? I inspect the flagged sites, examine char patterns, search the ground. Nothing but trampled ash. The char patterns are more confusing than the first time I looked this area over and I spend an hour walking in ever-widening circles, not sure what I'm looking for, frustrated the physical evidence has vanished. Someone tore down my flagging, perhaps by accident. Removing the fusee slag is another thing — firefighters all have basic training regarding origin protection. It makes no sense that a firefighter would deliberately sabotage the origin. It had to be the arsonist, hidden in the trees, watching the fire. He sees me hang the flagging, waits for me to leave, and quickly pulls it down, pocketing the fusee slag.

But why take the risk when a fusee is so common?

And how did he get out of here? We didn't encounter any vehicles.

I look around. There are only two ways out of here: the road or the forest. The timber is dense with understory — perfect cover for a getaway. The arsonist could have been on horseback, on foot, or had an all-terrain vehicle stashed somewhere. There must be trails and cutlines through the forest, same as anywhere. Or the arsonist didn't have far to go, I think, looking at the smoky outline of the northern ridge. But what motive would the squatters have? A fire this close could risk burning them out.

I head back to the road. It's time to meet the hippies.

The road drops around the toe of the northern ridge, then slowly begins to rise again, meandering like a riverbed among the tall trees. There are enough gullies and rills to discourage a hunter, and I can scarcely imagine anyone travelling this route frequently. But maybe that's the idea. I watch for some indication that a vehicle was turned along the trail, but find nothing. No broken branches, no tread marks, but there are several spots where a vehicle could have turned without leaving evidence and I drive on. A half-hour of thumping and rattling and I reach a crude gate, built of heavy poles. Pieces of plywood have been painted into signs with homey messages like: KEEP OUT, VISITORS NOT WELCOME and THIS MEANS YOU. The road beyond the gate bends so I can't see how far the old wellsite might be and I hesitate. What was it Brashaw said when I suggested we evacuate them?

"You can try, but you might get shot."

The road doesn't go much farther, so I park and continue on foot. The gate is positioned to block the line of sight into the small settlement. They probably didn't need to bother — the sight of this place would turn back all but the most intrepid. Three old trailers are set on blocks along one side of the clearing. The trailers are well past their prime, aluminum siding peeled back like half-opened sardine cans, pink fibreglass insulation hanging out like ragged tissue from a wound. Several vehicles are in various stages of demolition, one riddled with bullet holes. Empty tin cans and scraps of wood are littered everywhere. In the centre of the clearing is an old wellhead, next to which sits a toilet, spray-painted gold and propped on an immense chunk of ponderosa. A bathroom sink, complete with cabinet, has flowers growing in it. You know you're on the fringe when bathroom fixtures serve as lawn ornaments. I wander toward the wellhead and I hear voices — children playing in the dirt next to an old truck. They see me and stare, then scramble to a woman on the far side of the clearing, working over an old stock tank. I'm surprised I didn't see these people before; they sort of blend in with their surroundings.

"Hello," I say, raising a hand in greeting.

The woman stares at me — not an encouraging stare. She's sturdy, has the ageless look of rough living. Her long hair is pulled back in a ragged ponytail and she sports a pair of immense rubber boots. She's been doing laundry and wipes her hands on an apron as the kids cluster around her.

"Could I have a word with you?" I ask, walking closer.

She watches me approach, her expression stony. The clearing is wide enough she may not have heard me and I'm about to repeat my question when she shoos away the children, who dart under a trailer like frightened moles. With a few quick strides she makes it to a nearby trailer, yanks open a door and heaves herself inside.

Friendly people. I stand near the old wellhead wondering what to do.

It occurs to me, as I'm gazing at the wellhead, that there are hoses and tubes hanging from it. Crude fixtures have been attached, connected with sections of bicycle inner-tube and green garden hoses that snake across the dry ground to the trailers. They're running natural gas here, which is ingenious but more than a little frightening — if there's a leak, or one of the kids pull out a hose, the northern lights will be awfully bright around here. As I look around, I realize this isn't the only adaptation — there's a satellite dish mounted on one of the trailers, which means they're getting electricity from somewhere — a generator probably. All the comforts of home, which makes me wonder how long they plan on staying — and where they get their money. Social assistance? Or something a little less social?

I'm admiring the lawn fixtures when a trailer door slaps open and a creature steps out. He's wearing army boots, dirty sweat pants, and a tattered plaid shirt that hangs over his belly. Brown hair reaches to his elbows, braided into an immense beard. And he's big, in height not just girth.

"What'd'ya want?" he bellows.

I've come face-to-face with the Sasquatch, and he's armed. A sawed-off, double-barrelled shotgun hangs in his greasy hand. Maybe he thinks I'm going to steal his golden toilet. "I was working on the fire," I say, careful to enunciate so he doesn't misinterpret anything. "I just wanted to stop by and talk for a few minutes."

"Talk?" He scowls. "Your people already been here."

"I need to ask you a few questions anyway. It won't take long."

"I don't feel like talkin'. Best you just get going."

"Is there someone else I could speak with?"

His eyes widen and there's a dangerous silence. I watch the gun, dangling along his leg. He shifts on his feet, tightens the grip on his gun. If I'm going to ask him anything, it has to be now.

"Has anyone been up here recently? Even just to turn around?"

"Best you just back yourself outta here and leave us alone."

He gives me his best intimidating look, feet planted wide, shotgun a little farther forward. It's pretty convincing. Behind him, a row of curious dirty faces peer from under a trailer. In a window above them, I see another face — a woman, younger than the laundry lady and strangely familiar. Our eyes meet and she ducks out of sight.

"Go on!" he says, stepping forward, trying to shoo me away.

It takes a little resolve — or maybe stupidity — but I stand my ground.

"I'm not messin' around," he says, hefting the shotgun.

"Look, there's no need for alarm. I'm not with the government."

He frowns, his expression uncertain. Then his eyes narrow.

"I'm from up north," I say. "I was working —"

Suddenly, there are two very big holes staring me in the face. The gun is an old coach style weapon with double hammers, and when he cocks both hammers I begin to walk backward as quickly as I can, my hands lifted in a sign of surrender. "Listen — just relax buddy —"

The Sasquatch takes a step forward. "You're goddamn stupid, comin' up here."

"I don't know who you think I am, but I have nothing against you people."

I put the wellhead between myself and the Sasquatch. Hopefully, the risk of blowing himself up will deter him from firing, but he doesn't lower the weapon and I keep backing away. With the sawed-off barrels, the greater the distance, the safer I'll be.

"You come back," he hollers, "and I'll bury you."

I reach the road, walk quickly along the rutted trail. At the curve I glance back.

The Sasquatch is still there, watching.

I'm a little distracted on my drive back to town; it's been a while since someone shoved a gun in my face. Now I understand Castellino's reluctance to force the squatters off public land — you'd need a SWAT team. It would also create bad press: government versus the little guy. Best to leave them alone, which is why I doubt they started the fire — the last thing they want is a lot of attention. Maybe someone wanted to get rid of them and thought a fire would force their evacuation, or at least draw enough attention that they'd leave on their own. But why? There's nothing out there but empty, rugged country and a cursed canyon.

I'm still puzzling over this when I pull through the gates of Lakeside Estates. Aslund is waiting for me, his ball cap pulled low. I'm needed at the ranger station, so I follow Aslund's truck with my own borrowed unit. The Carson Lake Ranger Station is a few miles north of town and the drive doesn't take long. The parking lot is full; I hope they're not all here for me.

It's a nice ranger station, modern open-beam with lots of dead animals. A stuffed cougar menaces a strutting grouse. An elk head stares blankly at me from above the door. Fibreglass trout swim in a case below the reception counter. We walk through an area of open cubicles where people pretend not to notice us, then down a flight of stairs to the ready room. The last time I was here, I was playing cards with Brashaw and his men. Today, there's a different crowd.

"Thanks for coming," says Grey, seated at the head of the table.

Another inquisition. I pull up a chair and look around. Noble gives me a slight nod. His jacket is off, his tie loosened; he's ready to liaise. Aslund rummages for a pad of paper. There are two new faces; an older guy with wispy white hair and a short, intense-looking fellow of about forty-five.

"This is Don Turner," Grey says, indicating the older guy. "Don's with MTDC."

Turner must read my blank expression. "I'm with the Missoula Technology Development Center," he says. "We look at the equipment you used in the burnover. The Nomex clothing and the fire shelter — those sorts of things, to see how they performed."

Not well enough, I'm thinking. At least for Brashaw.

"And this is Neil Ursulak," says Grey. "Neil's with the Fire Center in Missoula."

Ursulak gives me a curt little nod.

"The purpose of our meeting today," says Grey, looking at me, "is to discuss events pertinent to the entrapment of Bert Brashaw and yourself. We need to hear from you what happened, to supplement what we already know, so we can prevent this sort of catastrophe in the future." He glances around. "Sorry about having so many bodies here — we usually interview with only one or two people, but we thought it best that everyone concerned heard you out right away. So we don't have to keep you here any longer than necessary. I'm sure you're anxious to get home."

The faces around the table are expectant. I nod, perhaps to reassure them; I'm not sure. In the centre of the table is a tape recorder. I take a minute to collect my thoughts, steady my voice — I keep seeing the black mummy in Brashaw's shelter.

"When I arrived at the fire, smokejumpers were on-scene and fire behaviour was moderate, with vigorous ground fire and some candling. In my opinion, direct attack was not feasible, so I started the dozers on line cutting along the rear flanks, with engines and personnel in support. Approximately forty-five minutes after this, the wind picked up and so did fire behaviour. I needed a better look at the fire and requested a helicopter, but was told none were available."

Noble raises an eyebrow toward Ursulak, who ignores him.

"Without aircraft, I had no way of knowing what the fire was doing. The smokejumpers had jumped-in to a ridge along the south flank, which they assured me had good visibility. Given wind direction and terrain, the ridge appeared safe, so I decided to use it as a vantage point. An old trail along the backside of the ridge provided partial access. Brashaw and I drove as far as we could, then hiked the rest of the way to the jumpers' landing zone."

"Why did you take Brashaw with you?" says Ursulak.

"I thought he needed an overview of the fire."

"But you had a radio. You could have called him. Why separate him from his men?"

Despite his small stature and slim build, Ursulak has an aggressive air about him. His hair is unnaturally black for his age and his cheek muscles keep clenching. Coming from Missoula Dispatch, he has a lot of his own concerns to defend — the denied helicopter and the bombers that took so long to make it to the fire.

"I customarily orient my crew leaders to the overall fire situation."

"Really? And what did Mr. Brashaw think of your trip to the ridge?"

I hesitate. "He had a few reservations."

Concerned glances are exchanged across the table.

"He was superstitious," I add quickly. "He was afraid of the canyon."

"Afraid?" Ursulak gives me a skeptical look.

"Some people believe the canyon is cursed," says Grey, coming to my rescue.

Ursulak isn't pleased. He tries to press the point but doesn't get a chance.

"Was visibility adequate from the ridge?" says Grey.

"Yes. We had an excellent view of the canyon."

"What did you do, once you were on the ridge?"

I sigh, ordering my thoughts.

"I assessed the fire and requested a bomber drop across the canyon."

"And what response did you receive?" says Grey.

"The bombers were tied up on a higher priority fire."

"But you did get the bombers," Ursulak says quickly. "We promised you a drop."

"Yes. After several requests. Unfortunately, they didn't arrive in time."

Ursulak bristles. "That wasn't our fault."

"No one said it was," Grey says evenly. "Did you order any other resources?"

"No. We were doing all we could on the ground. We needed air support."

Noble shoots Ursulak another critical look. Ursulak passes it on to me. Grey watches this exchange and chews his lower lip. "When did you first become aware that the fire had jumped the dozerline below you?"

"I received a call from Sue Galloway."

"You didn't notice anything before that?" says Noble.

"No. Our attention was on the fire in the canyon."

There's a pause as notes are taken. I can picture what they are writing — all actions on a fire are weighed against established operating procedures: the Ten Standard Fire Orders and Eighteen Watchout Situations. Like every firefighter, I have them memorized. Now, they're writing up my mistakes. Failing to post a lookout. Failing to determine safety zones and escape routes. Allowing unburned fuel to come between myself and the fire. My only defence is the fire seemed unlikely to pose a threat to the ridge. Today, it doesn't seem like much of a defence.

"What did you do after Galloway's call?" asks Grey.

I picture the curling fist of smoke rising above the treetops, how we stood riveted to the ground, held captive by its power, but it doesn't seem like a good thing to mention. "On the way up the ridge, I'd flagged a route back to the vehicle. We began to follow this downhill."

"But you were found on the ridge," says Ursulak.

"Yes, if you'll allow me to finish — we started downhill. Brashaw twisted his ankle and we had to reassess. Given the speed and direction of the flame front, it now became apparent the only safe location might be on the ridge, in the open, where we could deploy shelters. I assisted Brashaw and we returned to the ridge, where we deployed."

There's a lengthy pause. No one is clapping me on the back today, calling me a hero.

Ursulak breaks the silence. "What experience do you have, fighting fire in mountainous terrain?"

"I've been on several mountain fires in Alberta."

"I see. Is the terrain comparable?"

"It's similar."

Ursulak frowns, refers to a notepad. "You mentioned previously, in an interview with Mr. Noble and Mr. Grey, that you were unable to determine the origin of the fire strictly from the burn indicators on the trees." He looks at me, his expression intent. "Is that correct?"

I nod, with a sinking feeling. I know exactly where he's taking this.

"Given the inconclusive nature of fire travel patterns in the canyon," he says, giving me a severe look, "did it occur to you that the wind direction in this area was unpredictable? That it was possible the fire could spread to the ridge?"

Strike four — unfamiliar with weather and local factors influencing fire behaviour.

"Apparently, I failed to take that into consideration."

"Apparently," says Ursulak.

There's an uncomfortable silence. My head is throbbing and I'd like to shoot Ursulak. But the worst of it is, he's right. In his shoes, I'd be asking the same questions. Grey clears his throat. "We're not trying to assign blame here. We're just mapping out the sequence of events and contributing factors. The emphasis is on developing recommendations to prevent future occurrences."

"I've got a recommendation," says Ursulak, staring at me. "Stop using out-of-country service people."

Grey looks annoyed. "You know that isn't going to happen, Neil —"

I can't take this anymore. The guilt. The finger pointing.

"Don't worry," I say, standing and glaring at Ursulak. "I won't be back."

I leave through the backdoor. Footsteps behind me — it better not be Ursulak. I start walking.

"Porter ... Jesus Christ, man ..."

It's Grey, his stubby legs working hard to catch me. When he does, he's puffing and his face is pink. I stop and grit my teeth, not trusting myself to say anything.

"That was a crappy thing for Neil to say. Totally uncalled for."

I nod, stare at the ground.

"Come back in. The other guys have a few questions."

I take a deep breath, glance at the ranger station. "I don't think so."

Grey gives me a long look. "Okay," he says finally. "We can finish up later."

"I wouldn't count on that. I might need to talk to a lawyer."

Grey looks worried. "No — I don't think you'll find that necessary. Neil Ursulak has his own axe to grind and will no longer be participating in the entrapment investigation."

There's an awkward silence. Grey looks pained.

"Anyway," he says. "You don't worry about that."

I've missed lunch, and all I want to do is get away from the Forest Service and find something to eat. I go foraging for a restaurant in town. There's quite a selection along Main Street. I pick the place with the fewest vehicles in the parking lot.

The Filling Station is a restaurant-and-bar combo with high ceilings, hardwood floors, and old gas pumps against the stucco walls. I slide into one of several crescent-shaped booths. The only other customers are a group of middle-aged bikers, sitting at a wooden table close to a window so they can admire their Harleys. The bikers all wear the same uniform: blue jeans, red bandanas, and black leather vests that no longer fit over their big bellies. A waitress with white poodle hair and skin aged to the same deep walnut as the furniture offers me a menu. She tells me the special today is the Pioneer Burger with fries and a drink, which I order, then sink back against the cool vinyl and watch the big ceiling fans.

From where I'm sitting, I can see across the entrance hall into the bar, where a big-screen TV has a football game on. My Pioneer Burger arrives: three patties the size of a plate, and the fries in a wicker basket — this'll take me a week to eat. I get started, work on my Harley physique.

Someone switches the channel on the big screen in the bar and the news comes on. A talking head with perfect hair tries to look both appealing and serious. She's talking about the Holder's Canyon Fire, shown on a map over her shoulder. Suddenly, I'm looking down at the ridge where Brashaw died. A quick close-up of two crumpled silver shelters, then the view begins to swing around and I watch, transfixed, expecting to see the black mummy in Brashaw's shelter, but someone with more taste than the cameraman has edited that out. Instead, I see Grey pointing toward the camera, his features tense. Then my face fills the screen, in an unflattering close-up, my name in red letters at the bottom. *Porter Cassel — Incident Commander and survivor of the Holder Fire Burnover*. A new message flashes at the bottom of the screen: *Memorial service, tomorrow at ten*. I set down the burger, half-eaten, take a deep breath, and stare at the dessert menu until I realize someone is standing by the table.

"How is everything?" says the waitress, glancing down at the half-eaten burger.

"Fine," I mumble. "Just a little too much food for me."

"Are you done?"

"Yeah." I try to give her a good-natured smile. "I'm through here."

She reaches for the plate, looking at me. "You're that guy from the fire," she says. "The one that had to stay in one of those little silver tents, right?"

I nod reluctantly. "One of them, anyway."

"What was it like?"

"You don't want to know."

She gives me an appraising look, clearly wondering how much more to ask. "Tell you what," she says. "It's on the house. You want some dessert? On the house too. Blueberry pie. That must have been something, being in the fire like that. Would you mind giving me your autograph?"

"My autograph?"

"Yeah. We don't get many celebrities here."

"Maybe after the pie."

She brightens, heads for the kitchen.

I toss a ten on the table and get the hell out of there.

7

●

THE NEXT MORNING I eat breakfast at the cabin. No television. No waitresses. No reporters. Only drawback is I have to cook for myself, so I eat cold cereal. I dress in a clean shirt and jeans, wishing I had something more formal, and drive the borrowed Forest Service truck toward town. There's a traffic jam at the intersection with the highway, cars and trucks backed up all the way to the sawmill. It might be a while — the drivers are out of their vehicles, wandering along the road or standing in groups along the shoulder.

I shut off the truck, join the crowd at the intersection.

A convoy of fire engines inches its way toward town, lights strobing. Men and women stand along the highway, hands solemnly clasped. Children stare at the bright, silent procession. It's a parade without the noise and excitement. Drivers in dress uniform gaze grimly at spectators as they pass, returning the occasional salute. I count eighty-three engines from towns and cities all over the state. It's an impressive sight — a procession worthy of a king. The crowd begins to disperse, returning to their vehicles. I wait for my turn in the queue and follow the convoy.

The memorial service is at the Carson Lake Community Center. Streets are jammed and I park halfway across town, walk the remaining distance, my hard-soled work boots clacking on pavement. Two fire engines stationed at the entrance to the centre grounds have their long derricks extended toward one-another, an American flag hung between them. There must be several thousand people massed on the grass in front of the building. It's likely only a small percentage of them knew Brashaw, but all are mourning — typical of a profession where you face danger every day and rely on the skill of your co-workers. I doubt the crowd would be as large if Brashaw had been an accountant, or a lawyer. Near the big double doors, technicians are setting up loudspeakers for those who will have to remain outside. Close to them, a dozen Forest Service staff stand in rigid lines, dressed in crisp green uniforms, white gloves, and broad-brimmed hats. I circle around a cluster of reporters and their camera crews, spot Aslund among the crowd. He looks official this morning.

"Cassel, we've been looking for you."

Not very hard, I'm thinking. I was at the cabin all morning.

"We've got a spot up front for you, if you'd like."

I'd prefer a spot farther back, where I'd be anonymous, but Aslund leads me inside and offers me a seat a few rows back from the stage, among Forest Service staff and officials. I recognize Grey; the rest of the faces are largely unfamiliar. On the other side of the aisle are Brashaw's relatives, most of them wearing black, and it occurs to me how little I know about his family. A little red-haired girl sits swinging her legs and I have a sudden impression this is Brashaw's grandchild. Grey is behind a podium. There must be a platform behind there, or he's on his toes. He taps the mike, looks out over the crowd.

"If I could have your attention please, we'd like to get started."

Grey introduces himself, describes how Brashaw provided decades of leadership, friendship, and guidance to those he worked with. He speaks of tragedy, of loss to both Brashaw's immediate family and the broader family of the Forest Service and firefighting. Grey is a good speaker — his voice strong and filled with emotion. He's a striking figure behind the podium, white-haired and distinguished. Pine saplings have been set up on either side of the podium. A shovel and Pulaski are crossed behind an enlarged photo of Brashaw, grinning, covered in soot and ash — a good picture of a man I barely knew. On either side of the stage stand the honour guard, rigid and solemn.

A string of dignitaries follow Grey's stirring introduction, reading their prepared speeches. The mayor. A fire chief. Higher officials from the Forest Service. Even the governor takes the stage, after which he presents a folded American flag to Brashaw's daughter, Delise. The governor places a hand on her shoulder, offers a few words, then kneels and takes the hand of the red-haired girl. Flashes pop as reporters zoom in to capture this touching moment. The ceremony wraps up with the honour guard playing a piercing tune on their bagpipes as they march down the aisle and out of the building. Brashaw's relatives follow, his daughter and grandchild first, holding hands.

Outside on the lawn is a large crate, filled with balloons. The wind has shifted and a smell of woodsmoke is in the air now, drifting in from the fire. The crowd stands silent, purple ribbons on their chests rustling in the breeze, while a final ceremony takes place. The crate is sprung and a flock of balloons rise into the air. The honour guard close ranks behind Delise Brashaw. In front of her a line develops, starting with the dignitaries and Forest Service officials. She shakes their hands, accepts their few words, her expression grim and determined. I hang back, wanting to meet her, to say something but not sure what that might be. No doubt, she'll have a few words for me. Grey sees me hanging back.

"You holding up, Porter?"

"Yeah." I try to look reassuring. "Good eulogy."

He doesn't say anything, just looks at me until I wander over, join the line. The line inches closer and soon I'm only a dozen yards from Brashaw's daughter. She's in her early twenties, with a strong jawline and handsome features. She has her father's sturdy build, without his bulk. She nods after each handshake, wincing a little with each attempted smile. Suddenly, it's my turn. I can tell she doesn't know who I am.

"Porter Cassel," I say quietly. "I'm so sorry for your loss."

I extend my hand, hoping she'll just give it a quick shake and I can be on my way.

"Porter Cassel?" she says, then her eyes narrow. Here it comes.

"You were up there with BB when it happened," she says.

"Yes. I just ... wanted ..."

She leans forward, gives me an unexpected hug. I'm not sure what to do and stand there like an idiot, my arms frozen at my side. Suddenly, her voice is an urgent whisper in my ear. "Come to Del's Greenhouse." Then she lets me go. Confused, I try to catch her eye, gauge her intention, but she's already busy with the next mourner.

Grey catches up with me as I stand next to the empty crate.

"You got a few minutes, Porter?"

I nod, still a bit disoriented by Delise's unexpected invitation. Grey leads me to a small conference room at the back of the community hall where Noble is waiting. He's wearing a charcoal grey suit and very wide red tie. His tanned scalp reflects the fluorescent lighting. He leans back in a cheap stacking chair, his legs loosely crossed, a sheaf of papers on the table in front of him. He doesn't bother standing when I come in.

"Cassel — we've got a chronology of events on the fire we'd like you to review."

"Sure. When do you need this back?"

"Take a seat. We're on a tight timeline."

I'd like to take the papers with me, or make a copy, but neither seems likely so I sit down, pull the papers closer and start reading. It's pretty thorough, contains dispatch information prior to my arrival at the fire. I read this section twice. Reported by Kershaw Lookout at 12:37, well into the daily burning period. This means, if it was a half-hour fusee, the arsonist lit up right after lunch. If he was from town, he would have to leave a half-hour before this — all of which is interesting but useless without a suspect. Smokejumpers were dispatched from the Aerial Fire Depot in Missoula at 12:41 and jumped in about twenty minutes later. Brashaw's crew was dispatched about ten minutes after the smokejumpers. Nothing especially revealing here.

Further along, I see my call requesting a fire investigator logged into the dispatch record, which makes me feel a bit better considering the disappearance of all the evidence at the origin. So are my repeated requests for aircraft. I reach the end of the lengthy summary and flip back a few pages. Grey is staring out a window. Noble is cleaning his nails with the end of a bent paperclip.

"There's no mention of the origin disturbance," I say to Noble.

He shrugs, looks unconcerned. "That's a separate matter. This is just chronology."

"That's part of the chronology. The evidence vanished within two hours of my identification."

Noble uncrosses his legs, pushes himself upright. "We've purposefully left out all reference to the arson in this report, other than your initial call. We don't want any particulars getting out at this point. In fact," he says, pointing the paperclip at me, "we'd prefer if you didn't discuss this with anyone."

"Why? Do you think Forest Service staff could be involved?"

Grey turns and looks at me. He isn't impressed with my suggestion.

Noble shakes his head. "Anything's possible, but at this point we doubt it. As you're probably aware, withholding crime scene details is a routine practice. We don't like the bad guys keeping up on what we know. And it makes it easier to sort out the copycats and crackpots."

"What about your own determination of origin?"

"I think I mentioned before that it was inconclusive."

"The pin flags you left out there — were they potential origin locations?"

Noble glances at Grey, who shrugs. "Yes, they were."

"What about the squatters? Did you question them?"

Noble frowns, looks irritated. "They don't claim to know anything."

I picture Noble showing up in the clearing, wearing his suit, questioning the Sasquatch.

"What about an evacuation? Was that ever considered?"

Now Grey looks irritated. "Of course. The squatters told us to piss up a rope."

"They didn't want to leave?"

"Apparently not."

"And you don't know of anyone who might want to get rid of them?"

"Everyone would love to get rid of them," says Grey. "Myself included."

"Why?" says Noble, looking at me. "What are you thinking?"

I hesitate; I don't like discussing my theories without something to back them up, but I probably won't be around Carson Lake much longer. "The squatters resent authority, and this fire is bringing them into conflict with plenty of authority. The Forest Service, the sheriff's department. Probably the BLM. The fire may have been set specifically to make them uncomfortable, draw attention to them so they'd pull up and leave on their own."

"Maybe," says Grey. "But it didn't work."

"You haven't dealt with the kind of squatters we get here in the States," Noble tells me, tapping a pen against the table. "They're not easily frightened. You ever heard of the Freemen? They're anti-authority. Don't pay taxes. Don't recognize government. And they're heavily armed. There've been a few confrontations in the past and the results have been disastrous, particularly for the FBI. In most cases, if they're not hurting anyone, it's better to leave them be."

"Even during a wildfire?"

"We've had our people shot at."

I picture the Sasquatch and his coach gun. "On this fire?"

"Others," says Noble, looking bored.

"You seem quite interested in these squatters," says Grey. "Any particular reason?"

"I was there today," I admit, and Noble shoots Grey an annoyed look, but I have a few comments before I'm shuffled out of the way. "What about energy interests? Is there some way the presence of the squatters could influence mineral rights or drilling or something like that? Because that wellhead is active — you should see what they've done to it. Talk about a safety concern."

Noble raises an eyebrow, gives me a serious frown. "I know you're a fire investigator, Cassel, and you have a personal stake in what happened, but I would prefer it if you didn't involve yourself in this arson investigation."

"I'm only offering an opinion."

"Good," says Noble, leaning back. "Let's keep it that way."

Del's Greenhouse is about twenty miles southwest of town at the end of a winding maze of gravel roads. It's not hard to find; there are signs everywhere with little hand-painted pictures of azaleas and broccoli goading me on, telling me I'm almost there. I arrive at Del's Greenhouse shortly after at eight o'clock. The sign says closed, but the gate is open.

The driveway is long, meanders amid treed hummocks and dugouts filled with aquatic plants. Small handmade signs near the ponds offer sedges and lily pads. Vehicles are pulled over along the side of the driveway like the lineup at an auction sale. I create a parking space near an army of fruit bushes standing guard in plastic pots.

The greenhouses are long A-frames and arches of varying vintage and design. Most are built over a base of weathered log, covered with corrugated sheets of plastic roofing. The main building, serving as office and store, is also log, low and quaint, with carved gnomes sitting on crossbeams, wind chimes dangling everywhere. Bales of peat moss and vermiculite are stacked by the door. Trays loaded with snacks sit on a nearby picnic table. Visitors in dark suits and dresses wander among the flowerbeds.

"Glad you could make it," says a grey-haired woman, shaking my hand.

She looks to be in her early sixties, tall and gaunt, hair pulled back by a heavy comb. I don't recognize her, but she seems pleased that I've come, squeezing my hand and giving me a companionable pat on the shoulder.

"I'm Del's aunt," she says. "Gertrude Steinhauser."

"Porter Cassel," I say, but it doesn't register. She gives me a wince of a smile and moves on, greeting other guests. I wander along cobbled paths among beds of produce. The greenhouses are humid, crowded with lush green leaves and colourful blossoms. I work my way between tables and slow-moving visitors, looking for Delise, my head throbbing with damp, earthy smells. Her daughter appears, carrying a green plastic watering can. She stands on tiptoes to water flowers, enjoying her little chore. With her freckles and red hair, she looks like one of the lilies she's watering. I envy her smile. At her age, distraction comes easily. I squat in the aisle between the tables to talk with her.

"Hi, I'm Porter. What's your name?"

"Melissa," she says, holding the heavy watering jug with both hands.

"Melissa, do you know where I could find your mom?"

"She's in the other building. The one with the big plants."

I thank Melissa, who skips off, and start to look for a building with big plants. A door at the end of the greenhouse warns that whatever lies behind is for staff only. I can't resist and take a quick peek. There's nothing more than trays and bags of fertilizer. Someone taps me on the shoulder.

"Can I help you?"

It's Aunt Gertrude, with a look like my high school English teacher. I close the door, feeling guilty, like I was caught peeking into the girls' shower room. "I was just looking for Del."

"Well, she's not in there," says Gertrude. "Follow me."

She leads me into the next greenhouse, where Delise Brashaw is sitting at a small wooden table, surrounded by friends. I wanted to pass on my condolences — and apologies — right after the fire, when Grey notified the family, not in such a public forum, but this may be my last chance and I steel myself for what can only be an emotional scene. Heads turn as we near the table. Delise looks up, as do her four female friends.

"This young man was looking for you," says Aunt Gertrude.

"Yes, I expect he was," says Delise, giving me a hard look. "Take a seat."

There's one empty chair, like they've been expecting me, and I sit down, feeling awkward. Her friends are all in their late twenties or early thirties, wearing long formal dresses and wide-brimmed hats. Delise is in the same simple black funeral dress. Her hair is down, shoulder-length, wavy, and rust-red. Against a backdrop of banana leaves and ferns, she's sensory overload. She sees her companions staring at me, waves a hand at them.

"Give us a little room, will you."

The ladies exchange curious glances, make a production of pushing back chairs and standing up. Aunt Gertrude herds them away and Delise gives me a look that's not easy to hold.

"How are you today, Mr. Porter Cassel?"

"Delise, I feel horrible about what happened."

She nods, almost imperceptibly. I've more to say but am not sure where to go from here and glance at the table. Anger wells up — not at her for asking me here, but at myself. I need to blurt out everything or I'll explode. Get it into the open. Then I can leave and we can both try to get on with our lives. I meet her gaze. Her eyes are unbelievably green.

"Look — I brought BB up to the ridge with me, so that makes it my fault. He didn't want to go up there, but I insisted. I should have known better. I made a mistake — a big mistake — and your father paid for it with his life. I know this probably doesn't help, but I wanted you to know."

She stares at me and I feel heat creep up my neck.

"You done?" she says.

"What? Yes, I'm done."

"Good. First off, call me Del — I hate Delise. Secondly, I know what happened and I don't blame you. Firefighting is a dangerous business and BB knew the risks. He's been doing this for a long time — longer than you. If he really didn't want to go up there, he wouldn't have."

She pauses, watching me. I can't believe her. No one is this forgiving.

"You don't believe me?" she says.

"Well —"

"I can see it in your face. You think I'm in denial."

"It's only been a few days," I say.

"It doesn't really matter what you think," she says, waving a hand in my direction. "Not to me, anyway," she says. "That's not why I asked you here." She clasps her hands together on the table, pointing them at me like a battering ram. "What I want to know is who started the fire — that's who I'm mad at. That's who killed my father."

She stops, a little breathless, gives me an inquisitive stare.

"I'm sorry," I say. "But I don't know who started the fire."

"You're a fire investigator, right?"

"Yes." I shift in my chair, a little uncomfortable with what she's asking. "I am a fire investigator but I wasn't on the fire in that capacity. I was there as a suppression resource. I located the origin of the fire and determined it was arson, but that was the limit of my involvement in that aspect of the fire."

"I know all that," she says, waving away my explanation.

"Well, I'm not sure there's anything else I can tell you."

Del frowns, thinks about this for a moment. When I first saw her at the memorial service, she seemed pale and weak. Now she seems aggressive, her face full of colour and emotion, filled with an anxious energy. She's on the warpath and wants me to point her in the right direction. "Look, Del, I wish I could help you, but I'm really not in the loop here. They have people on this from the sheriff's department and the Forest Service. If there's some way of catching the creep who did this, they'll find it."

"You really think so?" she says, looking uncertain.

"Sure. They're professionals." But once more, my look gives me away.

"You don't think they'll catch him, do you?"

I hesitate. "It's a tough case, Del. They don't have physical evidence or a motive."

"But you saw the evidence," she says, looking hopeful. "You saw the evidence at the origin and when the other investigators arrived, it was gone. That gives you an advantage, doesn't it?" She looks dangerously optimistic.

"It was just fusee residue. I'm not sure that helps."

For a minute, neither of us say anything. I hear the drip of irrigation, the sigh of forced air.

"I want to hire you," she says suddenly.

"I'm not sure that's such a good idea."

"Why not? You're an investigator, and I have money."

The pause this time is longer. I don't want to get her hopes up. An isolated arson is difficult to solve — even when the evidence hasn't vanished — but from the determined look on her face, I can see she won't let this go without a fight. I take the easy way out.

"I'll look around a bit. But I'm not taking your money."

She nods. She seems fine with this.

It's dusk as I drive the winding road back to town, a rising moon casting craggy shadows. Cool air scented with woodsmoke blows in the open window, tugging at my hair — smoke from Holder's Canyon. Cursed smoke. I want to catch the bastard who started this fire, for my own peace of mind as much as Del's, but being excluded from the official investigation is a definite handicap. And sitting around waiting for a report from the investigators would be pointless — it could be weeks before they make an announcement.

Once again, I'm on my own. But where to start?

I brake as a shadow flickers across the road, catch a glimpse of the ruby eyes of a deer. Where there's one, there's usually more, so I wait.

Sure enough, three more trot across the road, their backs lit by moon-
light, and vanish into dark underbrush. Lots of game around here;
I'll bet the squatters do a little poaching to supplement their grocery
bill. I ease the truck into gear and it comes to me suddenly where I've
seen the face in the trailer window. I was drunk and more than a little
distracted, but I'm sure it was the waitress from the bar at the Paradise
Gateway Motel. She must work in town to help with the bills and, if
she was there once, chances are she'll be there again.

The motel parking lot is full and I park in the alley, step around broken
glass to get to a metal fire door announcing in faded red letters that
Minors are Not Permitted. The thump and twang of country music
seeps through the wall. I enter next to a bank of video gambling
machines, temporarily blinded by the gloom. Men in cowboy hats
materialize, hunched on chairs, staring at digital displays, waiting for
the big payoff. I glance around the bar, looking for the waitress. She's
not here — maybe it's her night off. Maybe I'm just early.

"Well, if it isn't the Canadian fuck-up —"

It's Cooper, standing by the bar, swaying unsteadily. He's rumpled
and unshaven, a bottle of beer in his hand. A crescent of stitches
track across his glistening cheek, a souvenir from his fall off the table
two days ago. His eyes are glazed, his jaw hanging slack; he's on an
extended holiday — a look I've seen in the mirror a few too many
times. He gives me a wicked grin, drapes a sweaty arm over my shoulders, breathes sour beer and pretzels in my face.

"How you been, buddy?"

"Just dandy, Mr. Cooper. They released you from the fire?"

"Oh yeah," he says leaning heavily on me. "All of us, thanks to you."

The room is full of firefighters, all watching me. Even the boys from
the volunteer fire department are here — Hutton and his sidekicks.
Hutton is still wearing his dark, wrap-around sunglasses.

"Wassa matter?" says Cooper, still hanging on me.

"Oh, nothing. I was just going to buy a round."

Cooper straightens himself, more or less. "Hey guys, the Canadian is buying."

There's a cheer — I've been elevated to hero status again, for a few minutes anyway. I take the opportunity to distance myself from Cooper and bump into the waitress I'm looking for. Her long brown hair is pulled into a ponytail and she's wearing a black skirt, white shirt, and green apron with the motel logo on it.

"How will you be paying for this round?"

"Plastic, I guess. I didn't catch your name."

"I didn't give it to you," she says, smiling professionally.

"Well, that would explain it."

I rummage in my pockets for a wallet. "That's quite a bumpy drive you have, getting to work."

She frowns. "What do you mean?"

I hand over my abused credit card. "I could have sworn I saw you yesterday."

"Really?" She slips the card into her apron.

"Out of town, up a long winding road."

"I doubt it," she says. "I live here, at the motel."

"That's interesting, because I would have sworn it was you, looking out a trailer window."

"Maybe it was my evil twin," she says, grinning, but it's not a very good grin. I'm about to call her on it, explain what I'm after, but she interrupts me, asking me what I want to drink. Rye and Seven, I tell her automatically. She's moving away already.

"Just the one round," I call after her.

She nods — at least I think it was a nod.

Cooper is searching for me when Hutton flags me over.

"Hey, I just wanted to thank you for the drink."

"You're welcome," I say, wishing I had my own drink.

He gives me a crooked smile. "You find what you're looking for?"

"What?"

"The other day, at the fire, you were looking in peoples' pockets."

"Right. No — I didn't find anything."

"That's not what I heard," he says, glancing toward Bickenham.

The kid sees us looking and turns away. Hutton takes off his sunglasses, tucks them into a shirt pocket. Must be a special occasion. He has shadows under his eyes.

"I hear you're a fire investigator."

"Occasionally."

"Is that why you were on the fire?"

"No," I say, looking for the waitress. "I was just another grunt."

"Another grunt?" Hutton looks amused. "I thought you were the commander."

"Yeah, well, it's just another job."

There's an awkward pause. Hutton's two companions sip their drinks. One guy is stocky, with a balding brush cut, looks to be in his early forties. He's got a fleshy, pocked face the texture of pumice, skin burned brick red. The other fellow is younger, late twenties, with limp black shoulder-length hair and a lot of stubble. They're both very quiet, no doubt waiting for a cue from their leader.

"I do a little of that myself," says Hutton. "Took some training a few years ago."

"Incident command?"

"Fire investigation. I do most of the investigations for the department here."

"You ever have a fire started with a fusee?"

"No. We do building fires. Kids with matches goofing around in abandoned houses. People smoking in bed." He shakes his head. "You'd think they'd learn. You see those charred corpses in the bedsprings man, you'd never light up again. They should do commercials, show them on TV."

"Sure. That'd go nicely on prime time."

Hutton gives me a humourless smile. "You investigating the Holder fire?"

"They've got plenty of people on it already."

"Yeah, but are they getting anywhere?"

"Who knows," I say, watching the waitress balance a loaded tray as she manoeuvres through a labyrinth of tables and groping hands. I'm positive it was her I saw at the squatters' camp and wonder why she's being so evasive. Maybe she's just ashamed of living like that — I hope she doesn't think I was hitting on her. I nod toward Hutton and his buddies, start to move in her direction.

"You need anything," Hutton calls after me, "you let me know."

I wave an acknowledgement, circle around as the waitress stops to pick up empties.

"Oh right," she says when she sees me. "I forgot your drink."

"No problem. Look, I wasn't trying to hit on you. I just need to talk."

"Sure," she says over her shoulder as she walks away. "That's how it starts."

She's playing hard to get. I circle around a group of tables so I don't have to talk to her back, but she diverts left. I alter course to intercept but she's weaving and dodging, stopping to deliver another round at a busy table. But she's out of booze now, so I meet her in front of the bar.

"I'm investigating the fire in the canyon, and I need to talk to you."

"Rye and Seven," she says. "Right? Roy, give me a Rye and Seven."

The bartender, a young guy with a pencil-thin moustache that looks drawn on with mascara, hands her a drink, which she hands to me. Customers are piling up at the bar like waves hitting the beach and I'm pressed closer to the waitress, nearly upsetting her tray, which she's loading with the efficiency of an assembly-line robot. "And three more draft, Roy —"

It's noisy enough I nearly have to shout.

"Look, maybe we can talk later. When do you get off?"

She gives me the briefest look. "For you buddy, never."

"Look, like I said, I'm not hitting on you."

"Hey, Roy." She jerks her head toward me. "This guy is bothering me."

Roy gives me his best tough guy look. "Leave the lady alone."

"Mind your own goddamn business, Roy."

Roy looks shocked, tries to puff up, but I turn my attention to the waitress. "I'm sorry, but I'm getting a little cranky. We need to talk. I need to know why your friend chased me off at gunpoint. If that fire had anything to do with your friends being out there, it could just be the beginning. Things could get worse. Look, I'm not a cop or anything, I'm just helping the dead guy's family."

For a second, she looks scared, then shakes her head. This is where a real investigator would relent, offer her a card so she could call if she thought of anything, but I don't have a card. I don't even have a pen. I pluck one from her shirt pocket — her hands are full — and look for that pad of paper she had earlier. I don't get a chance to find it. Roy's little army has arrived: two guys in cowboy hats and sleeveless denim shirts. "This the guy?" says the biggest of them.

"Yeah, that's him," says Roy, from behind the safety of the bar.

"Okay buddy, I'm going to have to ask you to leave."

Bouncers everywhere have the same expression when they deliver that line, but most of them really don't want to deliver what their faces are promising. It's hard work doing this all night, and there's nothing wrong with a walk-out. "Just a minute fellas —"

"Dump him!" shrieks Roy. "Toss his ass."

The big guys are paid to move, not think, and they grab me by the arms and drag me through the crowd, much to everyone's delight. I'm tossed on the ground outside the back door, just like you see in a western. Only in a western, the street is dirt, not asphalt. I roll a little, take it mostly in the shoulder.

"Stay out!" says the bigger bouncer, pointing at me, trying to look mean while he wheezes.

"Where's my card?"

"What?"

Now I've gone and confused him. "My plastic. My credit card. The waitress has it."

"You just stay here."

The door slaps shut and I lay on the asphalt a moment longer, wondering if anything is broken. I want to go back in, kick Roy's ass, talk to the waitress, and get my plastic back, but I don't think my lower back will agree. So, when the door opens again and the bouncer flicks my card at me, I just let it go.

At least I only paid for the one round. I hope.

When I finally scrape myself off the pavement, my truck doesn't start. I groan, pop the hood, peer into shadow. Whatever is wrong, I won't see it tonight and debate checking into the motel. I'm somewhat disenchanted with the hospitality here and decide I'll hitch my way back to the cabin. Or walk — it's just a few miles and I'm only half-crippled. If I don't make it, I'll just roll into a grassy ditch somewhere and catch a few winks — it wouldn't be the first time.

"Toss his ass," I mumble in falsetto. You'll get yours, Roy.

I head through town on a course parallel with the highway, which bends somewhere up ahead, where I'll cross, thumb a ride at the intersection by the sawmill. I don't go far before my shoulder and back begin to ache and I question the wisdom of walking. I could use some anaesthetic right now, but I never had a chance to drink my Rye and Seven. The bouncers knocked it out of my hand when they dragged me from the bar. I'll find a pay phone, call a taxi. I think there's one at a gas station a few blocks from here.

It's dark now, stars visible between streetlights as I walk. Tires squeal as a truck somewhere up ahead takes a corner too quickly. Air brakes rattle on the highway. Then it's silent again and I feel very alone. I wonder what Telson is doing right now. Home, watching the tube? Or out, dancing with the boys? I wonder if she misses me, and I remember the vow I made, when I was trapped in the fire — that I'd spend the rest of my life with her if I survived — and feel a longing ache deep in my chest. Suddenly, I'm very tired.

I'm cutting through an alley behind a grocery store when I hear the soft putter of a badly tuned engine, followed by a faint squeal of brakes and the arthritic creak of a vehicle door opening. It sounds close, at the far end of the alley. I don't hear the door close and the motor is still running: someone planning a quick getaway. Next, I'll hear a brick crashing through a window, or the groan of a crowbar against a locked door, teenagers looking for cash or smokes. The only sound, though, is the steady putter of an idling engine, like a sleeping cat; probably just someone who couldn't find the restroom. Then I feel the crowbar — across my middle back.

A searing flash of pain and I drop. My back feels broken; they must have snuck up from behind in the dark. I fall forward onto hands and knees, look around, raise an arm protectively, expecting the next blow will be to my head. But my attacker must see that he can take his time and the blow doesn't come right away. I'm in so much pain it's hard to breathe and I strain to see through the dark. Cowboy boots and jeans — that narrows it down. There's two of them, maybe three. Suddenly, a black ski mask bobs into view, close to my face.

"We don't like outsiders makin' trouble."

The voice is harsh, strained, excited. A kick comes from my right side, hitting me in the ribs, knocking the air out of me. Another kick, just to make sure I get the point. The ski mask floats closer.

"Get your fuckin' ass back to Canada — *eh.*"

The ski mask ascends and the blows rain down. I don't feel the crowbar, so they must not intend to kill me. I roll to the side, try to scramble to my feet while I still can. A boot glances off my cheek, nearly breaks my nose. Another hits me in the lower back and I'm down again. They'll take this as far as they want.

A beam of light plays across a stucco wall. The cops — thank God.

"Stop! Stop, you crazy bastards! You'll kill him."

It's not the cops — it's a woman's voice, nearly hysterical.

There's a bright pop of light and the pain goes away.

8

WHEN I COME to I'm on my back, bright specks of light shimmering above me. Stars. Everything hurts, which is a good sign — my spine is still intact — but I'm in no hurry to move. There's a fan of light low on the ground to my right: the flashlight. It moves suddenly, blinding me, and I lift a hand to shield my eyes.

"Sorry."

It's a woman, brown ponytail hanging over her shoulder as she kneels over me. She's still wearing her work uniform, complete with apron. Did she follow me here, or was she on her way home? Then I remember — she lives at the motel. Or so she says.

"Are they gone?" I ask, groaning as I lift my head.

She glances down the alley. "Yeah. They ran when I started screaming." Her face is pale and worried. "Can you move?"

"If I have to."

"Here, take my hand —"

She helps me to my feet. It's a lengthy, multi-stage process involving a lot of groaning. When I'm standing, I have to lean on her. It hurts to breathe.

"Thanks for coming," She's silent as we hobble down the alley.

"Are you finally going to tell me your name?"

She glances up from under my arm — a wistful smile. "Karalee. But call me Kar."

"So, where are we going, Kar?"

"Back to the motel."

"Great. I've got a score to settle with Roy and his bouncers."

She laughs a little. "I don't think so. I've got a room upstairs."

"Our relationship is deepening. First you tell me your name, now you want to go upstairs."

We step off a curb a little harder than necessary and pain shoots up my back. "Steady there, big boy," she says, in a way that leads me to believe the jolt was intentional. "I'm just going to patch you up a bit, then you're on your own. I've got to get back to work, or Roy is going to kill me."

"Let me deal with Roy," I say, as we reach the motel.

Kar directs me up a metal staircase to a room on the second floor, not far from where I spent my first night in town. Her room is homier than mine. Stuffed animals are everywhere, lounging on cabinets and shelves. It's like being in a toy store, but at least everything here is soft. I sink down on a corner of the bed; the only area not covered with critters. Kar vanishes into the bathroom and I hear water running. She returns with a damp towel.

"Take off your shirt." Obediently, I unbutton my shirt. She helps me pull my arms out of the sleeves. "Oh my God —"

"How bad is it?"

"Not too bad," she says quickly, but her face says otherwise.

She starts sponging and wiping, cool water trickling down my back. I hold still, just glad she's here — the angel of the Paradise Gateway Motel. I have a few questions but now doesn't seem the best time. I wait until she's sewing up a cut above my left eyebrow.

"Where did you learn to do this?"

She's biting her lower lip, concentrating like a jewel cutter. "You pick things up."

She's very close and I have a good view of a fairly attractive face, powdered on the cheeks with freckles. No make-up, unusual in her profession. "That's quite a handy skill, suturing and sewing. Who taught you?"

She tugs through a little more line, more firmly than the last stitch, and I wince. She gets physical when she doesn't want to answer questions. "My brothers got into a lot of fights when we were growing up. We didn't go to the doctor unless we were nearly dead."

"How many brothers do you have?"

She doesn't answer, just concentrates on her work. A few more tugs, a snip, and she's done. She leans back, her expression critical but satisfied. "That should hold you. Go to the doctor to get them out in about a week. And get some antibiotics."

She stands, collects her things. "I've got to get back to work."

"Look —" I reach for her hand, to catch her attention, but any physical closeness we had is gone and she pulls her hand away. Around here, you can drink the alcohol, but don't rub the nurse. "I just wanted to thank you for helping me out. If you hadn't come along, I'd still be lying in the alley. Or worse."

She nods, frowning a little, staring at the floor.

"Can I ask you something?"

The frown deepens but she doesn't say anything. I forge ahead.

"How was it that you happened to come along, when you're supposed to be working?"

"What difference does it make? You needed help, and I was there. That should be enough."

"You're right. It's just that when I get beat to a pulp, I want to know who's responsible."

"How should I know?" Her voice is sharp. Defensive.

"You managed to scare off three men."

Her hands are on her hips. She's downright hostile now. "You think I'm involved?"

I raise my hands, try to smooth things out. "That's not what I'm suggesting. I'm grateful for everything you've done for me — don't get me wrong. I'm just curious how you happened along at the right time. Did you see someone leave the bar right after I was tossed out?"

"You think I knew those guys were going to jump you?"

"You were three blocks from the motel."

She stares at me, stooped a little, her hands still on her hips. She's trying hard to look outraged, but her determination is flagging and I get the impression she knows more than she's letting on. For an instant she looks as though she might say something, then shakes her head and begins to pace. Irritated, she starts to pick things up, tossing towels at a sink in the kitchenette, rearranging her stuffed animals. "This is what I get," she says to a purple, two-headed dragon. "Try to help someone and they start accusing you of things."

"Kar, I wasn't accusing you of anything."

"Put your shirt on."

I tug on my shirt, filthy with dirt and blood.

"I'm just trying to make a living here," she says, turning suddenly, pointing an accusing finger at me. "It's not much of a living, I'll admit, but it's honest and it's what I do."

"You don't have to justify —"

"You're damn right I don't," she says, her eyes flashing. She crosses her arms to hide her trembling hands. She's too emotional not to be hiding something more. "I was just worried about you. After you got thrown out, I went to check on you. Those guys can be kind of rough. You were staggering down the street like you were going to fall over."

"So you came after me," I say quietly.

"To make sure you were okay."

"Good thing you did." I smile and she seems to relax a little.

"Well," she says, wiping her hands on her apron. "You seem fine now."

She comes around the bed, out of her safety zone, picks up her first-aid kit. It's quite a kit, filled with pressure bandages, hemostats, pill bottles. A pro's kit. She snaps it shut, slides it into a cupboard over the sink. She's tidying up, getting ready to leave. The meter has just about run out and I still know nothing about her or the squatters. I may not get another chance to speak privately with her, so I make one last effort. "I know it was you out at the camp, Kar. If that fire is in any way related to the camp, you or your friends could be in danger."

She pauses, one hand on the edge of the cupboard, quietly closes the door and turns to look at me. She wants to talk — I can see it in the uncertain way she stands. In her frown and the way she fiddles with the edge of her apron. She's scared and, if I don't press, I'm going to lose her. "Kar, that camp is about the only thing up there," I say quietly, "and that fire was started for a reason. If you know something about it, you should tell me."

Her frown deepens and she stares at the floor.

"Who are those people out in the bush, Kar? Friends? Family?" She cringes at the word family. "Is that guy with the beard your father?"

Her expression hardens. "I think it's time for you to go."

"Why did he chase me off at gunpoint? What is he afraid of?"

"I don't know what you're talking about."

"Is someone using fire to threaten your family?"

"You're nuts." She points at the door. "Get out."

"If you know something, you need to come forward."

"Out!" she yells, and starts throwing things at me. Fortunately, she's surrounded by stuffed animals. I take a troll to the side of the head and, sensing that further conversation is unlikely, retreat to the door. An old couple on the walkway with matching poodle hair and bifocals are frozen, watching me retreat. Something heavy thuds against the door just as I close it. Kar must have run out of stuffed animals. The couple stare at me like I might be a serial killer.

Given my appearance, I can't blame them.

Turns out, there's a pay phone in the lobby of the motel, which would have been handy to know a little earlier. Just my luck. I call a cab, spend most of the night tossing and turning from one bruise to the next. I wake in a cold sweat late the next morning, rummage through the cupboards of my Lakeside Estates cabin. Breakfast is complimentary instant coffee and oatmeal, which I find arranged in an ashtray. What I really need is a complimentary morphine drip.

There's a knock on the back door. Grey and Noble stand like watery ghosts on the other side of a frosted glass window. They look grouchy and out of sorts. Their disposition doesn't improve when they see my face.

"Christ, Cassel," says Grey. "What the hell happened to you?"

"I was just out picking up a little local colour."

"Yeah," says Noble. "Black and blue."

They come in, uninvited. Of course, they are paying the rent.

"What can I help you guys with this morning?"

Noble gives me a hard look. He's in a dark navy suit and sunglasses. Grey, in a brown work uniform, is quite a bit shorter and stouter than Noble, who takes off his shades, folds them, and tucks them neatly into his vest pocket, probably next to his gun. "We have a few questions, minor stuff really, but I'm more interested in what happened to you last night."

"I'm not really sure," I admit, leading them into the kitchen. I offer them a packet of instant coffee, which they decline.

"You were at the bar last night," says Grey. "The Pine Room at the Gateway."

"Yes."

"Not a good idea to park a Forest Service vehicle in front of a bar. Gets people's noses out of joint when they see a government decal in front of an establishment like that."

"It's also a motel," I say, wondering how they found out so quickly. Maybe Roy called.

"Is that where you had your altercation?" says Noble.

"It happened in an alley a few blocks away."

"Any idea who's responsible?"

I shake my head — a bad idea considering how stiff my neck is — tell them some of what happened last night, leaving out any reference to Kar. Makes it sound like I was just out for a beer. When I get to the part about the truck not starting, Grey frowns, tugging at his moustache. "That's strange," he says. "We had someone move it this morning. It started fine."

Which can mean only one thing: someone wanted me on foot. Someone planned this.

"Why, exactly, were you in the bar?" says Noble, giving me his best special agent look.

"I just wanted a beer. It was a long day."

Grey gives me an understanding smile. "It was, at that." But Noble isn't fooled.

"Come on, Cassel, don't bullshit me. I know how you operate."

"What?" I say, a little offended.

"I know all about that mess you were involved in last summer up in Canada. That bomber — the Lorax, I think he called himself — and those serial arsons. You were a fugitive for a while, if I recall. And they never caught the bomber, which they partly blame on your interference."

"We caught the arsonist," I say, feeling the blood rise into my cheeks.

"Your friend? He was hardly caught. He died, didn't he?"

There's an uncomfortable silence as Noble and I glare at each other.

"What, exactly, are you trying to say?"

Noble shrugs. "Just that your methods are not compatible."

"Not compatible —"

Grey steps in, like a good referee. "This is going nowhere. Just simmer down, both of you."

Noble glares at me a moment longer, then we both look away, simmering.

"Important thing here," says Grey, "is your safety. Obviously, there are people that have issues with you being here. And right now, that's our primary concern — we're not questioning your professionalism." He gives Noble a cautionary glance. "We're pretty much through the initial leg of our investigation, the part that involves you at any rate, and you're free to go back to Canada. In fact, there's a flight this afternoon, leaving from Missoula at four thirty, and I expect you to be on it. So does your boss back home. So relax. Try to get a little rest. Someone'll pick you up here at three."

I'm thinking about Del, about how I'd like to stay a little longer, but I'm not sure there'd be much point. I can't expect much co-operation from Noble or the other investigators, and Kar, even if she does know something, isn't talking. It's not going to be easy telling Del.

"Have you been to a doctor?" says Grey, looking concerned.

I shake my head.

"Well, you're going then. I'll drop you off on my way through town."

Grey drops me off at the hospital, a fairly recent addition to Carson Lake by the looks of it, modern but small. After an hour in a little white room, a doctor turns up to inspect my bruises, check my reflexes. He orders X-rays of my chest and spine. When I see him a half-hour later, he tells me I've got a cracked rib and bruised vertebrae. No heavy lifting and get plenty of rest.

What about something for the pain? I ask, by now not caring how wimpy I sound.

He smiles, prescribes a muscle relaxant, painkillers, and an anti-inflammatory. Taken as recommended, he assures me, resting will not be a problem.

I visit the pharmacy, call a cab.

The driver circles the motel parking lot twice before I see the green truck with the Forest Service decal. It's parked as far as possible away from the bar and I ask the driver to wait as I check the doors. Locked. Fortunately, the keys are under the gas-cap hinge — the universal Forest Service security precaution. I pay for the cab with the last of my American dollars, then start up the truck, which turns over nicely.

The trip to Del's Greenhouse seems shorter this time, maybe because I'm driving faster, maybe because I know it's the last trip and I want to get it over quickly — there won't be much to say. In the main building, Aunt Gertrude is minding the till. She looks at me over a set of half-glasses, smiles when she recognizes me.

"Mr. Cassel. How are you? Nasty bruise on your cheek there. What happened?"

"Long story, Gertie. Is Del in?"

"Oh, yes. She's been awaiting your arrival with great anticipation."

Gertrude directs me to the house, a doublewide trailer behind the office. It's apparent most of Del's energy has gone into the business, not her home, which sits unskirted on pilings, plumbing and electrical wires visible beneath. I walk up steps slapped together with rough lumber, weathered grey. I'm about to knock, when I hear Del's voice.

"No!" she says loudly. "Forget it!"

Other voices, lower, barely discernable but, from their tone, trying to soothe. This goes on for a minute and I look around, feeling conspicuous, standing outside the door, but I'm not willing to walk in on an argument. What I have to tell her will be hard enough.

Del's voice, clearly irritated: "I'm going to have to ask you to leave."

A pause, then a scrape of chairs. A woman's voice. "Well — really! We were just trying to help."

"Call if you reconsider," says a man's voice.

The voices are moving, approaching the door. I take a few steps back, so it looks like I just arrived. The trailer door opens. A man in a burgundy suit and a woman in a long dress emerge. They're an older couple, early fifties, his suit matching her hair. "She's just not listening to reason," whispers the woman, a pale, freckled creature. They see me, both force a smile. The man is vaguely familiar; I've seen his rotund face somewhere before. We pass each other silently on the landing.

I wait a minute before pressing the buzzer.

"Look —" Del's voice floats to me as she approaches. "I told you —" She sees me at the door, looks startled. "Porter — your face. What happened?"

"Bit of an accident." I try to smile reassuringly.

"Are you okay?"

"I'll be fine. Just a few bumps and bruises."

She opens the door wider. "Please, come in." There are nearly as many plants in her trailer as in her greenhouse. They crowd shelves, growing around books and appliances.

"So ... how are you holding up?"

She's a little distracted, frowning, looking around. "Well, you know, life goes on."

"Yes." I'm not sure how to begin.

"Have you had lunch?" she says. "I'll make you something."

"No — you don't have to do that. I just dropped by for a minute —"

But she's gone, in the kitchen by the sounds of it. I hear cupboards open.

"I've got tons of stuff left from yesterday," she calls. "I'll bring out a tray."

I'm about to protest again when she comes around the corner holding a tray loaded with cheese, rolled cold cuts, veggies and dip. The instant oatmeal I had this morning has long since evaporated and I start to salivate in a way that would impress Pavlov. "Come into the kitchen," she says. "I'll put on some coffee. Or do you like coffee? I could make tea. Or juice, or something."

"Coffee's fine."

I take off my boots, walk in damp socks to her kitchen table, where the deli tray sits, waiting to be desecrated. Del's at the counter, her back to me, furiously hand-grinding coffee beans. I quickly gobble a half-dozen slices of rolled ham before she turns. She pops open the grinder, spills coffee grounds all over the counter and swears. Wiping the mess together, she scoops it into a filter.

"I'm just a little tense," she says over her shoulder. "If I slow down, I'll fall down."

"I know the feeling," I say, around a mouthful of cheese.

"It's been nuts. So, tell me about the accident."

"Nothing special. Someone cut me off in a parking lot." She starts the coffee machine, turns to face me, leaning against the counter. "Who were those people leaving just as I arrived?" I say quickly, before she can ask more questions about my supposed accident. "They weren't in a very good mood."

"Oh — them." Del waves an annoyed hand toward the door. "Parasites."

"What did they want?"

"Everything," she says bitterly. "That was Bob Capsan, big-time real estate developer. He's wanted this place ever since he moved here from Missoula, thinks it's a waste, putting a greenhouse here." Del is still clearly agitated, talking with her hands like she's practising a new form of martial arts. "He wants to tear this all down, build a resort out here, a hotel or something."

Bob Capsan — the face on the sign by the new subdivision at the edge of Carson Lake.

"Why would he want this place? His little subdivision by town isn't doing so good."

"No wonder — you see the size of those lots? They're crammed together like teenagers in a sports car. And the old dump is right next door. But this place has a natural hot spring out back."

"A hot spring?"

"Yeah." She smiles, pleased by her ingenuity. "I use it to heat the place."

"That must be quite a spring."

"It's pretty handy. Without it, we'd never be able to afford the utility bills."

"So he was offering to buy the place?"

"That was the idea. He tried once before, years ago, right after he moved here and found out about it, but BB literally chased him out of here. This piece of land has been in the family for a long time. I grew up listening to my dad talk about doing something with that hot spring. Then I took horticulture and it just seemed perfect. Grow plants year-round using the sun and the earth's own internal heat. BB was going to work here full time in a few more years, after we got the setup paid for. It was going to be his retirement project."

She glances at the floor, her brow twitching. I give her a moment. "Why would Capsan think you'd sell now?"

A bitter, crafty look comes over her. "Oh — he's a sneaky bastard. He knows this place is struggling and the only thing that's kept it going is BB's firefighting income. So he comes in, pretending he's doing me a big favour, buying me out. But he's just a vulture, circling, waiting for the movement to stop." She's got a fiery look in her eye. "But he's going to be disappointed."

I can't help making the connection. "Del, could he have had something to do with the fire?"

She scowls — the possibility never occurred to her. "What do you mean?"

"I'm just curious. What do you know about him?"

She shrugs. "Not much. He built a few subdivisions around Missoula, then moved here. I think he had a car dealership there too. But even if he started the fire for some reason, he couldn't have known it would kill my father. Could he?"

"No," I say, thinking. "Probably not."

It occurs to me as I drive back to town that I didn't accomplish anything I'd set out to do — I didn't tell Del that I was leaving, or that I was done with the investigation. Maybe it's the painkillers and muscle relaxants — I'm feeling a little woozy. Maybe it's Bob Capsan. Despite my assurances to Del, the situation has me wondering. I do have a few hours before I'm evicted.

It's a stunning summer afternoon as I drive the winding highway past the ranger station. The lake is a shimmering blue. Distant mountains look cut out of frosted glass. Achingly white cumulous boil upward in towers. If this continues, there may be lightning, although with the low cloud base it'll probably be accompanied by rain. The last thing we need is another fire. I pass a church, then a sewage lagoon at the edge of town, ringed by cattails. A sign by a narrow side road announces an acreage for sale only a few miles up from the highway. Perfect. I use the pay phone next to the back door of The Filling Station.

"Hello, is this Western Alliance Realty?"

"Yes, this is Western Alliance. Can I help you?"

"I'm interested in an acreage a few miles north of town. The sign for it is just past the church."

"Oh, yes, it's a lovely place," replies a woman, her voice coarse with the timbre of a smoker.

"I know this is short notice, but I'm just passing through and was hoping I might be able to take a quick look. Do you have any agents available at the moment?"

A ragged cough. "Pardon me ... we only have one agent and he's out at the moment."

"What a shame. Oh well, that's all right. Maybe next time."

"I can call him," she says quickly. "He could meet you there in about twenty minutes."

"I don't want to trouble him —"

"It's no trouble," she says, a little desperately. "Really, it isn't."

"Twenty minutes then? I'll meet him at the gate."

The receptionist hangs up, sounding relieved. I get the impression sales aren't booming. From The Filling Station, I cut across the street to a small place along the boardwalk advertising thirty-two flavours of ice cream. In this weather, ice cream is about the only food I can stomach. Despite the looming clouds, it's deadly hot and the humidity is up. I buy a large vanilla, which immediately starts to melt, running down the cone and onto my hand as I walk across the street to my truck. I eat faster, drive to the real estate office fighting an ice cream headache. There's a car next to the little building, but it's not the car I saw at Del's Greenhouse, so I go in.

A door chime announces my arrival. A chubby, middle-aged woman looks up from behind her counter. Her hair is dark, returning from some strange shade of red to black, another failed experiment. Her glasses are heavily rimmed. Her eyes widen slightly, alarmed by my Frankenstein appearance, but she recovers quickly.

"Good afternoon. How can I help you?"

"I'm interested in acreages."

She frowns. "Did you just call?"

Oops — should have picked something else. "No. Is an agent available?"

She smiles; things are certainly picking up this afternoon. "I'm sorry, but he's out."

A bulletin board by the counter is papered with listings. I step over, pretend to be interested.

"We have a binder you could look through," offers the receptionist.

"That would be lovely."

She heaves an oversized binder from a shelf below the counter, leads me to a small room with a tiny table. Pictures on the wall are of immense log houses, set amid idyllic mountain scenes — I feel broke just looking at them. She sets the binder on the table, explaining that the listings are arranged by cost, starting with the more modest properties. Since I'm broke but not modest, I flip right to the back. The receptionist smiles again, asks if she can get me anything.

When she's finally gone I spend five minutes actually looking at the listings, while she gets comfortable up front. There's nothing cheap about getting back to the land around here — even the cheapest listings start in the low-to-mid six figures. Maybe that's why real estate isn't moving. I peer cautiously toward the front counter. The receptionist is busy flipping through a *Glamour* magazine. I slip into a short hall. Three doors. One leads to a toilet, one to a furnace room. The other is Capsan's office. I step inside, quietly close the door and start looking.

Listing books. Business books. Framed agent's licence on the wall. Pictures of chubby offspring. I'm opening file cabinets, rummaging

in his desk, looking for whatever plans he might have drawn up for
Del's land. Plans, and the detail of them, would be a good indication
of his level of interest and, therefore, motivation. A chair scrapes
floor and I hear footsteps: the receptionist coming to check on me.
Thankfully, this building is old and the floor creaks — the creak
stopping just up the hall. I step behind the door, barely make it into
position when the handle turns and the door opens halfway. I'm
sweating — she wouldn't do that unless she was suspicious. I hope she
didn't recognize me when I came in; I've been on the news quite a bit
lately. The door closes and the creak recedes to the front of the building. I wait a moment, then sneak into the short hall, making a lot of
noise as though I'd just come out of the restroom.

"Find anything you like?" she asks, as I pause in front of the small
hospitality room.

"There's a few."

She's about to stand but I bring her the book, flip at random to
several listings, have her make photocopies so it looks good. The agent
should be back right away, she says, handing me a sheaf of papers. I
tell her I'll do a drive-by, narrow it down before I come back. I'm just
about out the door when she asks my name.

"Phil Stanton."

"Thanks for coming in, Mr. Stanton."

Outside, I drive away but circle back to within a block, then stand
across the street in shadow and wait. I didn't find any plans involving
a hot spring, but I did notice a scanner under his desk, turned on but
the volume down. I'm not sure if they're legal here, but I'm pretty
sure it would allow him to listen to the Forest Service frequency. He'd
know that Brashaw's crew was on standby, to be dispatched to the
next local fire, and he'd hear the dispatch call. He'd hear my call for a
fire investigator, my caution to the crew leaders that the origin was
marked with pink ribbon, and he'd know when Brashaw was on the
ridge. It may just be a coincidence, but it's worth a harder look.

Capsan returns a half-hour later — he waited longer than I would have — and parks his big New Yorker in the gravel lot at the side of the building. He stalks to the front door, his expression tense and irritated — not the same cheerful face advertising the new Lazy Pine subdivision.

When he's inside, I cross the street.

The New Yorker isn't locked. There's a scanner in here too, under the dash. Nothing interesting in the glove box. The trunk, among other things, holds a bundle of fusees, which isn't uncommon. Lots of people carry them as emergency roadside flares. Not everyone has a scanner, however; fewer yet would benefit from Brashaw's death. I doubt Capsan knows anything about fire behaviour, which he'd need if he set the fire outside the dozerline with intent to kill Brashaw, but expertise can be bought. Maybe someone like Cooper, eyeing a promotion. He would have control over his men —

"Hey, what are you doing?!"

My senses are a bit dulled. Capsan is coming around the corner of the building. I do what any self-respecting investigator would do when caught conducting an illegal search.

I hide my face and run like hell.

I drive fast enough to arouse the concern of a cop going the other way on the highway. He flashes his lights but doesn't bother turning when he passes and sees the Forest Service logo on the side of the truck. It's going to be tight, but I should have just enough time for another trip to the fire. I roar up the Blood Creek Road, nearly fly into the trees at one curve. They've got security at the trail leading to the canyon, but the rent-a-cop sees the logo and waves me past. I've got immunity, at least for the time being. Smoke lingers like fog, but no flames are visible from the toe of the southern ridge, and the fire is considerably more docile now, with the still air and rise in humidity. I park and head straight for the area where the fire jumped the dozerline.

After crossing the dozerline, the fire backed into the wind, down to the road. Trees that were green when I first arrived at the fire are now black spikes. The dozerline windrow — a ridge of tangled trees, roots, and earth pushed by the dozer — has been reduced to ash. Nothing looks the same. I stand at the junction of road and dozerline, picturing what it looked like when I first arrived, trying to project where it must have crossed. Impossible from here. I'll have to track it back, like any other origin.

At first, deeper within the fire, there isn't much to see as entire trunks are deeply burned. Closer to the road, there's a noticeable transition as the char line drops on the trees. Wind blowing around a tree will form a slight vacuum along the lee side of the trunk, sucking flame and char upward in a chimney-like vortex, and I trace the height of this char to where it drops and finally vanishes, indicating the fire backed into the wind. Fifty yards from the road, and ten yards from the dozerline, a cluster of a dozen trees have very low char lines. Somewhere among these trees is a secondary origin and I study the ground, looking for fusee droppings, the spine of a matchbook — anything that might indicate arson — but there's nothing, which is consistent with an airborne ember or firebrand. Perfectly normal, predictable fire behaviour at the head of a fire. But this isn't the head; this is the tail. Wind here should have driven any firebrands harmlessly into the interior of the burn, suggesting it could have been a secondary arson — a theory I find appealing as it implies I hadn't misjudged the safety of the ridge.

I sigh heavily, stare at the ashen ground of this second origin, at black tree trunks marching up the ridge. Have I developed a numbed sense of danger — the curse of the overworked firefighter — or is it conceivable someone took advantage of the situation, removed Brashaw for some personal gain? At this point, I'm not prepared to accept either explanation without more evidence.

9

●

IT'S A QUARTER past four when I arrive back in town. I've missed my plane. I'm expecting Aslund or Grey at the cabin, a little pissed off, but when I pull through the gates of Lakeside Estates, I'm greeted by a somewhat larger delegation. Grey is here, but so are Castellino and Noble. They're sitting on the veranda, two suits and a uniform, and stand when I drive in. Nobody is smiling. I feel like a teenager caught playing hooky with his father's truck. I'm tempted to turn around and drive back to Canada.

I park, brace myself for the inevitable. Grey pointedly looks at his watch. Noble has a sort of wistful expression on his broad face. Castellino appears intent, lips pressed tightly together.

"I'm sorry I'm late," I say quickly. Always best to cut them off at the pass.

"Yeah, you're late," says Grey. "And you're not packed. Any special reason?"

"No, I just lost track of time. I'll grab my gear."

I move toward the door, thinking there'll be another flight soon enough, but Castellino lifts an arm, blocking my retreat. He motions me aside, without saying anything, leads me around a corner along the veranda. There's a hanging bench with a lovely view of the lake.

"Have a seat, Mr. Cassel."

I sit, watching Castellino. He props himself on the handrailing. His dark face is composed. He seems very calm. I try to match his repose, so I don't look as nervous as I feel, but I could use another fix of painkillers. He clears his throat, glances toward the lake, then at me.

"How is your investigation going, Mr. Cassel?"

I've been told not to investigate on my own, but there seems little point denying that I have.

I shrug. "Not so good."

"Is that why you missed your plane?"

"Yeah, pretty much. I was following up a lead. Took a little longer than I thought."

Castellino purses his lips, frowns a little. "Is this lead going anywhere?"

"I'm not sure. It could go either way."

He allows himself a small smile. "I admire your ambition, Mr. Cassel. Your resolve. I'm handicapped by procedure. By laws. You, on the other hand, are a take-charge kind of guy. As misguided as you are, you get things done. You don't let a little thing like breaking and entering stop you. Or invasion of privacy."

Damn. He knows about the real estate agent. I'm about to say something, but he cuts me off.

"Mr. Capsan is quite upset. Conducting an illegal search is a serious matter."

"It wasn't really a search —"

"Just as withholding evidence is a serious matter."

Another pause. Castellino waits, hands clasped over one leg. He's warning me about my methods, yet he's ready to accept whatever information I might have dug up. Another testimonial for tacit consent. Not that I want to push his limits — it doesn't much matter any longer; I'll be home on the next available plane.

"I went to the fire again," I say, leaning forward so the swing will stop swinging. "I wanted a look at the origin of the secondary fire, which ran up the ridge. It occurred to me, after visiting the real estate office and seeing the scanner, that Capsan would know Brashaw was on the fire. He'd also know where the origin was, and that Brashaw was on the ridge."

Castellino looks thoughtful. "You're suggesting there are two arsons?"

"It's possible. Char patterns indicate a second origin. It could be —"

"Just a minute," says Castellino, holding up a hand. "I want the others to hear this."

He calls for Grey and Noble, who join him at the rail, looking politely inquisitive. "Mr. Cassel was just explaining his suspicions about Bob Capsan," says Castellino. All three give me an expectant look. I recap my visit to the fire, which has Noble frowning.

"You didn't actually find physical evidence of a second arson?"

"Nothing physical, but it seems to be a point source ignition."

"Like a spot fire."

"Yes, but spotting is a little unusual at the tail of a fire."

"Perhaps in your experience," says Noble. "The winds in that terrain are pretty variable —"

"Look — we've been through this before. You think I screwed up, going onto the ridge. If you're right, then it's something I'll have to live with. But you have to admit there's a possibility the burnover on the ridge was set intentionally. The flagging I hung at the origin vanished, and so did the fusee residue. Someone was messing around up there. It's not such a stretch they'd light a second fire, particularly if they saw some gain."

"It's possible," Noble says reluctantly.

"What's Capsan's motive?" says Castellino.

"He's wanted Brashaw's land for years, but Brashaw wasn't selling."

"Why would he want Brashaw's land?"

"There's a natural hot spring out there that he wants to develop."

A moment of silence as all three ponder what appears to be new information. I'm surprised they didn't know this. But then again, they wouldn't unless Capsan made his plans public, or Brashaw told anyone of the offer. Castellino asks how I know this and I tell him of seeing Capsan on my visit to Del's Greenhouse, finishing by telling them of the financial straits the greenhouse is in as a result of Brashaw's death. Castellino looks thoughtful. Noble looks puzzled. Grey is shaking his head.

"I don't buy that," he says.

"Why not?"

"Because of the Public Safety Officers' Benefits Act. The families of victims who die in the line of duty receive a considerable compensation package. I'm willing to bet that whatever Delise Brashaw owes on the greenhouse could pretty much be paid out with that."

There's a thoughtful silence. "Unless Capsan didn't know that," I say quietly.

"Well, we'll look into it," says Castellino.

I want to point out that Capsan did make an offer of some sort after Brashaw's death, but I'm not sure they want to hear it; the mood of the group has already shifted from thoughtful to relieved — they're clearly glad to be rid of me. "There's another plane tomorrow at ten," says Noble. "In the interests of preventing an international incident, I suggest you make every effort to be on it. In fact, we'll make sure someone is here, bright and early, to pick you up."

Grey holds out a hand. "I'll take your keys, since you won't be needing the truck anymore."

"What about supper?"

"Call a cab," says Noble.

I need to say goodbye to Del Brashaw, again. This time though, she'll have to come to me. I call her from the cabin at Lakeside Estates. She sounds exhausted, but she's glad I called. She'll be right over. She picks me up with a van that has a big plastic carrot on top. We go for supper at the smallest A&W franchise in existence. We get our food, then cram into a booth without enough leg room.

"You look tired," I say. She has dirt under her fingernails. Her face is sunburned.

"Oh, Porter, you don't know the half of it."

"Tough day at the office?"

She gives me a trooper's smile. "You know, when you do a little gardening, it seems pretty nice, and you think to yourself — hey, it wouldn't be so bad doing this full time. What you don't realize is how truly backbreaking it is to seed, weed, water, and transplant thousands and thousands of plants." She sighs, blowing a strand of red hair away from her face. "Maybe I should just sell the whole damn thing to Bob Capsan. If I talk nice, he might give me a good rate on a room in his hotel."

She looks tired enough to be serious. "Are you worried about the money?"

"Money? Bah." She waves the thought away.

"I understand the Forest Service will provide compensation —"

"It's not the money, Porter. It's BB. This was just as much his dream as it was mine."

"I'm sure he'd want you to carry on."

"Yeah. I know. But it's just not the same. So, what have you been up to?"

I'm not really sure how much to tell her, because I'm not sure any of it means anything, and I don't want her jumping to conclusions. But if anyone has a right to know, she does. I shift in my seat, lean forward, and look around. Her body language changes subtly as well. She folds her napkin, tucks it under an empty mug, tidies up a bit. We're like an old married couple, gossiping about the neighbours. I wish it were that harmless.

"I went to see Bob Capsan this afternoon."

"You saw him?" she whispers. "You talked to him?"

"Not exactly. I waited until he was out and looked around his office."

Del doesn't say anything, but her eyebrows are up. She's impressed with my bravado. After what happened, she shouldn't be. But then again, she doesn't have to know. "I was looking for whatever plans he might have drawn up for your place. I figured they might indicate how motivated he is."

She's nodding, following right along.

"I didn't find any, Del."

"Nothing?"

"Nothing. But I was still curious, so I went back to the fire and had a look at where it took off and ran up the ridge. There was a good dozerline there, and I was pretty sure the ridge was safe when I went up there with your father. If I'd've had any doubt, believe me, I'd've stayed away from there."

She places her hand over mine on the table, gives me an earnest look. "I know, Porter."

Her hand remains on mine — warm and a little rough, and she gives me a look fringed with pain. It occurs to me just how strong she is, dealing with the horror of her father's death while working and taking care of her kid. I know from experience I wouldn't hold up as well.

"It took a while, but I found where the fire jumped the line."

She stares at me, frozen. Looks horrified.

"There was a distinct origin area —"

"Which means what?" she says, pulling back her hand.

"Nothing, maybe. It could have been a windborne ember."

"Or someone could have started it. Like Bob Capsan."

She has a look in her eye that makes me uncomfortable. "Let's not jump to conclusions," I caution her. "All I'm saying is that the fire that killed your father had a distinct origin area. More than likely, this is the result of perfectly normal fire behavior."

"But what do you think, Porter? You don't think it's just a spot fire, do you?"

I sigh, knowing it had to come to this — she doesn't want hints and possibilities, she wants answers. "It doesn't matter what I think Del — and I'm far from certain either way. It's what can be proven. The original fire was arson, but the evidence at the origin was removed. That stuff doesn't just dissolve. At any rate, it's gone, which makes solving the initial fire more difficult. Trying to prove the fire didn't spot over the line on its own is something else."

Del thinks about this, rubbing a hole through her napkin.

"It's not that I don't want to help. There's just nothing to go on."

She looks at me. "Who could have started it? The second fire?"

"Assuming there was a second fire, it would have to have been someone who was either already on the fire, or watching it and monitoring the radio."

"So there are suspects."

"Sure. Anyone with a scanner. That's why the police use so many codes."

"But it's a place to start." Her anger is gone, replaced by the fiery determination I saw during our first encounter at the greenhouse. She's leaning forward, elbows propped on the table, features etched with concentration. I'm leaning back, or our noses would be touching.

"It's a place for someone else to start."

It takes her a minute, then she frowns. "What do you mean?"

"They're sending me home, Del."

She's shaking her head in a way that makes me uneasy. "You can't go."

"I have to. They're not exactly thrilled with my contribution thus far."

"To hell with them. I need you here."

I take a moment to consider how best to leave this — it's a little like breaking up, a skill for which I've never had much need.

"I'll pay you."

"No, Del — no. I don't want money. As it is, I could never repay you for what happened."

"Maybe not," she says quietly. "But you could stay a little longer."

She gives me a look — she knows she has me.

Del offers her spare room for the night and gives me a ride to the cabin at Lakeshore Estates, where I pack my bedroll and sneak out like a bad tenant. Now that Del's talked me into staying a little longer, it seems best not to be around the next morning when the Forest Service come to pick me up.

The next morning I'm up early, feeling guilty for standing up the Forest Service. I call the ranger station right at eight o'clock to speak with Grey, but he's in a meeting. So is Aslund. I leave a message — I can't make the flight, something's come up. I'll have to reschedule. The receptionist asks if I want to leave my number but I decline.

Del cooks breakfast. Bacon. Sausages. Eggs. Waffles. Now I know why BB was three hundred pounds. After, she gives me a choice of transportation. I can use the company truck — the van with the big plastic carrot — or a relic sitting in the weeds. Since the bright orange carrot might be a little conspicuous, and because the company truck is needed for deliveries, I go for the clunker. It's a 1966 International panel van.

"BB was going to restore it," she says, as we contemplate the brooding hulk.

"An optimist." It gives the term vintage new depth.

"Do you think it'll work?"

I peer under the hood. "I don't know. When was the last time it ran?"

"He starts it up every once in a while," she says. Like he's still here. I check the rad. Pull out the dipstick. "Well, there's oil in it."

"He changed it this spring. Ordered some parts too, I think."

"Whatever possessed him?"

"He won it in a card game a couple of years ago."

"Or he lost," I mumble. "And they made him take it home."

We crank. We boost. We prime. Finally, it runs. I check the back for plates — it's registered. The glove compartment could double as a safe, the way you have to pound on it to get it open, but there's a treasure inside — the Cornbinder is insured. Thankfully, no one wasted money on collision coverage. I pump up soggy tires with an air compressor Del lugs out of a shed, check fluid levels, say a small prayer to the god of internal combustion. Then I'm off to town. Halfway there, I notice the gas gauge either isn't working, or I'm out of gas. I'm also out of money.

I'll have to find a bank.

"Try Carson United," says the kid working at the Conoco. "Just up the road."

The bank is an immense log building a few blocks farther south along the highway. At first, I think it's a hotel or lodge and have to double back, wasting precious fumes. I shut off the Cornbinder, which coughs and sputters to a halt. I'm lost in thought, thinking about the curse, when a van rushes past me. It's an old blue VW camper van. I catch a glimpse of a man's face, young and intent, looking over his shoulder like he's watching me. The van lurches around a corner, merges into traffic on the highway. I make a note to watch my back trail. It seems a little odd, the way he took off after passing. Nervous, like he didn't want me getting a good look at him. I'm pretty sure I'll be able to spot him again though — the windows of the van were hung with bright towels printed with comic book covers. I caught a pretty good look at Spider-Man and the Toxic Avenger.

The interior of the bank is like something out of a western movie. Lots of wrought iron, in the chandeliers, the bars over the windows. I can imagine a rack of Winchester lever-action rifles in a backroom, loaded and ready in case there's a holdup. I make a modest withdrawal and, coming out of the rear of the bank, see the blue VW van lurking in an alley a few blocks away, trying to hide. Sure enough, as I wheel the Cornbinder out of the lot, the van pulls out of the alley.

I head downtown, keeping an eye on the comic book van. The van hangs back, makes a bad pass, fights into position behind me. I watch in the rear-view mirror until I lock eyes with a young guy who looks vaguely familiar. Startled, he hits the brake and is nearly ploughed over by a log truck, which honks at him and roars past in a parallel lane. I can't believe anyone could follow this badly, and I have a little fun with him in the back alleys. Finally, I get tired of playing and shake him, then pick him up at the edge of town and start to follow. He heads south on the highway, turns onto a gravel road, vanishes in a dust cloud. After a few miles, he hangs a right and pulls into a small yard. I accelerate, pull in right behind him, and jump out before he has much of a chance to do anything. He sees me coming but he's too surprised to react. I shove him hard, slamming him against the side of his van.

"Hey!" he says, rubbing an elbow. "What'd you do that for?"

"Why were you following me?"

"Following you? What do you mean? I wasn't —"

I'm not crazy about the rough stuff — with my cracked ribs, this is hurting me more than him — but I shove him again and he thumps his head against a window.

"Take it easy dude. I don't know what your problem is, but I wasn't following you."

He's just a kid, maybe nineteen. I raise my hand like I'm going to hit him and he cringes.

"What's your problem, man?"

"Look, kid, there's a few things you need to learn about tailing someone."

"But I wasn't —"

"Like hanging back a bit farther instead of sticking your nose right up my ass."

He looks offended. "Just because I was behind you doesn't mean I was following you."

"And don't use a vehicle you could pick out of a Superbowl parking lot."

There's a silence as we size each other up. He's bigger than me but I can see right away he doesn't have the confidence to use this to his advantage. He's more than a little familiar. He's a firefighter from Brashaw's crew. I can't believe I didn't recognize him earlier. As much as it's nice to see a familiar face, my concern increases.

"Whose squad were you on at the fire?"

"Cooper's," he says, looking a little embarrassed.

"What's your name?"

He hesitates, sticks out a hand. "Lyle Harnack."

I ignore the proffered hand. "Why were you following me, Lyle?"

Harnack looks uncomfortable. "I was just a little curious."

"Curious, huh?" I give Harnack a hard look. "Don't bullshit me. You were following me around like that van of yours was on a tow rope. That's more than curiosity. That's obsession. Or guilt. You feeling guilty about anything, Lyle?"

"No." Harnack shakes his head, but his cheeks colour a little.

"Then what was it? Puppy love?"

He gives me a grim look, doesn't answer.

"You can talk to me, Lyle, or you can talk to the cops."

He frowns. "Okay man, I'll level with you. But you gotta promise not to laugh."

"No problem there."

Harnack shifts on his feet, frowning, looking at the ground. "I heard you were a private investigator or something. That you were just working on the fire by coincidence. After what happened, with BB getting killed and all, I figured you'd want to investigate the fire."

"The Forest Service is doing that."

"Yeah," he says, kicking dirt. "I know."

"So what's any of this got to do with you?"

He gives me a cautious glance. "If it were me, I'd want to help."

"Well, it wasn't you on that ridge, Lyle. And for your sake, I hope it never is."

There's a pause filled with the sound of distant traffic. Harnack leans against his van, scuffing dirt with his boot, not looking at me. "That's what you're doing though," he says quietly. "Helping out. Investigating the fire."

It's my turn to be uncomfortable. "What gives you that idea?"

He looks amused. "Everyone is talking about it. They know you missed your plane. Twice. There's only one reason for that. You're running your own investigation."

"Really?" I try to sound surprised.

He makes eye contact — he's regained most of his confidence. "Sure," he says, watching me, sensing my anxiety. "They know you're doing your own thing and it's making them nervous." He tosses hair out of his eyes. "This fire is an embarrassment. They want you sent back to Canada."

He pauses, seems to enjoy the effect he's having. I grit my teeth.

"So I figured, if they're sending you back, you'd like to keep your investigation going."

It takes me a minute to catch on. "What?"

"I figured you'd need some help."

"Help? For what? To pick up where I left off? You going to become a private investigator?"

He nods. I look at Spider-Man staring at me from the window, and try not to laugh.

"Yeah — that's what I was going to do," he says, finally.

"And that's why you were following me?"

Another nod, not so confident anymore.

"Why Lyle? What's so special about this fire?"

"What do you mean?"

"Why start your investigative career here?"

"BB was like a father to us."

"I'm sure he was. What else?"

His eyes narrow. "What do you mean?"

"Come on, Lyle. This isn't a comic strip. What's your real interest?"

He tries to look puzzled. "What are you talking about?"

"You're going to have to act a lot brighter to be a detective."

For a minute, Harnack doesn't know what to do. I can see it in the way he stands, the blank look on his face. He might be torn up enough about the fire and what happened to his crew leader to ask a few questions of his own, but he wouldn't need to follow me around. There's another agenda here, something deeper. He gets an ugly look on his face, takes a step forward, his hands clenched.

"Fuck you, man."

He's getting himself worked up to do something. I don't wait for him to take the first swing, and shove him hard against the side of the van. I lean against him, one elbow in his solar plexus — a move designed to be particularly uncomfortable — my other hand on his throat. My side and back are throbbing. I hope he'll co-operate soon, because I can't do this much longer. He squirms, but stops when I cut off his air. "Listen, Lyle. I was nearly incinerated in that fire. The local welcoming committee gave me a cracked rib and bruised vertebrae. And, yeah, I'm going back to Canada, so I don't much care if I hurt your feelings a little before I leave. So no more bullshit. Why were you following me?"

The kid looks terrified. He tries to swallow and I loosen my grip; I was pressing a little too hard. I hear a car on the road and reluctantly let him go. We're enveloped by a cloud of dust as the car roars past. Harnack slumps against the side of the van, coughing, his face pale.

"Jesus Christ, man ..."

"Why are you so interested in my investigation, Lyle?"

He slides down the side of the van, squatting, and rests his head against the metal, his aggression spent. "It's kind of personal," he says quietly. "Between me and Del." He watches, breathing hard, waiting to see if this will be enough. When I don't budge, he sighs, swallows noisily. "We went out for a while, after her husband left. She was pretty messed up and I kinda felt sorry for her. She's a great lady, but I had to cut it off. She had a lot of issues to work out."

"You and Del?" I'm trying to picture this.

"You don't believe me?" he says, with a faint sneer. "Ask her."

"Count on it. So what does this have to do with you following me?"

"I know she asked you to look into the arson."

"She told you this?"

"It's not hard to figure out. You're driving BB's panel."

We both look at the Cornbinder.

"If you didn't talk to her, then why are you doing this?"

"I just want to help her, man. I thought she'd appreciate it."

He hangs his head, looks dejected. It really is puppy love. He's infatuated with Delise Brashaw, wants to score a few points. It's pitiful enough I think I believe him — about everything except who dumped who. "Obviously, we both want to help her," I say, and he looks up at me, a dawning hope in his eyes.

"Maybe we can work together."

"I don't know about that, Lyle."

"I'm local. I know the area. I could help."

"Tell you what, Lyle. If I can use your help, I'll let you know."

I go to the Filling Station for lunch. I'm halfway through my burger when through the window I see a Forest Service truck pull in next to the Cornbinder. It's Grey. I can't help but think it's a bit of a coincidence, his coming here for lunch. Maybe he recognized BB's panel. Sure enough, he comes in, sees me, and slides into the booth. He sets his elbows on the table and gives me a hard look.

"I got your message a little late, Cassel."

"Sorry. You hungry? I'll never be able to eat all these fries."

He frowns, his moustache twitching. "You think this is a joke? You're pissing off a lot of people, ignoring them like this. We keep telling your boss back in Canada that you're coming home. Only, you never arrive. We're seriously thinking of charging you for the two wasted tickets. Letting you find your own way north."

"I can handle that."

His scowl deepens. I'm expecting a harsher reprimand, but he smiles suddenly. "That was my official message, Porter. Unofficially, I think you've got a lot of guts, pushing on with this. Bert was my guy, so I can understand your determination, but most fellas would have packed up as soon as they could, put some distance between here and home."

I try to hide my surprise. "Well, thanks."

The waitress pauses on her circuit. "You want anything, Herb?"

Grey glances up. "No thanks, Dolores. Wife's got me on another diet."

Dolores gives Grey her condolences and moves on. Grey sighs heavily, starts picking french fries out of the basket.

"Anyway," he says, waving a fry at me, "God knows not everyone feels like I do, but I appreciate your bull-headed stubbornness. Kirk Noble is a good enough guy, but he's about as by-the-book as they come. Which is fine to a point, but this situation isn't in any book. An arson and a death — that's never happened that I know of, not in the Forest Service anyway. And that spot fire, at the tail, that's pretty strange too."

"You think so?"

He gives me a speculative look. "It's not impossible, just strange."

"I'm relieved to hear you say that."

He munches thoughtfully, calls over Dolores and orders a Coke. He waits until it's arrived, then takes a long drink, setting the glass down with exaggerated care, asks me how my investigation is going. Not terribly good, I admit, but I'm working on a few things. He nods but doesn't press. This seems like a good time to ask about the entrapment investigation.

"Well, honestly Porter, it doesn't look so good. They're not assigning blame to you specifically, but it's pretty clear who they're talking about. You were unfamiliar with the terrain and local weather conditions. You didn't post a lookout. You were unaware of what the fire was doing behind you and you didn't have an adequate escape route."

"I shouldn't have needed an escape route. It looked safe."

I'm a little loud and Grey glances around, gives me a hand signal — keep it down.

"This isn't my first fire," I say, a little defensively.

"Yeah, I know that, Porter. Hindsight is 20/20. But that's what they're saying."

"What do you think?"

Grey sits back, takes some time. "Some of your actions were a little careless."

There's a thoughtful silence. I'd like to discuss this in more depth, but I'm not sure he's prepared to do that, which is fine — I'm just thankful he's being straight with me. "So, what happens now?"

"Not much, for a while. They have thirty days to submit their report."

Thirty days. "Will they consider new evidence before then?"

"Sure. Right up until release. Do you have any?"

I tell him no and there's an awkward silence. Grey drains his Coke and gives me a serious look. "You keep plugging away at it, Porter, but don't mention I said that to anyone. If there's anything I can help you with, unofficially of course, give me a call at home. I'm in the book."

I thank him and he leaves. I finish my burger and slip a five under the plate.

The parking lot at the Paradise Gateway Motel isn't exactly crowded at this time of day. I park next to a lonely tour bus, climb metal stairs to the second floor. I'm determined to talk with Kar again, to get some answers. I was jumped after trying to talk with her at the bar and I'm positive now that I saw her at the squatters' camp. There's no answer to my knocks.

I knock harder. Maybe she's sleeping off a long shift. Still no answer.

I retreat to the panel, temporarily stymied. I don't have a lot of investigative options at this point — I've been over both origins at the fire and a return to the squatters' camp would be less than healthy. So I wait; she'll come home sooner or later. When she does, I'll ask her again about the Sasquatch, why he ran me off at gunpoint. If she refuses to talk about it, maybe she can set up a safe meeting with him.

I'm not very good at waiting and am just weighing the benefits of coming back later when Harnack's old VW van sputters into the parking lot and pulls up beside me. He cranks down his window, hangs an elbow over the sill.

"You staking out this place?"

"No, Lyle, I'm not staking out anything."

"'Cause I could spell you off. Just tell me what we're looking for."

He looks so expectant I'm tempted to accept his offer, just so I know he's in one place and not following me around, but then he'll know I'm interested in Kar and I don't want to do that to her. He grins at me, waiting for instructions, like a faithful hound. I get an idea, a little reckless, but it would give us both something to do. "You really want to help, Lyle?"

"Yeah, you bet."

"This could be risky."

"Bring it on, man."

"Okay, here's the plan. I need you to distract the clerk at the office over there."

Harnack looks toward the motel. "How do I do that?"

"Go into the washroom and stuff paper towels into a toilet until it backs up, starts to make a mess. Then go tell her. Make it sound bad. I'll only need a few minutes, but you gotta keep her busy and away from the counter, so make sure there's some water on the floor. Think you can handle that?"

"Piece of cake."

I take a circuitous route to the side of the office. Nothing happens for a long time. Either Harnack can't figure out how to plug a toilet, or he's doing such a good job we're going to need an ark around here. Finally, I hear his murmured voice, followed by an expressive female curse. Soon after, the small office is empty and I slip in.

There's a long counter, cash register, and debit machine. A shelf under the counter is loaded with stacks of fraying phone books. I pull out a couple of drawers without finding what I'm looking for — a spare key for Room 212. There's a smaller office behind this reception area, scarcely large enough for a desk, single file cabinet, and antique safe. If the keys are in the safe, I'm out of luck — it would take a stick of dynamite to open. I rifle very quickly through the desk, find nothing, then notice a metal cabinet behind the door, mounted on the wall. It's wide, shallow, and unlocked. Inside are spare keys hung on hooks — rows and rows of them. At one time, they were organized numerically.

Now, it's random access, necessitating I look at each tag for the correct room number. I look as quickly as I can, expecting the clerk, but Harnack must have done a good job. I hear a door open, and the sound of a woman's irritated voice.

"— plumber. Fucking teenagers."

I'm out of time and just about to give up, when there it is. I grab the key, shut the cabinet, and step quickly out of the office. The clerk is in the hall, nearly at the front counter, and I hesitate. If she sees me passing from the counter she'll be suspicious, but I don't have a lot of choice. Harnack steps out of the washroom, saying something, distracting her enough that I slip past the hall and out the front door. I take the metal steps three at a time, so Harnack won't see where I'm going. I nearly forget to knock first, but there's still no answer.

Her bed is neatly made. Stuffed toys stare vacantly from shelves. I'm not sure there's anything here worth risking break-and-enter for, but you never know. I look in cupboards and drawers for pictures, or a diary — anything that might tell me who she is and how she's connected to the squatters. On the nightstand is a photo of a younger Kar, surrounded by a half-dozen people. They all look a little ragged and wild, and one of them could be the Sasquatch, in his summer fur. They're standing on a concrete pathway against a backdrop of ferns, a touristy sort of setting I'd expect the squatters to avoid. I set the photo back on the nightstand. In a cabinet below the TV is a hardcover book: a school textbook. She's taking physics by correspondence. This girl isn't planning on spending her life as a waitress, or living in a shack in the woods. I rummage a bit more. Thick brown envelopes contain returned lessons; she's doing pretty good. The name on the envelopes is Karalee Smith. The address is General Delivery. I return the book and envelopes, check the window. I've been doing this every few minutes, pulling aside the heavy drapes to scan the parking lot — I don't want to get trapped. A truck veers off the highway, coasts into the parking lot. It looks like a truck I saw at the squatters. Just to be safe, I let myself out and peer cautiously over the second floor railing.

The truck is an old GMC of roughly the same vintage as the Corn-binder. Big rectangular mirrors jut from the sides. Paint peels from the hood like bark from a cedar. Spare tire and junk in the open box. It's parked just below me, near the office, and I can see the side of a man's head. Ball cap and heavy, lamb chop sideburns. A door creaks open, then slams. Kar walks around the front of the truck, passes a few words with the driver, which I don't catch. Then she nods, heads for the stairs. I head the other direction, descend an opposing staircase. I hear the hollow clonk of her boots overhead as I reach pavement — I'll talk with her later. The old GMC turns left onto the highway.

A few minutes later, so do I.

10
●

I HAD EXPECTED the GMC to turn right and head north, toward the canyon and the squatters' camp, but it's going south, out of town. It's easy to follow here, plenty of curves and only a few gravel side roads, so I hang back. Once again, I'm driving a conspicuously distinctive vehicle. Everything rattles, from the floorboards to the roof, popping and warbling. The steering wheel is as big as a ship's tiller.

After an hour, we're on the big highway, headed toward Missoula. When the GMC takes an off-ramp I groan; I'm not real good at following in the city, but he stays on the outskirts like a country boy. When he stops at a Conoco, I ease in behind the station, find an air hose to fill a soggy tire, then watch from around a corner as he fuels up. He's a big guy in his mid-twenties, broad-shouldered without a lot of fat. Unlike Harnack, he looks like he'd know how to use his size. He's wearing dirty jeans and a couple of shirts with holes in the sleeves. Most striking are his dense brown lamb-chop sideburns, ending just shy of his nose. Thick curly hair crests from beneath a ball cap. He looks like Hugh Jackman playing Wolverine in the X-Men, complete with the antisocial frown. It occurs to me that he bears a striking resemblance to the Sasquatch. He must be the ape-man's son. When he goes in to pay, I go into his truck, rummage in the glove box. There's a pair of tin snips and a crescent wrench, but no registration or insurance. I retreat. The licence plate says Florida. I jot down the number.

From the Conoco, he goes for lunch at a drive-through, then stops at a grocery store. He's inside for a while and I consider another pass through his truck, but there isn't much point. He wheels out a heavily-loaded cart, slings bags in the back of the truck, then we're on the road again, passing through an industrial area. I'm pretty sure I've wasted an afternoon watching him buy groceries, but he has one stop left — a feed store. He tosses in a couple large bags of fertilizer. So much for high intrigue.

I let him get way ahead of me on the drive back. Rain spits on the windshield. The wipers are old and missing most of their rubber. To see where I'm going, I lean over the steering wheel, peering through a single two-inch clear arc of windshield. It doesn't improve my mood. I've pissed off the Forest Service just to waste the afternoon and fifty bucks on gas. Then it occurs to me that I didn't notice a garden at the squatters' camp. In fact, the old wellsite is clay so hard you could play tennis on it. There could be a garden out in the trees though, but it seems strange to drive all the way to Missoula to buy groceries and fertilizer, when both are available in Carson Lake.

Unless you don't want anyone in Carson Lake to know you're buying fertilizer.

Suddenly, it all makes sense — the squatters, the canyon, the curse, and the fire.

It's raining steadily when I stop on the Blood Creek Road. The rent-a-cop on the trail leading to the canyon is in his truck and doesn't look real happy when I lurch to a stop in the muddy intersection. He makes a show of pulling on his hood and wading through the muck. "This is a restricted area," he says, when I roll down the window.

"Yeah, I know. I'm headed to the fire."

He glances at the panel. "What's your business up there?"

It seems a little absurd, after all I've been through, to have to justify why I'm here, but it's a different rent-a-cop today so I don't get by on recognition. "I'm delivering commissary."

He hesitates, then shrugs and waves me through.

The steep uphill grades have not improved in the rain and the panel slides and spins. By the time I make it to the fire, there's so much mud on the Cornbinder I could park in the middle of the road and it would be invisible. Base camp looks deserted, the tents dark and slick. Nothing more depressing than fighting fire in the rain. I drive on. The road past the fire hasn't been graded but hasn't had a lot of traffic to churn up the mud — a single set of vehicle tracks meander up the hill. Water runs in rivulets down eroded gullies, collecting at the bottom of dips. I plough through these little ponds, muddy water splashing the windshield, seeping through rotted floorboards. I pull over, nose the panel as close to the trees as I can and pocket the keys.

As soon as I step onto the road, mud begins to collect on the soles of my boots. I take half a dozen steps but quickly collect twenty pounds of gumbo on each boot. My bruised vertebrae and cracked rib let me know just what a fool I am. I pop a few painkillers, swallow them dry as I'm pelted with rain, and head into the bush. It's not much better in here. Dense alpine fir loaded with moisture slap water over my arms and legs but since I'm soaked already, I plough through. At least I can walk and I'm not leaving an obvious trail. I parallel the road as much as possible, following the line of least resistance. It takes over an hour to reach the edge of the squatters' wellsite. I nearly blunder right into the open.

Wolverine's truck sits close to one of the trailers. Everyone must be inside. Rain drums softly on trailer roofs and old vehicles. Puddles dance. I shiver — I forgot how cold it gets at this altitude during a good rain, even in the middle of summer. All I have is a thin denim coat. No hat. I should turn back before I get pneumonia. I breathe into my cupped hands, which are turning a little blue.

Better keep moving.

I circle the camp well back, searching for a trail. There's a nasty-looking outhouse without a door, and a lot of garbage — old mattresses and empty, rusting fuel drums. I walk past the trail twice before noticing it; it's been well preserved, very few branches broken off. But it's impossible to completely hide a trail that receives any sort of regular use and, glancing back to make sure no one is watching, I start to follow.

The squatters' camp is in a valley about a third of the way up the mountain. The valley is wider and shallower than Holder's Canyon, which it roughly parallels, separated by a high ridge. It's hard to imagine anyone lugging heavy bags of fertilizer along a trail this rugged and the farther I go, the quicker I push on, cursing myself for wasting more time. I top the main ridge after what seems an eternity and have a sudden view of the fire. Or what used to be the fire — now just a black smear in the valley below. Burned branchless trees look like stubble. The perimeter, well up the valley, is a sharp line of green.

I stand for a while, staring at the ridge on the far side of the valley. It's a long black hump, like a whale coming to surface. I can see where Brashaw and I were trapped. From here the cliff looks low, like you could just step off it. I'm no longer certain what I'm doing out here, slugging through cold bush in the pouring rain. Cold, wet, and discouraged, I head downhill. At least it'll be easier to walk back through the burn.

The trail forks in several places on the way down. I stick with the route that heads most directly toward the fire, walking quickly, sliding in the steeper areas. I almost don't see the trap, and save my eyes by the merest coincidence as I slip on a greasy patch and fall painfully onto my back. When I look up, there's a series of fish hooks strung across the trail at eye-level. They're big barbed hooks, hung from monofilament fish line, bare of any lure and nearly invisible against the surrounding forest. I'm not sure how effective they might be, but they get their message across well enough — stay the hell away. I continue on, walking slower, my heart beating a little faster. In the dense green jungle it would be easy to hide more booby traps and I search the ground and branches, keep checking my back trail. It feels like someone is following me. The trail drops sharply and there's a pale grey snag at a downhill bend. I stop. A dead tree is nothing unusual, but it bothers me, at the side of the trail like that.

It's a marker. The users of the trail would need to know where their booby traps were set, so they wouldn't stumble into them. I'm willing to bet there was a marker by the fish hooks. I leave the trail, work my way downhill through dense green branches that scratch my hands, slap me with their load of moisture. My detour pays off. Nailed to the side of the dead tree, at just below head level and positioned to be invisible from uphill along the trail, is a heavy-duty spring-loaded rat trap. A short section of pipe is clamped to the trap and inside the pipe is a 12-gauge shotgun shell. A stub has been brazed onto the jaw of the trap, to align with the primer of the shotgun shell — a firing pin. Heavy fish line runs down along the side of the tree, around a thread thimble anchored to the trunk, and across the trail, about eight inches from the ground. It's a pretty deadly looking trip gun. I cut the line, releasing slowly as I do the jaw of the trap. The firing pin lines up perfectly with primer and I shudder. I walk very slowly now, paranoid I'll trip another wire or fall into a spiked pit.

I make it to the edge of the burn without further incident.

The fire didn't make it very far up the slope on the northern flank, due to wind direction and higher local humidity. A dozerline winds its way along the lower slope. It takes me some time to climb over the windrow of toppled trees on the outside of the line. The ribbon of bare brown earth is muddy and slick. The dozer operator wouldn't have seen the narrow footpath. Neither would firefighters patrolling the line — the trail in the green is obscured by the windrow and nearly invisible in the burn. But it's there, if you know what to look for. I follow the faint impression, still cautious despite the certainty that the fire should have destroyed any remaining traps. The trail becomes indistinct, then peters out completely. Retracing my route, I search for another trail or some sign I have arrived at my destination, but find neither. The trail had to go somewhere of importance, or why bother with the precautions and booby traps? I take a moment, stand in the charred skeletal forest and gaze around. It's raining harder now. No sound but the patter of rain; air filled with a pungent scent of damp smoke and baked earth. A forgotten graveyard at the end of the world.

I keep looking. Answers are here, somewhere.

The trail clearly does not continue and I'm forced to conclude the squatters purposefully took differing routes to obscure their destination. It seems an extreme precaution, unnecessary as they can't have located far from water. I walk quickly through the burn now and find the narrow channel of a creek. It doesn't take long to find what I'm looking for.

The gardens are small and numerous, close to the creek and connected by a pattern of faint foot trails. The clearings are fairly obvious — open patches of lightly scorched ground. The underbrush was cleared out and irrigation increased soil moisture, decreasing fire intensity, but not enough to save the crop. I wander among the clearings, looking for evidence. Even after a fire there should be plenty — melted blobs of plastic from transplant containers, irrigation line, remnants of more booby traps. But like the fire origin, there's very little here; someone cleaned up. The stalks of the plants, loaded with moisture, should have survived, but even these are gone. This was a big clean-up job and something had to have been missed. Finally, I find several unburned sections of plastic pipe, the blade of a small hand shovel. Not that I needed further confirmation of what was going on here. Until the fire, this was a perfect setup. Free land, a reliable water source, and privacy, courtesy of a local superstition. I'm too cold to stay any longer and head back through the wasteland of the burn.

Finally, I have something to tell Del.

Even with the heater rattling on maximum, the old panel doesn't warm up much and I'm shivering when I climb the stairs to Del's trailer, the back of my hands blue as I fumble with the door latch. Del meets me at the landing, where I drip onto her floor.

"Porter! My God, you look half-dead."

My teeth are chattering. "Just need ... dry clothes."

"I have something better than that," she says, her face assuming a look of motherly determination.

"Oh my —" Aunt Gertrude has joined the crowd. Del turns to her.

"Can you take care of Melissa? I'm taking him to the spring."

Gertrude nods and Del leads me back outside, into the rain. It's coming down like nails and she doesn't have a coat or hat. I try to protest but she leads me across the yard to a small log building behind one of the greenhouses, next to a treed slope. Even in the pouring rain, I can smell the sulphur. She opens a heavy wooden door, ushers me inside.

It's cramped and dark. I don't go far before thumping my boot against something hard. Del clicks on a low-watt bulb. In the dim yellow light, a wide octagonal tub built of heavy cedar planking. Steam rises from dark water like a witch's cauldron. On shelves around the tub, plastic jugs of chemicals. Tools propped in a corner. A combination garden shed and sauna like a workshop from a Grimm's fairytale.

"This will warm you up."

I hesitate, looking at the dark water flecked with foam.

"Strip down and take a soak," she says firmly.

I dip my hand in. Heat burns through skin, scalding cold flesh, but it feels good and I fumble with my shirt buttons. My hands are stiff and clumsy. Del brushes aside my ineffectual attempts, quickly tugs open the buttons. I stand, helpless and more than a little grateful. Droplets of rain nest in her red hair like transparent pearls. Her breath is warm on my chest. So are her hands as she helps me tug off the clinging shirt. It peels away like saran wrap.

"Porter — oh my God ..."

She's behind me, looking at my back, her fingers lightly tracing tender topography. The burn line from the branch that landed on the fire shelter. The bruise from the tire wrench. Assorted abrasions and contusions. I feel like a medical chart; an exhibit in gross human anatomy.

"You didn't just get into an accident with your truck, did you?"

"I ran into the Porter Cassel fan club the other night."

Behind me, a deep sigh. "This is my fault."

"No. This would have happened anyway."

Del drops the soggy shirt, unlaces my boots. She kneels in front of me, reaches for my pants. I'm a little hesitant — it's been a while since a strange woman tugged at my zipper. She tells me to relax.

"Don't flatter yourself. I prefer my men at room temperature."

Pants come off, slapping coldly against my legs as I stumble, reaching for balance. The underwear stays on. Her hand is warm on my arm as I fumble my way into the pool. The water is even warmer and I suppress a gasp. My skin prickles as the heat works in. The burn on my back blazes with pain.

"Do you mind if I join you?"

I hadn't realized until now, but Del is soaked to the skin. I shrug, slide deeper into the fiery water. She unbuttons her shirt and I glance away, try to look casual, focus on the pain in my back. She notices my discomfort, laughs lightly as she pulls off her shirt. I can't help glancing over. She's wearing a bra, lacy on the edges. It's wet and I can see her nipples.

"Relax, Porter. You never went skinny dipping with the girls?"

"It's been a while."

She tugs off rain-spattered pants and boots, slips into the tub in bra and panties, sits on the far side, and slides down in the water, until her breasts are covered. Red hair floats around her.

"That better?" she says.

"That's just fine."

She smiles, a little amused, a little dominant. I think all women enjoy watching a man squirm. God knows, Telson does. I focus on her, and the fact that Del is Bert Brashaw's daughter. It helps a little. So does the hot water; I'm suddenly very tired.

She leans back, sighs deeply. "Where were you all day?"

"I went for a little walk in the woods, out by the fire."

"You find anything new?"

"I think I found why the fire was started."

She stares at me from across the cauldron, wet hair plastered to her neck and shoulders.

"What did you find, Porter?"

"Do you know about the squatters up near the fire?"

Del frowns. "A little. I heard there were some old hippies up there."

"They're more than just hippies."

"What do you mean?"

"They're growing pot in the valley."

Del sits up, exposing well-shaped breasts beneath a very thin, wet bra. "Are you sure?"

I try not to stare. "Definitely."

"How did you find out?"

"I got to wondering why the squatters were there, on a hardpan old wellsite in the middle of nowhere, next to a canyon that's supposed to be cursed. At first, I thought they just wanted to be left alone. Then I started to wonder why they would want to be left alone. I went for a hike, worked the area around their camp until I found a trail leading to the burn."

"You found their gardens?"

"Yes, but the fire had wiped them out."

"Shit!" Del looks furious. "They were after the pot gardens."

"Why would someone burn the gardens, if they wanted the pot?"

"I don't know, Porter. Maybe they wanted to get rid of them."

"They could have just called the sheriff."

"Whoever started that fire killed my father."

Whoever started the fire wouldn't have known that BB would be killed. At most, they wanted to destroy the marijuana crop, or chase away the squatters. I'm about to bring this up, to caution her, but change my mind. She doesn't want her father's death to be without reason. I'm not sure it makes it any easier.

"So, what's next, Porter? What do we do next?"

"We go to the police. Tell the sheriff. They'll look into it."

Del shakes her head. "Not yet."

I give her a questioning look and she floats across to me. "What are the police going to do?" she says. She's very close, practically kneeling between my legs. I don't think she realizes how uncomfortable this makes me. "Look how much more you've done already."

"I haven't done that much, Del."

"Sure you have. You know why the fire was started."

"I don't know anything for certain."

"But you could find out."

I'm about to tell her once again how much better it would be to go to the police, let Castellino and Noble make the connections, but Del has a pleading look on her face and I close my eyes for a minute. She wants me to stay so she'll know what is happening — what the police won't tell her until their investigation is concluded. Or she has far more confidence in my abilities than is justified. Either way, I don't have the information she wants, just different pieces of the puzzle. When I look again, she's still in front of me, waiting and hopeful. Vulnerable in her passion for the truth.

"Del, anything I've accomplished has been a result of defying the authorities or conducting illegal searches. This is an open homicide investigation. At some point — and I think that point is now — I have to stop doing things the way I do. If I find out who started the fire that killed your father, whatever evidence I uncover may be inadmissible. There isn't a court in this country that will accept evidence obtained through an illegal search. Instead of catching the arsonist, he could go free."

Her gaze doesn't waver. "At least we'd know who did it."

"That's not enough," I say, gently placing a hand on her bare shoulder. "We have to go to the sheriff. Tell them what we know."

"Okay," she says, looking at me. "But not yet."

"Del, there's no point waiting —"

"Yes, Porter — there is." Her gaze is steady, makes me a little nervous. "What happens if the police become involved with the squatters and they disappear? They're growing marijuana up there and they've got nothing to gain from working with the police. But they might talk to you."

I think of the Sasquatch and his sawed-off shotgun. "No, Del, we have to go to the police."

Her jaw clenches and she gives me a look that makes me feel trapped. "Just a little longer, Porter. Please."

I sigh, wondering how I can make her believe this isn't a good idea. She's so close now I could lean over and kiss her. "I ran into one of your old flames earlier today."

She looks puzzled.

"A guy by the name of Lyle Harnack."

Del's smile is reluctant, wistful. "Oh yes — Lyle."

"You two actually went out? He seems a little young."

Del lays an arm along the edge of the tub. Steam rises from her skin. "I met Lyle at a barbecue, here at the greenhouse. BB used to throw them all the time, for the crew. He'd cook the burgers and steaks himself, then sit in a big log chair, sipping his beer and watching his children. Said he felt like a father with twenty adolescent teenagers. The guys would bug him, call him BB the King, sitting on his throne."

"I wondered where he got that name."

"Yeah." Del is smiling. "It just stuck. Anyway, Lyle started on the crew that spring — he's from Colorado originally. He seemed naive and sort of helpless among the other guys. I guess I felt sorry for him. He was so sweet, always bringing me things."

"Like a puppy."

She gives me an amused look. "He used to help at the greenhouse during his off days. After a while, I sorta got attached to him."

"That happens with puppies. Then they grow up."

"Yeah, well, no danger of that with Lyle."

"I got that impression. That why it didn't work out?"

Del shakes her head. "It never would have worked out. We had a thing for about a month, but he really isn't my type." She frowns, looks away. "It happened at a bad time, close to the anniversary of when Jack left. It was just a rebound thing."

"No explanation needed."

"Well, you asked."

"True. You know, Lyle said he was the one who broke it off."

Del chuckles, without much humour. "Yeah, he'd say that."

There's a pause. Somewhere, something is dripping, steady as a heartbeat.

"Where did you run into Lyle?" she says suddenly, looking at me.

"At the fire, initially. Lately though, he's been following me around."

"Following you?"

"When I stopped him, he said he was trying to help you."

"How could following you help me?"

"I'm not sure, but Lyle seems to think it might."

She looks puzzled.

"He wants to catch BB's killer. He thinks you'll appreciate that."

Del sighs. "That'd be Lyle. Doesn't know when to quit. Is he helping any?"

I think of the plugged toilets. "I've given him a few things to take care of."

Del looks amused. "That'll keep him happy."

There's a sudden scrape as the door opens and a cool breeze wafts in.

Christina Telson stands in the doorway. "I'm sorry," she says. "I thought you were alone."

I take my hand off Del's shoulder and she retreats to the far side of the tub, a questioning look on her face. Telson's look is questioning too, but in a different way — she's surprised and more than a little angry. I try to think of something to say but I'm too slow, fighting heat, fatigue, and painkillers. The door closes before I get out the first words.

"Christina —"

"Who was that?" Del says quietly.

I don't bother answering and charge after Telson. She's halfway across the yard when I make it outside, in my underwear, dripping and steaming. It's not very dignified, but I've gotten past dignified a long time ago. "Just wait," I holler, and she turns around. She's wearing tight black jeans and a red plaid flannel shirt. Her curly brown hair is getting wet, sticking to her face. She looks fantastic.

"It's not what you think," I say. The most overused line in history.

"Whatever," she says, turning away. "You're obviously busy."

"Just hang on a second!"

Telson is nearly to her rental car and I consider sprinting across the yard, but notice I'm now in plain view of the greenhouses. Two old ladies stand under an awning, watching me with great interest. I back away, watching Telson's car splash through puddles as it turns. It stops for a few seconds, the window coming down.

"I'm in town," she hollers. "Drop by, when you're not so busy."

I find Telson at the Super 8 at the edge of town. As I park the Cornbinder, it occurs to me that I should bring flowers or something. There's a lovely arrangement waiting in the motel planters but I restrain myself, avoid becoming a cliché. I'll take her out for a nice dinner, maybe do a little dancing. When she answers the door, I wear my best make-up smile. It's a little rumpled from storage, but it's a classic.

"What are you grinning about?" she says.

"I'm just happy to see you."

"Really." An eyebrow goes up. "You didn't seem so happy when I found you in the hot tub. In fact, you seemed a little scared."

I'm a little scared now. She's shorter than me, and half my weight, but she's a woman scorned.

"What you saw in the tub was nothing. We were both just cold, and she's a client."

"A client?" The other eyebrow goes up. "She hired you?"

"In a manner of speaking."

"For what?"

"She's Bert Brashaw's daughter."

The name has a sobering effect. Telson's frown softens. "Really?"

"Yes. I thought you would have figured that out already, being the big investigative reporter."

"I might have recognized her with her clothes on."

"Look," I say quickly, putting an arm around her shoulders, "I explained that already. Let's go for something to eat, maybe do a little dancing."

"You don't know how to dance."

"You can teach me," I say, attempting to direct her out of the room. But she's not ready to go. Her mood has changed and she looks at me with an unusual expression. Her brow furrows.

"I heard about a wildfire in Montana that killed a firefighter and I started to worry. I always worry now when I hear about wildfires. They mentioned a Canadian was involved. Naturally, I assumed the worst."

"I called you, left a message."

"I got it on my way up." She hugs me suddenly, whispers into my shirt. "Christ, Porter, for a while there, I thought I'd lost you."

A tremor runs through her. I hold her, standing in the doorway of the motel room. Her hair smells like peaches and she feels good, pressed up against me. I remember thinking about her in the fire shelter, how I swore to myself I'd marry her if I made it out alive. After a few long minutes, Telson lets go and sighs, looking at me.

"Porter ..."

"Yeah?"

"Nothing." She frowns. "I'm just glad you're okay. Let's get something to eat."

We drive around for a while. I'm not keen on returning to the Filling Station just yet — too many people recognize me there and I want a quiet supper with Telson. It's a toss-up between Pop's Family

Restaurant and Mom's Grill and Souvenir Shop. Telson picks Mom's, saying she doesn't trust a man in an apron. It's a nice enough place, built with milled logs. Souvenirs are tacked to the walls. We select a table next to a four-hundred-dollar framed print of a cougar. I hope the food here is cheaper than the mementos. The menus are bound hardcover. The tablecloths are real.

"The lobster and steak sound good," says Telson.

I look for the lobster and steak. Forty-five dollars.

"I think I'll just have the child's plate."

"Live a little," Telson says, peering over her menu.

"Okay. I'll have a side of gravy."

She sets down her menu and gives me a benevolent look. "I'll buy."

"Well, then, for starters, I'll go for the rack of ribs ..."

Telson tells me she's expensing it back to the paper she's working for. They never know where she is — one of the benefits of being a roving reporter.

"What happened out there, Porter?"

I'm suddenly reluctant to tell the story again, but she has a right to know. I tell her most of what happened at the fire, my decision to go up on the ridge, but skip over the worst of it — being trapped in the firestorm, finding Brashaw. Her expression goes from concern to horror.

"You blame yourself, don't you?"

I shrug, try to look noncommittal. Which doesn't fool either of us.

"It's not your fault, Porter. Fires are unpredictable."

I nod, don't want to argue. Thankfully, the main course arrives, bringing the usual lull. When the waitress leaves, I quickly change the subject. "How did you find me, at the greenhouse?"

"Oh, that was easy," Telson says, waving a fork in my direction. "I just called the local Forest Service office, asked for the guy in charge and told them I was your sister. He said you were staying at a place a few miles out of town, even gave directions."

Grey. It could have been worse. She could have found Noble.

"This client of yours, Brashaw's daughter — what did she hire you for?"

"Well, she didn't really hire me," I say, trying a rib.

"So, this hot tub thing is pro bono?"

"Let's forget the hot tub. She just wants me to investigate a little, keep her up-to-date. It was her father that was killed, after all. She seems to think that since I was on the fire, I have some sort of advantage over everyone else."

"Do you?"

"Not really. I saw the origin before it was disturbed, but other than that, I'm pretty much working blind." I don't tell her about Kar, or the marijuana gardens. I don't really want her involved in what I don't fully understand. That she's here to see me is enough. "In some ways, I'm at a disadvantage. I'm an outsider and don't know the system or any of the local politics."

"I didn't know the origin was disturbed," she says, chewing thoughtfully.

"Well, if they haven't let that out, you'll have to keep it under your hat."

"No problem. What else haven't they released?"

I hesitate. She seems relaxed, confidently inquisitive. Same old Telson.

"Look, Christina, don't take this the wrong way, but I don't want you involved."

She shrugs. "Okay — but I'd love to help. I thought we made a good team."

"I almost got you killed the last time."

She shrugs again, pops a piece of lobster in her mouth. "An occupational hazard."

She's so nonchalant it's infuriating. "I'm glad you're here to see me. I appreciate your concern — and your offer to help — but this is something I need to do on my own. Let's not talk shop tonight."

She nods, smiling. "Whatever you want, sweetheart."

I relax a little. There's only one thing left to do tonight, and tomorrow I'll see Castellino. Then I'll take Telson away from here and go for a little holiday. Maybe we'll see the Grand Canyon, do a little rafting. After supper, I'm ready to head back to the motel, but Telson tells me to slow down a little.

Didn't I promise dancing?

I tell her I know just the place.

11
●

TELSON LOOKS DUBIOUS when we pull into the parking lot of the
Paradise Gateway Motel. I thought we were going dancing, she says. I
assure her there will be dancing tonight — I just want a place where
my ineptitude won't be so conspicuous. Her mood doesn't improve
when we go inside. It's not that busy this early in the evening. Men
with ball caps on backwards sit at gambling machines. Older men sit
hunched at the bar, nursing drinks. A one-man-band is setting up in
the corner. Country music seeps from a jukebox.

"This isn't quite what I had in mind, Porter."

"One drink," I tell her. "I was here a few nights ago. People were
dancing on the tables."

"Table dancing. How romantic."

We find a table in the corner, away from the gambling machines. I
ask her what she wants and go to the bar to get the drinks. It makes
me look like a gentleman and I get to ask about Kar — nothing wrong
with accomplishing two things at once, but Roy isn't very co-operative.

"She's not here," he says, rubbing his imaginary moustache.

"Is she working tonight?"

"I thought I told you to stay away."

"How would you like to get arrested, Roy?"

Roy freezes. If he knows as much as everyone else around here, he
knows I'm an arson investigator. Obviously, he doesn't know that I
can't actually arrest him because he looks very suspicious. Maybe he's

on parole. "I don't want any trouble," he says, raising his hands like he's surrendering. "She's on in like a half-hour. I can get her down earlier, if you need."

"No problem, Roy. I'll wait. Now give me a beer and a red wine."

He hands me the drinks. "On the house, man."

On the way back to the table, one of the guys at the bar gives me a nod.

"You're a regular already," says Telson. "I can see the attraction."

She gestures toward my frosty mug. "Are you drinking again?"

"Not seriously. I'm past all that."

"This has got to be pretty stressful — the fire and the fatality."

"I thought we weren't going to talk shop."

She apologizes, hesitates for a second before she excuses herself, heads for the ladies' room. I head in the other direction, out the door. If I'm quick, I can catch Kar before she starts her shift. I don't want to talk with her inside the bar — that didn't work out so well last time. I run up the metal stairs to the second-floor landing, knock on her door. There's a delay, then the bolt rattles.

She peers at me through the crack allowed by the safety chain. "You again," she grumbles.

"I need to talk to you, Kar."

"I'm just getting ready for work. And I don't want to talk to you, anyway."

The door closes and I knock again. Her response is muffled but unmistakable. "Go away!"

"I know about the gardens, Kar."

For a minute there's no sound from within, then the bolt rattles again. This time, the door opens further. She doesn't exactly invite me in, just leaves the door open and stands by the bed. Textbooks and papers are scattered over the sheets — a little last-minute cramming. She's in her work uniform, hair pinned back, her expression tense. I close the door. Looks like it's my move.

"I know about the pot-growing."

"Yeah?" she says. "And what do *you* want?"

"I just want you to be honest with me."

She laughs. "Right."

"Was the fire started to burn out the pot gardens?"

For a few seconds she watches me. "How should I know?"

"Because you know the people that are growing the pot."

She gives me a blank stare — a good one; she's had some practice.

"Kar, look, you're a smart girl. Obviously, you have plans." I gesture toward the books scattered on the bed. Kar follows my gaze, begins to collect her books, her gaze averted like someone found out her dirty little secret. She shoves the loose bundle of papers into a nightstand and regards me cautiously from across the expanse of her bed. Waiting for me to leave. I don't move.

"It's getting late," she says. "I have to go to work."

"Those people you know, Kar, out in the bush, don't have plans like you. How do you think it's going to look when you finish your schooling and apply for a job, and you have a criminal record? Do you think it's going to help your chances? Because sooner or later, you'll have one if you keep hanging around with those kind of people."

"Those kind of people," she says bitterly, shaking her head. "What do you know?"

"Nothing. I don't know anything. Tell me about them, Kar. Who are they?"

"Nobody," she says. "They're nobody. Now I *really* have to go to work."

She moves toward the end of the bed. I step back, blocking the door. Her voice is sharp. "I'm going to be late."

"If the fire was set to burn out the gardens, that may be the least of your problems."

"Listen buddy — you're the only problem I got. Now get out of my room."

There's a tense silence as we face off. I glance at my watch. We're both running out of time.

"Why won't you talk to me, Kar?"

"Listen," she says slowly, so I don't miss anything. "I don't know what you're talking about."

She's made her decision and I've lost her. One more try.

"Kar, I know you're involved. I saw you get out of that truck."

"What truck?" she says. Smoothing her hands on her skirt.

"This morning. I was watching when you came back to the motel."

"Oh — that." She laughs, but it sounds strained. "I hitched. Caught a ride."

"Really? Where were you coming from?"

"None of your damn business."

"You helped me, Kar. I just want to return the favour."

"Look — I gotta get downstairs."

"What are you afraid of?"

She won't look at me. I try to meet her gaze, but she glances away.

"Just one minute, and I'll be gone. I just want to talk for one minute. You heard me the other night, in the bar, so you know who I am and why I'm so interested in who set that fire. I'm going back to Canada real soon, in fact, I'm out of this tomorrow. I know the squatters are growing pot in the canyon, and probably several other places, and I'm pretty sure that's why the fire was started."

She's staring at me now, her voice scarcely a whisper. "What are you going to do?"

"Tomorrow morning, I'm going to the sheriff and tell him what I know."

Kar's eyes widen and she shakes her head. "You can't do that."

"I can and I will. And then what do you think is going to happen? That fire killed someone, so it's a homicide. If you're covering for the killer, for some misguided reason, you may as well give up on your studies, because you'll be travelling in a different direction. And your friends out in the bush won't fare much better. At the very least, they'll be charged for growing. So, if you know anything about who started the fire, you need to tell me. I won't use your name and I won't mention the pot growing. You can prevent a lot of problems for your friends. Or you can talk to the sheriff tomorrow."

"Shit!" she says, staring at the floor. "I *knew* this would happen."

"Talk to me, Kar. Who would want to wipe out the gardens?"

Kar paces for a moment, then sits on the edge of the bed, begins to massage her forehead. Her hands are narrow, delicate, but calloused. She's trembling, trying not to cry. I pull up a chair, sit across from her. She flinches away when I touch her elbow.

"Kar, please believe me — I'm just trying to help."

The phone rings, shrill and demanding, and we both jump.

"Shit," she says, "it's Roy. I'm late."

She reaches over and grabs the phone. "I'll be down in a minute —"

It's not Roy — I can tell by the look on her face, the way she suddenly glances at me.

"No," she says, shaking her head. "No — no, he's not ... I would never ..."

I take a quick step, grab the phone, pulling it from Kar's grasp. She shrinks away from me, backs onto the bed. "Who is this?" I say into the receiver. A few seconds of breathing on the other end, then a click. I stab in the numbers for call trace, get nothing but a loud buzz — they must route through a switchboard. Whoever was calling knows where I am and must be close. I dart outside, peer over the second-floor rail. Nothing. They might have called from the lobby, and I thunder down the metal steps and yank open the door. The lobby is empty, the handset on the phone cold. Discouraged, I return to the bar, glance around. Nothing has changed. Telson is at the table, staring at me. I want to search the parking lot, but there isn't much use — the caller was probably on a cell and miles from here by now.

I wander back to the table, trying to come up with a good story.

"Where were you?" says Telson.

"Had to use the can by the lobby. Plumbing problems."

She nods, but I'm not sure she believes me. I sip my beer, try to slow my heart rate; I'm definitely in the target zone. A few minutes later Kar comes in, gives me a sharp look. I pretend not to notice and she turns away.

The one-man band steps onto the stage, taps the microphone, introduces himself as Rusty something-or-another, and asks for requests. I holler for some Clapton and he grins, starts playing "Knocking on Heaven's Door." Rusty can play. I pull Telson to her feet, create a dance floor. Kar watches. Telson holds me tight and I stop worrying about tomorrow.

The world seems a better place the next morning when I turn over in bed and find Telson next to me, all warm skin and curly hair. Yawning, I search for the clock. It's late — nine — but I take my time getting up. After a shower, Telson is still sleeping. I lean over, kiss her on the cheek. Her eyes flutter open and she smiles.

"Porter ... you're dressed."

"I've got something I need to do. You want to get breakfast first?"

She shakes her head, tells me to do my thing. She's asleep again before I reach the door.

I warm up the Cornbinder and head to Lakeside Estates. My plan is simple: tell Castellino everything I know, then see Del and tell her I've done all I can. Then back to the motel for brunch with Telson; maybe plan a holiday — I need some distance from recent events.

When I knock on the door of the cabin that Castellino and Noble use as an office, there's no response. Come to think of it, there're no vehicles here either. I divert to the ranger station, thinking they might be there, but Grey is the only familiar face.

"They're out on a call," he says. "Someone found a body."

"A body? Where?"

"I'm not sure. Some motel in town."

I get a bad feeling, which worsens as I approach the Paradise Gateway Motel. The parking lot is filled with sheriff and emergency services vehicles. A crowd has gathered and a cordon has been established. Deputy Sheriff Compton stands in the parking lot, wearing reflective sunglasses, his arms crossed. Half the Carson Lake Volunteer Fire Department are doing crowd control. There's even a media van here already — how they hear about these things so quickly, I'll never know. The door to Kar's room stands open. I park half in the ditch at the edge of the highway and watch. There's a lot of activity on the second-floor balcony; uniforms coming and going. I want to talk to Compton, find out what happened, but I'm a little reluctant. After the phone call Kar received last night, it occurs to me that I may have been the catalyst for what happened. Remembering I still have Kar's room key in my pocket, I feel sick, clench my jaw hard for a few minutes, and fight a rising panic.

Another death that may have been my fault.

I ease the Cornbinder back into traffic, return to the Super 8. I need to think.

Telson is in the shower. She comes out wearing a towel, smiling.

"Howdy, stranger. Want to borrow a towel?"

I shake my head, sit on a corner of the bed.

"What's wrong, Porter?"

I hesitate. "You know that waitress at the bar last night?"

Telson pulls the towel tighter around herself. "The one who was making eyes at you?"

"Yeah. I think she's dead. They found a body in her room this morning."

Telson sits on the bed next to me. "What happened?"

"I'm not sure. I just heard about it."

"Did you know her?"

"I talked to her a few times, about the fire."

"What's she got to do with the fire?"

"Long story. But somehow, I think she's connected to the arson."

We're both silent for a minute, thinking. No doubt, she's wondering why I didn't tell her earlier.

"I need your help," I say, finally. "I need you to be a reporter."

"Okay. But I thought you didn't want me involved."

"I don't. I just need this one little favour."

She smiles wistfully, watching my face.

"I need you to go to the motel and find out what you can. If it's really her. Who found the body. Signs of a struggle. The usual reporter questions. Then come back and let me know."

She stands, ready for action. "I'll head right over. What're you going to do?"

"Wait for you," I tell her. "And worry."

Telson doesn't take long to dress and hurry out the door. When she's gone, I dig Kar's room key out of my pocket and toss it into a dumpster behind the Super 8. I should have known better than to think this was all over for me. Then I sit and wait by the phone. Telson returns a half-hour later, beads of sweat on her forehead.

"She's dead, all right," she says, slinging her bag onto the bed.

"And?"

"Not so fast, sailor. You go first."

"What?"

"You asked me to be a reporter, but you won't tell me what's going on."

Telson is wearing her work face. I should have known. "This has to be off the record."

"You know it's never off the record with a reporter."

"Today, it had better be."

She reads my expression. "Okay, okay, I was just kidding. They were pulling her out when I got there. We're talking body bag, so I didn't get a look, but I did manage to squeeze in a few questions. They didn't tell me much, though. But from the talk in the crowd, it sounds like suicide — pills and booze."

"She killed herself?"

"It was just talk, Porter."

"Just talk? Who was talking?"

"Everyone. Apparently, someone at the motel found her."

"And had to tell their friends."

"You know how it goes. Big news, in a town like this."

I sigh, thinking about Kar and her correspondence course. Telson sits beside me, slides her hand onto my leg. "I'm sorry this happened, Porter. I want to help you, but I need to know what's going on. What did you talk to her about?"

I stand and Telson gives me a questioning look.

"Come with me. You're not the only one that needs to know."

We drive in separate vehicles to the greenhouse. The idea is to leave the Cornbinder with Del, stick with Telson's rental. This works well with my other plan — tell Del what happened, then go to the sheriff. Leave the investigation to the authorities. I gear down for a pothole, pondering how to explain to Castellino my involvement with Kar in a way that won't get me arrested for any number of things. Breaking and entering. Interfering in a police investigation. Stupidity. If I'm lucky, they'll just send me home. Telson's little blue Honda splashes through puddles ahead of me. The sun is out again and everything is steaming. When we arrive, Del is in the back, up to her armpits in an aquatic tub. She looks up at us as we walk in.

The women size each other up. Del stands, wipes water and wisps of root onto a rag, and offers her hand. "We didn't start off very well, did we? I'm Delise Brashaw."

Telson shakes her hand, and I breathe a silent sigh of relief.

"Christina Telson. I'm Porter's friend."

"I gathered that much."

There's an awkward silence.

"Del, something's happened. We need to talk."

Del glances up the aisle of the greenhouse, to where Melissa is sitting on a pallet, filling trays with soil, then herds us into a room at the end of the building. It's small, stuffy, and filled with bags of fertilizer. "What's the matter?" Del says, looking worried. "What happened?"

"You know how I told you the squatters were growing marijuana in the canyon?"

Del nods.

"Well, I didn't tell you the whole story about how I got the idea to start with. When I went to see the squatters the first time, I noticed a familiar face in a trailer window, watching me. Turns out, it was a girl working in town as a waitress. I didn't have any luck with the squatters, so I figured I'd give her a try. She didn't want to talk. I'm pretty sure someone else didn't want me talking to her either — that was the night I was jumped."

"Those bruises," says Del. "They gave you those?"

I nod. Telson shoots Del a vaguely annoyed look.

"Anyway, I returned to where she's staying in town, to talk to her again, but she wasn't there. So I waited around for a while. When she showed up, it was with one of the squatters." I pause. "At any rate, she's connected with them, so I tried once more to talk to her, but she was even less co-operative. Then, this morning, she turns up dead."

"What do you mean — dead?" says Del. As if there's more than one kind.

"The cops aren't saying much, but we've heard rumours of suicide."

"Suicide?" Del lets out a heavy sigh, sits on a stack of vermiculite. "Why would she do that?"

"She might not have," says Telson. "We can't rule out that this was a murder, and is somehow connected to the fire." From the look on her face, I know Telson won't let this go — this is her story now. So much for one small favour. Del looks at her.

"Do you think she knew who set the fire?"

"We're not sure of anything right now," I say, shooting Telson a cautionary glance.

"What about the police?" says Del. "What do they know?"

"That's a little difficult to determine. We're not talking."

Del gives me a piercing look. "You haven't told them about the pot gardens?"

"Not yet."

"Good." She looks determined. "That's good."

"No, Del, that's not good. The police are the ones in authority here — they're the ones who will solve this thing in the end. I'm just running around, trying to find out what little I can. All I'm really doing is trying to soothe my conscience."

Del places a hand on my shoulder. "Porter, you know this wasn't your fault."

I brush the hand away. "If I hadn't come, none of this would have happened."

"If you hadn't come, who knows what might have happened. Maybe no one would have called for the bombers, and the fire would have gone over the ridge and killed those squatters. Whoever set the fire would have set it anyway. Without you here, there's a better chance they might get away with it. But you *are* here Porter, and you have to stick with it."

Telson nods. "I agree, Porter. Let's stick with it."

I look at both women, wanting me to keep things from the police — each for different reasons. Telson wants an exclusive. Del has unrealistic expectations about what a man can accomplish on his own, with little-to-no resources. Both of them seem unaware of the very real danger.

"It would be better to turn this over to the sheriff."

Telson nods, like she knew I would say this. Del looks disgusted. "That's it, then?"

"You're dealing with people who won't hesitate to kill to protect themselves."

"Which is why we have to catch them," Del says, her eyes flashing.

I return Del's challenging look. "I'm flattered that you think I'm that good Del, but the reality here is the sheriff is in a much better position to catch whoever started the fire, and whoever might have killed the woman in town. Given what I know, their chances will be even better."

"Not if the squatters leave," Del says quietly.

"What do you mean?" says Telson.

Del looks at me. "We've talked about this before, Porter. They're growing pot, probably enough to put them into federal prison if they're caught. Do you think they'll co-operate with the police? They're the only people that might know who started the fire, and they could be packing up right now."

There's a heavy silence. Telson looks at me. "You know, she's right, Porter."

Both women watch me expectantly. I'm outnumbered.

"Okay," I say, reluctantly. "I'll try to talk with them again, then that's it."

12

ON THE DRIVE up from the Blood Creek Road, I'm half hoping the old wellsite will be abandoned. Another part of me is hoping they're still there, and I can get them to talk. Del is right about the squatters being the only other people that might know who started the fire, and the only way to put this behind me is to leave Montana knowing I did everything I could. The gate on the rutted trail is still closed and my heart beats a little faster. After what happened when I last approached them, I take the time to heave aside the heavy poles and open the gate.

I want the Cornbinder handy for a quick getaway.

Wolverine is working on his truck when I nose the Cornbinder onto the wellsite. He looks over from the open jaws of the engine compartment and frowns. I'm not encouraged by the way he picks up an oversized wrench, hefts it as he watches me leave the safety of my vehicle. I try to look harmless as I approach. Given the situation, it's not difficult.

"I need to talk to you for a minute."

He steps away from the truck, gives me a cold, appraising look.

"It's about the woman you dropped in town the other day."

No response. I should have brushed up on my Neanderthal.

"She was found dead this morning."

His look darkens. He turns toward a trailer and hollers: "Pa!"

When he stares at me again, he looks dangerously upset. A trailer door slaps open and the Sasquatch appears, toting his sawed-off shotgun. He gives me an ugly sneer as he steps down from the trailer and ambles over. I'm struck again by the similarity of their features. The Sasquatch's beard and moustache glisten with grease. They're both wearing over-sized rubber boots, caked with clay.

"He says Karalee is dead."

The Sasquatch's brow twitches. "That true?"

"Yes. They found her this morning, at the motel."

For a minute, neither squatter says anything. Father and son look at each other. Something passes between them. I'm thinking they'll want to know more — how she died, who found her — questions anyone would want answered. But when the Sasquatch looks at me, he has only one question.

"Where do we pick up the body?"

"I don't know. I'm not with the police."

"Then why're you here?" says Wolverine.

I hesitate, wondering how to come at this. By the look on their faces, straight-on is best. "I'm not with the sheriff or Forest Service," I tell them, to make sure this is perfectly clear. "I'm here for my own reasons. I was on the fire in the canyon. You've probably heard about what happened there, about the guy that was killed."

The Sasquatch is silent. Wolverine gives me an impatient look.

"I'm responsible for the fellow that was killed. I want to know who started that fire."

Sasquatch and son exchange glances, then Sasquatch looks at me. "Thanks for lettin' us know about Karalee," he says, his voice flat. They turn away, walk toward one of the trailers. I'm not sure what I expected, but it wasn't this. It comes to me that Kar is the Sasquatch's daughter.

I call after him. "Your daughter may have been murdered."

They stop, turn around. "What?" says Wolverine.

"I know about the gardens. I'm willing to bet someone else did, too."

For a moment, both men stand rooted, then look at each other and exchange a faint nod. They have ugly, determined looks on their faces as they walk closer. Sasquatch stops about three feet in front of me.

Wolverine keeps going, gets behind me, which makes me nervous. I turn, try to keep them both in view, but Wolverine knows the dance, keeps a step ahead. Sasquatch scowls.

"How do you know about the gardens?"

I back away, try to sound calm. "It wasn't that hard to figure out."

Sasquatch points the coach gun at my belly. "You made a mistake, showing your face."

"Listen, I'm just investigating —"

Sasquatch nods and Wolverine grabs my arms, pinning them behind my back in a way that quickly becomes uncomfortable. Sasquatch gets very close, the muzzle of the gun presses against my belly.

"You should have stayed away," he growls. "Don't you know this place is cursed?"

"It's cursed, all right," I say, grimacing, wondering if I can shake Wolverine, make a run for it.

"Then why'd you come back?"

"Whoever started the fire killed a man I'm responsible for. And probably Karalee."

Wolverine tightens his grip, giving my back a jolt of pain. "How do you know my sister?"

"I don't," I grunt, trying to keep my breathing even. "But I owe her. She helped me. A couple of guys jumped me. Would have finished me off if she hadn't stopped them."

The Sasquatch inspects the stitches on my face, the bruising on my neck, as though I'm an injured horse. It's a toss-up between shooting me and seeing if I'll still be of some use. He nods thoughtfully but doesn't remove the muzzle of the gun from my belly.

"Why would she help you?"

"I think she knew who started the fire, and was scared."

The Sasquatch stares at me for a painfully long second, during which my heart thumps in my ears and I'm convinced he's going to pull the trigger. Then he steps back and lowers the gun, nodding toward his son. "Let him go."

My arms are released. "What did she tell you?" says the Sasquatch.

"Not enough." I test my arms, line them up with my shoulders.

"Why do you think she knew who started the fire?"

"For the same reason you do."

They look confused, and it occurs to me that they don't know who started the fire, which might explain why they were so suspicious when I mentioned the gardens — they probably thought I was trying to extort them. They might, however, have some idea why the fire was set. I take a step back, so I can keep an eye on both of them. "I know you're growing marijuana in the canyon, and I have no issue with that. I'm also pretty sure you picked this area because of the curse, so people would stay away. My only interest is finding who started the fire. If we know that, we may also find who killed Karalee."

"Yeah?" says Wolverine. "How you gonna do that?"

"With your help. No reason we can't co-operate. We want the same thing."

Wolverine sniffs, wipes his nose on his sleeve. "I doubt that."

"I give you my word I'll say nothing about the gardens."

"What if we just send you off with a load of buckshot in your ass?"

"You may never find out what happened to Karalee."

Sasquatch and son walk a dozen yards away, confer in whispers, glancing at me. From the trailers, grubby faces watch from behind grubbier windows. There might be a dozen or more people here, judging from the line of laundry sagging at the edge of the wellsite. Father and son give me a hard look. I'm sure it's occurred to them that getting rid of me is the safest way to protect their gardens and I glance toward the Cornbinder, wondering how quickly I could cover the distance, fire her up and back down the trail. What I'm counting on is that they're not really killers — that their earlier threats were based on their suspicion that I might be involved in whatever transpired in the past. Wolverine seems to be doing most of the talking now, glancing toward me and gesturing with his hands. His father listens, scratching under his beard. Finally, he nods.

As they walk closer, I catch a few whispered words.

"— damn well better ..."

They stand in front of me, give me foreboding looks.

"Okay," says the Sasquatch. "But we call the shots."

"Not a chance. That'll never work."

Their eyes narrow. Their stances become more aggressive. I try not to look at the gun.

"You're not the reason I started this investigation," I tell them. "And you won't be the reason I finish it. I'm here to find out who started the fire. I can promise you I won't mention that you're growing dope, but you gotta understand that as soon as the sheriff's people connect you to Karalee, and they will, they'll be up here asking questions. You've been here long enough that people will have seen Karalee leaving town, getting dropped off at the motel. How do you think I figured it out? All I'm offering is a chance to help find her killer while you collect what's left of your crop and get the hell out of here."

The men stare at me, livid, jaws clenched.

"You can deal with me, or you can deal with the cops."

Wolverine looks at me in wonder, waits for his father's reaction. The Sasquatch frowns, thinking, tapping the muzzle of the shotgun against his leg. He chews his lower lip, glances around at his ramshackle kingdom. The trailers. The wellhead, sprouting hoses like a plant putting down roots. No doubt he's reluctant to leave such a well-serviced site, but he has to know the end is near.

"Okay," he says finally. Wolverine looks disappointed.

"Pa, I don't think we should —"

The Sasquatch turns on his son. "Shut up, boy! I have to think of us all."

Wolverine obviously has more to say, but bites his tongue, glaring at me.

"You got three days," says the Sasquatch, pointing the gun at me like a teacher might point a yardstick. I nod and he lowers the gun, gestures toward his son. "Erwin will fill you in. But there's a condition.

Non-negotiable. I don't know you from a hole in the ground, so I'm sending Erwin to be your right hand. Consider him your partner for the next three days."

Erwin's eyes widen. "Aw, come on, Pa!"

One look from the Sasquatch silences him. Erwin sizes me up, scowling; he doesn't look impressed. Neither am I — he'll be like taking the proverbial bull into a china shop. Hopefully, he can tell me enough of what's going on to make this worthwhile. I don't have much choice, if I want answers.

"All right, I'll take him with me. But he's gotta behave."

The Sasquatch looks amused. "You two will get along just fine."

Erwin gives me a wicked grin. "Let's get to work ... partner."

On the drive down from the wellsite, Erwin lays it out simply enough. Someone wants them to sell their crop at a ridiculously low price — the plight of farmers everywhere. Unlike other farmers though, they don't have to — they have their own sales department.

"Really?" I'm impressed. "Isn't that a little unusual?"

Erwin shrugs. "We don't like middlemen."

"So you run the whole show yourselves?"

"Pretty much," he says, glancing out the window at the fire camp.

"I think I ran into one of your salesmen the other day."

"I doubt it. We don't sell around here."

"No? Why not?"

He looks at me with disdain. "Never sell where you're growing, man."

The kid at the gas station must not have read the rule book. "So where do you sell?"

Erwin gives me a look that clearly indicates this is not up for discussion. I gear down to let a lowboy pass, crawling up the hill. The fire is in mop-up stage now, the flame gone. Nothing to do but wander the black, looking for any coals that might still burn in the ground or under some root. Boring, tedious work. On any other fire, most of the manpower and equipment would have been released by now, but there are still plenty of men in yellow Nomex fire shirts wandering the burn; dozers and water trucks neatly lined up in camp. This isn't just a fire, this is a media event, and although it's too late, the Forest Service wants to look like they're throwing everything they have at the beast. As if that might somehow compensate for what happened.

"How does your sister fit in?" I ask Erwin.

He shifts in his seat, looking uncomfortable. "She wanted to work in town — didn't like staying at camp very much, which is okay, because we can always use more bread until the crop is ready." He's silent for a few minutes, staring out the window as we grind down the long, winding trail to the Blood Creek Road. I don't press, let him tell the story in his own time. He shifts again, sighing heavily, his shoulders slumped. "They used Kar," he says finally. "They must have figured out she was with us, and used her to deliver their message. Bastards. They didn't have the balls to come face us."

"You never met them?"

"No."

"You have no idea who they are?"

Erwin gives me an evil look. "If we did, they wouldn't be walkin' around."

He falls silent again, morose. He's a big kid, wide in the shoulders, with a dangerous air about him, but he's subdued right now, grieving for his sister. This might make him more talkative. Or he could just withdraw.

"How did they contact her, Erwin?"

He looks at me suddenly, frowning, trying to cover the emotion I see written in his features.

"Notes," he says. "Or on the phone. They never contacted her directly."

"You believe that?"

"What do you mean?" This time, his frown is sincere.

"Well, it might be a little difficult to deal with these people if you never meet them. How were you supposed to sell them your product? I mean, we're talking some volume here, I'd assume, or it wouldn't be worth their trouble. What are you guys growing? A couple of tons?"

Erwin gets a suspicious look. "Yeah, maybe. Something like that."

"You weren't going to just leave the stuff in a drop box for them to pick up, were you?"

Erwin's expression grows cold — he doesn't like being challenged. He's about to say something when we come around a corner at the bottom of a hill. A vehicle is parked at the junction with the Blood Creek Road. It's the rent-a-cop and, although he couldn't care less who we are, the uniform clearly makes Erwin nervous. The guard nods as we drive past. Erwin doesn't nod back.

"Relax, Erwin. Act natural."

"Fuck you."

"Not that natural."

The sun is out again and it's dry enough that we kick up dust on the Blood Creek Road. Erwin is kneading his knuckles, rolling them back and forth, like he's impatient to hit someone. Since I'm the only one within range, this is not a good sign. "You think Kar knew who these guys were?" he says.

"Maybe. What do you think, Erwin? You think she killed herself?"

He scowls; the scowl goes good with the heavy sideburns. "No. She was pretty together."

"So she was murdered. Why would someone do that unless she were a threat?"

Erwin massages his knuckles a little more furiously for a moment, then swears and thumps both fists on the dash, hard enough to make something crack. The gas gauge on the Cornbinder flickers, then begins to rise. Erwin's fixed it, and I have a full tank. I suppress an urge to share this good news.

"Sons-a-bitches," Erwin says through clenched teeth.

I wait some time before saying anything, let Erwin cool down. He's slumped in his seat, his jaw clenched. "Okay," I say cautiously. "If we assume she knew who was moving in on you guys, she might have given you a clue. She might have let something slip."

Erwin looks at me, his expression blank.

"Did they talk specifics? Prices? Harvest date? Where the drop was going to be?"

He shakes his head. "No, man, we never got that far."

"Why not?"

"Because we told them to screw off."

Apparently, Kar passed on the message verbatim. "How soon after this did the fire start?"

He thinks, massaging his knuckles again. "About a week."

"Did you have any contact with them in the interim?"

"Yeah. They sent a message, through Kar." He hesitates, frowning, perhaps wondering how things might have been different. "They said that if we didn't deal with them, we wouldn't be dealing with anyone."

"How did they contact your sister?"

"By phone. At work."

We think about this for a few minutes as the gravel road unwinds ahead of us.

"Erwin, they didn't wipe out your entire crop, did they?"

He hesitates. "We got some left."

"So you still might be able to deal with them."

He looks at me like I'm crazy, then nods slowly, comprehension dawning. "Yeah, we could deal with them, all right. Then we might be able to figure out just who the hell they are."

"Now you're catching on."

"Except for one thing," he says quietly. "Kar is gone."

He's thinking what I am: if they killed Kar, they've covered their tracks and no longer want to deal. With Brashaw's death, this isn't just arson, this is homicide — they hadn't planned on anyone dying. So they cut their losses and have probably vanished.

"Erwin, who could know you're growing?"

He shrugs. "Hard to say."

"What about your customers?"

He gives this some thought. "That's a long ways away."

"Could your competition have followed you? Figured out where you're growing?"

"Maybe," he says. "But anyone could have stumbled across one of our patches. It can happen anytime. Hikers. Hunters. Timber cruisers. It's an occupational hazard."

"That's why you chose this canyon? Because of the curse?"

"Yeah." He rolls down the window, spits. "Not that it helped much."

"They'd have to connect the pot to you guys," I say. "And know it was worthwhile."

Erwin thinks about this, but no further information is forthcoming. We're on the highway now, the grip tires of the Cornbinder humming. Erwin stares blankly at the road. I think furiously about what to do next, but when we reach town, I'm no further ahead.

We drive around for a while, talking, then go see the clerk at the Paradise Gateway Motel. She's an older lady with thick glasses and a thicker waistline — the same clerk the night I checked in. She peers over her glasses at me. "Ah — the elusive Mr. Johnson."

Erwin gives me a puzzled glance. "The name is Porter Cassel," I say, trying to look friendly.

"Yes," she says. "I know. I saw you on Channel Seven."

I nod, drum my hands on the counter. "You've had a bit of news here lately too."

"Oh — yes." Her wrinkled face looks concerned. "That poor girl."

"A horrible thing," I say, glancing at Erwin. He's standing beside the counter, looming like an approaching hail storm. I give him a subtle gesture to back off. He hesitates and I repeat the gesture, not quite as subtly. After a threatening look, he wanders away, pretends to read a bulletin board. I return my attention to the clerk.

"Were you working last night?"

"Uh huh." She's watching Erwin. Even at a distance, he makes people nervous.

"Do you run the switchboard as well?"

"Yes." She looks at me. "I do just about everything here. Why?"

"I was wondering — when someone calls, do you manually transfer the call to the room?"

"Yup." She glances at a call transfer phone board, just under the lip of the counter, almost out of my view. "I just pick up the phone, like any regular call. They ask for the room number and I hit transfer, key in the room. Then I hang up."

"Do you have call display?"

"No. Are you working with the police?"

I hesitate. Sometimes it's best to let people jump to conclusions.

"I thought you might be," she says. "When they said your name was Mr. Johnson —"

I look appropriately solemn. "Last night, did you transfer a call to the girl's room?"

"Yes." She leans forward, lowers her voice. "Are you undercover?"

I return her whisper. "If I was, I couldn't tell you."

She glances at Erwin. "And that gentleman?"

"Deep, deep undercover."

She's impressed. I give her a stern look. "What can you tell me about that call?"

"Well, not much," she says regrettably. "He just asked for the room number."

"It was a man's voice?"

She nods.

"Do you ever listen in, when you're bored?"

"Heavens no," she says, looking shocked.

"Pity. Can you see the pay phone in the lobby from here?"

She glances toward the lobby, shakes her head.

"Anyone unusual come through last night?"

"Not that I recall."

"Karalee Smith — did she get a lot of visitors?"

The clerk adjusts her glasses, thinks about this. "No — not really. She was pretty quiet. I don't think she went out much either, spent a lot of time in her room, studying. She told me she wanted to be a teacher. She was taking courses, you know." The clerk gives me a meaningful look. "She was quite a determined young lady — I can't believe she would have done that. Just doesn't seem right."

"Did you hear any ruckus last night?"

"No," she says, without hesitation. "Police asked the same thing already, this morning, and I've been thinking about it ever since. I seen her, you know, lying there on the bed, all messed up. The chambermaid found her, young kid, was pretty upset. Karalee was helping her with some schoolwork. Summer classes. That's why she was by so early in the morning. Hit her pretty hard."

"What do you mean when you say she was all messed up?"

"Threw up all over herself," she says, shuddering. "Awful mess."

There's a sudden, uncomfortable silence. The clerk glances away, out a window, frowning. I'm frowning too. Vomiting is the body's way of purging poisons — I've had enough hangovers to confirm that — and it seems odd she died after purging her stomach. Then again, I'm no pathologist, and I make a note to look into this. Maybe someone loaded her up again, for a second round. Erwin stands by the bulletin board, arms crossed, staring at us. I give him a cautionary nod. Reluctantly, he turns back to the board.

"What time did the chambermaid find her?"

"Quarter past six," the clerk says mechanically, then gives me a sharp look. "Shouldn't you know this already? I talked to the police this morning."

"I know you did," I tell her, thinking fast. "And I read your statement. We just like to confirm what people tell us." The clerk gives me an offended look. "Just to check if you missed any details," I add quickly.

"In case you might have thought of something you hadn't previously mentioned."

"I see," she says, nodding gravely. "No — that's about it."

"How'd it go?" Erwin asks as we cross the parking lot.

"Not so great," I admit. "We know it was a man who called, but that's it."

"What about phone records?"

"Not a chance, unless you have a court order."

He broods about this as we drive through town. "So what do we do now?" he says.

"You meet my girlfriend."

"What?"

He looks concerned. So am I — I don't want him anywhere near Telson, but I can't see this working any other way. They're both far too suspicious to play separately, running back and forth, making up excuses. So I'll introduce them, carefully.

"Girlfriend? No way. Not part of the deal."

"Relax. She's not involved."

"Bullshit."

"She was worried. She heard about the fire."

Erwin broods a moment longer. "What have you told her?"

"Nothing. And I intend to keep it that way."

"You damn well better," he says, massaging his knuckles. I take a few extra laps around town while Erwin calms down. After the third lap, Erwin becomes impatient. Reluctantly, I pull the Cornbinder into a slot at the motel. I offer to put him up in a room for the night, which he graciously accepts.

Telson is waiting in the lobby when we pull in. She gives me a tight little smile, her eyes following the unkempt, oversized stranger behind me.

"Who's your friend?" says Telson.

"This is Waldo," I say, gesturing toward Erwin. "My fishing guide."

"Fishing guide?" Telson's eyebrows go up.

I give her a look — just go with this, please.

"Well, pleased to meet you, Waldo. I'm Barbie."

"Barbie, huh?" Erwin gives me an amused look as he shakes her hand. I shrug.

"What are you guys fishing for?" asks Telson.

"Trout," I say quickly.

"Really? What kind?"

"Cutthroat," says Erwin, grinning.

"Sounds like fun." There's a silence as Telson stares at me, waiting for me to crack. I'm starting to realize what a mistake this was. Her reporter instincts have been aroused and she'll be like a pitbull. I'm going to have to get her out of the picture, for her own safety. How, I'm not sure — I'll worry about that later. We leave Erwin to find his own room as we head to ours. When we get there Telson sits on the edge of the bed, arms crossed, staring at me. I play dumb. She doesn't buy the act for long.

"Who is he, Porter?"

The look on her face tells me her patience has worn thin — playing Barbie has not improved her mood. "I can't tell you, Christina."

"Oh, that's bullshit."

"I made a deal with this guy. I can't talk about it."

"Can't, or won't?"

"I don't think you should involve yourself any further."

She gives me a look — angry and determined. "Let's get something perfectly clear here, Porter. I came to see you. There was no hidden agenda, no ulterior motive — I was just worried. Then you needed a favour, and you brought me in."

"Well, now I'm bringing you out."

Telson's eyes narrow.

"For your own good," I tell her. "The less you know, the better. To say this guy is a little unbalanced would be an understatement. It's best he believes you're just my clueless girlfriend."

"Thanks," she says bitterly. "My ambition in life."

"Look, we both know you're anything but clueless. It's just that I'm worried about you. This guy, Waldo, is dangerous. He's angry and he has a lot to lose. But for the time being, he's on our side. I'd prefer to keep him there."

"You think I'm going to change that?"

"He's nervous enough without you asking questions."

"Why would he be nervous?"

I don't say anything.

"He's one of the growers, isn't he?"

"Never mind who he is. Believe me, there are people even more dangerous than him involved, and we don't know who they are. They probably didn't intend to kill Bert Brashaw, but when they lit that fusee, they did. So now we're talking homicide. When I started asking questions they jumped me, cracked my ribs, bruised my vertebrae. I'm pretty sure they were ready to take it further, because when I didn't give up they killed the waitress I was talking to. Whoever they are, Christina, they're watching me. As soon as they figure out that we're together, they could come after you."

"So you're worried about the case. I'm just baggage?"

"No, I'm worried about you. I swore I would never put you in that position again."

I'm sweating, breathing hard. Telson gives me a hug, which only strengthens my resolve.

"I want you to leave this place. Get away from Carson Lake."

She holds me a little longer, then lets go, stepping back so she can look me in the face.

"Porter ... I know you're worried, but I can take care of myself. I'm a big girl, and I carry a gun, remember." She places a hand on my chest. "But, I am concerned about you. I know you're not going to give up on this, no matter what you say, and you need help."

I take her hand off my chest. "I've got so much help, I'll never get anything done."

"I'm staying to help you. It's my decision."

I shake my head. "Let's not fight about this."

"Okay," she sighs. "But it's a pity. Now I can't tell you what I found."

I close my eyes, count to ten. "Okay. What did you find?"

"I can't tell you," says Telson, looking serious. "It wouldn't be fair."

"I hate it when you do this."

She grins.

"Okay," I say, resigned. "We share a little information, then you leave."

"No deal. We talk, I stay."

I think about this for a minute. Whatever she found may or may not be important, but if she stays, she won't be able to keep her nose out of this and she won't be safe. "It's about the waitress, Karalee," she says. "I did a little digging, talked to the other waitresses. Had one of those girl-to-girl talks. You could try it, but I don't think it would work as well for you."

Damn her. "Okay. But if you stay, you do what I tell you."

She gives me a sweet smile. "Don't I always?"

13

WE HAVE BREAKFAST together the next morning: Telson, Erwin, and I. Other than noting that eight o'clock is pretty late for two avid fishermen, Telson is quiet. We went for a walk last night, away from Erwin, discussed current events; Telson revealing what she'd learned from Kar's co-workers. They all claimed they got along fairly well with her. She'd been working the Gateway since spring, which fits with the squatters' planting schedule. Kept to herself, rarely socialized after hours, but was friendly and hard-working. Talked about becoming a teacher, living in the city. Never talked about her family and they didn't know her last name. She was from someplace down south, they said, but were a little vague on specifics; maybe Florida or California. An employment record might fill in a few gaps, but when Telson snuck into the motel office to take a quick peek in the file cabinet, she couldn't locate anything on Karalee. Which could mean the cops have the file, or that she was being paid under the table. All told, it's not a lot of information — certainly not enough to keep Telson here, but, as she pointed out, we had a deal. I told her about my visit to the squatters; that they don't know much more than we do. And about the arrangement with Erwin.

"You can't get rid of him?" she asked.

"Are you kidding? I couldn't get rid of you."

"But you didn't really want to," she said, snuggling close.

At the time, I didn't much feel like arguing, but this morning as I watch the two of them, I wonder how this could ever work. Telson is big-city; a modern career woman with a chip on her shoulder. Erwin is backwoods, prehistoric, and all chip. Three days, I keep telling myself. That was the deal. I try for three days — two-and-a-half now — then I say goodbye to Del and turn everything over to Castellino and Noble. If Telson behaves herself, and I can keep Erwin on a leash, it could work. I might even stumble across something useful.

"Where are you boys fishing today?" says Telson, sipping her orange juice.

"I've got a spot picked out," says Erwin. He's eaten a triple order of bacon. Maybe I'll get lucky and he'll have a coronary before he kills someone. He polishes off a half-pound of hash browns, four cups of coffee, and Telson's toast, then belches loudly. "Time to get to work," he says, standing, wiping his nose on his sleeve. "Let's catch the little bastards before they get away."

Telson wishes us luck and we head out. I pull the Cornbinder into the lot at the Filling Station, wrestle the shifter into neutral and look at Erwin. "What's your plan?"

"My plan?" he says, frowning.

"You said you had a spot picked out."

"That was just talk, for your friend Barbie. You're the investigator."

"Right. Look, Erwin, I have to level with you — I was kind of hoping you guys had at least some inkling who was moving in on your operation. Then we'd have a place to start. But right now, I don't have jack shit. So you'd better think back, give this some serious consideration."

Erwin's expression darkens. He begins to massage his knuckles.

"There must be something you haven't told me."

"We've been over this," he says, scowling, rolling his knuckles back and forth. "So let me level with you. We talked to you for a reason — we want to know who killed Karalee. We expect results. You got three days to figure this out. And you'd better figure it out. Believe me," he says, giving me a hard look, "we're not fucking around here."

"You expect me to catch the killer in three days?"

Erwin nods. "That's the deal."

"No, Erwin, that's not the deal. The deal was you guys tell me what you know and I do my best, based on what you've told me. But you've told me shit. You don't even know for sure that the fire was set by whoever is trying to move in on you. If they'd have followed up with a message, such as deal with us now or lose the rest of your crop, then at least that would be something."

"They did send a message," he says, staring at me. "They killed my sister."

"We think they killed your sister," I correct him.

"She didn't kill herself."

Like Del, Erwin has unreasonable expectations regarding what one person can do outside the system. I want to point out that I don't have access to forensics, fingerprinting, police databases. Nor do I have the authority to conduct searches or question reluctant suspects, but Erwin has lived his entire life outside the system, and pressing the issue isn't likely to help my situation. The only thing I can do for now is go along. Erwin must sense my reluctance, because he gives me another of his trademark stares.

"Don't be thinking about going to the cops, or Barbie will have to find a new playmate."

"Never crossed my mind."

"Good. So what's our next move?"

"Now we start shaking the tree," I tell him. "See what falls out."

It's a different clerk this morning at the Paradise Gateway Motel, younger and less interested in who we are. She's pale, plump, looks a little hungover. She gives us a blank stare when I ask what room Roy is staying in. "Roy who?" she says.

"The bartender. Is he staying here?"

"Oh, that Roy. Naw, he's a townie."

"Do you know where he lives?"

"Couldn't tell you," she says with a yawn. "But he's probably in the book."

We get Roy's last name — Draytor — and start flipping through a phone book anchored to the pay phone in the lobby. There are three Draytors listed. Two have no idea what I'm talking about. The third is an old man who says his son works at the Gateway, but doesn't live at home. Try the dump behind the car wash, an old two-storey with arches in front. I thank Mr. Draytor Senior, hang up, and signal Erwin, who's abusing a vending machine in the lobby.

"I remember when you could trick these things," he says.

"It's easier," I tell him, "if you put in some money."

We drive around for ten minutes without finding the car wash. Erwin is getting impatient and I'm just about to ask for directions when a light flashes behind me, blue and red. My first thought is they know about Erwin, and I begin to sweat. By the time I've pulled over, Erwin is in the back of the panel. I try to look relaxed when Deputy Sheriff Wayne Compton comes to the side window.

"Cassel," he says. "What a surprise — you're still here."

"Just tying up a few loose ends."

"So I've heard. I need you to follow me."

"Okay," I say hesitantly. "Where are we going?"

"There are some people who need to speak with you."

I think about Erwin, crouched behind me. "Give me a few minutes. I'll meet them."

Compton shakes his head. "You have a habit of disappearing. You better follow me."

I want to argue but it might look suspicious, and I can't withstand a lot of scrutiny at the moment. So I nod, follow Compton as he pulls into traffic. Erwin remains hidden, in case Compton happens to glance in his rear-view mirror, but I hear him breathing heavily in the back.

"Fuck, this is the shits," he grumbles.

"Don't worry, I won't tell them anything about the gardens."

"You better not."

Compton swings off the highway, leads me to Lakeside Estates. We park in front of the cabin being used by the investigators as an operations centre. There are a lot of vehicles here now. Compton escorts me in. Castellino and Noble are leaning over some papers at a counter, both in identical dark suits, like matched bookends. Robert Haines, the sheriff's arson specialist, is sitting, drinking coffee, his thin hair plastered to his pale, damp forehead. New maps are pinned to a cluster of hastily hung corkboards. The big dining-room table is scattered with papers.

"I found him," says Compton, by way of introduction.

Castellino gives me a critical look.

"About time," says Noble.

There is a new face as well. Castellino suggests we all take a seat, introduces Scott Batiste across the table from me, an investigator from Missoula here to help with the Smith death. Batiste is tall and lanky, with thinning brown hair and hollow cheeks. He's wearing jeans and a blue work shirt, looks as if he might have wandered in from a construction site.

"This is Porter Cassel," Castellino tells Batiste.

"Mr. Cassel," Batiste says significantly. "I've been wanting to meet you." He raises an eyebrow. "I understand you've been running your own sort of investigation here."

I shift a little uncomfortably. "Well, not really."

Batiste smiles, as does Noble at the other end of the table, neither with a lot of humour. "I understand that twice now you've evaded transport back to Canada," says Batiste. "And that you've been making inquiries, even conducting a few searches. Sounds a lot like an investigation to me."

"I'm looking into a few things," I say cautiously.

"Indeed," he says. "And your investigation seems to have had some impact."

Batiste frowns, looks down at a sheaf of papers in front of him. I'm not sure what he intended by that remark, but it seems he's hinting I may have been the catalyst in Karalee's death. I've had the same thought, but have been holding it at the back of my mind. Hearing the suggestion from someone else suddenly makes me feel faint. A line of sweat breaks out just below my hairline.

"I'm particularly interested," Batiste says, giving me a hard look, "in your investigation involving a young lady by the name of Karalee Smith. Not that we're sure that's her real name, but perhaps you can shed some light on that."

"I met her once or twice," I say carefully. "She works as a waitress at a place in town."

"Yes," says Batiste. "She worked at the Paradise Gateway Motel — a motel you yourself occupied for one night, directly after the incident on the fire. It is also the motel where we found her body just recently. It was made to appear that the young lady took her own life."

"You think it was a homicide?"

"There seems to be some indication."

"Really?" I say, glancing at Castellino. "Like what?"

"That's confidential," says Batiste. "I'm sure you understand."

Noble is staring at me like I might have crawled out of a manhole cover.

"What about your investigation?" says Batiste. "What have you uncovered?"

"That's confidential," I say, returning his gaze. "I'm sure you understand."

Batiste gives me a dry smile. "Bear in mind, Mr. Cassel, that we do not have to share any of the details of our case with you. You, on the other hand, have a legal obligation to share anything that might, if withheld, hinder our investigation."

"Understood," I say.

"Good. You don't have any such information, do you?"

I shrug, but get an uncomfortable feeling they've set a trap for me.

"Because if you did," says Batiste, pausing to consult his notes, "it would be best to bring this forward now, when it might do us all some good." He gives me a critical look, as if to convey this is my last chance. I wait, wondering if they know something or if they're just fishing. "Such as, Mr. Cassel, an explanation of why your fingerprints are in Miss Smith's motel room."

I swallow, try not to sweat so hard. "There was probably some of my blood there as well," I say, succeeding reasonably well to keep my voice level. Batiste's eyebrows go up and I hasten to explain. "Several nights ago, I was at the bar in the Gateway, having a few drinks with the firefighters. After I left, I was jumped by several individuals who beat me with what I think was a tire iron. I staggered back to the bar. The waitress, Karalee, took me to her room and bandaged my wounds, stitched the cut above my eye. I'm not surprised my fingerprints are all over the place."

"They certainly were," says Batiste.

"Why would she help you?" says Noble.

"Felt sorry for me, I'd imagine."

"Where were you attacked?"

"In an alley, a block or two from the bar."

"What happened?" says Castellino. I give them the basics — where it happened, about when. Two, maybe three masked attackers. Their generic message: we don't like outsiders makin' trouble. Batiste listens, impassive, taking notes. I don't mention that Kar found me in the alley. I'm not sure how much I can tell them about her without revealing her connection to the squatters and their gardens.

There's a silence after I finish. Batiste chews his lower lip for a moment.

"This attack have anything to do with your getting tossed from the bar?"

They've done their homework. "I have no idea."

"Why'd they toss you out?" says Noble.

"A personal disagreement with the bartender."

"Ah, yes," says Batiste, referring to his notes. "A Mr. Draytor. He claims you were harassing the waitress. Karalee Smith. And now she's dead. An interesting coincidence."

"I had nothing to do with her death," I say, with a twinge of conscience.

A trickle of sweat crawls like a spider down my back.

"Why were you harassing Miss Smith?"

"I wasn't harassing her," I say, my tone becoming alarmingly defensive.

"Mr. Draytor was mistaken?"

"It was a misunderstanding. I was trying to order a drink."

"Really," says Noble. "You were just ordering a drink."

"Yes. Are you accusing me of something?"

Noble gives me a smug look.

"No accusations are being made," says Batiste, calmly, pausing to give me a reassuring glance. They're using standard interrogation protocol — good cop, bad cop. I've been on this see-saw ride before; it never fails to leave me a little disoriented, but that's the idea. "We're just trying to understand how your fingerprints came to be in Miss Smith's motel room."

"Well, now you know. Were there anyone else's prints in her room?"

Batiste doesn't reply. Castellino gives me a bitter smile. I get the impression that whoever else was in Karalee's room cleaned up after themselves — much like the origin at the fire — leaving the police little to go on. There's an ominous silence. Batiste has a calm, curious expression. The others are all frowning slightly. Like the origin, they have little choice but to rely on my version of events and this clearly makes them uncomfortable. I get the feeling they don't believe my story, or suspect there's a lot more to it than I'm letting on. Batiste sits forward, places his elbows on the table, and knits his hands together as though he's preparing to pray — a little ceremony no doubt designed to give weight to what comes next. He fixes me with a baleful glare, one eyebrow jacked up. "Mr. Cassel, we know you're running an unofficial investigation here, and we know that, among other things, you've searched Miss Smith's room. Your fingerprints were found on drawer and cupboard handles. That alone places you in a very precarious situation. I'm not going to go into the many concerns I have regarding the way you operate, but I will tell you that you are way out on a limb. There's no established support network documenting what you're doing, why, or with whom, which leaves you wide open."

Batiste pauses to let this sink in, then leans back and crosses his arms.

"I'm only going to ask this once. What, exactly, is your interest in Karalee Smith?"

I have the distinct impression I'm being offered a limited-time deal. Co-operate now, or face the consequences. I think of Erwin, his threats, and consider telling Batiste and Castellino everything, let them deal with the squatters, but I'm not sure the squatters will deal. I'm also more than a little worried about what they might do if I expose their pot growing operation. There's Telson to worry about, as well as Del and her little girl Melissa. I've got to get them out of harm's way. Until then, I'll tell Batiste and Castellino as much as I can without breaking my deal with the Sasquatch.

"I thought Karalee Smith might know something about the arson."

Batiste frowns. "Why might that be?"

"I thought she might be linked to the squatters."

"Based on what?"

"I saw her in a vehicle that I noticed at the squatters' camp."

"You've talked with these squatters?"

"Yes. Shortly after the burnover on the fire."

"And what did they tell you?" says Batiste.

"Nothing. They refused to talk to me."

"They haven't co-operated with us either," says Noble.

"So you tried to talk to Miss Smith instead?" says Batiste.

"Yes. Without success."

"That's when you decided to search her room?"

I hesitate, knowing I'd be admitting to break and enter. Not that it matters anymore — they've got my prints at the scene. I nod reluctantly and Castellino sits up a little straighter. Noble gives me a thoughtful look. Haines has his bony fingers tented together.

"What did your search reveal?" says Castellino.

"Nothing of substance, unfortunately."

I can feel the frustration around the table. Noble sighs heavily, cranes his neck as he loosens his tie. His forehead glistens with sweat when he turns to look at me. "You still haven't told us why you think there might be a connection between the arson and these squatters."

"Just a hunch," I say. "Based on their proximity."

"You conduct illegal searches on the basis of a hunch?"

There's an awkward silence.

Batiste gives me a patient look. "Let's remain focused on the issue at hand."

"Good idea," I say. "Why do you think Karalee Smith was murdered?"

Noble looks disgusted, as if he can't believe my audacity. Castellino has a wry smile playing at the corners of his mouth. "I think we can share that with Mr. Cassel," he says. "In the spirit of co-operation."

"You can't be serious," says Noble. "He hasn't told us anything —"

Castellino cuts him off. "This is the sheriff's investigation, Mr. Noble, and as such I will determine what information is released, and when. I'm sure Mr. Cassel will treat anything we tell him with the greatest confidentiality," he says, cocking an eyebrow significantly in my direction. "Isn't that right, Mr. Cassel?"

I nod. Noble gives me a poisonous look, stares furiously at the table.

"First things first," says Castellino. "Did Miss Smith strike you as a drinker?"

"Not particularly."

"And you base that on what?"

"On her appearance. On talking with her. She had plans for the future."

"Plans — yes," says Castellino. "You found her correspondence course."

I hesitate again, uncomfortable discussing my search, but nod. If they're planning on charging me, they'll do it anyway. And Castellino seems ready to offer information I can't get anywhere else.

"When you searched her room," he says slowly, "did you find any alcohol bottles?"

"No," I say, a little surprised.

"And you conducted quite a thorough search? You checked her bureau?"

Now I understand why he's willing to deal. They found bottles in Karalee's room and want to establish her character — if she was a closet drinker. On one hand, they're ready to condemn my methods, but on the other, they want to know what I found. It's a thin line, this tacit consent. It makes me wonder just how sure they are this wasn't a suicide.

"If there were bottles in her room," I say. "I would have found them."

Castellino nods, seems satisfied.

"What did the autopsy reveal?" I ask cautiously.

Castellino considers, leaning back, watching me. I try my best to look co-operative and after a moment he nods toward Batiste, tells him to relate the autopsy findings. Batiste rummages in his file, pausing to put on half-glasses — the discriminating scholar. "There were bruises on the right upper arm, and some bruising on the right side of the ribcage." He glances around the table. "This could be the result of blundering into hard objects while in an intoxicated state. Or it could be ligature marks, as a result of restraint."

"What sort of restraint?" I say, thinking about Karalee. She wasn't a big girl.

"Well, they puzzled us at first," says Batiste. "There were also bruises on her lips. Taken together, they seem consistent with someone lying across the victim, pinning her down and holding her right arm as they pushed a bottle into her mouth, forcing her to drink."

"So it looks like one attacker?"

"We're not prepared to speculate on that," says Batiste, glancing at Castellino as if for a cue when to stop. Castellino waves a hand at him, signalling for him to continue. Batiste scans the report, frowning. "No foreign fibres or hair found on the body. Negative for semen. Nothing under the fingernails."

"Isn't that a little strange?"

"Yes." Batiste gives me a knowing look. "Usually, during a struggle, the victim has traces of skin under the fingernails. In this case though, the nails were cut short and recently cleaned."

"Recently? You mean, after the attack?"

"We think it was post-mortem. There were traces of a solvent in the cuticle area."

Someone cleaning up once again. "What was the cause of death?"

"The cause of death is attributed to acute alcohol poisoning."

"What about toxicology?" I say quietly. "Were there pills involved too?"

Batiste lifts a sheet from the pile, examines it carefully. "Yes, there were non-prescription sleeping pills in her system, but not enough to kill her on their own. She had a blood alcohol level of 720 milligrams percent," he says, giving me a meaningful look.

"That's quite high, I take it."

"Very high," he says, glancing again at Castellino. "Which is one of the prime reasons we believe this may have been a homicide. At 250 milligrams percent, most people pass out. Death usually occurs at around 500 milligrams percent. This means it should have been physically impossible for the decedent to have consumed that volume of alcohol on her own."

"Which explains the bruises," I mutter.

"Yes." Batiste sighs wearily. "The evidence thus far suggests Miss Smith, either wittingly or unwittingly, consumed several sleeping pills, after which she was forced to consume a considerable amount of alcohol — the equivalent of about 40 drinks. Her attacker would have had to keep feeding this to her after she passed out, which, if she wasn't a serious drinker, would have occurred fairly quickly."

"What type of pills did she take?" I ask, but Castellino holds up a hand.

"That's more than enough for now, Mr. Cassel. Is there anything else you have to offer?"

"Yes, one more thing. I spoke with her the night before her death."

"When?" Batiste says sharply.

"I talked with her shortly before the start of her shift, in her room. I questioned her once again regarding a possible link to the squatters — if they'd received any threats, if someone wanted to chase them off. She was agitated and appeared nervous."

"Did she tell you anything?" says Noble.

"No, unfortunately she didn't, but we didn't get a chance to complete our conversation. We were interrupted by a phone call. Judging by Karalee's reaction, and by what she said, someone was aware I was in her room, talking to her. After that, I couldn't get through to her."

"Do you know the substance of their conversations?"

"Based on her response, I think she was being threatened."

A heavy silence as the investigators exchange glances, take notes.

Batiste peers at me over his half-glasses. "Do you know the identity of this caller?"

"No. I grabbed the phone, but the caller hung up. Can you trace the call?"

Castellino nods. "We're sure going to try."

"Can you let me know what you find out?"

Castellino smiles. "Thank you for your time, Mr. Cassel. Rest assured, we'll be talking with you again. Until then, consider yourself a resident of Carson Lake. A law-abiding resident. And if you happen to recall anything further, don't hesitate to bring it to our attention."

I nod — they know they have me.

When I return to the Cornbinder, Erwin is gone. It's a relief, until it occurs to me he's probably in town, interviewing Roy the bartender. I'm not particularly fond of Roy, but I'd like to talk with him while he's still in one piece. A few frustrating moments of cruising back alleys before I find the house. It isn't much to look at — an ancient two-storey, stucco faded and stained. Crudely built veranda with a sagging roof. Aluminum foil in the windows. The backyard is a patch of dandelions, going to seed, decorated with an obstacle course of rimless tires and rotting couches. Several inmates lounge outside, also going to seed. I lean out the window.

"Does Roy Draytor live here?"

No reply — doesn't matter where you are, tough guys all lounge the same way, be it Hell's Kitchen or Carson Lake; but on closer inspection, these tough guys have been tenderized. They're a bit flushed, sprawling on the couches as though their insides hurt. Several have fresh scrapes on their faces. I may already be too late. I get out of the Cornbinder.

"Is Roy here?"

A kid of about eighteen with a scraggly goatee blinks at me. "Yeah, he's here."

"Top or bottom?"

The kid points, without looking. I start toward the stairs leading to the second floor.

"You don't want to go up there, man," says a guy with a bad mohawk.

"Why not?"

"There's a fuckin' psycho up there."

"Anybody dead yet?"

He shrugs, which evidently causes some pain, watches suspiciously as I pick my way through the obstacle course. The stairs creak, rotten like everything else around here. Sheets of stained plywood surround a tiny landing. A door hangs open from a peeling frame. I hear scuffling sounds. A whiny, desperate voice, like something you'd hear in a mob movie when the enforcer finally catches the rat.

"Look, man, I told you ..."

A short hall is crowded with empty beer cases. The carpet is multicoloured, from use not design, covered with cigarette burns and spilled food. Another door hangs open. Roy is face down on a messy bed. Erwin has a knee in Roy's back, a hand in his hair. A black revolver is pressed against Roy's temple.

"I'm running out of patience," Erwin snarls at Roy.

The floor creaks. Erwin turns, without releasing Roy, swings the revolver around at me. His lips are pulled back and he has a wild, excited look in his eyes. I raise my arms and freeze, and for a moment we remain like this. Then Erwin presses the muzzle of the revolver into Roy's cheek, continues as if I wasn't there.

"One last time, asshole. What the fuck happened to my sister?"

Roy squirms, breathing heavy. "I don't knowww ..."

"Look, Waldo," I say carefully. "Let's just take a breather here."

Erwin looks at me like I've lost my mind, then down at Roy, who may be suffocating, Erwin has his face pushed so deep into the stained pillows. He slaps the back of Roy's head, then releases him, stepping away from the bed, the revolver held casually against his side. "I'm just asking him a few questions."

"I see that," I say, trying not to stare at the revolver.

"He's not very co-operative," Erwin says, matter-of-fact.

"Maybe it's your technique. Let me try."

Erwin looks disgusted. "Yeah, whatever."

Roy is cowering on the bed, eyes wide. A small circle is temporarily tattooed on his temple, from the muzzle of Erwin's gun. "Look, Roy," I say, as friendly as I can. "I think maybe we got off on the wrong foot. Let's try again."

Roy nods slightly, staring at Erwin, who's flopped onto a crooked recliner, the gun hanging over an armrest. Erwin sneers at him and Roy decides it's better to look at me. I give him a reassuring nod, try to dissipate some of the tension.

"Karalee Smith worked for you, right?"

"Well, sorta," he says, breathless. "I was the shift supervisor."

"Did she drink a lot?"

"What?"

"Did she drink a lot?"

"Karalee? No, man. Little goody two-shoes."

"Did any customers give her a hard time?"

He shrugs. "Not really."

"Think hard, Roy," says Erwin.

Roy's gaze flickers toward Erwin, then back to me. "Guys sometimes paid her a lot of attention, you know, especially when they were drunk. A lot of guys tried to pick her up. I mean — it's a bar, right? Everyone's trying to get lucky. And she was pretty hot."

Erwin growls.

"Sorry." Roy raises a hand defensively toward Erwin. "I didn't mean that."

"You mean she was ugly?" says Erwin.

Roy looks stricken. "No, man —"

"Relax," I tell Roy. "He's just playing with you."

"Fuck you both," says Erwin, toying with the revolver. Spinning the drum. This doesn't help Roy's state of mind. He watches, transfixed. For a moment the smooth, metallic clicking is the only sound. Erwin looks up, realizes no one is talking, points the gun at Roy. "You were saying?"

"No one gave her a hard time that I know of," he says quickly.

"Good," I tell Roy. "Now we're getting somewhere. What about boyfriends?"

Erwin gives me a dark look. Roy shakes his head. "Not that I know of."

"Phone calls?"

"You mean, like — did she make some?"

"No, dipshit," says Erwin. "Did she ever get any? Like, at work?"

Roy thinks about this real hard for a moment, then brightens. "Yeah, there was this one time, she got a call, just after her shift started, and she looked real upset, broke three glasses right away. And she spilled a drink on herself too, a Bloody Mary, had to go change."

"Do you know who called her?" I ask.

"Naw, she never said. Look, man, I told all this crap to the cops."

"We're not the cops," says Erwin. "You should wish we're the cops."

Roy looks at me, then Erwin, then back at me, terrified.

"Roy, that night you had me tossed out —"

Roy winces at the memory, looks like he might cry.

"Do you remember who was in the bar?"

"Lots of people, man."

"Could you be a little more specific?"

"Firefighters, locals — I can't remember all of them."

"It would be good if you could," I say. "We'd appreciate that."

As if on cue, Erwin starts to spin the drum of his revolver again. It's the auditory equivalent of his knuckle-cracking. I decide it would be a good idea to wrap up the interview. "You just give it some thought, Roy. Make up a list. Ask around. Go back to the receipts, for the people that used plastic. We'll be by later to pick it up. Say, tonight, at the bar."

Roy is staring at Erwin, who's giving him an evil grin as he spins the revolver drum.

"Just nod your head," I prompt Roy.

He nods.

"Okay — Waldo, let's hit the road."

For a moment, Erwin remains seated, staring at Roy cowered on his messy bed, and I think I've lost what little control I may have over the situation. Then Erwin stands, snaps his fingers, and points at Roy, grinning. "See you later, Roy."

The backyard couches are empty — no one wants to be a witness. We climb into the Cornbinder, Erwin casually tucking the revolver into his pants, covering the butt of the weapon with his coat. I slam my door, sit gripping the oversized steering wheel for a moment.

"What's the matter?" says Erwin. I'm breathing a little harder than him.

"Nothing," I say tightly.

"Good. Let's get some lunch."

I ease the old wreck into traffic, glancing at Erwin as I shoulder check to change lanes. The rear windows are dirty and I cut off a small car, which swerves, honking. The car roars past, a teenager in the passenger side giving me the finger, and I swear.

"You okay?" says Erwin. "You seem a little tense."

"I'm fine," I say through clenched teeth.

"What'd you tell the cops," he says, wiping his mouth with the back of a sleeve.

"Nothing."

"Don't bullshit me."

There's a lengthy silence as I weave through back alleys. Erwin watches me, quickly losing what little patience he has. "They're treating your sister's death as suspicious."

"Damn right it's suspicious," says Erwin. "What do they know?"

"Not a lot. The autopsy says booze and pills, but it was the booze that killed her."

"She died of alcohol poisoning?" The disbelief in his voice is clear. "Did she drink much?"

Erwin shakes his head. "Just a beer, now and then. Nothing hard."

"Well, she drank a lot that night. You sure she didn't have a boyfriend?"

Erwin gives me a speculative look. "Why?"

"Well, it's hard to imagine a girl who doesn't drink much taking in that much booze on her own. Someone might have gotten her started on the hard stuff, or slipped the pills in to get her defences down. It could be anyone, but it makes more sense if she knew the person."

Erwin gives this some thought. "What kind of pills?"

"Sleeping pills. Non-prescription."

"She didn't use sleeping pills," he says, then falls silent.

"How well did you know your sister?" I say. "Could she have had a friend that knew about your growing and wanted in on the action?"

"Maybe, but I doubt it. What about this call my sister got?"

"The cops are going to check the phone records."

Erwin nods. I'm hoping he doesn't realize I would have had to tell the cops how I knew Karalee received the call. Which would naturally lead them to wonder why I was interested in Karalee.

We're on Main Street, headed out of town. A flock of bored teenagers roost in a patch of shade next to an ice cream stand, slouched and sipping sugar water, waiting for something to happen. They're not the only ones waiting; I'm stalled for clues, unsure what to do next. We pass the last few buildings and Erwin sits up.

"Where are we going?" Erwin's expression is not encouraging and I explain that, although we had a little fun, we're no further ahead. What the hell am I doing, he says, wasting time, driving around town? I have two days left — don't I realize the clock is ticking.

"Oh, I hear it," I tell him. "Every time you open your mouth."

"Fuck you," he says, pointing a stubby finger at me. "You better start thinking."

"Look —" I say, trying to find words to convey the impossibility of solving this puzzle in two more days. "I'm doing my best here, Erwin, but I'm just one guy, out of the loop. There isn't a hell of a lot I can do without access to the official investigation. I don't hear you coming up with any brilliant ideas, either. Give me something I can use, or get off my back."

For a minute, Erwin just stares at me. "Fuck it. Turn around." he says, pulling out his revolver, examining it. "You want access?" says Erwin. "I'll get you access."

I'm worried about what Erwin has in mind. His gun is tucked in his pants again, but he hasn't told me just how he plans to gain access to the official investigation. Subtlety is not his specialty. I have visions of him storming into the ranger station, gun drawn, dragging me along, followed by a nationally televised standoff, before we go out in a blaze of stupidity. I ask once more what his plan might be.

"Just drive," he grumbles.

"Okay." We reach the highway intersection. "Anywhere in particular?"

"You know the place."

I act dumb.

"The cabin by the lake," he says irritably.

"Why there, Erwin? What good will that do?"

Erwin turns in his seat, gives me a look that would make the Terminator proud. I shrug, as if this is no big deal, pop the Cornbinder into first and lurch onto the highway. Erwin is sullen as we drive through town. The teenagers are still at the ice cream stand. Tourists line the boardwalk. Erwin pulls out his revolver, holds it below the window, idly spins the drum.

"Do you have to do that?"

"Yeah," he says. "Helps me relax."

"It's not exactly doing wonders for my concentration."

He spins for another minute before putting it away. We turn off the highway, pass the sawmill. Carson Lake flashes through the trees. "What are you going to do?" I ask Erwin. "Just walk in and demand the cops tell you everything? Wave your gun in their face? That ought to go over well."

Erwin doesn't respond. A moment later he points to a driveway. "Turn in here."

The driveway winds among dense timber. The house isn't clearly visible from the road. It's a nice house, log, two-storey with lots of dormers. There's no one home and I wonder if Erwin knew this, or was just taking a chance. Then I remember that he made his own way back to town earlier today, probably on foot, cutting through the acreages around here. He directs me to park behind the garage, then ushers me out and leads the way through the trees. We cross the road and follow a gully dense with alder and young fir until we're close to the lake. Erwin seems to know this area remarkably well. Suddenly, he stops, holding up his hand. He's watching the cabin at Lakeshore Estates. Four vehicles are parked in front: two sheriff's black-and-whites and two unmarked.

"Now what?" I whisper.

"Shut up," says Erwin. "I'm thinking."

I hope he only wants to get into the building, not actually talk to anyone.

"It's close to supper time. If you have to go in, let's just wait until they leave."

He grunts and we wait. I try to talk Erwin out of this and he pulls out his gun, jams it into my ribs, then puts it away without saying anything. I'm a little worried the investigators will just order in, and Erwin will lose his patience, but they come out, all at once — Castellino, Noble, Aslund, and Batiste — and pile into a minivan. They're barely out the drive when Erwin makes his move, grabbing me by my shirt collar like a truant kid. Hang on, I tell him, as we cross the yard. There might still be people in the cabin.

"We'll find out soon enough," he says.

He drags me to the door facing the lake, hidden from the road. Erwin tries the door. It's locked.

"Too bad," I say, starting to move away.

Erwin grabs my arm, yanks me back. He pulls out his revolver, taps a glass pane with the butt. The pane pops out with a loud tinkle, shatters on the floor inside. Erwin reaches in, opens the door. I hesitate but he prods me inside, where I stand like a thief caught in the act.

"Come on," he hisses. "Get to work."

I look at the door, at the broken pane. What if there's a silent alarm? Erwin still has the revolver in his hand, which he uses to urge me forward, toward the large kitchen table, cluttered with documents. The only way to get out of here quickly is to make it look like I'm doing something, so I lean over the table, scrutinize the paperwork. Now that I'm here anyway, I'm more than a little curious.

There are a lot of files here, in neat piles on the table. All the documents pertain to the arson and the entrapment — Karalee's death is being investigated elsewhere, or the documents have been secured. I glance around, note a small file cabinet in a corner, which I find locked.

"You want me to open that?" says Erwin.

"No — I don't think it'll be necessary."

"Bullshit," he says, and goes to work on the metal cabinet, leaving his fingerprints everywhere — something I'm going to great lengths to avoid. The cabinet yields in about ten seconds. Inside are three slim files, which I open using the tip of a pen. Erwin, impatient, pulls them out, lays them open. The pages are stamped: *Confidential Information Pending Anticipated Litigation; Exempt from Freedom of Information Act*. This must be the good stuff. I use a bulldog clip as tweezers, flipping through carefully. Brashaw's autopsy report is here, indicating he died of asphyxiation due to the searing of his lung membranes — hopefully, it was quick. Negative on drugs or alcohol.

"Now that's brutal," says Erwin, looking at the pictures.

I quickly close the file, move on. Another file contains witness statements from various staff on the fire — far too much information to read now. I consider photocopying the works, but they're stapled and it would take a lot of time. It would also be a little awkward to explain why I have them, if they were ever found. So I set them aside. Erwin stands beside me, shaking his head, holding Brashaw's autopsy report. I snatch it out of his hands and vigorously try to wipe off any prints.

"What'd you do that for?" he says.

"Give the man some rest."

"Touchy, touchy."

"Just give me some space," I snap. "Let me work."

He backs away, stands in front of a map pinned to the wall, pretends he isn't interested. How long have we been here? I notice one of the witness statements is from a member of the volunteer fire department and I take a closer look, curious how they were dispatched. Sometimes the arsonist calls the fire department, so he can watch the show. Or, in this case, the arsonist might not have wanted the fire to go far — it was probably just a warning; if he was interested in the marijuana, he wouldn't have wanted the gardens to burn up. The statement is from Hutton, the VFD Chief who was on the fire. The smoke was reported by a motorist on the highway, which probably means it was called in on a cellphone. The last of the three files contains only pictures — the disturbed origin and Brashaw's removal from the fatality scene. I move to the table, for a quick look at the documents there.

Crunch of gravel under tires.

"Shit," says Erwin, glancing cautiously out a window. "We got company."

It's Compton and another uniform I haven't seen before. The way they exit the vehicle, and the fact that the lights aren't going, indicates there is indeed a silent alarm here. Compton nods to his partner and they vanish from sight, going in opposite directions around the cabin. There's nothing outside but manicured lawn and scattered trees. We're in big trouble.

"No shooting!" I hiss at Erwin, who quickly checks the other windows.

"Shut up and find some place to hide," he snaps at me.

I'm ready to walk out with my hands up, put an end to this ridiculous affair, but Erwin pushes me backwards, into the next room — a bedroom — and shoves me into a closet. The last thing I see before he closes the door is his face, and the muzzle of his gun. Seconds later, I hear boots on the landing, the rattle of a door slapping open, followed by a lot of stomping and a few thuds. There's a single gunshot, then a creak of floorboards, drawing closer. They've shot Erwin and now I have a lot of explaining to do, but when the closet door opens, it's Erwin, sweating and breathing hard.

"Come on!"

When I don't move fast enough, he reaches in, yanks me out by the arm. Dazed, I follow him into the kitchen, where paperwork is scattered like leaves. Compton and company are face down on the floor, not moving. I stop, looking for blood, but Erwin grabs me again and tows me out of the cabin, past the black-and-white and through the trees. We dash across the road, head for the acreage where we left the Cornbinder. Sirens and lights pass, a blur through the trees. We heave ourselves into the panel, wheezing and panting, then creep cautiously onto the road. Soon, we're back on the highway.

"Jesus Christ!" I shout at Erwin, finally able to breathe. "What happened?"

"I had to give them a little tap," he says.

"A tap? Did you kill anyone?"

"Naw, they're just sleeping."

"And the gunshot?"

"Don't worry about it. It was theirs. Just a wild shot."

14

●

WE'RE HEADED NORTH, into town. Parking lots along Main Street are full. Heat shimmers off the pavement, off vehicles and buildings. Girls in shorts saunter along the boardwalk. It'll take me a few minutes to decelerate to the groggy afternoon pace.

"Where are we going?"

Erwin is slumped against the door, catching his breath.

"Anywhere," he says. "Just keep driving."

We pass through town and continue north, past the sewage lagoon and church. Soon, we're in open country. I have no idea where we're going, or what to do next. I'm expecting Erwin to be full of questions, demanding to know what I found at the cabin, but he's strangely quiet. A few miles out of town, I glance over and realize why. He's holding his side. Beneath his hand, a large red stain has soaked through his jacket. He's been shot. How he made it from the cabin to the truck at a dead run, I'll never know. I pull over abruptly, gears grinding, come to a rocking halt on the shoulder of the highway.

"Jesus Christ, Erwin. Why didn't you say something?"

"It's not so bad," he says coarsely.

"Bullshit, you're bleeding like a stuck pig. I'm taking you to the hospital."

He starts to protest but I ignore him — I don't want another death on my hands. It takes a minute to turn the old beater around — trucks swooshing past — then I grip the big steering wheel and floor the old girl, glancing frequently at Erwin. Under the dirt, he looks pale but gives me a weak grin. He's got his revolver pointed at my side.

"I said no hospital."

"Put that thing away."

He cocks the revolver. "No hospital."

"Erwin, listen — you're going to bleed to death. You think Karalee would have wanted that?"

"Fuck you," he says, grimacing. "You pull into Emergency, you'll be the one needing it."

For a moment, I just drive. Maybe he'll pass out before we get there, but he hangs on, stubborn, the revolver resting on his thigh, his other hand pressed against his side. The hospital turnoff comes and goes. Erwin relaxes slightly. Either that, or he's going into shock.

"I'll take you to the motel," I tell him. "See what we can do."

He doesn't argue. The Super 8 looms ahead. As I pull in, I see Telson's rental car, beside which is a van with a big plastic carrot mounted on the roof. I had planned on keeping Del and Erwin apart, for safety and to avoid complicating matters. So much for planning.

Erwin insists on walking on his own. He staggers a little, leans on the door, which is locked. I knock and when the door opens Erwin falls into the room — on top of Telson. They both go down. Del gives a startled little gasp, from where she's standing at the far side of the room. Telson swears, hitting Erwin, thinking he's attacking her. She stops quickly when he doesn't fight back.

"Crap," she says, looking up at me. "He's bleeding. What happened?"

"Long story," I say. "Let's just get him onto the bed."

I pull Erwin off Telson and the three of us heave him onto the bed. Erwin opens his eyes and mumbles something. Telson and Del work off his jacket, unbutton his shirt. As the shirt is peeled back I'm worried what I'll see, but it's not too bad. Most of it's graze, with a shallow entry and exit. A lot of blood, but survivable.

"Jesus," whispers Del. "We should get him to the hospital."

"No —" Erwin opens his eyes, grabs Del's shirt. "No doctor."

He's pale, looks crazed. I'm thinking Del might lose it here, but she regards him calmly.

"You're shot," she says. "Do you want to die?"

"I'm not dying," he mumbles. "I just need a Band-Aid and some whisky."

Del snorts. "Yeah, right."

While he's distracted, I slip the revolver from his waistband, set it in a drawer in the nightstand.

"It's okay," I tell Del, giving her a cautionary glance. "We'll take care of him ourselves."

She pauses, then nods. "Let's get to work, then."

Turns out, Del is pretty handy. She has a kit in her van, from which she takes alcohol, thread, needle, bandages. She cleans the wound, sews it up. Erwin, laying on the bed, looks weak but seems to be coming around, watching Del as she ministers to him. "I'm sorry about your sister," Del says quietly, as she tapes on strips of gauze. "Horrible thing to happen."

Erwin grabs her wrist. "What?"

"Your sister — Karalee. She sounded like a good person."

Erwin stares at her and there's a dangerous silence. I shoot a questioning look at Telson.

"She asked," says Telson. "I couldn't exactly lie."

I'm thinking bullshit — she's lied plenty since I've known her — but keep quiet, giving Telson my best frown; I don't want Del thinking I've been holding out, even if it is for her own safety. Erwin watches this little exchange. He's got Del's wrist in a tight grip, as if this gives him some control over the situation. I feel for him — I'd like a little control myself.

"Her father was killed by the arsonist," Telson says defensively. "She has a right to know."

"Shit," says Erwin, looking at me. "You told her?"

Now it's my turn to get defensive. "She tortured it out of me."

"Torture." Erwin glares at me. "Now there's an idea."

"You're hurting my arm," Del says a little tersely.

Erwin looks at her, releases his grip. "Sorry."

There's a moment of silence as Erwin regards the three of us from where he's sprawled on the bed. He looks disgusted, but he's outnumbered, injured, and doesn't have his gun, which he realizes as he runs his fingers down his side. The bloody fingers hesitate where the gun should have been and he cranes his neck to look at the floor. There's nothing there. He sighs, lays his head back, and stares at the ceiling, his jaw clenched.

"I had to tell her," I say to Erwin. "I needed her help."

"I don't like it," he says. "Wasn't part of the deal. Too many people involved."

"They're fine," I say. "Besides, they don't know everything."

"What exactly don't I know?" says Telson.

I shoot her a look — just back off. She frowns, her jaw set.

"Don't worry," says Del. "No one's judging you. What you're doing is just agriculture."

Erwin pushes himself up on his elbows, glaring at me, a vein bulging in his forehead. I have a sudden urge to be somewhere else. "You told them about the gardens!" he shouts, remarkably vigorous for a downed man. "Are you fucking nuts?"

"It's no big deal. Just relax."

"Relax?" His face is red. "You better pray nothing happens to the rest of those gardens."

Del places a hand on his chest, gently urges him down. Erwin resists, scowling at her. She smiles — a nurse's gentle smile — and he yields, lying back and making anxious, irritated sounds. I'm impressed. If the greenhouse doesn't work out for Del, she can always take up lion taming. Or work on a psych ward. "It's just agriculture," she repeats softly. "Just growing plants. I'm in the same business. Third oldest profession. I've always wondered what it's like growing them, though — the marijuana. I hear they need a lot of moisture."

Del's tone is soothing, almost cooing, and I'm worried this will backfire, but Erwin seems to relax. "Yeah," he says distantly. "They're thirsty little buggers. Like a rich site too ..."

Telson and I watch, amazed, as they talk about fertilizer, transplants, hours of sunlight. Just two horticulturists, discussing their hobby. I crook a finger at Telson, motioning her outside. We walk around back. I sit on a picnic table, scattered with dead pine needles and, for a minute, stare at the trees. Like most men, I handle anger by bottling it up.

"What the hell happened to your buddy Erwin?"

I say nothing, just grind my teeth.

"Come on, Porter — this is serious. What happened?"

"It's always been serious," I snap at her. "Something you seem to have forgotten."

There's a tense silence. "You're angry with me," she says. "Why?"

"Why?" I glance at her, then look away. "Why do you think?"

"You can't be angry about my talking to Del."

"You had no right to tell her anything."

"Really?" Telson walks around the table so I'm looking at her instead of the trees, props one foot on the bench seat. She's wearing steel-toed work boots. "It was her father, for Christ's sakes. Her father. She has a right to know about the fire, and who might have started it."

"Of course she does. She's the reason I'm still here."

Telson throws up her hands. "So, what's the problem?"

"The problem," I say, a little icily so she'll know just how pissed I am, "is that *I'm* the one who should be telling her. It's difficult enough trying to run an investigation without resources. I don't need you complicating things. You told her who Erwin is, and Erwin is supposed to think you don't know what I'm doing. I made a deal with him, in order to get some information. Turns out the information was a little thin, but it's still a deal, my part of which was not to tell anyone for a few days."

"You think I'm complicating things?"

"You broke my deal with Erwin."

"You're the one who came crashing in with a gunshot victim."

"I didn't have much choice. Unlike you. You could have stayed away from Del."

Telson's body language becomes defensive. "Look, she came to me."

"And you told her —"

"Of course I told her," Telson says hotly. "We've both been talking to her about what's been going on. We went to the greenhouse together and talked to her about the gardens. Or don't you remember that I was there? Am I the third point in this triangle?"

"Don't be ridiculous."

"So, now I'm being ridiculous?"

She's angry, but she's also hurt — I can tell by the way her chin dimples a little. It makes me feel cheap. "Look, Christina, the only thing between Del and me is this fire. This tragedy. You know what I thought of, when I was trapped in that little aluminum tent, surrounded by flames? I thought about you. What a fool I am for not being with you more often. I was thrilled when you showed up here, but this isn't the best place for you. Erwin is dangerous. He beats up people, sets booby traps, holds guns to people's heads. And he's on our side. It's the arsonist I'm really worried about. He's still out there and one woman is already dead — maybe because I tried to talk with her. You go advertising who Erwin is and now I have the safety of two women to worry about."

"We're not exactly helpless, Porter."

"This isn't about equality. This is about staying alive."

We glare at each other. I was making progress when I was talking about the fire shelter, but now Telson is angry again. Her independence has been challenged — the ultimate insult. I should have known better than to let her become involved. The day she arrived I should have thanked her for her concern and sent her packing, but I wanted her here for my own selfish reasons.

"So that's it?" says Telson.

"I'm just worried about your safety."

"Well, I'm worried about yours, so we're even."

This isn't a battle I'm going to win, so I retreat and we return to the motel room. Before we go in, I grab Telson from behind, turn her around, and give her a hug. She resists for a few seconds — still angry with me — then yields, forming herself to the contours of my body.

"I'm sorry for yelling at you," I say.

She looks up at me. "I'm sorry you're such a bonehead."

"Now you're just getting mushy."

She gives me a squeeze, which hurts my cracked ribs. I try to make the grimace look like a smile and we go inside. Del is sitting on the bed, talking with Erwin. They both stop when we come in.

"Everything okay?"

"Fine," says Del. "We were just discussing hydroponics."

"I'm sure you were."

"Where's my gun?" says Erwin.

"I don't know. You must have dropped it. I'll keep an eye out."

He doesn't look like he believes me.

"I'm taking him to my place," says Del. "He shouldn't stay here."

I wonder how much Erwin told her. "You sure that's a good idea?"

"Yeah." She nods. "I have some antibiotics. And he wants to see the greenhouse."

I motion her outside for a minute. "I'm not crazy about this," I tell her.

"He's okay," she says, which makes me more worried.

"You don't know him Del, or who might be after him."

"Don't worry." She places a hand on my arm, which I carefully remove. Telson has followed us out and is watching. "He's just a big farm kid," says Del. "An overgrown puppy."

"He's a Rottweiler. You run into trouble, you call the cops."

"I don't think he'll be any trouble. And it's just for a day or two."

"Then send Melissa away with your aunt. Just for a day or two."

Del nods, gives me a reassuring pat on the arm, and returns to the room. Telson stands on the sidewalk, her arms crossed, a worried look on her face. "What happens in a few days?" she says. "After you've kept your part of the deal with Erwin. What then?"

"I don't know," I tell her. "I'm not sure anymore."

I go for a drive, on my own, the old AM radio in the Cornbinder turned up high. Sometimes a man just needs to drive. Clears the mind. Trees and mountains. Small lakes in the valley bottoms. After a half-hour, I pull into a campground, rattle around a loop filled with motorhomes, then head north again on the highway. I'd like to go farther but the gas gauge has stopped working again and my thumps on the dash are ineffectual; I don't have quite the same presence as Erwin. I don't want to be gone too long, either. I'm a little worried about Del, alone with the Rottweiler.

And Telson.

And what might happen when the Sasquatch finds out his son has been shot.

The Cornbinder starts to cough and splutter on the final hill. I pat its dash, whisper encouragement, and we make it back to town, stopping at the first gas station, where I treat the old girl to a quick oil change — you gotta maintain a good working relationship with a vehicle of this vintage. She purrs a little more smoothly as we roll through town. I pass a side road close to the lake, where I see fire engines gleaming in the evening sun, and double back. A sign at the intersection invites me to support my local community and become a volunteer firefighter. The doors on the small station are wide open, men sitting out front, cleaning equipment and stringing hose. I turn in, park by an engine I recognize from the fire.

No one pays much attention to me as I walk up.

"Had a little action?" I say to a young lad tinkering on one of the engines.

He looks down, blinks at me. "Yeah. Trailer fire. Shop went too."

"Anyone know why?"

The kid is about nineteen, tall and lanky, with haystack hair and lots of freckles. "Electrical, I think," he says, then looks thoughtful. "You a reporter?"

"Just visiting. I work fires too."

"Yeah?" he says. "Where you out of?"

"Up north. You mind if I look around?"

He shrugs. "Help yourself."

"Thanks." I pause. "Who does your dispatching?"

"I don't know," he says. "Mostly 911, I think. Ask the chief. He's in the office."

There's a small, shaded porch in front. Music from a local station drifts from an open door. Inside, Hutton is sitting on the corner of a desk, talking to a woman who's peering intently at a computer screen. Hutton, naturally, is wearing his dark sunglasses. He gives me a crooked smile.

"Porter Cassel," he says. "You still here?"

"Yeah, I'm still here."

"You buying a place? Moving in?"

"Maybe," I say. "The country is nice and the people are so friendly."

The woman looks up at me, no doubt catching the sarcastic edge in my voice. There's a casual arrogance about Hutton that rubs me the wrong way. "I was just looking for the chief."

"That's me," says Hutton, giving me another confident grin.

"You're that guy from the fire," says the woman. "The Canadian."

I nod. She's in her forties, sunburned, looks tired.

"I was wondering how you were dispatched to the Holder Canyon fire," I say, looking at them both. The woman probably does administration, might be responsible for dispatch records. She frowns, thinking about this. "I think it was 911," she says. "I could check."

"No need, Connie," says Hutton. "It was direct. Some guy driving past on the highway."

"You sure?" says Connie. "I thought it was 911."

"No." Hutton slides off the corner of the desk. "It was direct."

He wanders into the adjoining room and I follow, believing this to be some sort of cue, but he's just going for coffee. He offers me one, which I decline, then stands by the machine, sipping and looking at me through his dark glasses. "Why are you interested in the dispatch?"

"Just curious. Arsonists sometimes report their own fires, so they can watch the action."

He nods. "I've heard that. I doubt that was the case here, though."

"Really? Why?"

"It was just some guy, driving past and saw the smoke."

"And he knew the number here?"

Hutton shifts on his feet, glances toward the open door leading to the front office, like he's anxious to be somewhere else. "We have signs along the highway," he says. "You've probably seen them."

"Probably," I say, but I don't remember any.

"Are you on the investigation team?"

"Not really," I admit. "I'm just looking around."

"Ah." He sips his coffee, looks amused.

"You said it was reported directly here. Who took the call?"

"I did. I was in, doing some paperwork."

"What did the caller say? Did he leave his name?"

Hutton looks at the floor for a minute, then at me. "I've been through all this with the sheriff and the Forest Service," he says, with exaggerated patience. "But I'll go through it, a third time, just for you. The guy was driving on the highway and saw the smoke, so he called here. From the sound of it, he was on a cellphone. He gave us an approximate location, from the peaks he could see, and said the smoke was coming from somewhere low."

"What colour was the smoke?"

"White."

Which means the fire was just getting started. "What time was the call?"

Hutton smoothes back his already smooth hair. "I'd have to check."

From his tone, I gather he's not particularly eager to rummage through his files.

"Did you ask his name?"

"He didn't say. We're just glad they call."

"Of course. Did he say where he was calling from?"

"On the highway, north of town."

"Could you be a little more specific?"

"What difference does it make?"

"I'm just curious."

"Well, I'm busy. I don't have time for curious."

"Then could I see the dispatch record?"

"Hell no," he says. "We're not a library."

I glance toward the open door, where I'm thinking it would be easier just to ask Connie.

"It was a couple of miles from the Jack Creek Store," he says. "Now you know everything."

He drains the rest of his coffee, tosses the Styrofoam cup into a wastebasket, and walks out of the ready room. I follow past Connie, hard at work, to the front of the building, where Hutton begins to talk with several of his men, his back to me, as if to prove that he's busy. They discuss equipment, the trailer fire they were on, a training course that's coming up. It's becoming a regular staff meeting and I can't help feeling Hutton is doing this to put me off. Then again, they are all volunteer, and waiting to go home. So I hang back, decide to be patient. One of the other men from the Holder fire is in the group, a guy with a brush cut and a face like a ripe pomegranate. He keeps glancing at me. Finally, they run out of things to talk about and the men begin to haul equipment back into the building. Hutton heads for his truck. I head him off before he gets there.

"I was wondering — do you check with the Forest Service before heading to a wildfire?"

Hutton regards me as though I were an unexpected roadblock on the way home from the office.

"No," he says, stepping around me.

"Why wouldn't you do that?"

He ignores me, gets into his truck. I stand by the window.

"What?" he says, rolling down the window.

"Why wouldn't you check with the Forest Service before heading to a bush fire?"

"That's not how it works," he says, his patience clearly at an end. "We get a call, we roll. If someone else is already there, then that's wonderful, but we don't count on it. It's better too many people respond than not enough. Now, if you'll excuse me, I have a life to get back to."

I'm about to thank him for his time, but he backs away and roars off, leaving me in a cloud of dust. Fire engines start to move, returning to their stalls. Someone tells me to move my truck. I start up the Cornbinder, head back to the motel. Halfway there, I remember Roy and his list, pull into the parking lot of the Paradise Gateway Motel. I've been here so many times, it's starting to feel like home. Roy is less thrilled than Hutton to see me.

"Where's the gorilla?" he says, from behind the safety of the bar.

"Back in the zoo, for now. You have that list?"

"Yeah." He reaches under the bar. The list is on a napkin. It's not a large napkin and there's plenty of space left.

"Is this all you have?"

"Hey, man — it's a bar. People come and go."

"There were about a hundred people here that night. You have eleven names."

"That's all I could remember."

"I doubt it."

Roy looks insulted. "I did my best."

There are a lot of things I could say to that, but there isn't much use. I take the napkin, head back to the Super 8. Telson is there, reading a book. Erwin and Del are gone. There's a plastic garbage bag by the door. Telson snaps her book shut.

"About time," she says. "Where'd you drive? California?"

"It crossed my mind. What's in the bag?"

"Bloody bed sheets," she says, giving me a sweet smile. "The usual gangster laundry."

"Wonderful. What are we going to do with them?"

"What do you think?" she says. "Oh, I forgot — you're a man. We're going to wash them."

"I love it when you get domestic."

"Don't get used to it. I'm not that kind of girl."

We take her car, forage for a laundromat. Bored housewives give us strange looks as we stuff bloody sheets into an industrial-sized machine, but no one asks questions. Telson borrows some bleach, turns the machine onto the heaviest setting. Then we go for supper at Pop's Family Restaurant. The food comes quickly and the burgers are good — high-quality cholesterol delivery systems. Telson must be famished because she eats most of her burger before asking the question I know must be killing her.

"Now will you tell me how your buddy Erwin got shot?"

I chew my burger, ponder the wisdom of answering.

"Come on, Porter. You can't still be angry."

"He was cleaning his gun."

Telson watches me, trying to decide if I'm teasing her or really won't answer. When I continue to eat instead of saying anything more, she lets out a heavy sigh, shakes her head. "I thought we settled this," she says. "I thought we were working together."

"We are. But you don't need to know everything."

I've insulted her journalistic instincts. "It's all or nothing, Porter."

"What if it's illegal? Forces you to withhold evidence? Aiding and abetting?"

She laughs. "Give me a break. Our relationship is based on aiding and abetting. I didn't turn away from you when the cops were after you. I aided and abetted. I withheld evidence. Christ — I nearly got killed helping you out."

"I know," I say quietly. Telson stares at me, realizing she just made my point.

She leans forward, gives me her best serious look. "Treat me like a grown-up."

It's not a request — it's an ultimatum. I sense I've pushed this as far as I can, so I take a deep breath, wait until the waitress is out of earshot, and tell her the whole, bungled story of the break-in at the cabin. When I'm done, she leans back, thinking. "Are the two cops okay?"

"I think so. I haven't heard anything on the news."

"You want me to look into it?"

"Yes — if you can without raising suspicion."

"I can do that," she says, giving me an encouraging smile. I have to admit, it's a weight off my shoulders, knowing I don't have to fight with her over this anymore. Not tonight anyway. On the way to the laundromat, she asks the inevitable question.

"Did you find anything at the cabin?"

"Not much. The fire was reported by a passing motorist, but that's about it."

"And the Smith death?"

"Nothing. They must be running that somewhere else."

"Seems like a lot of risk for no payback," she says.

I nod, thinking she's pretty much summed up my entire trip to Carson Lake. I consider telling her about my visit to the volunteer fire station, but there's really nothing to mention. We arrive to find our bed sheets have completed their cycle, and we go back to the motel to mess them up again.

The next morning after breakfast we head out for a little road trip in the Cornbinder. Telson would prefer to take her car, but then she would miss out on a truly unique travel experience. The sides of the panel shake as I gear up. Everything begins to rattle.

Fortunately, we're not going far — just north to the Jack Creek Store. Hutton didn't specify in which direction the man who reported the fire was travelling, so I keep glancing to the side, try to pick out the fire. It's not easy — trees crowd both sides of the road most of the way, and the smoke is long gone. Finally, I find a spot where the road rises over the lake and the black scar of the fire is visible, on the lower slope of the mountain. I pull over, take a good look.

"Where exactly are we going?" says Telson.

"Right here, I think."

"Lovely. Why?"

"This may be where the guy who reported the fire first saw it. Do you have your cellphone?"

Telson does. I ask her to check for coverage. There isn't any.

"He could have called from anywhere," she says.

True, and a column of smoke would be visible from several locations. We drive to the Jack Creek Store, losing and picking up cell coverage intermittently. When we have coverage, it isn't for long — not long enough for much of a conversation. Which could be why the caller didn't bother to leave his name. Or the call was made from farther down the road.

I didn't notice any signs with the phone number of the volunteer fire department, just a generic Forest Service placard sternly reminding me to make sure my fire is out. But I might have missed it — the sign would likely be close to town and facing traffic travelling in the opposite direction. Regardless of whether or not there was a sign, the caller could have been local and knew the phone number to the fire station. Either way, I'm in no position to trace the call, which leaves me nowhere. We drive a few miles north of the store, make sure all the ground has been covered.

"Why is this important?" asks Telson.

"I'm not sure it is."

She props a boot on the dash. "Oh well, lovely day for a drive."

I agree. The sky is blue and cloudless, the trees vivid, the motor-homes white and sparkling as they blow past, rattling our windows. We keep checking — and losing — cell coverage. I try to imagine what the smoke would have looked like from this narrow, winding road, hemmed in with tall ponderosa. A puff here or there above the treetops. At first anyway — after it really started to cook you could probably see it from Missoula. But none of this means anything and, once again, we're at a dead end. I complain about this to Telson, who nods, doesn't seem concerned this morning. I think she's just waiting to step out of the Cornbinder again, return to good old terra firma. Nearly back in town, her cellphone rings. No problem with coverage here.

"It's for you," she says, raising an eyebrow as she hands me the phone.

It's Del, and she's a little upset. A group of strange, hairy cavemen appeared at the greenhouse and claimed Erwin, taking him away. He needs more rest. He needs the antibiotics they forgot to take. From her description, it has to be the Sasquatch and his clan. Did they say anything? No, she says — not really. Except they want to see me, right away. I'll know where to go.

I thank her, tell her not to worry. She tells me to stop by for the antibiotics.

"What did she say?" asks Telson, taking back her phone.

"Erwin went home."

"That's it?"

"She just wanted to let me know."

"I see," says Telson. "Sounds like crucial information."

"Don't start."

She's quiet for a moment. I'm not taking her with me to the squatters.

"I need you to do something," I tell her, handing her Roy's napkin. She takes it without saying anything. "Those are some of the people who were at the bar the night I was jumped, which I think happened because I tried to talk to Karalee Smith. Unfortunately, the list isn't very comprehensive. I'd like you to track down the people on the list, see how many more names you can add."

"Okay. What are you going to do?"

"See what I can find out about cellphone records."

It's not exactly the truth, but Telson doesn't question it. I drop her at the motel, then head to the greenhouse, where Del gives me the medicine for Erwin. I inquire how her night passed and she rolls her eyes, tells me Erwin was no trouble. He's a nice guy, really. She must be using a different yardstick; one with flowers on it. Maybe she's just attracted to misfits. I take the vial of antibiotics, head north to the Blood Creek Road, then up the winding trail to the fire. Base camp is quiet now. The rain a few days ago did most of the work and the fire is in babysitting mode. I drive past, take the time to heave open the squatters' heavy gate. There's no one in sight when I park at the edge of the old wellsite, but Erwin's truck is there so I get out, wander past the wellhead, which is oozing natural gas vapours. A trailer door slaps open. The Sasquatch stares at me.

"Come in," he says gruffly.

I hesitate, wondering what it is he plans to do that can't be done out here. He stands in the open trailer door, waiting. I trudge across the clearing, past the car riddled with bullet holes. The Sasquatch steps back and I heave myself into the trailer. Erwin is seated at a small, flip-down table, the sleeves on his hairy arms rolled back, idly shuffling a deck of cards. He glances at me, goes back to shuffling. He looks pale, but better than last night. The Sasquatch motions me to take a seat. I decide to stand, as close to the door as possible.

"The boy here tells me you got him shot," says the Sasquatch.

I look at Erwin. That's one version of the events I hadn't considered. "Not exactly."

Erwin glances at me, then back at his cards. One eyebrow twitches. He's more scared of his old man than he is of me, which is probably why he twisted this around. Given the stakes, it's not something I'm willing to let him get away with. "Erwin got shot," I say, looking the Sasquatch in the eye, "because of his own stupid idea. I tried to talk him out of it, but he wouldn't listen."

The Sasquatch looks at Erwin. "That right, boy?"

Erwin looks at his father, but can't hold his gaze. There's an ominous silence. I glance around the trailer. I was expecting a slum, but it's pretty tidy in here. The counters are clean and there's a picture of a younger Karalee beside a jar filled with wildflowers. There's also an old scanner and shortwave radio, turned way down. "We went together," Erwin says finally.

"These cops he knocked," says the Sasquatch, nodding toward his prodigy. "Are they okay?"

"You mean — are they going to live?"

The Sasquatch catches the sarcasm in my voice and his expression darkens. I make a mental note — no more sarcasm. "What've you heard about them?" he says.

"Nothing. But I haven't seen them around town, either."

The Sasquatch swears, points a thick, dirty finger at Erwin. "How many times do I have to tell you not to mess with the cops, boy? You hurt them, they take it personal. Every cop in the state gets excited. Last thing we need is more attention."

Erwin shrugs, looks uncomfortable.

"Kids," says the Sasquatch, shaking his head.

I nod in commiseration, edging toward the door.

"He's been talking to the cops," says Erwin. "That's why they came."

The Sasquatch turns on me, his eyes narrowed. "That right?"

"The cops came here?" I ask innocently.

"Damn right they came," growls the Sasquatch.

"What did they want?"

"What do you think? They asked about Karalee."

"I told you they would make the connection —"

"Take a seat," says the Sasquatch, grabbing me above the shoulder with a grip that causes a flash of pain. Shoving me toward the table.

I stumble, manage a half-decent landing on a chair. Fight or flight time — but the Sasquatch is right in front of me, and Erwin is already half standing. So I do neither, which is the classic cause of stress. I ease back onto the chair and, after a moment, Erwin sits down. The Sasquatch remains standing, his bowling pin forearms crossed over his chest.

"What'd you tell the cops?" he demands, scowling down at me.

"Nothing," I say. "Nothing important, anyway."

"Then why were they here?"

"I'm not sure. Maybe they developed a lead on their own."

Erwin sniffs at this — obviously relieved to see the Sasquatch's anger directed elsewhere. The Sasquatch considers me for a moment, stroking his beard thoughtfully. "Why would they come here, if you haven't told them anything?"

"Why wouldn't they?"

Both men looked puzzled.

"You're close to the fire, you're squatting illegally, and you're unco-operative."

"It's public land," says the Sasquatch. "No one can tell us we can't be here."

"See what I mean?"

I get a double-barrelled frown and remind myself again to avoid sarcasm. "Given recent events, you're conspicuous. You don't think the cops have been a little curious about why you're here, other than the free gas? They're going to have questions. Eventually, they'll figure it out, just like I did."

"And just how did you figure it out?" says the Sasquatch. "Karalee tell you?"

"No — Karalee was good at keeping secrets. Too good. I followed Erwin to the feed store, figured there was a reason you needed that much fertilizer. Then I searched the bush around your camp until I found the trail to the burn. It wasn't that hard."

The Sasquatch glares at Erwin, who glares at me.

"If he knows where the trail is —"

The Sasquatch nods, gives me a critical look. I get a bad feeling.

"I haven't told anyone about the gardens," I say, standing.

"And you're not gonna," he says, reaching into a back pocket and pulling something out. It's a picture — a Polaroid, curved and crimped. A Polaroid of Telson, taken in front of the Super 8. They caught her in mid-stride, walking to her car, and it's blurry, like a bad snap taken by the paparazzi.

He holds up the photo, so I get a real good look. "You make sure you don't let anything slip."

I meet his eye. There's murder there. "Anything else?"

The Sasquatch shakes his head and I back toward the door, feeling for the handle.

"Get out of here," says Erwin, waving me off. "Find my sister's killer. Do your job."

I hurry across the wellsite. In the Cornbinder, I stare at the cluster of old trailers, at the wellhead covered with parasitic hoses, the car riddled with bullet holes, and shake my head. Somehow, I have to get Telson the hell away from here. I turn the Cornbinder around, drive like a madman down the rough trail, jolting from rut to rut. On the Blood Creek Road, I remember the vial of antibiotics in my pocket, decide against returning. My concern for Erwin's well-being is at an all-time low.

I haven't calmed down much when I reach town and pull into the Super 8. I'm determined to make Telson listen to reason, talk her into leaving. Her car is gone, the motel room empty. I pace for a minute, manic with worry, then sit on the edge of the bed. She's in town some-where, running down that list I gave her, and it occurs to me she'll never leave on her own.

On impulse, I pull open the drawer in the nightstand. Other than a dusty bible, it's empty. Erwin's gun is gone — I should have tossed it into the lake. Not that it would make much difference; the Erwins of this world have an inexhaustible supply of guns. Which only fuels my resolve to get Telson the hell away from Carson Lake. I have a sudden idea, but it's not one I particularly care for. I lock the motel room, drive around town in the Cornbinder, mulling over the possibilities.

I pass Carson Lake Sporting Goods and it occurs to me again that whoever was leaning on the squatters somehow had to find out they were growing marijuana. They could be former associates of the squatters, or they could be local. If they are local, they probably stumbled across a garden or two and made the same connections I did. Considering the reputation of the canyon, I doubt there were many hikers or recreationists thrashing through the heavy understory, but a hunter is a definite possibility — they're always looking for that pristine area. That secret fishing hole or bluff. I make a U-turn in the parking lot of the Chicken Coop Casino and Lounge, head back to the sports store.

The store is in a new log building, stained dark brown. In the window, empty jackets and hunting pants are propped on wires, posed like ghosts gone fishing, holding rods and catching plastic fish. The clerk gives me an idle nod when I amble in. I'm the only customer and spend a few minutes perusing the inventory, which consists of fishing tackle, life jackets and game calls. They must still be in startup mode; shelves are made of unfinished plywood and sections of sub-floor are visible. After a few minutes the clerk sets aside his elk-hunting magazine to ask if I need help.

"Just browsing," I tell him.

He looks disappointed. I wait until he's turning away, then cast my lure.

"Beautiful area you got here," I say. "What's the hunting like?"

He circles back, takes another look. "Do you hunt?"

I jiggle the line. "You bet. Elk, cougar, bear. It walks, I kill it."

The clerk smiles, sensing a potential sale. He's a young guy, curly hair, lots of freckles.

"We got good moose and deer hunting here. Some of the best in the state."

"What about bear? I'd love to plug a big black around here."

"Oh, yeah — we got bear," he says. He's wearing a checkered plaid shirt and has his ball cap on backwards: the uniform of the young outdoorsman. "Had a record come out of here a couple of years ago. Can't remember the exact size, but it was a real monster."

"I'd like to do a company hunting trip. You have anyone around here that guides?"

"There's a few guys," he says. "I do a little myself, off the books."

"That area northwest of town looks interesting. Where they had that fire."

The clerk frowns a little. "Not many guys go out there."

"Perfect. Just what I'm looking for."

"There's better places," he says.

"I'm sure there is," I say, putting on my pushy, executive attitude. "I've flown over a lot of this area though, hired a chopper out of Missoula, and that mountain caught my eye. I know there's gotta be some good hunting in those draws and canyons. Especially that one that got burned. Give it a year or two and it'll be chock full of animals, moving in for the shoots that'll be coming up."

"Yeah." The clerk doesn't sound convinced. "I guess so."

"You know anyone that specializes in that area?"

My best cast, but he's circling, wary. I'll have to sweeten the deal. "Now, I understand your hesitation," I say, clapping a friendly hand on his back. "You're thinking you'd like to get my business yourself — and there's no harm in that, son -- but you don't know the area as well as you'd like. I'll tell you what. If I decide to take a group out there, I'll pay you a finder's fee to show you I appreciate you pointing me in the right direction. Off the books, of course. How does, say, five hundred bucks sound?"

Judging by the look on the clerk's face, it sounds just fine.

"Okay, you got yourself a deal Mr. —"

"Sneed," I say, shaking his hand. "Gilbert Sneed."

"Well, Mr. Sneed, there's only two guys I know of that've hunted that area."

The clerk is smiling, relaxed now. I reel him in without a fight. He jots down two names on a piece of paper. I give him a fictitious address and phone number on another piece of paper, which he carefully folds and slips into the pocket of his plaid shirt. Behind us, the door jingles. "Or you could hire Bob Capsan," says the clerk, as a man wanders past. "He's a big-time hunter."

I turn to see Capsan, the real estate agent, frowning at me.

"You name it," says the clerk, "he's shot it. Rhino. Cape buffalo. Polar bear."

"What are you still doing here?" says Capsan.

The clerk's smile falters. "You two know each other?"

"We haven't been formally introduced," Capsan says dryly. He's sweating, looks grumpy.

"This is Mr. Sneed," says the clerk. "He's looking for a hunting guide."

"I'll get back to you," I tell the clerk, and head for the door. I'm expecting Capsan to follow, to chew me out for searching his car, but make it outside and into the Cornbinder unmolested. On the street, I breathe a sigh of relief, drive a few blocks before pulling out the scrap of paper the clerk gave me. One of the names I don't recognize. The other is the chief of the Carson Lake Volunteer Fire Department.

I park behind a strip mall a few blocks from the fire station, walk back alleys between rows of trailers, cut across small treed spaces. The parking lot of the fire station is empty. I approach from behind, just to be cautious, peer in the side windows. Too much glare to see anything. I try the front door — locked, as I suspected. I knock anyway, just in case, get no answer. I'll have to go in the hard way but there's too much exposure in front; I'll try the back.

There's a single red metal door at the rear of the building. Heat ripples off corrugated siding. Grasshoppers whine and complain. It's so hot, I can hear pinecones popping. I hesitate, look around. Nothing behind me but trees and, much farther back, another industrial building. I slip on leather work gloves, take out my pocketknife. I'm no expert, but the door yields easily — no one expects a break-in at a fire station. It takes a moment before I see much of anything. Long blocky shapes emerge; I'm in the garage.

I pass through a small locker room into the ready room, where it's much brighter, moving straight into the front office where the records are kept. The computer, which I'm hoping will have everything I'm looking for, is password protected and I'm no hacker. I start looking for a hard copy of the dispatch record. It's a bit of a long shot, but I can't help wondering why the chief received the call, why he was so reluctant to share information, and why he was the one who went to the fire. It seems odd, on a fire in the bush, that he didn't contact the Forest Service before responding, or didn't scan the Forest Service frequency on the trip out.

There's a two-way radio in here, volume turned low. The dispatch log is on a clipboard, in a drawer below the radio. I flip back a few pages, find an entry signed by Hutton. The notes are brief but concise: public call, bush fire, Blood Creek. Time of call: 1137. There's no phone number or name of caller. I try to remember when I was dispatched to the fire but can't recall the exact time. It would have been about a half-hour earlier, judging by the time Hutton and his men arrived. Once again, none of this really means anything. I rummage in a file drawer, looking for anything on how they're supposed to respond to calls; fire organizations are inevitably heavy on operating procedure. I find their bylaws and standard operating guidelines, do a quick skim. It seems all dispatch communication should be routed through 911. This means Hutton should have called 911 before departing. A quick check in the radio log confirms he did. There's a very small section on wildland fires. Dress in appropriate wildland gear — and monitor the red channel on the radio for traffic from either the US Forest Service or DNRC.

If they were following procedure, they should have known the Forest Service was already at the Holder fire. Perhaps there's another procedure requiring them to show up to any fire within a certain radius of town. I look, but find nothing documenting this, switch to the personnel files, flip through. They each have a picture, and list the member's address, phone number, and place of work. I photocopy the files of the members who were at the fire. I'm putting the files back when I hear gravel crunching outside, and I duck away from the window. A sheriff's suburban does a slow U-turn in the parking lot. I break into a prickly sweat, my heart thumping. Fortunately, the vehicle is just patrolling and completes its circuit. I wait until it turns onto the road, then switch off the photocopier and head for the back door. In the garage I pause and, on impulse, climb into one of the trucks that was at the fire, check in the glove compartment, behind the seat. Fusees — the thirty-minute variety. A box of reflective hazard triangles. Under the seat is dust and grime. My hand brushes something, dangling from the seat springs — cobwebs or a filament of cloth. It's probably nothing, but I forage for a flashlight, take a look.

Hanging from where it's caught in the seat springs is a scrap of pink flagging.

15

I PULL OUT the flagging. It takes a little work because it's jammed in tight, caught in the coil of a spring like someone shoved a tangle of the stuff under the seat in a hurry, then yanked it out. The strip I finally manage to extricate is about three inches long and stretched out of shape, but it's plastic flagging, and it's pink. I'd like to search the lockers and storeroom to see if they stock pink flagging, but don't want to take that much time. I shove the ribbon into my pocket and slip out of the fire station. At the strip mall I find a pay phone, place a quick call to Del's Greenhouse. A man answers, his voice vaguely familiar. I ask for Del. The voice tells me she's not available.

"Do you know where she is?"

"At home," says the voice. "But she's not working."

"Who is this?"

"Lyle Harnack. Who is this?"

I hang up.

I'm not sure why, but it bothers me that Harnack is there. Maybe it's the proprietary air he has when he talks about Del. Maybe it's just that he complicates things. Either way, I need to see her, so I drive the Cornbinder to its ancestral home. Business is light — a minivan load of old ladies are the only customers, admiring the flowers. I find Harnack behind the counter at the main building.

"Lyle — where's Del?"

"At the house," he says mildly. "You want me to call her?"

"No thanks. I think I can find the way."

He nods, smiling a good-natured, farm-boy sort of smile. He's like a kid with a new box of Legos. I exit through the back of the greenhouse, crossing the yard, and ring the buzzer on the trailer. After a moment, Del comes to the door. She's wearing baggy shorts and a ratty old T-shirt. No bra. She looks tired, and a little distracted.

"Come in," she says.

She offers me coffee, which I decline — it's just too hot. Her kitchen table is scattered with papers, pencils, a calculator — looks like she's doing her taxes. "Cash flow," she says. "The bank wants an update. You'd think they'd give a person a little slack, after what happened."

"Maybe for a price," I say. "So, Erwin really wasn't any trouble?"

"No." She pours herself a glass of iced tea from a pitcher. "We had a good talk."

"Really?" I can't imagine Erwin talking much. "What did you talk about?"

"Just things. He's an interesting guy. You give him the antibiotics?"

"Sure," I say with a twinge of conscience. A very small twinge.

"Good." She drains the glass in one swallow. "He needs to get better."

There's a pause. Del leans against the counter, holding the empty glass in her hand. The last thing I want to talk about is what a great guy Erwin is. I dig the scrap of pink flagging from my pocket, drop it on the counter beside her. She looks at it. "What's that?"

"Pink flagging. The same type I used to mark the origin of the fire."

She frowns, then her eyes widen. "The same flagging?"

"I think so."

"Where did you get it?"

"From under the seat of a fire engine."

She thinks about this for a minute, toying with the glass. "A Forest Service engine?"

When I tell her no, she looks relieved, then puzzled.

"I paid a little visit to the Carson Lake Volunteer Fire Department."

"You found the ribbon in a VFD truck?"

I nod. Her green eyes narrow.

"They disturbed the origin," she says.

"Maybe. Maybe it's just coincidence."

"Maybe not," she says, frowning in a horrified sort of way.

"Let's not jump to conclusions here, Del. There are several possibilities —"

"Who was at the fire?" she says sharply. "Which volunteer members?"

Her jaw is set and she has an intent, possessed look in her eye I find a little disquieting. It occurs to me that it might not be a good idea to give her names until I have something more to go on. She's angry enough, she might confront these people. If they're innocent, it would be more than a little embarrassing. If they're involved, it would put them on their guard. "The only thing we really know is there was some pink ribbon under the seat of an engine. Anyone who was at the fire could have put it there. The arsonist could have been watching, waiting for just this sort of opportunity. It could be a deliberate attempt at misdirection."

"Maybe. Did you find all your ribbon?

"Just this scrap."

"So someone took out the rest."

"Apparently."

"Wouldn't the VFD people have mentioned finding the ribbon?"

"Someone else could have cleaned out the truck. Someone who wasn't at the fire, who didn't understand the significance of the pink ribbon. To them, it would just have been trash."

Del nods reluctantly. "Are you taking this to the cops?"

"Not yet. We don't know if it's the same ribbon."

"What are you going to do?"

"Try to find out who put the ribbon in the truck."

She rubs her forehead, frowning like she has a migraine, then looks at me with the sudden expression of someone who just remembered something important. "You've got to talk to Lyle," she says. "I'll call him over." Before I can say anything, she's on the phone, calling the green-house.

"What's Lyle doing here?" I ask, after she hangs up.

"He knows something," she says briskly. "He has some information."

"That why he's at the front counter?"

"No. He just wants to help. He used to do it all the time."

"Before you two broke up?"

"Before we got together," she says.

"You think it's wise, having him around?"

Del gives me an impatient look. "He just wants to help, and God knows I could use it. With Gertie and Melissa gone, it's just me and the two summer students." She must be able to read my expression. "Don't worry Porter. I can handle Lyle Harnack. You're sounding like my mother."

I'm about to say something more when the door opens. Lyle comes in.

"Hey guys, what's up?"

Del smiles at him. "Tell Porter what you saw at the fire."

Lyle gives me an earnest look. "I was walking along the dozerline when I saw someone where I think the origin was. One guy, all alone. So I hollered to him, thinking it was you. But he didn't answer, just sort of looked back at me and hurried away."

"Do you know who it was?"

Harnack shakes his head.

"Why didn't you mention this before, Lyle?"

He glances at Del, who gives him an encouraging nod. "It didn't occur to me until later that this was the origin area, because there was no ribbon. But when I started to think about how that guy just rushed off, it seemed a little strange. Anyway, I thought you should know, so I came here to tell Del because I knew she would tell you." Harnack looks self-conscious. "Turns out, she needed a little help, so I stuck around."

"And he's a godsend," says Del. Harnack beams. I'd picked him as the manipulator, but now I wonder who's being taken advantage of.

"Did you see him taking down any ribbon?"

Harnack shakes his head.

"Did you see where he went?"

"Just into the burn."

"Into the burn? Didn't that strike you as a little odd?"

Harnack looks uncomfortable. Firefighters avoid the interior of a burn because there's no danger of spread from within — unless there's a snag blowing sparks, a fire spreads from its perimeter. "I thought it might be you," he says again. "Doing your investigation."

"Fair enough." I give him a little slack. "Was there anything distinctive about the guy?"

"Like what?" says Harnack, scratching his head.

"What was he wearing? What did he have strapped around his waist? Did he look like one of the guys on your crew? Or could he have been a smokejumper? Or maybe someone else?"

Harnack gives this some thought, his young brow furrowed.

"Think hard," says Del. "This is important."

"He was dressed like everyone else," says Lyle.

"Was he wearing green pants?"

Harnack thinks some more, then looks troubled. "I'm not sure."

I look at both Del and Harnack. The only people at the fire not wearing green pants would have been smokejumpers. They wear jump suits, with big bulges in the legs. The difference in appearance is fairly distinct. Either Harnack is lying, just for an excuse to talk to Del, or he didn't get a good look at the guy — which is likely if he was on the far side of the creek. Neither scenario is very helpful.

"Did it look like a jumper, Lyle?"

"It could have been," he says, trying to help. But I need more than good intentions — the jumpers were the only ones I didn't check for ribbon. They're not local and I can't think of a reason they might want to tamper with the origin.

"I could do some checking," says Lyle. "Dig up some information on the jumpers."

"I'm not sure that would help."

"It couldn't hurt though, could it?" says Del.

I could get whatever information is available on the jumpers just as easily from Grey, but by the way Del is looking at Harnack, I can see she wants to throw him a bone. Which is fine by me, as long as Harnack stays out of my way. In fact, it's probably worth it for that reason alone. "Okay, Lyle," I say, trying to make this sound like another crucial assignment, "I think that would be a good idea. Get a list of their names. See what you can dig up about where they've worked so far this season. But be discrete. Don't tell anyone why you're doing this. Whatever you do, don't talk to the jumpers directly."

"I can do that," he says, watching Del. The phone rings. It's one of the summer students. The old ladies are waiting to pay for their flowers and they need someone to open the till. Harnack affects the air of a gracious but unappreciated mâitre d', tells us that duty calls, he'll see us later. I wait until he's gone before laughing.

"Where did you find that guy?"

Del looks wistful. "If only they could all be that naive."

My photocopies from the fire station identify Henry Dancey and Doug Bradley as the two firefighters who were with Hutton at the canyon. Dancey was at the station when I talked to Hutton, so I decide to start with Bradley. He's the youngest and, I'm hoping, the easiest to talk to. The personnel file lists him as working at the sawmill, but when I pull over and use the pay phone at the Filling Station, a polite receptionist tells me Bradley isn't working today. So I drive to his house, a small cedar-sided bungalow set amid the pines. There's a swing set in the yard, plastic toys scattered across the lawn. His wife answers the door in sweat pants and a loose T-shirt.

"Is Doug home?"

"He's in the garage," she says, brushing dark hair out of her face. "Hiding from the kids."

I thank her, walk around back, picking my way through a minefield of toys. Bradley is in a small garage, the door open. He's crouched next to a dirt bike, up on a stand. Most of the engine is in pieces on a cluttered workbench. Bradley looks at me, his ball cap backwards, a thoughtful frown on his face.

"Taking apart, or putting together?" I ask.

"Putting together," he says. "I think."

I introduce myself. "Porter Cassel."

"I know," he says, standing up. "From the fire."

There's a conspicuous pause. He doesn't offer to shake my hand, but then again his hands are covered to the elbow with grease and dirt. He's wearing jeans, equally soiled, and an old AC/DC T-shirt. He looks very relaxed. Either he doesn't think I'm a threat, or he doesn't know anything.

"You want a beer?" he says.

"No thanks, I better not."

He opens an old fridge next to the workbench. "You sure?"

"Maybe a quick one." A small sacrifice, in the line of duty.

He hands me a can and we crack our beers, sip for a minute staring at the disembowelled motorcycle. I get the impression Bradley would be happy to stand around drinking beer with me all afternoon, no questions asked. An endearing quality, but after a few minutes I bring up the ugly topic of work. "I'm assisting the Forest Service investigators, looking into the arson," I tell him, stretching the truth just a bit. "I wanted to talk to you about the fire."

"Okay." He shrugs. "What do you want to know?"

"How were you guys dispatched?"

"Air raid siren. That sucker goes off, you just about jump out of your skin."

"That's how you were dispatched on this fire?"

"Yeah. I was downtown, just coming out of the hardware store."

"And you went straight to the station?"

"Sure." He sips his beer, gazes outside.

"Does everyone normally head straight to the station?"

Bradley sniffs, carefully rubs his nose with a clean spot on his forearm. "Normally, we call on the radio first. We all got radios in our trucks, so we can call the fire hall, see how many guys are needed. That way, if they don't need you, you don't waste your time. We got a lot of members."

"Do you get a lot of calls?"

"Tons," he says, nodding. "But not everyone goes out each time."

"And you were called for this fire?"

"Naw," he says. "I was just close. Sometimes, we sort it out at the station."

"How many guys usually roll on a call?"

Bradley shrugs. "Depends on what sort of fire it is."

"What about a wildfire? Like the one at the canyon."

"Half a dozen, maybe."

"But there were only three on this fire," I say. "You and two other guys."

"That's all that showed up," says Bradley.

"Is that usual?"

"Sometimes. It's volunteer, and everyone's busy."

"So they couldn't get any more guys?"

"I don't think they needed more. They said they just needed two."

"Who said that?"

"The Chief — he was there. And Henry."

"But you went anyway."

"Sure." Bradley squats beside his bike. "I was ready."

There's a lull in conversation. Bradley spins the back tire of his bike, thrums his fingers on the spokes. It seems odd only two men would go to a wildfire, instead of the usual half-dozen. If the fire were reported by a passing motorist, they would have no idea how large it was, or what it was doing. Under similar circumstances, I'd send everything I could spare. Better to return a few resources rather than risk losing the show. Perhaps I'm jumping to conclusions. Wildfires aren't the primary concern of a volunteer fire department. They would want to keep the maximum resources in town.

"Were you aware the Forest Service was already on the fire when you were dispatched?"

Bradley shrugs. "No one said anything."

"Did you monitor the red channel on your way out?"

"The what?"

"The red channel. The Forest Service frequency."

Bradley uses the palm of his hand to slow and then stop the spinning tire. "I think so," he says thoughtfully. He stands, scratches his forehead, leaving a greasy mark above his eye. "Yeah, we had the radio going, like we always do. Come to think of it, I heard talk about bombers, even heard you call about the arson. Funny though — it never occurred to me that we should check with you guys."

"Whose call would that have been, Doug?"

"Chief's, I guess. He was with us."

"Telford Hutton?"

Bradley nods. He doesn't look quite so relaxed anymore.

"How often do you go out on a fire where the Forest Service is already there?"

"This is the first one since I been on the force. But that's only been two years."

"And how many wildfires have you been on?"

He frowns, concentrating. "About a dozen, I guess."

"If you're the first responder, what happens when the Forest Service shows up?"

"We head back to town." He hesitates, looks a little uncomfortable. "I don't know if I should say this, but I guess it's okay, since you're from Canada. The Forest Service around here is kinda arrogant when they take over a fire. It's like they're the big brothers and they're sending us to go play somewhere else. When they show up, we just reel in our hoses and take off."

"But you didn't at this fire."

"No. You asked us to stick around."

Not quite, I'm thinking. Hutton offered — but maybe that was just because I was a different face.

"Doug, do you receive training on protecting the origin of a fire?"

"Oh yeah," he says, his face lighting up. "We took a course. In fact, last year we had this house fire where it was obvious someone started it. Used an accelerant. We did such a good job of protecting the origin, we got a commendation from the investigators who come from Missoula."

I nod, duly impressed. "They catch the guy?"

"Yup." Bradley takes a big gulp of beer. "Insurance job."

"What about ribbon?"

"What?"

"Flagging. Do you guys mark things on a fire, using flagging?"

"Sure. Crime scene tape, for the origin."

"What colour is it?"

"Yellow," he says. "Don't you watch the movies?"

"What about pink ribbon?"

He gives this some thought. "Not that I'm aware of."

"On that fire in the canyon, did you see anyone take down any pink ribbon?"

He shakes his head — no hesitation there.

"Did the three of you work together the whole time you were at the fire?"

His expression clouds. "What are you getting at?"

I don't say anything, just watch his face. His brow twitches.

"You think one of us screwed up that origin?"

"I doubt it, Doug. Do you guys receive training on how to burnout or backfire?"

The change in direction catches him off balance. "What?"

"They never taught you about widening a fireline by burning?"

Bradley looks puzzled. "No man, we do structure fires."

"What about using in-draft to backfire?"

He shakes his head, seems genuinely flustered. I'm interested because if the fire on the ridge that killed Brashaw was a secondary arson, the arsonist would have needed more than a passing knowledge of how to use fire to fight fire. Bradley puts this together and his eyes narrow.

"What the hell are you talking about?"

"Nothing," I tell him. "Don't worry about it."

But Bradley is worrying. He throws back the rest of his beer and stares at his project bike, frowning, obviously thinking hard. Time to go. I thank Bradley for the beer, leave him to ponder the scruples of his co-workers. I'll drop by in a day or two, talk to him again.

Sometimes, a little worry is a good thing.

Telson's rental car is at the motel when I pull into the Super 8. She's inside, at a little table, poring over photocopies of old newspaper clippings. The shades are drawn and the lamp is on. "Did you know," she says, with a meaningful glance, "that canyon, where the fire started, has a bit of a reputation?"

"No — really?"

"Yes." She points to one of the articles. "Back in the early seventies —"

"Bear hunters. Vengeful Indians. That sort of thing?"

She looks deflated. "You knew."

"That the canyon is cursed? Of course. In fact, I'm starting to believe it."

"Did you know the Indians were killed by a fire?"

"I seem to recall someone mentioning it. Can we talk about something else?"

She hesitates, then folds together her newspaper clippings.

"How did you do with that list?"

"Pretty good," she says. "I did a little calling around. At first, no one would co-operate, so I told them I was with the CDC and that one of the patrons in the bar might have a highly infectious virus. Told them I needed the name of everyone who was there that particular night, so I could track them down, prevent an outbreak." She grins, pleased with herself. "Amazing how forthcoming people are when faced with a public health crisis."

"That's my girl."

"There's gonna be a hell of a crowd at the clinic tomorrow."

I try to smile, share her enthusiasm.

"What's the matter, Porter? You look a little pale."

"I'm fine. What else have you been up to?"

I haven't been able to think of anything better to get Telson out of harm's way, so I'm going to have to lie to her, which makes me feel sick. I force a smile as she talks about the list, about her theories, about Erwin, about everything. She's so lively, so optimistic.

"What did you do today?" she says.

"Poked around. Looked into a few things."

"Did you find out anything about cellphone records?"

"What?" I say, then remember with another twinge of guilt that I'd told her I would look into this today. It was just a cover, but I don't want to tell her about my visit to the squatters. Or my suspicions regarding the VFD. It doesn't leave us a lot to talk about. "Apparently, it takes a battery of lawyers and a few pretty good computer geeks to access cellphone records."

"Too bad. So, what's our next move?"

"There isn't a next move. In fact, this case has pretty much run its course. We should get out of here, turn over what little we have to the sheriff."

"You're giving up?"

"I have to."

Telson stares, trying to read my expression. I'm not good at lying, so I glance away, grab a handful of clothes, and stuff them into my duffle bag. "I'm done," I tell her. "Finished. Which is all for the best, because I'm needed back home in Alberta. There's another fire."

"Another fire? Can't they send someone else?"

"They could, but there's no need."

There's a long pause. I'm nauseous and sweating.

"When do you have to leave?" Telson asks.

I glance at my watch. "In about an hour."

Telson is still staring at me. I continue packing, trying not to look as guilty as I feel.

"Have you told Del yet?"

"No, but thanks for mentioning it." I look at my watch again. "I better run up there quick."

Telson chews her lip, watching me. "You want me to come with you?"

"This is something I need to do alone."

There's an uncomfortable few minutes, with a minimum of small talk and a quick goodbye, then Telson is gone. No kiss. No see-you-later. She's pissed and I wonder if she saw through me. I tell myself it doesn't matter — she's gone and safe. I try to believe it. Then I climb into the Cornbinder and head to Del's, not to say goodbye, but to plan our next move.

"What did you find out about the volunteer fire department?" she says.

"I talked to one of the guys."

"What did he say? Any clue as to who might have put that ribbon under the seat of the engine?"

"Nothing on the ribbon, but the two guys he went to the fire with weren't real thrilled about taking him along."

"Which two guys?"

"Henry Dancey and Telford Hutton."

"Hutton is the chief," she says quietly.

"It could be nothing," I caution. "My experience with volunteer fire departments is they never know how many people are available, and they always want to maintain coverage in town. They're generally hard-working, community-minded individuals. Not arsonists."

She nods, pensive for a moment. "So, now what?"

"We keep looking."

I'm distracted on my drive back into town. I'm feeling shitty about deceiving Telson and the way we parted. I'm not thrilled about the progress of my investigation. I'm not going to accuse the chief of the volunteer fire department unless I have something solid. And a scrap of pink ribbon under the seat of a truck is hardly a solid lead. It's barely circumstantial.

I'm still not thinking clearly when I reach the highway, nearly blowing past the stop sign into the path of a log truck. I take a few deep breaths, steady myself, ease into the flow of traffic. Coming to the intersection leading to the sawmill, I start to brake. The pedal goes all the way to the floor without meeting resistance. I panic, grab for the gearshift, manage to ram it into a lower gear, overshooting the turn as I do and realizing too late that I never should have tried to turn. I slew sideways, narrowly miss a loaded lumber truck, and lose the surface of the highway. There's a roar of overworked gears, a blur of trees, then something abruptly stops my progress.

A sound of shattering glass.

A crunch of metal.

Darkness.

16

I WAKE WITH a start, still hurtling toward the trees, breathing hard, my muscles tense. Instead of the impact my body has suddenly braced for, I see white walls, a heart monitor, hear the gentle sigh and bleep of a hospital ward. An accident. I was in an accident, but I'm alive. My head is throbbing, my cheek burns, my ribs ache with every breath. When I lift a hand to explore a lump on my forehead, a tube running from my wrist brushes across my face. I'm plugged into a machine. A cord hanging conveniently close by invites me to press a bright red button for the nurse. I give it a try. A minute later, a smiling nurse appears.

"You're back with us," she says. "How do you feel?"

"Like a soccer ball. What happened?"

She leans over, shines a light in my eye. "You had a bit of an accident."

"I figured that part out. I just don't know why."

"What do you remember?"

"It's still a little fuzzy. Was anyone else hurt?"

She frowns thoughtfully. "Not that I know of. You're the only one they brought in."

That, at least, is something. I recall an intersection, a car travelling the opposite direction. The memory is distant, like the flash impression of a blink.

She finishes taking my vitals. "Any dizziness? Loss of coordination?"

"Nothing more than usual. How long have I been out?"

She consults her watch. "An hour and forty minutes since arrival."

"And when was that?"

"Just after seven."

She finishes up, updates her clipboard. Something occurs to me.

"Who's paying for this?"

"A Mr. Grey from the Forest Service has taken care of all the paperwork."

Grey — my guardian angel. I thank the nurse, who assures me the doctor will be along shortly. Then I'm alone, listening to the patter and moan of the hospital. I struggle out of bed, hobble to the small bathroom, towing my IV stand. I'm bruised, have a few cuts along one temple. Sutures not stitches — always a good sign. There's a goose egg on my forehead, no doubt from the steering wheel. All in all, I didn't fare too badly; I'm sore but mobile, anxious to get out of here. I splash a little cold water on my face, towel off, smooth down my hair as best as possible and return to my bed to await the doctor.

He tells me I have two more cracked ribs and a mild concussion, and that I'll be here overnight, as a precaution to make sure there's no swelling in the brain. I can't help thinking what Telson might say to that, smile a little sadly. Then, once again, I'm on my own.

Not for long. Castellino comes in.

"Mr. Cassel — back to the land of the living."

"For the time being."

Castellino nods. In his dark suit, he looks like an injury lawyer, doing his rounds, looking for customers. "Tell me about the accident."

"I was driving, minding my own business, and the brakes failed."

"Any prior indication? Any warning they might not be fully functional?"

"Not that I can think of," I say, then pause, my mind going back to the near-miss as I entered the highway. The logging truck that blasted its horn at me. "Well, actually, the brakes did seem a bit spongy when I stopped to enter the highway, just prior to the accident. I drove to the intersection by the sawmill and turned east. The brakes failed as I was turning."

"Nasty timing," he says, stroking his moustache. "Hazardous thing, driving an old vehicle like that. Never know what might go wrong." He props a foot on a plastic chair near the bed, gives me a hard look. "So is shaking every goddamn tree, just to see what might fall out."

"What are you talking about?"

Castellino allows himself a small, unamused smile. "Knowing the way you operate, I figured you might have pissed someone off, so I had your wreck towed to our yard. One of our mechanical contractors looked at it. It seems the brake line was loose where it connects to the reservoir. Every time you pumped the pedal, you squirted out fluid until there was none left. Did you notice anyone lurking around your motel room?"

"Not that I recall. Could it have been the result of wear?"

Castellino shakes his head. "Our mechanic didn't think so. Said he could tell where the grime on the fitting had been recently disturbed. There's a puddle of brake fluid in your motel parking lot. Looks to me like someone wanted you out of the picture, and nearly succeeded. Is there anything you might want to share? Anyone in particular you've pissed off lately?"

Telson is the first to come to mind, but she wouldn't do something like this. And Erwin needs me, for another day or so anyway. That just leaves Hutton, with two strikes against him already. But I've barely spoken to him, so he would have little reason to get that nervous. Castellino is waiting, watching me with X-ray eyes. Maybe I should tell him my suspicions. Maybe he'll take it more seriously than the Bob Capsan fiasco. I'd better wait until I have something a little firmer.

"Nothing substantial."

Castellino leans forward, rests his arm on the bedrail and lowers his voice confidentially. "You know, if I really wanted to, I could find out what you've been up to. But that would be a lot of work, would waste valuable resources which should be spent doing real police work. Mr. Noble warned me that you have a reputation for doing whatever you want, regardless of the legality. Something about an investigation into a string of bombings up north, and an arson. I hope that isn't the case here."

I shrug, try to look harmless. Right now, it isn't that difficult.

"When I'm certain of anything," I tell Castellino, "you'll be the first to know."

"You intend to continue investigating?"

"Within the limits of the law."

Castellino sighs heavily, rubs his temples as though he suddenly has a migraine. He's haggard, aged these last few days. He glances into the hall as a nurse whispers past and shakes his head.

"I can't talk you into just going back to Canada?"

"I thought you wanted me to stick around."

"I'm starting to regret that."

The next morning, the doctor seems pleased. My eyes are equally responsive to light and my goose egg is down to extra-large. He'd like to keep me another day, but I'm too restless for further captivity and check myself out, stopping on the way to fill another prescription for painkillers. While I wait for the narcotics to do their magic, I call Del from a pay phone in the hospital lobby, explain what happened, and apologize for destroying her father's truck.

"Don't worry about that," she says briskly. "Are you okay?"

"I think so, but I'm never quite sure."

"Are you still at the hospital? I'll come pick you up."

I tell her no thanks — not yet anyway. I'll call her in a few hours and we'll do lunch.

Heat coming off the parking lot envelops me like fever. Everything ripples and shimmers. Quarter past nine in the morning and the pavement is already hot enough to fry bacon. I walk as quickly as my ribs will allow, planning my route based on the availability of shade. Score one for old-fashioned verandas. I find a pay phone, flip through the wrinkled pages of a directory. I could get the same information from the photocopies I left at my motel room, but that's too many blocks in the wrong direction, and the address is right here.

Hutton, Telford. 201 Larch Street.

I stop at a tourist booth, get a town map, and have the lady there point out Larch Street. It's eight blocks away. I'm feeling a little faint but fortunately there are more trees closer to my destination, more patches of dappled shade. I rest frequently, wishing I'd had the foresight to bring a water bottle. Number 201 is a small, vinyl-sided bungalow with matching garage. What looks to be a '68 Corvette Stingray convertible is the only vehicle parked outside. The car has seen better days, the paint badly chipped, upholstery cracked and peeling like an old bandage. A set of booster cables are curled on the passenger seat: the car has been recently moved. No licence plate. I confirm there's no one home and start with the garage, gaining entry by using my credit card as a shim.

The garage is full of motorcycles, Harleys — five of them. Rather a lot of pig iron for one guy. Closer inspection reveals a lack of serial numbers; they must have been ground off and painted over. It's a little hard to register them that way, so I can only assume the bikes are for parts. But this is no chop shop, just a holding area. If nothing else, I could turn Hutton over for possession of stolen property. Maybe he'll talk if they give him a deal, tell the cops about the arson. Then again, if he's involved in the arson, he could be looking at a manslaughter charge — worse if they connect him to the death of Karalee Smith. A few stolen bikes are small change.

The back door on the house is a little more difficult — there's a deadbolt I can't get around. I try the windows, find one not quite locked. Using the tip of my pocketknife, I edge it loose, slide it open. Checking to make sure no one is looking, I push in the mosquito screen, heave myself into Hutton's bedroom. It's immediately apparent that Hutton lives alone. The bedroom is scattered with dirty clothes, empty bottles, and biker magazines. The rest of the house is marginally cleaner — no underwear hanging from the lampshades. The living room is almost civil; this must be where Hutton entertains his more respectable company. Not that he'll ever be featured in *Good Housekeeping*. A small hobby room has a computer, scanner, and printer. A fantasy poster occupies one wall: a futuristic soldier in a swamp, shooting a massive serpent as it rises out of the mire. Facing this is a movie poster that makes me shiver: Woody Harrelson, shaved bald for *Natural Born Killers*, looking sufficiently demonic. I turn on the computer but there isn't anything particularly interesting. Lots of games. I'd love to read his email but it's passworded and, once again, I'm no hacker. I know just enough to check his Internet files, scan the list of cookies posting the addresses of the sites he's recently visited. Porn. Bikers. Guns. More porn. No startling revelations here. I rummage around a little, listening for the sound of an approaching vehicle. In a cardboard box under the computer table is a collection of photos Hutton no doubt eventually intends to scan. Biker trash. I keep looking, sitting on the floor, while trying to find a position that'll ease the ache in my side.

Hutton must be the photographer because he isn't in most of the pictures. I notice him occasionally, hanging with a crowd that would make the Sasquatch feel right at home. I flip through a little faster, anxious to get out of here. Near the bottom of the box a particular photo catches my eye, not due to editorial content, but because of a sudden similarity, and I look a little harder. It's another group shot — a dozen of America's smelliest hoist beer cans toward the camera. Most are wearing colours but, from the angle, I can't make out the fraternity. Hutton is plainclothes. He's off to one side, his arm around a big bald guy with a beard. The bald guy is a few years older but their features are almost identical. I'm no genealogist, but it's obvious the men are related and it finally sinks in. Hutton is hanging out with his big brother. Idolizing him. Trying to impress him. So the bikers give him an odd job or two. Store a few stolen Harleys. He's got a perfect cover: community volunteer, chief of the fire department. Respectable citizen. Then one day Hutton is scouting the canyon and comes across the pot gardens. Naturally, he calls big brother. Baldy is interested but there's a problem — Hutton doesn't own the pot. He could just cut it, like any patch pirate, but that's dangerous — he just wants to be the middleman. So he goes looking for the owners — not difficult when you know the pot is there — and uses Karalee Smith to send his offer, which is not well received.

Why wouldn't Erwin have known that Hutton was behind the offer?

Hutton was operating anonymously. He probably contacted Karalee through the phone, or slipped her a note. Maybe he approached her directly, threatening her if she revealed his identity. Either way, she figured out who was leaning on her, which is why she was so evasive in the bar that night, with Hutton watching. So nervous when I talked to her later.

She was biding her time, doing her correspondence, hoping it would all blow over.

Hutton, however, became impatient, made his point by starting a little fire in the canyon. Just to let them know what he's capable of. But he underestimated the terrain and weather conditions, and the fire developed into something bigger than anticipated, ran up the ridge and killed Brashaw. Now everything is different. The pot is gone — some of it anyway — and the squatters will never co-operate with him. The sheriff is gunning for a manslaughter conviction and everything is fucked up. Then I come along, questioning Karalee in the bar in sight of Hutton and his buddies. They introduce me to their tire iron but when I don't leave, they get nervous and take out Karalee.

Damage control.

I'm suddenly covered in a prickly sweat. If I hadn't gone blundering around, asking questions, talking to Karalee, she might still be alive.

One careless moment leads to another, and people keep dying. I've got to get this mess under control. Got to make things right. I stand, woozy, shove the photo of Hutton and his brother into my pocket. The other photos go back into the box under the computer desk and I exit through the bedroom window, replace the screen, and slide it shut. Then I'm in the alley, sweating, breathing hard, holding my side as I walk. I'm halfway back to Main Street when I remember I left Hutton's computer turned on.

Fuck it — I'm not going back. I have more important things to do.

I stop at a pay phone next to a Conoco on Main Street, look up Lyle Harnack's number. He sounds surprised to hear me but quickly recovers. Where am I? He'll be right over. I buy a bag of ice from the cooler out front, sit in the shade with the ice pressed to my head. I get a few strange looks but the ice feels good. The parking lot shimmers like a desert mirage. The Volkswagen van pulls into the lot, parks in front of me. Harnack hangs out the window.

"You okay? I heard you were in an accident."

"I'm fine," I say, staggering as I stand up. Water trickles down my neck.

"Really?" says Harnack. "Because you look like shit."

"Thanks." I climb into the passenger side of the van. "You'd make a great doctor."

Harnack looks a little uncertain as I buckle myself in. "What're we doing?"

"Just drive," I tell him. "I need some wind."

Harnack drives. Wind blows in through the window, not cooling me much. The bag of ice melts at my feet. Harnack thumps the steering wheel. "So, what happened?" he says, glancing over at me. "What's with the accident?"

"I'm not sure. Something went on the old beater. I lost the road."

Harnack nods. "I saw them loading it on a truck last night. Nasty."

I ask him how he made out on the smokejumpers. He frowns thoughtfully. "Not that good. I had a friend in Missoula check the flight manifest — those guys are from all over."

"And gals," I add, thinking of Sue Galloway.

"Yeah — right. Anyway, I tried to get some info about them, but those records aren't in Missoula. Or, if they are, not somewhere I can get access. You think it's worth digging deeper?"

Harnack gives me a look of exaggerated nonchalance. The role of detective is new to him and he's going by what he's seen on TV. With his long hair and adolescent manner, it's a little comical. I try to keep a straight face. "I think we can drop that. I have a more promising lead."

"Really?" His face lights up. "What is it?"

Ever since the idea occurred to me, I've been debating the wisdom of involving Harnack, but I need a local for this to work. Someone young, about Karalee's age.

"I've got a suspect," I tell him.

"Right on," says Harnack. "Who is it?"

"That's not important right now. The less you know, the safer you are."

Harnack's face drops. I'm worried that if I tell him, he'll do something stupid.

"But I need your help," I say, and he cheers up a bit. "I need you to make a phone call."

"A phone call." He was expecting something a bit more daring.

"A very important phone call, Lyle. One that might break this case wide open."

"All right," he says, nodding. "Now we're talking. Where do we make the call?"

"From a pay phone. The one back at the Conoco will be fine."

I brief Harnack as we drive. It's a simple plan — shake the tree, see what falls out. As much as Castellino despises my methods, they work more times than not; you'd be surprised how many rotten apples can fall from a tree. Harnack listens intently, which is good because he has a script to follow. We drive around the block a few times as he rehearses. If he sticks to the script, he'll do fine.

"That's good," I tell him, after the third recital. "I think you've got it."

We park at the Conoco. I don't want Harnack to know who he's calling and ask him to keep an eye on the highway traffic while I look up the number — Hutton's work number at Precision Log Homes. I motion Harnack over and when Hutton comes on the line, hand the receiver to Harnack.

"Hello."

I hear Hutton's voice. Harnack freezes, a look of horror on his face. He's forgotten his lines.

"Who is this?"

The silence lengthens. I'm pretty sure Hutton won't wait long and reach for the phone — we'll have to try this later, after a little more practice — when Harnack comes to life. "This is Lyle Harnack," he says. "And I got a message for you."

I groan — he wasn't supposed to use his name. I reach for the receiver again, to stop this before it's too late, but Harnack turns away, blocking me.

"I know what you did to that waitress," he says, segueing into the script.

Hutton's reply is muffled but harsh. "I don't know what the fuck you're talking about ..."

"Lyle —" I whisper, but it's too late. Might as well let him finish.

"And I know why you started that fire. I know everything."

"Bullshit ..."

Harnack is holding the receiver too close to his ear now to hear everything Hutton is saying.

"She was my girlfriend, asshole," says Harnack, and I'm impressed with his sincerity. "And she kept a diary," he says. "She was pretty thorough. Your name comes up a lot. You want me to read some?"

Silence. Then I hear Hutton's reply, muffled but distinct. "What do you want?"

"Not much," says Harnack, really enjoying his role. "Just a little compensation."

A pause, then Harnack says, "Twenty grand."

Another pause. I can hear Hutton arguing, but can't make out more than the tone.

"Fuck you, too," says Harnack. "Now it's thirty, or the book goes to the cops."

I'm waving at Harnack — he was supposed to ask for ten. Now he's haggling. He gives me a wicked grin, like I'm supposed to be impressed with his negotiating skills. "Okay," he says into the phone, "so it's agreed then. We'll do it tonight, at the grocery store. Somewhere nice and public. You bring the cash, I'll bring the diary. Six thirty in the produce aisle."

There's some murmuring from the phone, a little more subdued.

"Damn right," says Harnack. "And don't fuck us around."

Then he hangs up, beaming, proud of himself. "How was that?"

"You idiot!"

His grin falters.

"You told him your name. You haggled over the price."

"I got him up to thirty grand," Harnack says defensively.

"We're not selling him a car. The diary doesn't even exist."

"So what?" says Harnack, regaining his composure and looking offended. "He doesn't know that. I had to make it sound real. Now we know he's really interested."

I close my eyes for a moment, try to regain my own composure. The worst mistake is what Harnack added toward the end, to sound like a tough guy. "Don't fuck us around."

Us. Hopefully, Hutton wasn't paying attention.

"Okay," I say finally. "It's done."

"Now what?" says Harnack.

"Now we get the players together."

"I can't believe you did this," says Castellino.

I'm in the parking lot of the grocery store, in a motorhome with Castellino, Batiste, and a surveillance technician wearing headphones. It's nearly six o'clock and still hot enough to roast a lizard. The cops are not enjoying the sunshine — they've both got flak jackets under their plainclothes and, even in the air-conditioned motorhome, they're sweating. More plainclothes officers are camped in the parking lot. One is bent over an open hood, pretending to have vehicle trouble; another is dressed like a tourist, resting in the shade. And there are more in the store, ready to pounce. I can see them on the monitors, dressed as store clerks, pretending to stock shelves. The inside of the motorhome looks like the bridge of the Enterprise. Four monitors are on a feed from the store's security cameras. The scene on a fifth monitor keeps bobbing and weaving, showing shoppers in unflattering close-ups. Everything is grey, like watching an old high-school yearbook come to life.

"The produce aisle," says Castellino, shaking his head as he watches the monitors.

"I needed someplace public, someplace a nineteen-year-old might pick."

"Well, you outdid yourself."

The technician adjusts a knob on the soundboard, looks at Castellino. "They're ready to send him in, sir." Castellino nods and the tech relays the message. A moment later, Harnack appears on one of the monitors, glancing around, trying very hard not to look conspicuous. He's wearing a loose jacket with big pockets and is pushing a shopping cart.

"How's the feed?" says Batiste.

"Good. Coming in five-by-five," says the technician.

Harnack is wired for sound. The plan is to get Hutton to say something incriminating. To do this, Harnack is going to change his mind, ask for fifty grand. Hopefully, Hutton will be pissed enough to let something slip. "Because we sure as hell can't charge him on the basis of a call in which we had no involvement," Castellino had explained earlier. "A call that we don't even have a goddamn record of." He wasn't happy about any of it — my explanation that Hutton was trying to pressure the squatters into selling their pot through him. My theory that Hutton killed Karalee Smith to cover his tracks, or that I'd been talking to the squatters and had known about the pot gardens for days without telling him. When I wouldn't reveal how I came across some of this information, he grumbled about withholding evidence and obstruction of justice, but he was willing to cut me some slack because my plan — as misguided as it was — was now in play and he didn't want anyone else to get hurt. In other words, it was time for the professionals to step in. Which suited me just fine. I've had enough of Carson Lake and this curse. I just want this to be over.

"He's in Produce, sir," says the technician.

"I can see that," snaps Castellino, staring at the monitors.

Harnack was thrilled the cops were following through on this. They tried to talk him out of it — it was too risky — but they might as well have been talking to a lemon. Harnack wanted to be in the middle of the action. He wanted to make the drop. He wanted to be wired for sound. He wanted a gun.

"Not a chance," said Castellino. "There'll be plenty of guns there already."

It was a bad location, the tactical leader had explained. Terrible. Too many civilians. Too many cover areas. So the idea is to get Hutton to follow Harnack outside the store, where he'll be more likely to say something incriminating, then grab him.

That's how they set it up, anyway. Now it's all up to Harnack.

We wait, watch Harnack linger in the produce aisle. Castellino has him do some shopping in the rest of the store, so he won't look so suspicious. Harnack pushes his cart off one monitor and onto another. Inside the motorhome, the two cops stand behind the technician seated at the control panel. I try to watch without getting in the way.

Very little happens. Time begins to slow. A digital clock in the control panel reads ten past six. Then quarter past. No one moves.

"Where's Special Agent Noble?" I ask Castellino.

"Gone back to Washington."

"Where the real crooks are?"

Castellino ignores me, staring intently at the monitors, still firmly pissed off. Twenty past six. I pull aside the drapes, peer out the window, and am reprimanded by Batiste. Suddenly, Castellino swears, frowning at the monitors.

"What the hell is she doing here?"

Del is on one of the monitors, pushing a cart along an aisle in the store.

"Shopping, by the looks of it."

"You didn't tell her about this," says Castellino. "Tell me you didn't tell her."

"I didn't tell her." It must have been Harnack. He wanted her to see him in his moment of glory.

"Get her out of there," says Batiste, and Castellino makes the call. One of the undercover grocery clerks moves from Produce, intercepts her in Dairy. The two grey figures converse. Del shakes her head, pushes her cart away. The clerk takes a few steps after her and stops. We hear his murmured voice on a speaker set into the control panel.

"Three here. She refuses to leave."

Castellino keys a mike. "Does she know what's going on?"

A brief hesitation. "Yes sir. I believe so."

Castellino grinds his teeth, looks at me like it's my fault. "Keep her away from Produce."

"Copy."

We watch the monitors. Del passes from one to another, pushing her cart, tossing in the odd can or box. She edges toward the produce aisle but holds in Bakery. Harnack looks toward Bakery and smiles like a schoolboy. Castellino leans on the control panel, frowning intently.

Six thirty-five. Harnack is getting bored, poking melons. Del's cart is full of bread.

Castellino checks in with tactical, who inform him that absolutely nothing has happened outside. The suspect's vehicle is nowhere in sight. Castellino sighs heavily, wipes sweat from his brow. "He did say he was coming, right?"

I nod. We continue to wait. Radios hum. The tension is unbearable.

Castellino is grumbling under his breath. Something about idiots, amateurs, and wasting resources. Suddenly, I see a familiar face on one of the monitors. A balding brush cut and a dark, pocked complexion. "That guy," I say, pointing at the monitor. "He works with Hutton and he was on the fire. I think he may be involved."

The three of us crowd over the control panel. Castellino has the technician zoom in.

"That's him," I say. "Henry Dancey."

Castellino alerts the officers in the store. We watch, transfixed, as Dancey shoves his cart from Dairy to Produce. Castellino gives Harnack a heads up and Harnack freezes, a cantaloupe in his hands, watching Dancey. Dancey pushes his cart past Harnack, without stopping.

"Did you see that?" I say. "Did you see the way Dancey looked at him?"

Castellino says nothing, eyes narrowed as he stares at the monitors.

"He was scoping him," I say. "He'll probably make another pass."

Without taking his eyes from the monitors, Castellino holds up a hand in the universal gesture for silence, and I shut up and content myself with watching the show. Harnack watches Dancey retreat. Del watches Harnack. The undercover grocery clerk watches everyone. Dancey makes a few more trips down the aisles, from monitor to monitor, then he heads for the checkout, pays for his groceries, and leaves the store. Seven fifteen.

"That's it," Castellino says softly.

"You're giving up?"

"Yeah," he says, fixing me with a cold look. "We're giving up. One of two things just happened. Dancey was sent in and suspected something was amiss, or your buddy Hutton was pulling your leg, to make you look like a fool. Either way, it's over."

Castellino calls tactical, who call in their men. Harnack is told to report to the motorhome, and to bring Delise Brashaw. In a few minutes, it becomes crowded in command central. "What happened?" says Harnack, looking concerned.

"Nothing," says Castellino. "Nothing happened."

"But he said he'd be here," whines Harnack. Castellino ignores him, looks at Del.

"Why were you in the store, Ms. Brashaw?"

Del looks around, wide-eyed. "I was shopping."

"Shopping," Castellino says sarcastically.

Del begins to protest, as does Harnack as a matter of principle, until Castellino shoos them out, along with everyone but Batiste and me. Batiste sits in the vacant technician's chair, crosses his long legs and stares at me. Castellino frowns and strokes his moustache. "Tell me again," he says, "why you think the chief of the volunteer fire department set the fire that killed Bert Brashaw."

"He wanted to make some money on the squatters' marijuana."

"Yes," says Castellino, chewing his lower lip. "So you said. And you know this how?"

I hesitate, thinking about my promise to Del, my deal with Erwin. Then I think about Telson, and Bert Brashaw and Karalee Smith. I was wrong to think that I could make up for any of this. I pull out a rumpled photo from the back pocket of my jeans and hand it to Castellino.

"Hutton has a brother in a bike gang."

Castellino glances at the photo, then looks at me. "You set it up on the basis of this?" he says, holding the picture like it might be covered with cat litter. "You put people's lives at risk on the basis of an old photograph?"

"He knows the area," I say, plowing on. "He guides hunters —"

"Coincidental," says Castellino. "Tell me you have something more."

Anything more I have isn't much — the scrap of flagging, Hutton's reaction when I questioned him about the call that dispatched the volunteer fire department. And it's all based on hunch and illegal searches. Castellino has a challenging look in his eye. Batiste is watching me with clinical disinterest.

"Where did you get the photograph?" says Batiste.

"From a friend."

"A friend?"

I nod, wondering what their reaction would be if I told them exactly how I got the photograph, or the scrap of flagging. Or how Erwin coerced me into breaking into their cabin. Best not to bring it up — they don't much believe me anyway.

Batiste gives me a hard look. "You know what I think, Mr. Cassel?"

He doesn't wait for me to answer, which is just as well.

"I think you're playing a dangerous game." He sits up, his expression cold. "There are only two sides in this game and they are divided by the rules. The side that doesn't play by the rules does the killing. The side that does play by the rules tries to stop them. There's no middle ground. If you can't decide what side you're on, you had better get out of the game."

I'm in the Hogshead Pub when Del finally catches up with me. Her long red hair is back in a ponytail and she's wearing a work shirt and jeans. She takes a seat beside me at the bar, gives me a long, knowing look. "I'm sorry this didn't work out," she says. "It sounded like a great plan."

"It wasn't that great. Can I buy you a beer?"

She nods. I motion to the bartender, who draws a glass of draft, sets it in front of her.

"Don't blame yourself," she says finally. "You tried."

I give her a wry smile. "The ultimate excuse."

She takes a sip of her beer, sets it carefully on the counter. "It's not an excuse, Porter — you really did try. And I'm thankful for that. The police wouldn't be nearly as far as they are without you."

I can't help chuckling. She actually seems to believe this.

"No — really," she says. "Think of everything you've accomplished."

"I'd rather not. I got your father killed, and probably Karalee Smith. I broke every law in the book. I'm surprised they haven't tossed me in jail."

Del starts to protest, but I cut her short.

"Look — just save it, Del. If you think I did some good, well, that's something, I guess. But I can't help thinking everyone would have been better off if I hadn't showed up."

She gives me a searching look. "You don't really believe that?"

"I'm not sure what I believe. Except this place is cursed. For me, anyway."

Del watches my face until I become uncomfortable. I know I'm feeling sorry for myself, wallowing a little, but every man has an inherent right to wallow. I take a gulp of beer to hide my discomfort. "Anyway," I add, "I told the sheriff pretty much everything, although I'm not sure they believe me."

"So, now what?"

"Nothing. I go home. Finally."

She nods, like she knew I would say this. I raise my glass. "Cheers."

She doesn't meet my mocking toast. Instead, she stands, giving me a hard look.

"Fine," she says. "I'm going now. You just sit there and drink yourself stupid."

She's gone and I'm left wondering what happened. I drain my beer and consider her suggestion.

Outside, it's finally starting to cool. Everything hurts. My ribs, spine, and head. My soul.

I go two blocks before I cave in and call a cab. I fumble with the key — I can barely wait to get into the room, to lie in bed and pull the covers over my head. To sleep. The light on the phone indicates I have messages. I hesitate, then think maybe it's Telson. But it's nothing but hang-ups.

I'm just getting into bed when the phone rings. I lunge for the receiver.

It's Harnack. He's hysterical. They're going to kill him.

17
●

"CALM DOWN," I tell him. "Tell me what happened."

"What happened?" he shrieks. "I stepped inside my house and they grabbed me. Knocked me cold. Now they're going to kill me! Jesus fucking Christ ..."

He starts to sob. It's not a pleasant sound.

"Where are you, Lyle?"

"I don't know." He sniffles, his voice catching. "Just some place."

It seems odd they're letting him talk like this. "Put them on the phone, Lyle."

There's some scuffling and I hear Lyle telling someone that I want to talk to them. His voice is a little distant, shaky. Then the phone goes dead and I stare at the receiver in disbelief. I set it carefully in the cradle, like it might explode. A minute later the phone rings and I jump.

"Hello?"

"They don't want to talk," says Lyle, his voice filled with suppressed fear.

"Well, then, you talk, Lyle. What the hell is going on?"

"The diary," he says tearfully. "They want the fucking diary!"

"What, exactly, did you tell them?"

"I told them you have it." He's nearly hysterical again.

"Yes," I say slowly, as it dawns on me they're probably listening. "I have the diary."

"They want you to bring it, or they're going to kill me."

"No one is going to kill you, Lyle. Where am I supposed to bring the diary?"

There's a crinkly sound — paper being shoved into Lyle's hand. He reads mechanically.

"142 Aspen Grove Estates."

Aspen Grove. I try to think where that might be. Then I realize the conversation is nearly over, and I don't have a diary to give them — Harnack had a bible in his pocket at the store. He also had half the Missoula County Sheriff's Department in the other pocket. I have neither. I need time.

"Lyle, the diary is in a safe deposit box at the bank. I can't get it until tomorrow morning."

"What?" He can't believe this.

"Just tell them, Lyle. And trust me. I'll get you out of there."

"Okay," he says, sounding marginally calmer. I hear him repeating the message to his captors.

"He says the diary is at the bank —"

There's a thud and a crash, followed by Lyle's whimpering. He's crying, begging for them not to hit him again. It's pathetic and more than a little heart wrenching. I listen hard to make out the response — deeper, like bass on a bad radio. Someone picks up the phone.

"Get your ass down here!"

"Who is this?" I inquire politely.

"The tooth fairy. Don't bullshit me about the diary."

Too late, I'm thinking. "It's at the bank," I say flatly. "You're going to have to wait."

There's an ominous silence. I'm pretty sure it's Dancey, but I've never heard him on the phone.

"The bank opens at nine," says the voice. "I'll call you at nine fifteen."

"That's not enough time —"

"You don't answer and your friend dies. Any cops and he dies painfully."

The line goes dead. I wish I still had the Cornbinder so I could look for 142 Aspen Grove Estates, although I doubt that would help much; I'm sure there'll be a different location for the meet tomorrow. Instead, I call Del at the greenhouse. She sounds surprised to hear from me.

"Aren't you drinking yourself stupid?"

"Apparently I don't need to drink for that. I need your help. Something has happened."

She agrees to meet me at the motel in a half-hour. In the meantime, I go for a walk to the drugstore, buy a cheap diary — the type I imagine a waitress would use. When I return to the motel, Del is waiting. I unlock the door, usher her in. She looks confused as she sits on the bed, her hair down, framing a tense, worried expression.

"What's happened, Porter?"

"The VFD guys have Lyle. They're going to kill him if I don't give them the diary."

She looks dumbfounded. "You're kidding."

"I wish I were."

"But there is no diary," she says, frowning.

"Not yet." I hand her the blank diary from the drugstore. "I hope you're a good writer."

She looks at the thin booklet in a dubious, puzzled sort of way.

"Avoid using dates," I tell her. "And when you do, smear them a little. Start with a month or two ago. Put in references to Telford Hutton, but start with anonymous contacts, and make sure those dates are the hardest to read. Talk about Erwin — her brother — and how she can't wait to get away from the pot-growing lifestyle. And put in lots about Lyle — he was supposedly seeing her, so make it convincing. Use details that he can confirm. I'm sure that won't be too difficult."

Del gives me a cold look.

"And spill some coffee here and there. Make it look used."

"No problem," she says quietly. "How long do I have?"

"All night. The swap will happen tomorrow morning."

"Maybe we should go to the sheriff."

Now she wants to go to the sheriff. "I'm not sure that's a good idea."

She frowns. "You're probably right. I'm just worried about you and Lyle."

"We'll stick to the plan. When Lyle is safe, we'll bring in the cops."

"What if it's a trap? What if they don't let either of you go?"

"Don't worry — I've got a trick or two up my sleeve."

We work on the diary until three in the morning, trying to make it specific enough that Hutton will believe it should he decide to flip through before releasing Lyle, but vague enough that he won't catch any obvious errors. It's trickier than cheating on your taxes. We dribble a little coffee on it, toss it around for a minute or two. By the time we're finished, it looks pretty authentic.

"Thank God that's done," says Del, rubbing her wrist. She's got carpal tunnel syndrome and we're both a little frayed. We agree it would be best if she spent the rest of the night here — I don't want to lose track of her until this is over. She takes a shower while I take a crescent wrench to the bright orange carrot on the roof of the van, make it a little less conspicuous. By the time I'm done, Del is in bed, sleeping.

I take the floor.

I didn't think I'd be able to sleep but at some point I must have dozed off because the ringing phone jars me out of a blurry dream. I scramble off the floor, paranoid I've slept in and Hutton is calling to tell me it's too late — Harnack is dead — but it's just my wake-up call from the front desk. I hang up and collapse into a chair. Del props herself on her elbows and looks at me.

"Is it time?"

I nod and she pushes herself up, swings her legs out of bed. She's quite an attractive woman, long legs and red hair, even first thing in the morning. No wonder Lyle is so obsessed with her. No wonder

Telson was jealous. I notice the way her lacy bra cups her breasts, the way her panties cling to her thighs, and force myself to look away, give her time to dress.

"What now?" she says from behind me. "Do we just wait for them to call?"

"No, I have to go to the bank. Keep up appearances. They may be watching."

I slip out while she's in the washroom, before she has a chance to ask more questions. Or ask to come with me. I park the van in the lot next to the log bank, wait for Carson United Trust to open its doors. At exactly nine o'clock I head for the bank, glancing around as I walk across the warm pavement. I don't see anyone watching. I ask the teller if I could use the washroom; I must look guilty because she gives me a suspicious glance as I cross the lobby. I wait in the can for a few minutes, then leave the bank. Still no visible observers. I peer into the van from the back, in case Hutton or Dancey have snuck inside to surprise me and take the diary, but it's empty.

As I pull into traffic, an old Ford pickup swings in behind me. I make a few random turns and the truck follows. I can't be certain, looking back through the dusty windows, but it could be Dancey following me — the profile looks about right. He could be following to take the diary from me before the meet, but there isn't a lot of time to fool around and I head for the motel. The Ford slows behind me, like it's going to follow me in, then accelerates down the highway, showing its buckled tailgate. Del looks tense when I step through the door.

"How'd it go?"

"Fine," I tell her. I don't want to mention the truck. "They call yet?"

She shakes her head. The clock says quarter past nine. The phone rings at twenty past.

"You're late," I tell Hutton.

"Fuck you too. You got the package?"

"Yeah, I got the package. Let me talk to Lyle."

There's a moment's pause, then Harnack comes on the line. "Porter?"

"You okay?"

"Yeah." He sounds far from certain. "But come quickly. They're gonna burn me."

"Relax, Lyle, they're just playing with you. You'll be home in no time."

But Lyle doesn't have the phone anymore. "We're not playing," Hutton growls.

"Neither am I. Where's the meet?"

Hutton gives me directions instead of an address. It's someplace out of town, down a series of back roads, and the instructions are complicated enough that I write them on a little pad next to the phone, shielding it from Del's view. After I'm done — and Hutton makes the usual threatening overtures about involving the cops — I hang up and shove the piece of paper with the directions into my pocket.

"Is it set?" says Del, her features etched with concern.

"Yes." I head for the door. "I've got fifteen minutes to get there."

"Where is it?" she says. "In case something goes wrong."

"Nothing's going to go wrong."

"Porter, wait —"

I hesitate, expecting Del will ask me to reconsider, or call the cops, but she surprises me by pulling a revolver out of her handbag. "It was my father's," she says, urging me to take it.

I take the gun. It's loaded. "Thanks."

She gives me a hard look. "Don't be afraid to use it."

I tuck the gun under my jacket and head out to rescue Lyle Harnack.

The directions lead me south, out of town again, then east. I follow a gravel road, which begins to narrow as the ground rises toward a distant ridge. Spur roads take off everywhere. This looks like an old logging area. I take the third spur road to the right, little more than a set of dusty tracks between dense forest. In places, the trees are younger — second growth over an army of rotting stumps. The road splits in three directions in a small clearing, littered with rocky fire rings and broken bottles. I pause to check the directions, take the trail on the left. It rises steeply then levels out. A grey flash of boards around a curve in the trail and suddenly I'm there.

An old clapboard shack squats in a small clearing. The windows are gone, as are many of the wooden shingles. A veranda over a narrow front porch sags dangerously. An outbuilding has been flattened by a toppled tree. The rusting bed of an ancient sawmill sits in front of the shack. The grille and hood of an old Ford is visible at the rear of the shack: the truck that followed me. At least I know I have the correct address. I turn around so I'm facing back down the trail for a quick getaway, then walk into the clearing in front of the shack and holler for Hutton.

"Okay — I'm here. Let's get this over with."

No response. Birds twitter in the trees. I holler again with the same result. They want me to go in — a bad sign. It's always better to do things in the open, but I'll be damned if I'm going in through the front door, where they'll be expecting me. I stay close to the wall instead, where it'll be difficult for them to see me from inside. If they are inside. The weathered boards are coarse beneath my hand as I creep along the side of the house. I glance through a low, narrow window frame. A dry, musty smell wafts through the opening. The house has several rooms — this one holds only an ancient table, caked with a layer of grey pigeon droppings.

"Lyle?" I whisper through the window. "Are you in there?"

Nothing. I don't like this. If they wanted to trade, they should have come out already. They could be watching and waiting, ready to pick me off and just take the diary. Or they might not even be here — just booby-trapped the house. They don't really need the diary, just need to get rid of it. Hairs on my neck begin to rise as I glance at the surrounding forest — plenty of cover for a waiting sniper. Despite my assurances to Del, I don't have much up my sleeve. I'd expected to confront Hutton. I move quickly around a corner to the back of the house. A door, pushed in, hangs on its hinges. I dart over to the truck to see if there are keys I can steal, but it's locked. Maybe I should take the distributor lead so they can't get away.

A sound — a scrape, coming from the house.

I freeze, my heart thumping. It comes again, like a chair grating on a floor. Then I see movement, ever so slight, through the open back door. Past another doorframe, deeper in the house, I see cloth — an arm. Harnack. I abandon the truck, pause at the weathered doorframe, looking and listening. I can smell diesel, faint but unmistakable, and I remember what Harnack said on the phone.

"Come quickly. They're gonna burn me."

Nerves prickle down my spine as I step across the threshold into the gloom. The ceiling is low and dark. Ragged strips of peeling paint hang like fly paper. Patterns on the wall, faded, barely visible under the grime: flowers and bunches of grapes. A smell of pigeon droppings and dry rot. The waxy odour of diesel. Gun in hand, I move toward the narrow, vacant doorframe leading to the next room.

Harnack comes into sight. I see him from behind, framed by an empty window. He's seated, tied to an old wooden chair, hands bound behind his back, ankles lashed to the legs. The floor creaks beneath me and Harnack moves his head, trying to see who's behind him. I pause, taking a good look around. This is the main room, perhaps fourteen feet square. Other than Harnack, the room is empty. There's another vacant doorframe on the far side of the room and I'm willing to bet Hutton is waiting there. He'll come out as I try to untie Harnack, but it's too obvious. I should go outside, look for a view into that other room. Maybe a crack or —

"Don't fucking move!"

Dancey's voice. I look around — the room is still empty. Then a trail of powdered pigeon shit drifts down. When I look up, Dancey is staring down at me from the ceiling, his legs straddling a hole between the rafters. I have a fleeting urge to lift the revolver and start shooting, but the double-barrel coach gun pointed at my head makes a pretty convincing argument.

He grins. "Lay the piece on the floor. Real slow. This here gun don't have no choke."

I do as he says, squatting, setting the revolver carefully on the floor. "Kick it away."

I nudge the revolver hard enough it goes halfway across the room — not as far as it could, but out of Dancey's sight. Harnack struggles to look over his shoulder. In profile, I can see his mouth is duct-taped shut.

"Now, lie on the floor," says Dancey. "Face down. I wanna see your hands."

Reluctantly, I spread out on the floor. An odd thought occurs to me — the floor is grimy, but there's no dust, no loose bits of bird shit here. Like they swept the floor. There's a creaking of boards and Hutton towers above me. He squats, rolls one knee painfully into my lower back, does a quick search. He finds the diary, a Swiss Army knife, my wallet, and credit card. He takes everything but the wallet, which he shoves roughly back into my pocket.

"Might help identify the body," he says, grinning. He walks behind Harnack, picks up the revolver. "You can get up now, but stay right where you are."

I stand up, glance around. Dancey is gone from the hole above me. I hear him making his way down a staircase in the next room. He walks though the far doorway, on the other side of Harnack, levels the gun at both of us.

"Why are you involved?" I ask Dancey. "You getting paid? Or just another wannabe?"

"Fuck you," he says flatly.

"I was afraid you might be bullshitting me," says Hutton, flipping through the diary. "But damned if the little bitch wasn't writing it all down."

"You got what you wanted, Hutton. Now let him go."

Hutton snaps the diary shut and shoves it into his coat pocket. "Be my guest."

I hesitate, looking at Hutton and Dancey. Hutton gives me an impatient wave with the revolver. If they wanted to shoot me, they would have done it already, as soon as they had the diary. I circle around, in front of Harnack, watching the guns. Harnack's eyes are huge. He's breathing heavy, cheeks puffing against the duct tape. That's the first thing that'll come off. I step toward him, start to reach, when the floor gives way beneath me and I crash into darkness amid a clatter of boards, and see stars as a board hits me on the head. A cloud of dust rises around me. I'm in an old root cellar, half caved-in but still plenty deep. The floor joists above me have been cut, ends white and ragged against the aged wood. That's why there wasn't any dust on the floor — they cleaned up so the trap wouldn't be obvious.

Hutton looks down from the edge of the hole. "These old buildings are treacherous."

"Yeah," says Dancey, from somewhere overhead. "A real fire hazard."

There's a scrape, then I have just enough time to grab for Harnack as they toss him into the hole, chair and all. Catching him is like getting hit by a two-hundred-pound medicine ball. The chair shatters and Harnack grunts through his nose. I lay him on his side, yank off the tape. He curses, breathing hard.

"Fuck —"

"You okay? Anything broken?"

His voice is ragged. "I don't think so. Get these damn ropes off me."

My midsection is throbbing, pain blossoming across my back — I may have cracked another rib. I start to untie Harnack's hands, then glance up toward Hutton. He's watching, an ironic smile twisting his lips. He never planned on letting us leave. The hole isn't that deep — even with my cracked ribs I could probably climb out, but he'd shoot me first. Then I hear a gulping, sloshing sound, like someone pouring out of a large jug. The stink of diesel suddenly becomes overwhelming.

"You girls have a nice time down there," says Hutton.

I start to work in earnest on the knots holding Harnack's hands. Diesel dribbles through the floorboards above, pattering on the dusty earth of the cellar. Hutton laughs down at us — a hollow, evil sound. He's in no hurry. Diesel isn't that volatile and has a high flashpoint. It burns slow enough he can hold a match to the spreading puddle on the floor and then jump out the big window, but not slow enough that I'll get out of here in time. And it burns hot. Very hot.

"I photocopied that diary," I shout, tugging at the knots. "At the bank."

"Sure you did," says Hutton.

"I left a copy with the manager. In a sealed envelope, told him to give it to the cops if I wasn't back in an hour." Finally, the first knot comes free. "How do think it's going to look if they find us dead, after they read those photocopies?"

"That's a bitch," says Hutton. "But it's just a chance I'll have to take."

The stench of diesel is sickening. The last knot slips free and Harnack can move his arms. I point to his feet, signal him to get to work, then glance around the dim cellar. It's just a big hole in the ground, slumped in — there must be somewhere we could dig out.

Hutton steps back from the hole above us. "See you girls later."

"Fuck!" Harnack swears, struggling frantically with the knot at his ankles. I hear footsteps — Hutton and Dancey retreating, getting ready to light up. Then a curse of surprise, a scuffle, and a thud. It sounds like a herd of rhinos up there, thumping on the floor. Dust and bits of wood begin to settle around us. An arm flops suddenly into the hole and for a second Hutton is looking down at us, startled. Then I see an angry, hairy face above me and Hutton is dragged from view. The Sasquatch kneels, offering me a grubby hand. I gesture toward Harnack, still struggling with the knot. The Sasquatch pulls an immense knife from under his jacket, offers it handle-first. I take the knife, slash the cord around Harnack's ankles, and the Sasquatch lugs us out of the hole, one at a time. Erwin and two guys I haven't seen before — equally frightening — have Hutton and Dancey up against a wall. Erwin is holding Dancey's shotgun on them. He sees me and grins.

"These the guys?"

"Maybe," I say, wondering what Erwin is going to do.

"You want to go back into the cellar?"

"These are the guys," Harnack blurts out.

Erwin nods, signalling to his cohorts, who step forward and hit Hutton and Dancey low. The two men drop like melting candles, staring at their tormentors. Staring at me. It's the first time I've seen fear in Hutton's eyes. I take a step back, nearly slipping on the diesel-soaked boards. Erwin pulls a revolver out from his belt, hands it to me.

"I believe this is yours."

I take the gun, not sure I believe any of this is happening. The Sasquatch is standing on a dry section of floor, lighting a small propane torch, adjusting the flame. Hutton is crab-walking backward, trying to get away. Dancey looks like he's in shock. Erwin's buddies have baseball bats — why didn't I notice that before?

"Get out of here," says Erwin, glancing back at me.

Harnack doesn't need to be told twice — he heads for the big window, pausing long enough to urge me to follow, then jumps. I see him running across the clearing, then turn my attention back to the room. Hutton tries to stand and is knocked down again.

"Get the hell out of here," Erwin says savagely. "Forget this ever happened."

I take a step back, notice the gun is still loaded. The Sasquatch advances on Hutton and Dancey, a sharp little flame hissing from the torch. It occurs to me that I could stop them, hold them at bay while Harnack goes for the cops. Then I think of BB, beating me at cards. Walking with me up the slope. Dying beside me. And of Karalee and her correspondence course — trying to build a better life. I shove the gun into my waistband and follow Harnack out the window.

Harnack is silent as the van thumps down the narrow trail. His breathing is heavy and he's shaking — his big hands dance across his thighs. I glance in the rear-view mirror, not sure what to expect. Erwin's truck, a fireball maybe, but there's just trees — another peaceful day in the forest. We pass the clearing with the fire rings and broken bottles, head downslope to the secondary road. In ten minutes, we're on the highway, heading toward town.

"Where are we going?" Harnack says finally, his voice faint.

"I don't know. I haven't really thought about it."

"Maybe we should call somebody."

"Maybe," I say, looking back again. "Maybe not."

"What about the cops? We should call the cops."

"And tell them what, exactly?"

Harnack thinks about this. I'm expecting to see smoke in the direction from which we just came, but when I see a dense column, it's in the wrong location altogether — in front of us and to the west, in the direction of Holder's Canyon. But that fire is dead. A flare up? No — the colour of the smoke is too dark and oily, the base too small. More like an industrial fire — tires or oil or something like that. Then it hits me: the squatters' camp is burning. One of those crazy hoses leeching off the old wellhead finally popped. Or something more sinister; maybe Hutton made a quick stop at the squatters' camp before meeting me at the shack in the woods. Or his brother stopped by to collect the pot and clean up the mess.

I think about the dusty little faces I saw hiding under the trailers and get a sick feeling.

I pull the van around and head back toward the smoke.

"Where are we going?"

"To the fire. I have a bad feeling I know where it is."

There's a helicopter circling when we get there and the trail is congested with vehicles. Two fire engines and an ambulance from the Carson Lake Volunteer Fire Department are parked a good distance back. The medics wait, leaned against the grille of the ambulance, watching the show. Firefighters pull gear from a Forest Service crew cab. "Jesus Christ," Harnack mumbles as we get out of the van, his face glowing in the yellow light. The wellhead has blown, a jet of flame billowing straight up for a hundred yards, thundering like a waterfall. Trees at the edge of the clearing are burning. I can't see the trailers through the smoke and shimmering heat, just vague shadowy flickers.

"What should we do?" says Harnack.

I shake my head — he seems to think I have answers, a chronic problem around here — and approach a cluster of Forest Service men conferring in subdued tones. Most of them I don't know, except a local — Al Gunderson, from my brief sojourn on the Holder fire. They're talking about moving resources up from the canyon. I stand at the periphery, listen for some clue as to what happened.

"Cassel," he says, recognizing me. "What are you doing here?"

"Just trying to help. Anyone hurt? Anyone home when it went off?"

Gunderson frowns — he's a big guy, with a heavy chin and goatee. He glances over his shoulder, toward the fire. "We don't know. Haven't been able to get close."

"When did it start?"

"Twenty, maybe thirty minutes ago."

"You see anyone drive past?"

He shakes his head. "We weren't really looking —"

"Just stay out of this, Cassel," says one of the officers, staring at me. He's older, with dark bushy eyebrows and a lean, haggard face. I don't know him but that doesn't mean much — most of the Forest Service in Montana would recognize me by now. "We've got enough to worry about already," he says, turning back to the others. I bite my tongue, retreat — the message is clear enough. I've become a pariah. An embarrassment. I stand for a moment, a few paces back from Gunderson and the fire gods, frustrated and more than a little angry. They ignore me. Belt radios blare tinny voices. The helicopter reports the fire is creeping into timber. The voice, which sounds a lot like

Grey, asks for aerial support, dozers, water trucks, crew to cap the blow out, and to send an investigator. Gunderson shoots me a cautionary look and I turn away, find Harnack talking with the men by the VFD engines. They fall silent when they see me and I wonder what he might have told them. Then Doug Bradley gives me a friendly smile. "Hell of a thing," he says. "Got any marshmallows?"

I shake my head. "You heard if there was anyone in the trailers?"

"No." He looks concerned. "Nothing left on that wellsite but hot metal."

"When did you guys arrive?"

"A few minutes after the Forest Service."

I nod, thinking about the Holder fire. Bradley must read my expression.

"We called ahead this time," he says. "They asked us to lend a hand."

Nice to see everyone working together, I tell him. He grins and we watch the fire for a few minutes. Harnack is silent and I wonder what he'll say if Castellino turns those X-ray eyes on him. Will he blurt out the whole muddled story, twist it around so he looks like a hero for Del? Or say nothing, in which case Castellino will probably never know we were there. Either way, it won't make a difference for Hutton and Dancey. I watch as the helicopter lands farther back along the trail, stirring up dust. A uniform steps out, crouches as the helicopter augers away. Then Deputy Sheriff Wayne Compton strides up the trail, green and officious-looking. I fade back as he passes, watch him talk with the Forest Service men. They nod their heads, move in separate directions. Compton watches the fire for a moment, a hand up to shield his face from the heat, then turns abruptly and sees me.

"Cassel — what the hell are you doing here?"

"I saw the smoke and came to help."

"Just can't stay away from disaster, can you?"

"Not when it involves fire. Was there anyone in the trailers?"

"I don't think so. I was in the area before it went, looking for those pot gardens. I flew over the camp a few times, didn't see anyone. No vehicles either, just that shot-up old car."

"The ignition source had to come from somewhere."

He nods, staring at the jet of flame shimmering ahead of us.

"Did you find the gardens?"

"No." He gives me a dubious look. I want to ask him where he searched, if he found anything at all — clearings, trails, any indication — but he walks away, talks with Bradley and his group. I watch the fountain of fire through the rifle sight of trees, cautiously edge closer, trying to see what's left of the trailers. Burning pine pop and crackle. Barely visible, metal frames waver in heat rippling off scorched earth. The roar of the fire is frighteningly familiar and suddenly I'm back in the fire shelter, surrounded by flame. I force myself to take a deep breath — my heart is surging — and fight the panic that threatens to engulf me. Slowly, the impression subsides and I'm back on the narrow trail, dizzy and faint from the spent adrenaline rush. I lean against a tree as the memory ebbs, watch the fire. My enemy gropes blindly outward, reaching for fuel. Always reaching. Forever hungry. Growing until someone stops it. I take another deep, steadying breath and make a short foray into the timber, to get a better idea of how quickly the fire is spreading. Smoke drifts among the trees, stinging my eyes. The pungent odour of burning pine fills my nostrils. Flame creeps through underbrush, snapping and sizzling. When I return to the trail, a lowboy bearing a dozer lumbers to a halt. Busloads of Forest Service firefighters are arriving — Brashaw's crew, now under the stern leadership of Brad Cooper. Harnack joins them, suits up.

A burning tree crashes across the trail, sending a shower of sparks into the surrounding underbrush, igniting smaller fires, soon to be consumed by the larger conflagration, and it comes to me as I watch — this fire is just a diversion. The pot is gone. The guilty are being punished. Soon, the squatters will be nothing but a memory. Fire will cleanse the area of clues, leaving only ash and twisted metal.

I can't help an ironic chuckle. I should have seen it coming.

The helicopter is circling again. On the ground behind me, men begin to unload equipment. Trucks jockey for position. Engines beep as they back down the trail. Harnack approaches, dressed and ready for action. "We've got to move these vehicles back," he says. "Your truck is in the way."

"You okay?"

He frowns, looking down, then nods.

"What are you going to tell them?"

"About what?" he says.

"Nothing. Go do your job."

Harnack grins, returns to his unit. I watch him string hose into the bush. They'll stay back from the blowout, establish a perimeter, control the wildfire. The blowout will be left to another group of heroes. Soon, water is flowing onto the fire as firefighters stand face-to-face with the beast. Farther down the trail a familiar figure walks through the smoke. It's Grey, in fire gear and hard hat.

"Cassel," he says as he approaches. "Just can't stay away, can you?"

I shake my head, point. "There's a lot of understory on the north side —"

"But you'll have to," he says, watching me. "Stay away, that is."

Our eyes meet and a look of sorrow crosses his face. I nod, to show I understand.

"It would be best if you cleared the area. Before the media arrive."

I'm about to say something, apologize maybe, when his belt radio blares. He snatches it out of its holster. I hear him swear, then he comes over, snapping his radio back into place. "You better get going."

"What's happened?"

"We've got another damn fire."

18

DEL IS WAITING at the motel when I get back to town. She's been busy. The desk is covered with strips of shredded newspaper, like a gerbil has been making a nest. "What took you so long?" she says, raking a hand through her hair. "Where's Lyle?"

"Lyle is fine," I say, closing the door.

She stares at me like I'm crazy. "So where is he?"

"Working. There's another fire by the canyon."

For a moment she just stands there, her hand in her hair, trying to connect the dots. She can't and sits on the edge of the bed, looking at me, her hands in her lap. She looks confused and distraught, but I've begun to suspect she's good at looking whichever way best suits her need.

"The well at the squatters' camp blew out."

"What?" she says, frowning.

"Erwin and his buddies had lines tapped into an old wellhead. One must have been leaking."

Her frown intensifies. "Is anyone hurt?"

I shake my head. "I don't think so. The camp seems to have been deserted."

"Good," she says slowly. "That's good. But how did the meet go?"

"Not so good," I say, tossing my jacket over the back of a chair, scooping the gerbil strippings into a nearby wastebasket. I'm not in a hurry to talk about the meet because I'm not yet sure what I want to say. Del sits tensely on the edge of the bed, watching me. Waiting. "Well — tell me, for Christ's sakes," she says impatiently. "Were they there? Did you give them the diary? What happened?"

"Yeah — they were there."

"Was Lyle okay?" She's kneading the bed sheets.

"He was a little freaked out, but he was fine."

"And you gave them the diary?"

I nod.

"So what didn't work out so well?"

I hesitate, take a deep breath. I might as well tell her. Better she hears it from me, rather than Castellino. "They liked the diary — real top-notch work — but they weren't so keen on letting Lyle and me go. In fact, they had a little surprise ready for us."

"That's what I was afraid of," Del says, almost in a whisper.

I wait, to see if there's anything she'd like to add, but she just watches me.

"They were going to kill us, Del, just like you suspected, but the strangest thing happened."

I pause, watching her face. Her expression doesn't change. She's very good.

"Erwin and his buddies came along and saved us. It was amazing."

"Erwin?" she says, looking perplexed.

"Yeah — Erwin, and a few friends. They must have been following me, or Hutton, because they knew where we were. They set off the wellhead as a diversion, then swooped in and rescued Lyle and me. Very coordinated. Like a military operation."

Del manages to look stunned. "That's incredible. Have you told the police?"

"Not yet," I say, shaking my head.

There's a long moment as Del and I watch each other. I try not to betray the mix of feelings churning inside. Anger at her betrayal — at being used. Gratitude for being rescued. Annoyance that we have to play these games. Sorrow for everything lost.

"What happened after they rescued you?" she says, her voice catching just slightly.

"I don't know. I didn't hang around."

She nods, waiting anxiously. She knows there's more.

"I think you can bring Melissa home," I say, handing her the revolver.

There's a brief hesitation, then she lets out a sigh, sags a little. "Thank God."

It's done and I don't want to prolong our goodbye. There are a few things I have to do, I tell her. A few loose ends. She catches my meaning, excuses herself, tucking the revolver under her jacket and saying she has to get back to the greenhouse. Please stop by for supper. About six. I thank her for the invitation. Then I'm alone, staring at the phone. I wait a few minutes, until my pulse returns to something resembling normal, then rummage in the small trash can on the floor, pull out the strips of newspaper. At the bottom is a wrinkled nugget of a different kind of paper and I open it up, smooth it out. It's from the pad next to the phone, has the motel logo in one corner. It's been shaded grey with a pencil, like a kid taking a rubbing off a coin, but the message is more specific: directions to the meet. I shake my head. Another thing I should have seen coming. Del wanted me to continue investigating for a reason. She was the one who gave the gun back to Erwin. She kept him at the greenhouse overnight, worked out the details. She played me like a pro.

I flush the note down the toilet, along with most of the pad, tearing the sheets off one at a time, watching them swirl away. Del has her revenge and, in a way, so do I. But it doesn't feel like much. I pull a phone book from a drawer in the table, look up travel agencies. There's a flight tomorrow afternoon, at twelve thirty, leaving from Missoula. I book a seat, eat supper alone.

I sleep late the next morning, ignore the phone. Breakfast is a gourmet affair involving a fist full of coins and a vending machine. Home seems achingly far away. I can't wait to see my sister Cindy and her kids. But my simple morning is interrupted when Deputy Sheriff Wayne Compton calls, offering me a ride to the ranger station. I'm not keen on another tour, but participation is mandatory. Castellino, Batiste, and Haines are in a room downstairs, scowling over a table covered with photographs and reports.

"Cassel," Castellino says dryly. "Glad you could make it."

"I had a good chauffeur."

"You weren't going to leave without saying goodbye, were you?"

The men look haggard. Castellino is in jeans and a rumpled shirt, stained dark with sweat under his arms. Batiste is sullen and stoop-shouldered. Haines has bags under his eyes, hair plastered to his sweaty scalp. They're all grubby and unshaven. "We had a bit of an interesting night," says Batiste, waving at the table. "You wouldn't know anything about that, would you?"

I move closer, take a look. The photos on the table are the usual ash and blackened bits of wood. Grids and measurements. Burned-out truck. But there's something else here that makes me shudder — shots of a corpse, mummified to charcoal. Black on black. I think of Brashaw and my heart races.

"You all right?" says Castellino. "You look a little flushed."

"Fine," I mumble, staring at the mummy.

"You sure? You look like maybe you're going to faint."

I force myself to look away from the horrifying images. "Who is that?"

"Interesting question," says Castellino. "Glad you asked. Would you like to guess?"

I wait, wondering if it's Hutton or Dancey, and what happened to the other.

"No guesses?" Castellino walks around the table, picking up photos and offering them to me. Dropping them when I don't move. "Pity," he says. "Because I'm willing to bet you have a pretty good idea." When

I don't bite, he drops the last photo, looking disgusted. "Let me give you a clue. Male. Early forties. Worked for the Carson Lake Volunteer Fire Department. Still don't know?"

"Hutton?"

"Yes!" He slaps the table hard enough several pictures drift away. "Telford Hutton."

"Give the man a prize," mutters Batiste.

"What happened?"

"What indeed?" says Castellino, walking to the far side of the table, so he can stare at me across the grisly expanse of photographs. He seems a little melodramatic — a little manic — but that's what you get from long hours and too much coffee. "Well, so far as we can tell, Mr. Hutton was trapped in a burning structure outside of town. Exactly how he came to be there is a matter of some conjecture. When was the last time you saw him?"

"A few days ago, at the fire station."

Batiste raises an eyebrow. "What were you doing at the fire station?"

"You know very well what I was doing," I tell them, not bothering to keep the irritation from my voice. "I told you everything when we set up the sting at the grocery store. I was looking for some information on how the VFD were dispatched to the Holder fire."

"Ah, yes — the sting," Castellino says, giving me a humourless smile.

"You mentioned a structure," I say. "This didn't happen at the wellhead fire?"

Haines gives me a thoughtful frown. "No, this was an old house."

"Was anyone injured at the wellhead fire?"

"It appears the camp was empty," says Castellino. "Which I find interesting."

"Empty," I echo. "You're sure?"

"Reasonably. The vehicles were gone and the trailers appear to have been vacant."

I think again about the children. "That's a relief."

"Indeed," says Castellino. "Another interesting thing — there was no pot in the forest, none that we've found yet anyway, although we've found some interesting trails and a few unmistakable indications." He pauses significantly. "You know what I think, Mr. Cassel?"

I shrug — it's best never to answer a question like that.

Castellino wags a stubby finger at me. "I think you told these pot growers your suspicions regarding Mr. Hutton and his associate. They pulled up their crop and staged both of these fires, trapping the men in an old house and using the wellhead fire as a diversion."

He gives me an intent look, waiting for a reaction.

"I didn't tell them anything," I say truthfully.

"Really. When was the last time you saw them?"

"Days ago. I talked with one of them — a young guy with heavy sideburns — hoping he might give me some insight as to why someone would want to burn out the valley, but he wasn't very co-operative."

Batiste glances at Castellino. "Matches the description from the break-in."

Castellino nods. "I've seen him around. Not lately though. What's his name?"

"Erwin," I say. "Erwin Smith."

"Ah, yes," Haines mutters. "The ubiquitous Smith family."

"You did more than talk with him," says Castellino. "It seems the two of you were getting pretty chummy. You were seen driving around with him. Visiting the motel clerk."

He pauses, watching me carefully. "You sure you didn't visit our cabin together as well?"

"I was trying to work with him," I say, ignoring the question. "I thought I might be able to make some headway before the squatters became nervous and pulled up stakes. It didn't seem likely they would talk to anyone in law enforcement, and they seemed to trust me."

"Really?" says Batiste. "Why would they do that?"

"Because of what happened on the fire."

There's an uncomfortable silence. I avoid glancing at the photos on the table.

"What did you and Mr. Smith talk about?"

"Not much. He had no idea who was after his pot."

Castellino smiles, without much humour. "But you did, didn't you, Mr. Cassel? You were certain enough that Telford Hutton was responsible for the fire that you set up that little *Gong Show* at the grocery store. You sure you didn't let Mr. Smith in on your plans?"

I shake my head. "We parted ways long before that."

"Did you discuss Karalee Smith?"

"He confirmed she was his sister."

"That's it?" says Batiste. "He didn't tell you anything else?"

"No." I glance at my watch. I'm missing my plane. "What happened to the other guy?"

Castellino gives me a crafty, appreciative look. I think he was testing me, trying to trick me into revealing that I knew there was more than one man involved in the house fire, but he let it slip, and I pretend I just caught it. "At the house fire?" I prompt. "You mentioned an associate of Hutton's."

"Yes. Henry Dancey — your friend from the grocery store."

"What happened to him?"

"Mr. Dancey was rather badly burned," says Batiste.

I nod thoughtfully, wondering if Erwin intended to let him live.

"So, you haven't seen these squatters in the past few days?" says Castellino, trying again.

I shake my head. "Did you talk to Dancey?"

The three men exchange glances and I wonder if Dancey really did survive, or if they're stringing me along, waiting for me to slip up, but Castellino nods, his eyebrows tented together, as if he can't believe he's telling me this — doing me some sort of favour. "Dancey claims they got an anonymous tip that some kids were going to burn the place down, so they went for a look. No kids visible when they arrived, but they could smell smoke, so they went in. He claims they fell through a weak spot in the floor, into an old cellar. Before they could get out, the house went up like tinder."

I think of Dancey, pouring diesel.

"Who set the fire?"

"We're not sure," says Haines.

I glance at the pictures. "How did Dancey survive?"

"He must have pulled himself out. We found him on the ground, about forty yards away."

"Do you believe him?"

Castellino sighs. "What I believe is irrelevant — it's what I can prove. Both Hutton and Dancey weren't wearing fire gear when they were found at the fire. Nor did they bring any with them. They didn't record their trip in the dispatch log at the fire station and they didn't call 911, like they're supposed to. Seems a little odd, don't you think?"

I wait, keeping my expression carefully neutral.

"If they weren't there on a fire call, it was something else," says Batiste.

Castellino crosses his arms. "What do you think, Mr. Cassel?"

"I think Hutton and Dancey crossed the wrong kind of people, and it caught up with them."

Castellino watches me a moment longer, waiting for something more. I hold his X-ray gaze as long as I can, hoping he can't read my thoughts, then drop my gaze to the mosaic of photos on the table. Greed and revenge, reduced to ash. When I glance up, Batiste, Castellino, and Haines seem lost in thought. The confrontational tension is gone from the room. They know I was at the wellhead fire before the other fire was reported, and I have no revelations to offer.

"Do you have any leads?" I ask. "Do you know who these squatters are?"

"The squatters," Castellino says wistfully. "They're a mystery, these invisible people. No social security number. No driver's licence. Constantly mobile. Even Karalee Smith wasn't using her real name," he says, looking at me. "We checked back through her correspondence school, thinking she'd want a diploma in her own name, but she was operating under a false identity. The real Karalee Smith died in Minnesota, at two months of age, back in 1983."

"So they've just vanished? You have no idea who they are, or where they've gone?"

"We're doing roadside checks," says Batiste. "But so far, we're drawing a blank."

Perfectly orchestrated, I'm thinking. Erwin. Del. Even Harnack had a role to play. And me — the biggest fool of all, blindly charging ahead, believing I might make a difference. I almost chuckle, but Castellino and Batiste are giving me strange looks.

"What is it, Cassel?"

"A licence plate number," I say. "From Erwin's truck."

I concentrate, trying to remember, and they perk up. No harm in giving them the only real scrap of information I have on Erwin's identity — although even that is probably just a front. I dredge up the number from my trip to Missoula tailing the old truck, and Batiste hurries out of the room to use Compton's computer. He's back in minutes and hands a print out to Castellino.

"Typical," Castellino mutters, frowning. "Plate was stolen from a repair shop in Florida."

"Shit," mumbles Haines.

I wait a minute, but no further comment is forthcoming. "Can I go now?"

Castellino gives me a long look before answering. The look on his face — he doesn't quite believe I've told him everything, but he can't think of a way to keep me here. He nods and I wish them luck, take my leave, head up the stairs, and walk through a forest of cubicles, uniformed men and women working at their desks. A few stop what they're doing and watch me pass. In their eyes, I'll always be the stranger who screwed up, got one of their own killed. I hurry through but Grey intercepts me as I pass his office.

"Cassel! Hold up a second." He's loud enough I can't pretend I didn't hear him. "You all done here?" he says, scrutinizing me.

"Yeah. Back to Canada, with my tail between my legs."

His moustache twitches and he gives me his best chief ranger look. "Don't leave here thinking that," he says, standing in the hall. "This is a tough occupation and you did your best. You went through something we all dread, and came out the other side."

"Thanks," I say, not very convincingly.

"And," he says, lowering his voice, "I just want you to know, no matter how things turned out, that I appreciate your sticking around and trying to help on this thing. Most guys would have just packed their bedrolls and ran for the hills."

I nod, looking at the floor. He asks me how I'm getting home. I tell him I've booked a flight for tomorrow — I've missed my chance today. I'll be heading to Missoula tonight, to make sure I'll be on time, for a change. He tells me he's headed there himself — he'll give me a ride. Seems like a good way to save an expensive cab fare and we agree to meet at the motel later and retrieve my luggage. I finally manage to get out of the ranger station, and I stand in the baking heat of the parking lot, as it occurs to me I'm miles from town without a ride. I consider asking Grey, or Compton, but don't particularly want to go inside again, so instead hitch a ride with a local rancher. An old guy with a big hat, he doesn't say more than two words, which suits me fine — I've got more than enough to think about. By the time we reach town, I know what I have to do, and head for the hospital.

Dancey is the only customer in ICU, a small, three-bed ward just off Emergency. He's in an isolation tent — a plastic shroud hung around the bed to ward off bacteria — and is heavily bandaged. I have to check his chart to make sure it's really him. Half his face is all that is visible and, despite what he's done, I can't help feeling sorry for him; the possibility of burns like these haunt every firefighter. He's sleeping, or unconscious, and I watch him through the plastic for a few minutes, listening to the beep and sigh of life support. I want to ask him about the Holder fire. About Karalee Smith. I want to hear him explain why, but he's beyond reach — another victim of the curse.

"Dancey," I say quietly. Nothing. Then a little more loudly.

Movement behind the eyelid. I lean closer — as close as the shroud will allow.

"Can you hear me, Dancey?"

The eye struggles, slowly opens. It's disconcerting, like watching a corpse return to life.

"Can you talk? Concentrate, this is important."

The eye wanders, fixes on me. He moans and the rhythm on the heart rate monitor intensifies. There's a long silent pause. Beneath the edge of the bandages covering half his face, there's a tube going into his mouth. He talked to the police, but that was before they pumped him full of narcotics. And the tube won't help. He might not be able to speak — but I'm willing to bet he can hear me.

"I'm going to ask you a few questions. Blink once for yes, twice for no."

He blinks twice before I ask the first question.

"Did you start the fire in the canyon?"

Nothing. Then a hoarse whisper. "Fuck you ..."

I stand up, shocked. Half-dead and helpless, and still he gives me attitude. Then it occurs to me that he can talk, although with considerable effort. I hear voices in the hall as two nurses walk past. I'll have to make this quick, so I pull open the plastic shroud. "Listen Dancey," I say, leaning close, looking him in the eye, "I know what you told the sheriff, but it's just the three of us here now — you, me, and life support. I want a few answers, for my own peace of mind. Then, if you're lucky, you'll never see me again. Did you start the fire in the canyon?"

A long pause. Dancey turns his head slightly, toward the battery of equipment next to his bed, then looks at me. "Hutton," he whispers.

"It was for the pot, wasn't it?"

A single blink.

"And the waitress?"

A longer pause. His heart rate changes on the monitor again, a little faster, and he swallows painfully. His eye wells up. A tear trickles down his cheek. "Hutton," he repeats in a faint breath.

"It was all Hutton, was it?" I say angrily. "You had nothing to do with it?"

"Had to," he sighs. "The fire. Murder."

So there it is — the truth, as I had suspected. They murdered Karalee because of the runaway on the Holder fire, which killed Brashaw. They were covering their tracks. If no one had died on the Holder fire then Karalee would still be alive. I stand up, a little faint, my anger displaced by a sickening feeling of guilt. One last question comes to mind.

"You tried to kill me too, by cutting the brakes on my truck."

Dancey stares at me, then blinks — twice.

A sharp voice behind me. "What are you doing?"

I turn. A nurse stands just inside a closing door, tray in hand. I look at Dancey. The shroud hangs open. "He was trying to say something," I mumble. "I couldn't hear —"

"Well, you should have called," says the nurse, her expression changing from shock to annoyance. She sets aside the tray, quickly checks on Dancey, shooing me out of the way. I step back, glancing toward the door. "You shouldn't be here," she says over her shoulder. "He could get infected."

"I'm sorry. I just wanted to see how he was doing."

"We have procedures to follow," she says, closing the shroud. "For the safety of the patient." She checks the instrumentation, making nervous, clucking sounds, then looks over at me, her expression softening slightly. "I'm sorry — this must be hard for you."

"Is he going to be okay?"

The nurse glances toward Dancey, leads me out of the room, into the hallway.

"We're not sure yet," she says in muted tones. "He's pretty badly burned and there are a lot of unknowns. Infection is always a serious threat. But he's starting to stabilize enough that we can move him to Missoula, where they have a better burn facility." She hesitates. "Who did you say you were?"

"Just a fellow firefighter."

She smiles, pats me on the shoulder. "You're all such heroes. Keep up the good work."

My heart is pounding as I leave the hospital. Seeing Dancey burned like that. Admitting they killed Karalee. Confirmation that I was the catalyst for these events. And then the nurse, saying we're all heroes. I stand in the parking lot in front of Emergency, cloaked in sweat and breathing hard. I want to leave this place so badly I nearly call a cab, head straight for Missoula, but I think of Grey; I haven't yet thanked him for taking care of the paperwork at the hospital, after I totalled the Cornbinder. I walk in the blistering heat to the motel, where my luggage is waiting, stowed at the checkout counter. Grey shows up at half past six, parks his green truck in front of the small motel office. I grab my luggage, toss the bags into the back of the truck, climb in without saying anything.

We turn left onto the highway — headed north, instead of south toward Missoula. I assume Grey plans to stop for gas, but we pass the Conoco. I watch the church slide past at the north end of town.

"Isn't Missoula in the other direction?"

"Shortcut," says Grey. But he's grinning.

"Okay — I'll bite. What's going on?"

Grey shrugs. "Just a little barbecue at the greenhouse. Del made me promise to stop by with you. Threatened me with bodily harm if I didn't." He looks a little sheepish. "I never argue with a redhead."

I nod, with a fleeting urge to decline, but it seems best to go with the plan. We rattle up the gravel road to the greenhouse and I take the opportunity to thank Grey for his generosity at the hospital. It wasn't something he had to do — I wasn't employed by the Forest Service when I had the accident. He tells me not to worry about it. The parking lot at the greenhouse is crammed. We squeeze in next to a row of fruit bushes. Melissa is playing at one of the cribs filled with aquatic plants, up to her armpits in water.

"Uncle Porter!"

She runs over, gives my leg a wet hug. "I was on holiday," she says, beaming.

"Good for you. Did you have fun?"

She assures me she did.

Aunt Gertie comes out of the main building, looking around. "There you are," she says, picking up Melissa. "Mommy needs your help."

I follow them inside, past rows of hanging flower baskets and towering tomatoes, loaded with ripening fruit. Men and women wander among the aisles, chatting, carrying trays of cold cuts and crackers. Someone presses a beer into my hand. Outside, Del is talking to an old guy with a spatula in his hand. He's supervising a large, home-built barbecue and is wearing an apron with a picture of a flaming steak. Del sees me, thanks me for coming, asks if she can get me anything.

I show her the beer, tell her I'm fine.

"Are you, really?" she says, meeting my eye.

"I'm working on it."

She nods, tells me we'll talk later — she still has a hundred things to do. I wander off among the vegetables, thinking about marijuana. So much trouble over a plant. The firefighters arrive in their crew bus, still in yellow fire shirts, green pants, and White's fire boots. They're grimy, covered with soot, but joking and talking as they trickle into the greenhouse, comparing notes on the day's effort. I wait as they wash up, then mingle and ask them how the fire is going. The wellhead has been capped and the fire is contained at seventy acres. Dozerline around everything; should be mopping up in a few days.

"What about you?" says Cooper, sitting on a picnic table. "What have you been up to?"

Mopping up a different fire, I tell him.

Steaks are flopped onto the grill and the air fills with tantalizing odours. Garlic. Roasting meat. Potato salad. Grey lugs a keg of beer out of a van and offers me the privilege of tapping, drawing the first mug. I play bartender for a while. Finally, when everyone has a steak on their plate, Del takes a seat beside me. "I thought it would be nice to have a barbecue," she says. "Like BB used to."

I nod and for a few minutes we eat in silence.

"You see that chair over there?" she says, pointing with a fork.

I follow her direction. It's a massive wooden chair, built of logs; it looks like a medieval throne. That's BB's chair, she says. He'd sit there during these barbecues, watching his flock — it's how he got his nickname: BB the King. Now it's empty. As we watch, Cooper wanders past, holding a heavily loaded paper plate, looking for a seat. He's out of luck — the throne is the only vacant spot. He glances around, sees Del watching. She nods, waves for him to sit down. Cooper hesitates, but then acknowledges the honour with an abashed nod, and sits primly on the edge of the big chair. Del sees I'm watching her.

"Life goes on," she says, smiling wistfully.

She finishes her meal — she's just having salad and a baked potato — and moves off toward the grill, checking on the steaks. Checking to make sure everyone has enough to eat and is having a good time. Harnack is at the grill now, wearing the apron. He says something to Del and she laughs. He pulls her close, whispers in her ear. The firefighter beside me at the picnic table stiffens.

"I can't believe he's moving in on her again."

It's Phil, the guy with the bear claw necklace. He's cutting his steak with a Bowie knife. "After they broke up," says Phil, pointing his knife toward Harnack, "he followed her around for weeks. BB finally had to give him a talking to, to get him to lay off. Now he's in there again, like a dirty shirt. The old man would be turning in his grave."

I watch Harnack for a minute. Del pulls away from him and he reaches for her again. When she evades him, he forces a laugh — I can hear it all the way over here — but he looks a bit put off. Del waves at him, pretending it's a game, and moves into the crowd. As Harnack turns back to the grill, stabbing at the steaks with a pair of tongs, I remember what Del told me.

"I can handle Lyle Harnack."

But I wonder — who benefited most from BB's death? Harnack is the only clear winner here. With BB out of the picture he has a clear shot at Del once again. He had the means, motive, and opportunity. He knew Brashaw was on the ridge — just as any firefighter could have known. He had the training to set the fatal blaze. If he could get away from his crew long enough, he'd certainly have had the opportunity. It would be the perfect crime — an arson within an arson. Who would suspect? And once the deed had been done, Harnack followed me around claiming he wanted to help me investigate, no doubt to keep tabs on the investigation.

I've lost my appetite and sit frowning over my food, watching Lyle Harnack flip steaks. If he set the fire outside the dozerline — the fire that killed Bert Brashaw and nearly killed me — then he's responsible for everything that happened after as well. His actions led to the death of Karalee Smith — not mine. I take a sip of beer without tasting it, watching Harnack.

"Phil, can I ask you something?"

"Yeah — sure," says Phil, around a mouthful of steak. "What's up?"

"On the canyon fire, just before the blow-up, do you know where Harnack was?"

Phil thinks, chewing vigorously. "Can't say. Wasn't with me."

"Do you think anyone knows where he was?"

Phil turns in his seat, giving me a troubled look. "Why?"

I don't answer and Phil's expression turns ugly.

"Can you ask around?" I say. "Discretely?"

Phil pushes away his plate, sheaths his knife. "You got it."

Phil is gone for half an hour. My steak is cold and my beer is warm, but I barely notice, thinking about Harnack and BB and Karalee. Trying to convince myself I'm way off base. But I can't. I keep picturing Henry Dancey, burned and bandaged. Henry Dancey when I asked him about the brakes on the Cornbinder. He didn't know what I was talking about. Phil returns and heaves himself onto the seat next to me, breathing beer and garlic in my face.

"No one seems to remember," he says.

"No one saw him right before the blow-up was reported?"

Phil shakes his head. It could mean Harnack was going for some hose, or scouting ahead — or even just in the bushes relieving himself. Or it could mean Harnack is Brashaw's killer.

I thank Phil, start to leave. He grabs my arm.

"What are you gonna do?" he whispers hoarsely.

"Nothing," I say. "Just talk to him."

"You need help?"

I shake my head — this is something I need to do alone — and I find Del. She's helping Melissa load her plate with cake and cookies. I wait until she's done, pull her aside.

"I need a favour, Del."

"Sure," she says, brushing back her hair. "What's up?"

"I need you to invite Lyle for a little dip in the hot tub."

"What?" Her expression darkens.

"Just invite him. Tell him to wait a few minutes, then to meet you there."

Del frowns, looking at me suspiciously. "What are you up to?"

"I just need to talk to him. Alone. I'll tell you later."

Del hesitates, glancing toward Harnack, then nods. I watch her talk to him — the way he brushes his hand against her thigh. Then she wanders away, in the direction of the little building over the hot spring. I follow, taking a circuitous route through the greenhouses, meet Del going the other direction. She gives me a look — I'd better explain later — as she brushes past. I crouch inside the dark building, moist and heady with the vapour of sulphur and minerals. A few minutes later the door opens, casting a shaft of light across the steaming water, and Harnack enters.

"Del?" he says, standing by the door, peering over the wooden tub.

I wait. He closes the door, reaches for the light. A single bulb casts weak illumination in the steamy room. Harnack frowns as I stand; he's confused. "What are you doing here?"

"We need to talk, Lyle."

He glances around, as if Del might be hiding among the tools. "No we don't."

"She's not coming, Lyle."

He frowns a little harder, trying to decide what to do. I charge ahead, while he's still off-balance.

"Was it really worth it? Starting that fire? Killing her father?"

Harnack looks at me, shocked — not the sort of shock you see when someone is startled by the unexpected, but a deeper, guilt-ridden sort of shock. His expression changes quickly, covered with a hastily man-ufactured anger, but I've seen what I came to see.

"What the hell are you talking about?"

"You knew Brashaw was on the ridge," I say, advancing on him, forcing him back, away from the door. He's not going anywhere until I get the answers I need. Until he confesses. "You knew I was there too, but that didn't matter. You wanted Del so badly you were willing to kill to get her, so what was an extra body?"

Harnack is shaking his head, a panicky look in his eye. "You're crazy."

"Am I, Lyle? A perfect little crime — the secondary fire is put down to unpredictable winds at the canyon mouth. The real arsonist takes the blame. But there was a bit of a complication."

Harnack is at the far side of the big octagonal tub, bracing himself against the cedar boards like a kid in a game of tag, ready to make a run for it, but he's trapped and knows it, so he tries to talk his way out of the corner. "If you think I started the fire that killed BB, you're nuts," he says, his voice wavering, nearly choked with fear. "I was fighting that fire. I was trying to put it out."

"Where were you, Lyle, right before the blow-up?"

"I was ... going to get some hose. We needed another length."

"Bullshit!"

Harnack cringes, but quickly rallies, pointing a finger at me. "You better be careful what you say, accusing people. I've got rights, you know. I'll sue your ass."

"You'll sue me?" I can't help chuckling.

"Damn right." Harnack stands, sensing victory.

"Well, before you sue me, Lyle, let me tell you what your little fire did. It not only killed Bert Brashaw, and nearly me — it caused the real arsonists more than a little anguish. So much anguish, in fact, that they killed Karalee Smith, thinking they might go to jail for Brashaw's death. For a crime you committed, Lyle. Of course, you know all of this. You're getting mileage out of it."

"Fuck you," he says. "I've had enough of this bullshit."

But he doesn't move toward the door.

"And now the real arsonist is dead, which doesn't break me up much, but here's the kicker Lyle — you're responsible for three deaths. How do you think the cops are going to feel about that?"

Harnack gives me a nervous smile — false bravado. "You don't have any evidence."

"What do you think Del will say when she learns you killed her father?"

For a few seconds, Lyle just stares at me. It never occurred to him that Del could find out — that even without evidence, all he's worked for could be lost. The nervous, fight-or-flight look is replaced with cold, intense hatred. "You're not going to do that," he says, coming around the tub. Coming at me. It's a small building and I have about three seconds to decide what to do.

"You should already be dead," he says.

When he grabs a shovel propped against the wall, I take a step back, reach for the door, but his swing hits me in the shoulder and I stumble backward, pinning the door shut with the weight of my body. I manage to raise an arm to counter the second blow. The force nearly breaks bone and I cringe away, instinctively holding the injured limb close to my body, which is a mistake. The third blow is wild but glances off the door, hitting me in the temple, and I go down amid a shower of bright lights.

A hollow voice. "Slipped and hit his head ..."

Then movement, reeling, like I'm drunk, and hot water in my face, my ears, my mouth. I try to scream, swallow more water and panic takes hold. He's bigger than me, has me pinned against the side of the tub — I can feel the hard line of the wooden rim against my midsection — my head and shoulders underwater. I scramble, chest heaving, frantically searching for something to push against, touch the bench in the water, too far down to do any good, try to trace the wall of the tub up to the edge, but there's nothing. It feels like a car is parked on my back. The heat makes it worse.

Spots, grey against black.

I'm going to pass out ...

Have to breathe ...

Water, hot in my mouth, filling my nose, my sinuses. A buzzing in my ears. Blackness. I'm falling, turning, spinning. Cindy. Mom and Dad. Pressure on my chest.

Gone. All for nothing ...

Then I cough, violently, water bursting from nose and mouth. It hurts. I'm on my side, retching. A blur of colours. A face, close by. Lips over mine, pushing air into my lungs. Another spasm of water and pain and I can breath. Long hair tickling my face. It's Telson.

Oh my God — it's Telson.

For a minute, I just lie there, my chest heaving, staring into Telson's beautiful face. Maybe I died and this is a mirage, just a last flickering memory.

"How do you feel, Porter? Can you talk?"

I spit a little more water. "How — how did you get here?"

"Pontiac," she says.

For a moment she looks intensely serious and suddenly we both laugh, freed from the panic of near death. The laughter dies quickly as I remember Harnack. Despite Telson's protest, I struggle to my feet, looking wildly around, expecting Harnack will be waiting, hiding in the shadows. Then I see him, sprawled face down on the floor next to the tub, a bloody spot on the back of his head, the shovel lying close by. For a moment we both stare at the prone form.

"I think you killed him."

"Maybe," says Telson, kneeling at his side. I pick up the shovel, hold it ready, just in case.

"No," she says, glancing up at me. "He's still alive."

Telson uses her cellphone to call 911 while I stand over Harnack, waiting for him to move, to stand and come at me again. But he's out for the count.

"Why are you here?" I ask again.

Telson gives me a brief, ironic smile. "I could ask you the same thing."

I nod, feeling like a heel.

"I'm here," she says pointedly, "because I heard about the fires."

"You're here for work? As a reporter?"

"Should there be another reason?"

I frown, not sure how to respond to her loaded question. Are we done?

"I don't care why you're here," I say, glancing down at Harnack. "I'm just glad you came."

As we watch, Harnack moans, lifts his head a little.

"Me too," says Telson. "Now we're even."

There's a knock on the door — it's Phil, Cooper, and most of the rest of the crew. They've been talking about Harnack, explains Cooper, discussing my suspicions, and they want to talk to him. They look to be in a lynching mood, so I explain that Harnack is indisposed at the moment, open the door enough that Cooper can see Harnack lying in the dirt. I need Harnack in one piece, so he can explain to Castellino what really happened that day on the ridge. Cooper and company don't budge. Thankfully, we're rescued by the EMTs, who bundle Harnack into an ambulance. I'm bandaged; I have a nasty cut on my temple, an impressive swelling on my forearm. The EMTs usher me into the ambulance, where I sit on a vinyl bench, look down at Harnack strapped to a spine board. Then we're rolling, down the winding drive. A procession of vehicles follow, intercepted on the main road by a sheriff's black-and-white SUV. Harnack moans again, tries to lift his head but finds he's strapped down, in a cervical collar. An EMT, a young bald guy sitting across from me, leans over to check on Harnack.

"Just relax. You're in an ambulance, headed to the hospital."

Harnack blinks, looks a little confused. I lean over him, so he can see me.

"Hi, Lyle."

His eyes widen — both equally responsive to panic. "What are you doing here?"

"Just hitching a ride," I say, touching the bandage on the side of my head. The EMT watches both of us, frowning, no doubt wondering about the wisdom of conveying combatants simultaneously. "Don't worry," I assure him. "I don't think he'll attack again."

The EMT sits back but doesn't look particularly reassured.

"Soon, it'll be time to talk," I say to Harnack. "Time to come clean."

Harnack swivels his eyes toward the EMT. "I don't know what you're talking about."

I crouch, slowly, so the EMT knows I'm not doing anything threatening, whisper in Lyle's ear. His eyes widen. He's silent for a few minutes, then whispers a single word: "Okay."

Soon we're in town, backing into the ambulance bay at Emergency.

Harnack is rolled out, rushed away. I watch the ward doors swing shut. Then someone taps me on the shoulder. It's Castellino.

"We need to talk."

I nod. Finally, I have something to tell him.

EPILOGUE

●

WE MEET AT the Filling Station — Del, Telson, and I. We're seated at one of the wooden tables, close to a window. I'm on a side by myself, my arm in a sling. Telson and Del are on the other side. A waitress comes — the same one that requested my autograph — and starts to tell us the specials.

"No thanks," Telson says crisply. "We won't be here long."

"Just coffees," I tell her.

Coffee is poured in silence. Telson is still pissed that I lied to her. I struggle to find a way to break the ice and smooth things over. When the waitress leaves, I nervously clear my throat. "I thought it would be a good idea to get together, so we could talk about what happened."

"This should be interesting," says Telson, stirring her coffee.

"I lied to you, Christina, and I'm sorry, but there was a very good reason."

"Yeah, you've got the hots for Red over there."

I glance over at Del, with her rusty red hair.

"No, Christina, that's not it."

"Really?" She raises an eyebrow.

"Of course not. That's silly —"

"Silly?" She glares at me. "You two were naked together in the hot tub."

"We weren't naked. I had just been to the squatters' ..."

I'm stumbling badly. Bewildered, I start over.

"Look, Christina, the squatters were putting pressure on me to find Karalee's killer. I was worried what might happen if I didn't deliver. That's why we sent Melissa away —"

"You're comparing me to a child?" says Telson.

"I'm saying I wanted you safe. The squatters had someone following you. They showed me a picture of you, taken in front of the motel. They were going to come after you if anything happened to their pot gardens. They were using you as insurance."

"I thought you said it was because they wanted you to find Karalee's killer."

"Yes — that too. That was their first demand. They gave me three days."

Telson stares at me. "Well, which is it Porter?"

"It's both," I say, wishing this were less complicated.

Telson looks disgusted. "You can't even get your stories straight."

She pushes back her chair, reaches for her coat.

"Listen to me, Christina. I did it because I care about you."

"You lied," she says, giving me a murderous look. "Goodbye, Porter."

"No," I whisper, but it's too late. I've lost her. I cover my face, try to regain my composure.

Suddenly, both women are laughing. Then it dawns on me.

"Okay ... okay ... you got me."

Telson sits down, still laughing. "You should have seen the look on your face."

Both women laugh again, attracting the attention of the other patrons. I feel my face fill with blood, hot and glowing. Telson points out that I'm blushing and I blush harder, until I'm beet red. It's not the most masculine reaction and I shield my face, glare out the window.

"You deserve it," says Telson.

I nod, embarrassed but too weak with relief to be angry. "How did you know?"

"Del called me," Telson says. "Told me everything, invited me to the party."

"You knew when you got there?"

Telson nods. "But I had to teach you a lesson."

"Lucky for me you did."

There's a lull as we bask in a sense of relief and renewed companionship.

Telson looks at me. "There's just one thing I don't understand. Lyle admitted that he started the fire that killed Del's father. Basically, he confessed to premeditated murder. It's all over the news. He'll probably get a life sentence. Why would he confess if there isn't any evidence?"

I shrug. "Maybe he couldn't live with his conscience."

Both women clearly do not believe this. The waitress rolls past again, asking if we need anything. Telson requests a menu. We'll stay for lunch. I use the opportunity to slip away to the washroom, where I pull a piece of paper from my back pocket. It's the bill from the motel. I glance at it once more — at the service charge for the phone call I didn't make, the night I went to rescue Lyle. It didn't take long to figure out the call was made by Del. When I tried the number at a pay phone, Erwin answered. I didn't say anything, just hung up, but that number came in handy once more. I whispered it into Lyle's ear, as he lay on the gurney in the ambulance, gave him a simple choice. He could talk, or I could call Erwin and explain that Lyle was really the one to blame for the death of his sister.

Lyle wisely opted for the first choice.

I ponder the motel bill a moment longer. I could use it to confront Del about how she played me, or I could turn it over to the cops, so they could track down Erwin. But there doesn't seem to be much point. The guilty have been punished. Anything more is just paperwork. I crumple the motel bill into a little ball, toss it into the trash, and return to the table. Telson raises an eyebrow as I slide in beside her.

Del watches, grinning. "You two are such a cute couple."

"Yeah," says Telson. "Barbie and Butt Head."

But she smiles at me — a secret, endearing smile. I think about the fire on the ridge. Being trapped in the flimsy shelter. About everything I had to lose. "Christina," I say, and she meets my gaze. Her eyes are deep and open, and for a long moment we just look into each other. I'm sure she'll say something intentionally abrasive to break the moment, but she doesn't.

"Yes, Porter," she says finally. Her smile is wistful, a little afraid.

"Christina, there's something I've been meaning to ask you."

ACKNOWLEDGEMENTS

I would like to thank the following members of the United States Forest Service for their interest and friendly co-operation while I was researching this book. Without exception, every one of them gave generously of their time. Timothy G. Love, Chief Ranger, allowed me full access to his staff. Becky White, Assistant Fire Management Officer, answered my many questions on USFS fire operations. Jon P. Agner, Fire Management Technician, provided insights into district fire investigation procedures. Bill Oelig provided information on the use of fusees. Paul Steensland, Senior Special Agent, provided information on the criminal investigative branch of the Forest Service. Special thanks to Dick Mangan of Blackbull Wildfire Services, who provided me with a copy of *Investigating Wildland Fire Entrapments* (USDA 0151-2823-MTDC), for sharing his extensive experience in investigating these tragedies, including the investigation of the South Canyon disaster at Storm King Mountain. Thanks to Mike Dietrich for providing pictures of the USDA Honor Guard. I would like to extend my appreciation to Paul Broyles, Chief of Fire Operations for the US National Park Service, for providing information on fire investigation and incident management teams and a copy of the video NFES 1568; *Using Your Fire Shelter*. Many thanks to Mike McMeekin of the Missoula County Sheriff's Department for his detailed responses to my many questions regarding homicide and arson investigation. Deputy Sheriff Scott Newell provided valuable insight into crime scene procedure.

Pat Swan Smith, of the Seeley Lake Rural Fire District, provided information on the functioning of a volunteer fire department. Cpl Gordon Petracek, Forensic Identification Specialist, Royal Canadian Mounted Police, provided information on fusee residue. I would like to thank Marc Gamache of the Alberta Forest Service, a friend and former co-worker, for sharing his experience regarding fire operations in Montana. Also Blake Sproule, for his judicious editing.

Read how it all began!

DAY INTO NIGHT

A PORTER CASSEL MYSTERY

by DAVE HUGELSCHAFFER

• •

Porter Cassel can't hide from the tragedy of seeing his fiancée, Nina, killed by an ecoterrorist three years ago. Nor does he want to: the bomber calling himself "the Lorax" is still at large and may have struck again in the Curtain River area of Alberta, putting innocent forestry workers, campers, and bystanders all in jeopardy.

When he is framed for the murder of one of the suspects, Cassel realizes someone else may be behind the bombings, and the investigation becomes a race to clear his name as well as to catch those responsible.

And then there is the matter of Nina's killer — the real Lorax — who may be much closer to home than Cassel ever suspected …